CW01637366

"Sometimes It Happens that I come across a thoroughly enjoyable story that makes me laugh out loud at the antics of the characters within. This is one of them!"
Helen Hollick.

Dear Linda
Enjoy & I hope it makes you smile
Pauline
X
Aug 2013

Also by Pauline Barclay

MAGNOLIA HOUSE

SATCHFIELD HALL

Sometimes It Happens…

Pauline Barclay

www.paulinebarclay.co.uk

Published in 2012 by FeedARead.com Publishing – Arts Council funded

Cover Design by @Avalon Graphic

A CIP catalogue record for this title is available from the British Library.

To my husband, my best friend and soul mate, Clive, as always with love.

To mum and dad, loves you.

Acknowledgements

Special thanks to Helen Hollick whose patience and knowledge knows no bounds. A truly lovely lady, good friend and brilliant author.

Hugs to Sue Beveridge who has never given up on me despite the many times she has read, reread and read again all my writings over the years.
Thank you, dear one!

For an amazing book cover, thanks to Cathy Helms at Avalon Graphics

Sometimes It Happens…

Chapter ONE

Nothing in her wildest dreams had prepared Doreen Wilkinson for something like this. But then, nothing had prepared her for winning the lottery either.

Several *million*. *Several* million. Eleven million, three hundred and fifty four thousand, two hundred and ten pounds and nineteen pence to be precise.

She had giggled at the nineteen pence. "Break the bleedin' bank that will!"

The media had made the comment a headline, *"19p to break the bleedin' bank!"* splashed all over the *Sun* and *Daily Mirror* accompanied by her smiling face and a fountain spray of champagne. She had thought it a waste shaking that great big bottle and letting it fizz everywhere, but the reporters had told her to do it.

Giggling at the memory, dressed in her silk pyjamas, Doreen stepped out on to the terrace. The warm morning air that caressed her face was in stark contrast to the chilled champagne she was sipping. She giggled again at drinking champagne before the sun had got out of bed. Padding to the end of the terrace, her bare feet absorbing the heat from the ceramic tiles, she looked out in awe over the Villas Bonitas complex of luxury villas. Apart from in films she had never seen exotic plants and trees, meandering tiled pathways and white walled, red roofed villas with sprawling private terraces. But then, she told herself, she had never won the lottery or been abroad before either. In fact she had never had a proper holiday full stop.

As the sun began to rise the solar lights that lit the gardens during the hours of darkness began to fade. Doreen watched, mesmerized, as the colours of the neatly maintained gardens surrounding each individual terrace gradually turned from sombre shades to vibrant greens, reds, pinks and yellows, and the shadows darkening the walls of each villa changed to a dazzling white. In the distance she could just make out the silhouette of the volcanic mountains as the rising sun cast its morning rays against their dark, jagged shapes.

Drinking the last drops of her champagne Doreen sighed with contentment. She had not known such beauty existed. Even the air had a sweet fragrance to it. She closed her eyes and inhaled the heady perfume, a high pitched shriek pierced the stillness, startled, she opened her eyes to see a yellow parrot dart past, almost within touching distance, its wings fanning her face. No sooner had the parrot disappeared into the tall palm trees, another, more muted sound rippled through the sultry, morning, air.

She frowned as she heard it again; looked left and right to locate where it was coming from. Giggled. She had half an idea what was going on and was surprised that such naughty cries could be heard in such a posh place. Grinning she went to sip her champagne, tipping the glass to her lips, realised it was empty. Pulling a face, she ambled back across the terrace and stepping through the wide open patio doors, giggled. "Someone's enjoying a good time."

Blinking rapidly, her eyes struggling to focus after the brightness of the terrace, squinting, Doreen looked around the lounge. "Blimey," she cried seeing glasses and a couple of empty bottles on one of the low coffee tables. A makeup bag, its contents scattered on the dining table and an open magazine lay on the floor near one of the sofas.

"God, what am I like?" she muttered as she reached for a packet of cigarettes and a lighter.

Taking a drag from her newly lit cigarette, Doreen looked at her watch. It was still early, she thought as she paused outside her daughter Trisha's door. Should she peep in? Her only daughter had gone out clubbing the night before, no doubt got home in the early hours. Her hand half way to the door handle, she wondered had she heard Trisha come in? She tried to think, but could not remember hearing any sounds; but then, she had been dead to the world, her first decent night's sleep in weeks.

“Youngsters,” she giggled, “on the go all day, party all night. Don’t know where they get their energy from.”

Shaking her head, still giggling, she wandered to her bathroom. What she would give to be seventeen again!

Chapter TWO

Hands placed firmly on hips, a look on her face that would sour cream and a glare that was as piercing as a laser beam, Frau Hecks stared across the hibiscus gardens. Her steel like gaze travelled slowly across the scented shrubbery and stopped at the pool house. A yellow parrot screeched as it perched in one of the palm trees, its feathers ruffled. With distaste twitching on her lips, Frau Hecks listened to the muted noises coming from the small, highly ornate building that housed the equipment and machinery for maintaining the swimming pool and Jacuzzi.

Her nose wrinkled in disgust and with a resounding *tutt tutt* of disapproval she turned abruptly and strode back across the tiled terrace and disappeared into the sanctuary of her villa. It was too early to complain to Carmen, the manager, so settling at her desk she reached for her diary. Gripping a pen tightly she scrawled words that described the sounds she had heard. It had not been the first time *things* had happened and her written account of complaints was not a short one.

In the pool house, oblivious of anyone being around at six thirty in the morning the heavy breathing and panting reached a wild crescendo, then slowed and quietened.

"You are some babe," Ben sighed out of breath as he slowly rolled off Trisha and sprawled next to her, sweat trickling down his back and thighs. He twisted slightly and gazed at Trisha's incredible body, his heart rate continuing to race madly. Sliding his hand over her small, perfectly rounded breast, he bent down and kissed her hard nipple.

"Mmmm, you are just so wild and scarily sexy."

Trisha moaned as Ben's touch rippled through her trembling body. With gentle fingers she put her hand down and laced them round his soft manhood. Her smile, wickedly seductive, she whispered. “Let’s do it all again, hmm?”

“Again?” Ben laughed. “You’ll have to give me a minute or two, you greedy minx!”

With their lovemaking over and his need sated, Ben eased himself away from her, his left hand surreptitiously groping for his boxer shorts. In the aftermath of enjoyment he realised the stupidity of his actions. Not that making love to the sexy Trisha Wilkinson was a mistake, but the reckless stupidity of where they were. He should never have brought her here, but after leaving the nightclub, with the stars twinkling above and a pale, sickle moon hanging like a suggestive smile in the sky they had both known what they had wanted. And going home alone at dawn was not it. Intoxicated with the heat of the night and the desire for each other, he had thought only of finding a suitable place for them to end the exciting hours they had spent together dancing: The icing on the cake of an incredible evening.

The pool house at Villas Bonitas was ideal. It was attractive and secluded and had what they needed; a large, comfortable, leather sofa and cool air conditioning.

To this quiet, almost secretive, place he had brought Trisha, but now he was realising just how risky his idea had been. He must get them both out and away before the maintenance man, his grandfather, arrived. Granddad would have a fit. Maybe even lose his job. A rise of panic creeping in, Ben looked at his watch and frowned. He was going to be in serious trouble if they did not leave immediately.

Well tanned and well toned, at twenty one, Ben’s good looks attracted girls like bees to a honey pot. He flashed Trisha a sexy smile; she was amazingly beautiful, her jet black hair, now ruffled, shone like ebony as it touched the curve of her shoulders. Her skin was pale as milk, and, like her lips, was smooth. He wanted to touch her softness again, but knew they had to get out of here.

He reached down for his clothing, but giggling, Trisha pulled him back, hooking her arm around his waist and smoothing her foot along his thigh.

"You simply cannot leave," she purred. "You are so mine for the entire week. I'm on holiday."

Breathing heavily with rising alarm, not the intense excitement of an hour earlier, Ben guessed that if they did not leave straight away, making love with Trisha would become nothing more than a distant memory and a painful one at that. He winced at the thought of what his granddad would do if ever the old man found out. Reluctant, Ben stood and began hurriedly dressing. Had the time of day been different then this was the last thing he would be doing; putting his clothes on!

Trisha, slim, pretty and fun with a hint of danger, added an extra spice of excitement about her. It was the danger that had brought them here in the first place. That and lust. He gathered up her clothes; bra, pants and dress, more like a handkerchief than a dress it was so scanty, and threw them to her. Trying to keep the urgency out of his voice, he forced a cheerful grin. "Please babe, get dressed. We shouldn't be in here. I promise we are going to have so much more fun later. Fun that'll make this holiday one you will *never* forget." Leaning towards her he kissed her, adding, "It is not a promise, it is a threat."

Trisha giggled as she stepped into her panties. "I so love threats."

Ben felt another tingle of desire squirm through his stomach and into his groin and despite the urgency, the taste of Trisha remained frighteningly tantalising. Again, he placed his lips on her mouth and after a long and passionate kiss, pulled away. "Babe, surely that tells you I want to see you again and again and again?"

He strode towards the opaque glazed door, gingerly opened it a crack and, to his horror, saw Frau Hecks staring straight at the pool house. He froze. Had the old battle axe seen him? To his relief, she turned and marched back into her villa. He swore under his breath, added, *achtung, mein Führer.*

What was she doing on the prowl so early? Did the old bat never sleep? Trouble would follow very quickly if Frau

Hecks had any suspicion of his early morning entertainment. Turning to Trisha, he said in a voice that offered no argument, “I am leaving and you must too.” Added, in a softer, seductive tone, “I’ll see you tonight; I promise you I will be at your villa.” He grinned, stepped through the door, paused and tossed over his shoulder, “Naked in your bed.”

Disappointed that their night had come to such an abrupt end, Trisha managed the pretence of a little giggle then shrugged. Resigned, she watched Ben disappear. Hoping she would see him again, she smiled and adjusting her short dress, picked up her tiny handbag from the floor and strolled to the door. With her hand poised on the handle, she looked around at the little room and giggled then slowly, very slowly, opened the door. Stepping out into the warm, morning air, she could see and hear no one. Ben had gone, the sun was rising, birds were singing. She tossed her head, her black hair shimmering in the strengthening morning sunlight and clutching her handbag to her petit breasts, sashayed jauntily towards villa number four.

With every detail written down, Frau Hecks returned to the terrace, but paused within the open patio doorway, her eyes shrinking to slits and a hiss of outrage leaving her pursed lips. She recognised the boy ducking away through the hibiscus garden and a short moment later saw that little tramp from number four ambling along the tiled pathway, swaying her hips, tossing her hair and smiling.

Chapter THREE

Bob Preston sauntered through the security gates into the beautiful grounds of Villas Bonitas. He stopped, looked around, his gaze taking in the opulence. He sighed, he could never afford to live in such luxury, but had the next best thing; he worked here and most of the time he loved his job.

Whistling a tuneless sound he studied what he regarded as his domain and noted that the palm trees would not say no to another trim. The hibiscus also needed dead heading. The climate made it almost a daily task. He grimaced. He had more than enough to do today without having to worry about dead heading blooms, but *they* all expected not only perfection, but miracles. He chuckled to himself; so many of the owners regularly exclaimed in astonishment. "Oh God! What do you mean you can't do that?"

He would like the odd miracle to show these idle rich what *real* life was all about. Shrugging, he ignored the beckoning work and walked briskly towards the centre of his operations, the pool room.

Gazing down the wide, tiled pathway flanked by vibrant red hibiscus and fragrant pale yellow oleander, he spotted Frau Hecks standing at the edge of her terrace glaring at him. He stopped, pretended to examine a broken oleander branch as warning bells started to ring loudly in his head. Frau Hecks did not normally stand at the edge of her terrace, arms folded, unless she was waiting for someone. He sighed apprehensively, fished out a small pair of secateurs from his pocket and snipped off the remains of the broken branch. Putting off the inevitable, he snipped at another small branch. Past experience had taught him that Frau Hecks was not merely admiring the view of his beautifully maintained gardens, but waiting for him, to complain. She seemed to have got worse of late, Nag nag, complain complain.

Taking a deep breath, he knew he had no chance of a detour and his choice of avoiding the battle axe was limited. Inspecting the oleander bush for any further broken branches, he carefully considered. Rubbing his chin, pretending his attention was on the flowering shrub, he pondered two possibilities, find out what she wanted or quicken his step, walk straight past and ignore her. If he was steadfast and intent on an assumed urgent mission, he might just get away with it?

Slipping the secateurs back inside his pocket he convinced himself that maybe, after all, she was admiring the view. An unlikely conclusion, but thrusting his hands into his jacket pockets and averting his gaze from the annoying Frau, he strode onwards. Whistling in an octave higher, he added a longer and quicker stride to his step and headed straight for the safety of his pool house. His home from home, where he kept all his tools and maintenance equipment, where he ate his lunch and enjoyed the occasional quiet doze: His personal sanctuary. If only he could get to it without interruption…

That annoying, tuneless whistle, Frau Hecks could not believe something so irritating could actually come from a human. Annoyance growing, she waited at the edge of her terrace intent on accosting the wretched man heading in her direction. It was bad enough that he should shatter the early morning peace with his infuriating whistling, but she considered he was personally responsible for what she had heard. It was not acceptable, she would not have it and in no uncertain terms she was determined to tell Bob Preston so.

He had seen her. Fiddling with that oleander was a ruse. "*Dummkopf,*" she hissed and folding her arms scrutinised him with her keen, piercing eyes as he came nearer; pulling her shoulders back she moved her hands to her hips and waited for the perfect moment as he approached. He was walking quicker, striding out. With a sardonic smile twisting her mouth, she was ready to pounce.

To her horror he walked straight past! Did not even acknowledge her. Walked? *Pah*, scuttled more like!

Bob reached the pool house, curled his fingers round the door handle, relief flooding through him. He started to open the door. Two or three more steps and he would be safe inside.

"Bob, Bob. I talk with you. *Now!*"

With his hand frozen on the door handle, Bob silently counted to ten then slowly turned, startled he almost fell backwards. Frau Hecks stood right behind him.

"Good grief Flawline, you nearly gave me an 'eart attack!"

Hands on hips, her face set for battle, Frau Hecks snapped, "Pah! You have no idea."

Confused, shaking his head at such an early morning outburst, Bob spread his hands in bewilderment. "Blimey Flawline, it's not even eight o'clock yet. What can be so important that you need to frighten me half to death? You know today's a busy one for me, what with all the comings and goings." He was blustering attempting not to betray his anxiety. Wiping his hand across his soaking brow, it was going to be a hot day and with Frau Hecks breathing fire, he was already in a sweat.

A round face, with rosy chubby cheeks, a dimpled chin, Frau Hecks was naturally pretty, but time had cast shadows that darkened her blue eyes to suspicious pools and her once full lips to a thin line that sneered and curled in anger. "You think I am amused with what you say? You think everything a joke? I telling you, I live in this beautiful place and all the time put up with terrible people who come for holiday and spoil themselves and my home. And today it is, again, *your* fault that things happen."

A mixed expression of confusion and concern, Bob stared straight at the angry Frau Hecks as she trembled with rage. Having no idea what the old bat was fuming about, he looked down at the spotlessly clean tiled pathway then with an exaggerated movement of his head, gazed across at the lush gardens. Seeing nothing untoward, returned his attention back to Frau Hecks.

Wiping his hand over his face, baffled, he sighed. "You've lost me."

Annoyance on the verge of boiling over, her blue eyes flashing with anger,

her accent thickening with impatience, Frau Hecks snapped. "You are stupid man. No wonder he is stupid also." Removing one hand from her hips she pointed a long, straight finger at the door of the pool house. "Zat door, you not see it is the door?"

Bob swivelled round, stared solemnly at the door, what on earth was she on about? One of them had lost the plot and from where he was standing it was not him.

"Yes, Flawline," he said in response, trying not to sound sarcastic. "I can see the door. It looks fine to me and I can assure you, all is well behind it too."

"You talk nonsense. I tell you things happen there. Filthy things because you not lock zat door."

Ah! Was *that* it! Relief flooded through him and he smiled. "Why didn't yer say we've 'ad burglars?" Thinking the old lady had definitely lost her marbles, his reassuring smile broadened. "Don't worry Flawline, there's nothing to pinch."

Annoyed that he was a bigger idiot than she had thought, Frau Hecks leant towards Bob, her face almost touching his and spat one word. "Sex!"

Shocked Bob barked back. "*What!*"

"Sex! Zat is what happening in there." Frau Hecks glared at him and at the same time stabbed a finger towards the offending door. "This is high class place, I will not put up with it. I get you the sack."

Totally perplexed, determined to get to the bottom of whatever was causing the old basket to have another of her *wobblies*, asked. "What's the burglars got to do with sex?"

"Pah! You hear that noise? I tell you that noise is my patience it go *snap!* They are not the burglars, they are disgusting noise and *sex*."

Bob rubbed his clean shaven chin, with a mixture of concern and amusement, but could not resist a grin. "Cor blimey Flawline, how come I miss out on all the fun, eh?"

Her upper lip creased into a snarl, Frau Hecks turned abruptly and pointing in the direction of villa number four, hissed in a lowered voice. "You are a stupid man, it is the *fräulein* that tart who came yesterday to number *vier.* She been in there with that disgraceful grandson of yours doing … filthy stuff, because *you* do not lock zat door. I see them leave and I hear too. You no care, but you will. You will!"

Not waiting for a reaction or response, Frau Hecks marched away, straight backed and dignified, to her villa.

Chapter FOUR

Despite the sun brightening in the deepening blue sky, despite the rapidly increasing heat, despite the beauty of the day, Doreen did not feel bright or warm or beautiful. She felt as if a shadow was engulfing her, devouring her whole; she felt cold, sad, lonely and frightened.

Cigarette in one hand, champagne glass in the other, she stood unseen inside the open patio doors of her beautiful holiday villa, her robe pulled loosely over a sparkling purple bikini.

She wanted to believe that she had not overheard what that foreign woman next door had been shouting at the gardener. She wanted to believe none of it. In less than twenty four hours, spiteful, foul, words were being said. She thought she had left all that behind, all the bitching and snarling, nasty people looking for trouble.

She was shaking. Tears stung the back of her eyes. The champagne glass in her hand slipped from her fingers, dropped to the marble floor and shattered.

Unaware of the broken glass, she stood at the open door staring blindly out, a feeling of nausea and panic coursing through her. She wanted to be sick, wanted to cry, to scream, shout, she wanted to run and run and run. Instead, she stood there as if immobilised, a trickle of blood oozing from beneath her foot, forming a puddle on the expensive marble floor. She stood there, staring out at the past. A past that she had thought, naively, she had left behind: The malicious gossips, the arguments, the fights, her own screaming and shouting, the futility of trying to stand up for herself and her girl.

Taking a drag from her cigarette Doreen blew a stream of smoke above her head, watched as it curled and twisted in the warm air. She had stood there minding her own business, enjoying the clean, fresh smell of the morning air; had watched with amused interest as the foreign woman, whatever her name, had accosted the gardener. She had almost laughed out loud as he had scuttled past, head up, determinedly looking in the opposite direction, pretending for all the world that he could not see the woman planted on the edge of the terrace like a terrier marking a rat hole.

Bob, she thought his name was Bob, had seemed a decent bloke yesterday when she had briefly met him. A Londoner, like herself, although he sounded more posh not as common as her East End rabbiting. He was more south London, she guessed, or west: Where the classy folk came from. Her nails pressed into the palms of her hands. Nothing had changed. Even the rich and the posh liked to bitch. She turned her head at the muted sound of her daughter coughing. She was back then. But when had she come in? Before midnight? Before dawn? Or had she sauntered quietly in fifteen minutes ago, whilst she had been in the shower?

A tear welled in the corners of Doreen's eyes. She shut them, tight. For all the hardship and poverty of living as a single mother on a Council estate in the East End of London, for all the slagging and bitching and whinging and moaning, at least she had belonged there. A half strangled sob shuddered its way through her body as the past teased and tormented her behind her closed eyelids. What was she doing here among these la-di-da nobs? Who was she kidding? Did several million pounds make her talk proper, give her the charm and manners she was expected to have? If she kept her eyes closed could she hide away from the world she had always dreamt about being part of: A world which she had suddenly been catapulted into? A world of riches and privileges and appeared to have more bitches than Battersea Dogs' Home!

Even as she contemplated these foolish thoughts, a voice inside her head began to mutter and nervously giggle. A voice she knew only too well: her own, inner, voice. The same voice that had kept her afloat and fighting throughout the years, the one that had kept her head above water and the degradation of the poverty she had assumed she was destined to stay in. Born into poverty, grew up in poverty, bore a child in poverty and lived in poverty: The sort of poverty where benefits were swallowed up within a day just to feed the gas meter. And now that same voice yelled at her. "Keep your eyes tightly shut Doreen old girl and you can stay locked in the past forever or open them and face the world; your new world, the world you deserve. It's your choice girl!"

Snapping her eyes open she pulled herself together. What was she doing standing here moping like a wet washday? Living in the past was not an option. She had been one of the rare lucky ones. She had not only got out, but had been plucked out at a breathtaking speed. The days of fumbling down the back of the settee for a few lost pennies to buy a loaf of bread were gone, buried forever. She could buy as much bread as she wanted now, a whole bakery and a whole shop full of sofas! She sucked at the last of her cigarette and tossed the stub out onto the terrace. Let the cow next door complain about *that!* She took off her robe and swirled it like a toreador's cape.

"*Olez*!" she laughed then winced as she looked down and saw the blood on the floor. "Oh bleeding hell!" she muttered then giggled. "Bleeding indeed!"

The misery of the past was back where it belonged, behind her. She stepped out onto the terrace where a little pool of blood would not matter and felt in her pocket for her fags and lighter. Placing a cigarette between her lips, lit up and took a long, strong pull. Tilting her head backwards she exhaled the smoke and watched it plume above her head into the clear, blue, sky. Had it ever been this clear and blue in London? Her elbow resting on her arm she smoked the cigarette down to its stub. Walking to the patio table ground the cigarette out into the ashtray. The old Doreen would have ignored the gossip and, if necessary, deal with it later. But she was no longer the old Doreen. She was the new, vulnerable, Doreen nervous and out of her depth.

She asked herself: how would someone of her new wealthy status behave? With confidence? Course they would! Not with a fishwife shouting match, entertaining the neighbourhood over the backyard fence, while the laundry that looked as grey as it had before going through the washing machine, flapped in the smog laden breeze.

She sniffed, "Bleeding hell," then giggled as she cast her gaze towards the end of her terrace. The foreign woman had gone. So had the old gardener, but she could hear a chatter of voices. She braced herself to stand her ground. Two girls were in the distance each pushing a trolley along the pathway, the wheels gently rumbling; a noise as familiar to Doreen as a clock ticking. Was that another person walking behind the two cleaning maids? Doreen could not quite see.

Giggling again, what was the matter with her? She waved cheerfully at the girls, then realised they were too far away to have seen her. Trisha, she told herself, was in bed; sound asleep after her night out at the disco. This silliness had been nothing except overhearing a few angry words, her own nightmares and fear putting cockeyed ideas into her head, adding two and two and coming up with seven hundred and sixty three! So the German neighbour had been complaining about whoever had been having a bit of *hows yer father* in that pretty little building on the other side of the shrubbery? Jealous, probably, because no one was interested in tickling her fancy! Doreen giggled. A Doreen giggle that instantly turned into a full blown laugh. The nosey busybody had pointed vaguely in this direction. "Cor blimey," Doreen said out loud, looking over her shoulder at the three villas beyond her private terrace, "What made me think she was pointing at me?"

Turning her back on the sound of the clacking wheels coming nearer and the clacking tongue of a lonely old biddy she limped back into her villa in search of cotton wool and antiseptic. She giggled again. She had a new life to get on with and she must give it a try after she had swept up the glass and got the blood off the posh marble floor.

Chapter FIVE

Wearing a dark pencil skirt and white, short sleeved blouse, tailored exquisitely to fit her tall, slim physique, designed to portray her status at Villas Bonitas, Carman Santana walked closely behind the two cleaning maids. Her mind occupied with the busy schedule of the day. Several owners and guests were arriving and the demands on her and her staff were high. Though what sat in the forefront of her mind were the arrivals of yesterday, Mrs Wilkinson and her daughter.

As usual, Carman had welcomed and greeted the new guests, but nothing had prepared her for meeting Doreen Wilkinson. Petite and beautiful with soft blue eyes that flashed a mixture of mischievousness and sadness, blonde hair, exquisitely cut that bobbed above her shoulders and a tailored dress in shocking pink. Every inch of the woman an attractive lady that oozed wealth, but what Carmen had heard when those glossy pink lips parted was in stark contrast to the image of riches and beauty. A voice that momentarily took Carmen's breath away, reminding her of one or two of the characters in the old sixties comedy films; a plethora of *Cor blimeys* had been interspersed with several nervous giggles. The colour of the dress, Carmen realised afterwards, should have been a signal. But despite the shock, Carmen was aware that everything she had been told about the two new guests was confidential. Her instructions were crystal clear; Doreen Wilkinson must not learn that her fabulous holiday had been carefully and deliberately organised. Carmen had far too much on her mind for this to cause a problem. Though one thing did bother her and that was what she had seen earlier as she had walked through the entrance gates; Bob's grandson rushing past her mumbling a nervous good morning shortly followed by Trisha Wilkinson sashaying towards her villa. Despite her unease she knew that young man's 'Casanova' reputation all too well and decided to ignore the incident for now. The pair of them were of age and having a discreet liaison was not illegal, though it did lower the tone of Villas Bonitas.

She winced; a slight throb was starting to pound in her left temple. She glanced at her watch time for once was not racing at an alarming speed. Raising her hand to gently massage the area of pain in an attempt to ease the threatening headache, she heard her name spoken. Dropping her hand down to her side looked over at the two maids, a frown creasing her forehead. Had she been so distracted? They were already outside Villa number four.

"Carmen, I'll start here with number four so I can introduce myself." Tracey announced as she pushed her laden trolley along the villa's private walkway.

Ignoring the throbbing pain, Carmen nodded at the young woman. "Perfect. I need to make sure everything is comfortable for Mrs Wilkinson. We shall go in together."

She instructed the other maid, Cissie to prepare villa five. Guests were arriving later that morning. Unusual, she thought because the Judge's villa was only ever used by the Judge and his family. Shrugging the thought away Carmen added, "Please call me if you need any assistance," her mind already distracted as she walked towards villa four a few yards behind Tracey.

The knocking at the door caused Doreen to swear under her breath. She dabbed more antiseptic on her foot and hastily tied a bandage round it. The knocking came again. "I'm coming as fast as I bleeding can," she muttered.

Leaving the first aid box open on the kitchen table, its contents scattered as she started hobbling towards the entrance area, her robe opened to reveal her bikini clad trim figure. She stopped, startled as the front door swung open.

"What the…?" she started to call as she watched two women enter her villa.

Carmen entering the villa hastily explained, "Good morning Mrs Wilkinson, I'm so sorry if we have startled you, but as you didn't answer the door I assumed you were not in."

Doreen recognised her from the day before: The manageress who had greeted them on their arrival. What was her name? She noted the other person wore a maid's uniform, and beyond the open front door Doreen could see the cleaning trolley laden with bottles, brushes, polishes, dusters, buckets, mops: The Full Monty. She grinned as she took it all in, she knew all about that!

The spacious villa was expensively furnished in soft tones. Doreen in her sparkling purple bikini was the brightest object in the villa. Crossing her arms, almost pushing her small rounded breast out of the tiny top, in a nervous and defensive tone she cried. "Cor blimey we've only been here a day, the place isn't filthy or nothing."

Carmen half grinned at the woman's eagerness for the swimming pool. The bikini was a bit skimpy and very sparkly. She coughed lightly to ensure her voice remained polite and steady before saying in a friendly tone. "A daily cleaning service is fully inclusive Mrs Wilkinson. Bathroom, kitchen and of course clean towels and linen." Smiling added, "Please let me introduce you to Tracey. She is the maid who will be looking after you throughout your stay her at Villas Bonitas." Turning, Carmen nodded at Tracey who stood behind her, before adding. "Tracey is here to ensure that everything remains perfect for your stay."

Stepping forward, Tracey extended her hand. "Hello Mrs Wilkinson."

Hearing the friendly tone, Doreen relaxed slightly, but remained wary. Unfolding her arms self consciously she gathered her robe discretely around her body and politely offered her hand in response to the young maid. Relief spread through her, calming her startled unease as she realised the two women were not, as she had feared, here to harass her about that nasty piece of gossip she had overheard earlier. She giggled nervously; her resolve to not care about what others said or did had rapidly evaporated at the sight of these two women marching into her villa uninvited. Her

New Year resolutions had never lasted long: Seemed that her new life resolutions were no different.

Sounding more confident than she felt, Doreen cried. "Nice to meet you. Now I think about it, something was said about cleaning and all. Silly me, you must think I know nothing." Bleeding hell what did she sound like? she asked herself, embarrassed. Trying to hold a confident smile, knowing full well she had no idea how to live or behave in this style of luxury and worse she suspected these two women knew it too. God, she cried silently as she cast a quick glance around the room. Blimey it looked like a tip with empty bottles and make up scattered on the table, then spying her packet of cigarettes on the top of the lightwood coffee table, swooped over and pulled the packet towards her. Removing a long Dunhill, scrabbled in her robe pocket and pulled out her lighter and lit up.

Blowing a plume of smoke into the air, from the corner of her eye, noticed a half empty bottle of gin sitting on the breakfast bar and secretly wished she could have a nip of that instead of a fag. Mind, she thought that mixed with the champagne and all the fags she had smoked might not give the best impression. Tempted as she was to giggle, she drew on her cigarette instead.

Turning her attention back to Carmen who had wandered into the lounge area and appeared to be inspecting, "I was going to tidy up, but had a bit of an accident with me foot." She raised her leg up to produce the evidence.

"Mrs Wilkinson, I'm only here to check everything is perfect for you, now can I do anything to help with your foot?"

"Thanks, a bit of glass, nothing to worry about." She giggled. What must these two be thinking? The place in a two and eight and my foot in a bandage. She was supposed to be all refined and classy now she had money, not hobbling around and trembling with nerves. God, she had always dreamed of staying in such a fabulous place, but in reality it was turning out to be nothing like her dreams, nothing like the glossy magazines and TV soaps. Life for the rich, from where she had stood, permanently in the smelly stuff, had always seemed to be perfect. But so far with all her money, she was not composed and in control. Out of bleeding control more like.

Standing in silence, Carmen could almost feel the anguish that was rippling through Doreen Wilkinson. She had barely been in the villa for more than a couple of minutes yet she could see the woman was struggling, clearly out of her depth with her new life. Sympathy surged through her, stepping forward and in a tone, she hoped conveyed friendliness, broke the silence. “It is my job and my great pleasure, to ensure we make this holiday a memorable one for you. If there is anything you need, anything you are unsure of please, ask me.” Before she could offer more encouragement, Tracey interrupted.

“Excuse me, is it ok for me to go in and change the beds?”

Doreen ran one hand through her immaculate hair, her cigarette pivoting on her bottom lip. Were these two setting a trap to catch her out about the gossip she had heard? What was she to do? Trisha was in bed and as if on cue a low cough was heard coming from the bedroom. She inhaled another lungful of much needed nicotine then stubbed the cigarette out in the ashtray. Sighed with relief at her daughter’s coughing sound, then sharper than intended, said, “You can do mine, but me girl is still abed. Typical of her age, been out clubbing so best if you leave it ‘till later.” Rolling her eyes continued. “Time means nothing at that age, midnight, midday, they don’t know if the stars or the sun is shining. Teenagers, what do you do with them eh?”

Unaware of the worries swirling around in Doreen’s head, Tracey, turning towards the font door, called with bland ease. “No problem. Many of the guests never emerge until well after noon. After all, you are on holiday. I can always come back later to finish off.” Smiling she went to her trolley to fetch a bundle of clean linen.

Her arms laden with fresh laundry, Tracey walked down the hall towards the bedrooms.

Watching the maid head towards her room, Doreen had another fleeting attack of nerves, stepped forward as if to run after the girl, stopped, blimey, what if me knicks are on the floor? Oh God, the gin glass is still on the cabinet bedside me bed. Gordon Bennett, the ashtray is full! Bleeding hell what will the girl be thinking? This is ridiculous! Snap out of it Doreen, she castigated herself. The maid is only doing her job and ever likely me drawers are stuffed in the linen basket.

Noting Doreen's worried face and the temperature rising in the room, Carmen strode over to the air conditioning control panel. Adjusting the settings, turned to Doreen, she could see the lottery winner was uncomfortable with their presence. The temperature reset, she strolled back to where Doreen stood,

"It seems rather warm in here, so I've adjusted the settings," she pointed to the small control unit. "Would you like me to show you how to adjust it if it gets too cool in here?" She smiled as she spoke and hoped her tone conveyed a friendly voice. It was clear Doreen Wilkinson needed to feel less intimidated.

Doreen did not miss the affable tone and gesture, smiled back. "Thanks I'm not used to central heating let alone central chilling," she giggled. She could sense Carmen was trying to find a way to talk to her.

Reaching over, Carmen lightly placed her hand on Doreen's shoulder, "I'm here to make sure your stay is as perfect as we can make it. Tracey's job is to look after the villa for you and your job, Mrs Wilkinson, is to enjoy yourself."

Meeting Carmen's eyes, Doreen giggled, it might be a trap, she was not sure, but she liked this Carmen. Maybe she was genuine, time would tell. "Seems we've all got our work cut out then. You know we've never been in such a lovely place. I'm already loving every minute, you girls have done a great job with making it look so smart." She knew only too well how much effort was needed to keep a place looking this good. She giggled excitedly at the thought of not having to clean it herself. Staring at Carmen's manicured hand still resting on her shoulder added. "With those nice hands of yours, I doubt you've had to dip them in bleach and buckets of stuff."

Doreen looked at her own hands, not as soft looking at Carmen's, but not red and raw anymore. "To think you work in such a lovely place. When I was a cleaner, the holes I had to do were stinky and filthy. Even the people treated you like you were the muck you had to clean up. You're lucky. God very lucky!"

She stopped talking, her cheeks burning red. Cor blimey, what had made her say all that? She blushed crimson with embarrassment. Too late now, it was out. She had told this perfectly dressed and styled woman, a total stranger, that she was not rich in the proper sense and that she had been a cleaner and not even a high class cleaner like that Tracey girl changing the sheets. What on earth had made her say it?

Grabbing at her cigarette packet, she took one out, placed it between her lips and lit it. Blowing the smoke into the room she knew why, because despite all her anxieties, all the baggage and crap she carried about in her head, all the fear that pounded in her about the world she had entered, this pretty woman with her educated but pleasant accent was making her feel surprisingly comfortable and happy.

"I will do whatever I can to ensure you enjoy your time here." Carmen said her voice kindly and friendly.

Puffing on her cigarette, Doreen suddenly thought that if there were more people like Carmen around then maybe she would eventually fit in. With the smoke wafting around her, said. "I can see yer understand me. Funny, we've had to come all this way to meet someone nice like you. Fickle finger of fate, me old Nan would say. God rest her soul."

Resisting the urge to waft the smoke away from her face, Carmen reached her own surprising conclusion; she liked Doreen Wilkinson. She had been unprepared for the bluntness, the shyness, the nervousness and she knew it would be tough for someone from her walk of life to hold her own here at Villas Bonitas. More than a few eyebrows would be raised and some of the owners would not take easily to this new multimillionaire who was a little rough around edges. Looking across at the pretty woman, a very rich pretty woman, who smoked like a chimney, Carmen could not begin to imagine the world Doreen had left behind.

Chapter SIX

Simon Barrington and Chicky Wentworth stood together under the rich blue sky and blazing sun, a slight beading of perspiration from the heat on their foreheads and upper lips. The air was heavy with the sweet fragrance of jasmine, its perfume heady and intoxicating tickled at their nostrils. Standing outside the entrance gates, the two men watched as their chauffeur driven limousine disappeared around the curve of the shady tree lined avenue, the sound of the engine fading, leaving the twittering of birds and clicking sound of crickets echoing in the light breeze.

Officially, as junior partners, they were here to attend an important conference representing their legal firm of *Hardy, Gale and Pemberton*. Unofficially they were here for a holiday.

A car, they had been told, would be waiting at the airport to take them to the villa. A car! They had expected a taxi, not a limo with a chauffeur resplendent in uniform who had tipped his cap on greeting them. But then, when their friend Paul Denbie had offered his holiday retreat, he had said little about the place other than it was in a nice area and everything would be taken care of. And, as if the personal transport was not enough of a surprise, what their eyes were now taking in was breathtaking as they stared through the gates in amazement, totally unprepared for the luxurious flamboyance that beckoned.

Their expensive matching luggage stood in front of two tall, imposing ornate iron gates. Next to the gates, a magnificent mural in ceramic tiles depicted a calm blue sea and a golden sanded beach, dotted with tropical parasols and towel covered recliners, the name *Villas Bonitas* was boldly painted in the cloudless deep blue sky.

On the pillar to the right of the gates, an intercom built into the brick wall, gave off a low hum as Simon pressed the buzzer. Immediately an echoing voice answered asking their names, the spy camera staring at them rapidly rotated as if focusing. Chicky stepped back. Simon moving closer to the microphone answered confidently. "Simon Barrington and Christopher Wentworth." He winked at Chicky after announcing his name in full.

Leaning closer to the intercom, he listened to the voice of the receptionist as it crackled through the speaker. "Thank you," he added, beckoning to Chicky, "a porter is on his way to collect our luggage."

Following his words a loud buzz resonated through the air and the gates silently slid open, Simon and Chicky, pulling their luggage, stepped into the luxurious park of Villas Bonitas.

Spectacular gardens filled with rich, vibrant colours from exotic flowers contrasted with dazzling white walls of villas nestling amongst the vivid greens of palm trees and bougainvillea. In the distance a waterfall cascaded over rugged black lava rocks as it splashed down into a large kidney shaped swimming pool: Its deep blue water rippling and sparkling beneath the hot, semi tropical, sun. Sun loungers, with blue and white stripped cushions were set in a relaxed style around the pool's perimeter. The only sunbather appeared to be a black cat, who had sprawled out on the warm tiled surface washing its face.

In their early thirties, Simon and Chicky casually, but elegantly dressed, were tall and slim, exuding fitness and vitality. Chicky's fair hair, which readily took on a tousled look when hands ran through its thick mass was in sharp contrast to Simon's rich dark hair that was poker straight. Attractive, both men turned heads, female and male, of all ages. Neither of them noticed the surreptitious glances, the cheeky smiles or the *come on* eyes. They only had interest for each other.

Discretely curling his fingers into Chicky's, Simon murmured. "This place is incredible. How has Paul managed to own something like this and keep so quiet about it?"

His gaze taking in the magnificence of Villas Bonitas, Chicky tightened his grip on Simon's hand. "Paul obviously has hidden tastes and resources!" Standing transfixed. "It looks too exclusive for mundane numbers, how do we know which one is ours?" he whispered so not to disturb the tranquillity around them.

Silently, Simon removed his hand from his partner's and took a neatly folded piece of paper from the breast pocket of his jacket. Slowly, carefully, he unfolded the note and read the words written there, his lips moving soundlessly. Equally as slowly, his expression impassive, he refolded the paper and slid it back into his pocket. He sighed heavily. "Chicky, my dear, I am sorry, but I have to inform you..." he paused, "that despite such opulence. Paul's villa is a simple *number five*."

Laughing, Chicky counted. "That one with the flowering hanging baskets is the fifth from the left. Mmm, but that one over there is fifth from the right, or are those we can see the servants' quarters?"

Simon looked at his partner grinned. 'Now you are being silly."

"Hello! Can I help?" The man's greeting startled them both and stifled their bubbling laughter

Simon and Chicky swivelled round simultaneously to see a tall man, dressed in blue drill trousers and a light blue polo shirt, looking over the top of a flowering bush.

"Oh, yes. Hello!" Chicky answered. "We are a bit uncertain where to go. We're looking for number five, Paul Denbie's Villa."

Stepping through the foliage Bob pushed his secateurs into his pocket, removed his leather garden gloves and stuffed them into his other pocket then looked both men up and down. Sniffed, they appeared decent enough, but appearances could be deceptive, he reminded himself. "I take it you mean the Judge's place? Don't get many staying there. Only folks that go in there is the cleaners. Mind, he's had it since it was new and you can count on one hand the people he lets in: An important man."

Looking Chicky straight in the eye, added. "So how comes you knows the Judge?" Grinning cheekily added, "You look too decent to be in a courtroom."

Simon could not resist the offered temptation. "Interesting you should mention it, but as a matter of fact that is exactly where we met Judge Denbie. Yes, unfortunately far too many times. Courtrooms, the bane of our life, that's why we're here. It's a new idea of the Judge's. Rehabilitation!"

Chicky snorted, stifling his laughter.

Moving back a pace, with slit eyes glowering suspiciously, Bob looked at the two well dressed men in front of him. Bank Robbers? Thieves? Hood Winkers? What was the world coming to sending them here? Had he not got enough on his plate without having to keep a beady eye on these two?

A gentle drone announced the arrival of the porter in the electric buggy. Pulling alongside, the driver enquired. "Mr Denbie's guests?"

Receiving a nod of confirmation, he jumped out of the buggy, picked up the luggage and carefully placed it in the storage compartment. "Please gentleman, step into the buggy and we'll be away to villa five."

Watching them drive away, Bob felt a stir of unease that made him shiver, he ought not to have been so forward with those two. It just might bite him back.

As the buggy made its way along the wide pathway, passing immaculately kept gardens and expensively furnished terraces of the white single story villas, Chicky laughed. "You should not to have teased the poor old chap like that Simon."

"He was the one to talk about courtrooms and judges. I simply added a little something for him to think about. He'll know soon enough we are barristers and friends of *The Judge*." Grinning added, "Cheeky devil!"

He laughed. Feeling the heat from Chicky's thigh rubbing gently against his, he discreetly placed his hand on his partner's knee.

"We are here gentlemen," the porter announced, bringing the buggy to a halt. Jumping out, pulled the suitcases from the storage bin and carried them along the short walkway to villa five.

Following, Simon and Chicky suddenly stopped as the sound of giggling from the villa next door carried on the breeze. They caught a glimpse of a petite blonde woman wearing a gaudy purple bikini step through her open patio doors on to her terrace.

"It seems it's not only the gardens that are colourful!" quipped Simon, smirking at Chicky.

Stepping into Paul Denbie's villa the coolness enveloped the two barristers as their gaze travelled around the spacious accommodation. The marble flooring, the sumptuous long, black leather sofas, the large square coffee table, which appeared to be made entirely out of glass; the dining table, wide and long, a copy of the smaller table flanked by six high backed white leather chairs. The kitchen to the left, behind the dining area, fitted with pristine white units where concealed lighting reflected down on to jet black marble worktops. Everything exquisitely designed.

Chicky slid his arm through Simon's. "My, my, I think I have died and gone to Heaven," he said, nodding towards an open door that revealed a luxurious bedroom.

Naughtily, Simon rested his palm against Chicky's bottom. "Heaven, my dear boy comes later, when we are alone and *in* that gorgeous bed." Looking round the large open planned room, he added, "This bit is just the taster."

Chapter SEVEN

Sitting on her terrace in one of the comfortable heavily upholstered chairs, the sun dappling through the palm trees, warm on her face, Doreen hugged a large gin and tonic. She knew she had been nipping away at the champagne and gin all morning, and to her surprise did not feel the slightest tipsy. The only dizziness she felt was the overwhelming headiness of her new life. Ignoring her earlier nervousness and feeling like a fish out of water, when the maid and Carmen had waltzed in, she knew her story was rags to riches. Now staring fascinated, at a bunch of green bananas hanging from a tree at the edge of the terrace, she shook her head. She had only ever seen bananas in the shops. The tree with its unripe fruit was straight out of a magazine or a storybook picture. She almost felt as if she was in a story herself.

Sipping at her drink, she mentally counted the noughts on her bank account balance. There were at least seven. How on earth would she ever spend all that money? She grinned. She would most certainly be trying hard to find a way! She had never had a bank account before, let alone one like the one she had now! As far as she was concerned the visit by the maid and manager and the sniping, heard earlier, had evaporated. She was counting money not snide remarks.

Never in a million years could she have imagined that she, Doreen Wilkinson, of all people, would have won the lottery. If she had bought a ticket every week, she might have had a chance, be it a slim one, but a chance none the less. As it was, she had probably bought no more than six tickets in all the years the lottery had been going. Not because she did not want to win, but she simply could not afford even the one pound for such an extravagance: A duck's backside had more chance of taking in water than her purse had of having spare cash. Giggling, she tried to remember the numbers she had used on her heart stopping lucky ticket, but for the life of her could not. She remembered scribbling them down in a hurry because, as always, she had been late for work.

Sipping her gin and tonic, she noticed a tiny green lizard shoot across the terrace, stopping for a brief moment at the edge of the garden before darting off under a large rock.

She had only bought the ticket because her mate she cleaned with had told her, if she ever wanted to get out of mucking out for others, than the best thing she could do was to buy some lottery tickets, or take up bank robbing. At the time, desperate for a few extra quid, she had thought she would probably have more luck getting away with robbing a bank. On impulse when she had bought her fags at the corner shop where Mr Greedy charged more than anyone else, but allowed you to have things on the slate, she had bought a ticket: One single ticket with six randomly chosen numbers. One had been her birthday, one was Trisha's another had been.... She frowned. Twenty eight! Now why had she used that number? Huh, fancy remembering that... She took a larger swallow of gin.

"Fancy remembering that..." she said out loud and giggled.

Forty eight hours later, she was a multi millionaire. But despite all her money, she wanted to be better than she was. If only she could be *proper posh*, she knew everything would be perfect.

The sound of bare feet padding on the villa's marbled floor roused Doreen from her thoughts. "Good morning," she said cheerfully as her sleep tousled daughter sauntered on to the terrace.

"Is it really?" Trisha questioned as she set a glass of freshly squeezed orange juice on the table and plonked herself down into one of the chairs opposite her mother.

Through half open eyes, added, “I’m so fazed. You just can not believe.”

She had showered, but the refreshing jets of water had not revived her. She removed the towel wrapped around her head and rubbed at her wet hair, her black thigh length robe parting to reveal a flat stomach and skimpy bikini. Dropping the towel in a wet heap to the floor Trisha blinked repeatedly to help bring the world into focus, gave up trying and resting her head on the comfortable cushions and closed her eyes.

Raising a well shaped eyebrow, an amused look on her face, Doreen stared at her daughter and in a matter of fact tone said. “Can’t say I’m that surprised.”

Flashing a look at her mother, Trisha grinned before taking a long drink from her glass of juice. Letting the cold drink slowly slip down her throat, she ignored what she had just heard and what it was meant to imply. No doubt her mother knew what time she had arrived back. With an over exaggerated yawn, sighed. “I just need to chill, revite my energy levels.”

Taking a large sip of her drink, Doreen peered over the top of the glass at her daughter. She had missed nothing: The flash of her eyes, the dramatic yawn, even the heavy sigh. In a tone that brooked no nonsense, said. “You think I was born yesterday?”

Determined not to bite, Trisha sucked her lips and bit them in an attempt to stop herself from smiling. Through hooded eyes and in a sleepy voice, asked. “Is this a test? If so, I’ve failed. My brain has powered down and is now in energy save mode.” With a cheeky smile on her face, Trisha carefully placed her empty glass on the table and flopping back in the chair closed her eyes.

At seventeen Trisha was confident, pretty and very bright: According to her mother, a bit too clever and confident for her own good. But Doreen was not going to be put off by the show of avoidance. She knew her daughter *was* avoiding answering her and she had something to say, and say it she would.

Getting up and moving over to her daughter, Doreen perched on the chair arm. Crossing her legs realised that she did not like the fake tan that had been sprayed on at the beauty salon before they had set off for this holiday. What she needed was the real thing and sitting here in the dappled shade trying to make sure Trisha was not the one being talked about was not going to achieve it.

Irritation tinged with impatience caused her to snap. "You said you were going clubbing last night, but that ain't all you've been doing is it?" She noted the slight curve of a smile on her daughter's lips at the question. At least she had been heard.

With her eyes firmly shut Trisha answered. "Just tell me why would I say something and not mean it?"

From the direction of the pool came a peal of laughter and splashing sounds as someone jumped in.

Doreen wished she was dipping her toes into the swimming pool rather than sitting here trying to find out if her daughter was the talk of Villas Bonitas. A sardonic smile crept across her face. She was not going to be put off by Trisha's *closed eye* game either: A game her daughter had played enough times in the past. Doreen knew from experience that this was one of the signs that Trisha was trying to steer the conversation away from what she really wanted to talk about.

In a firm voice Doreen replied. "Because you didn't think I'd find out about what you've really been doing."

In her mind, Doreen could hear the foreign woman shouting *vier, vier*. German. She knew a little German, one of the old geezers she had cleaned for had been German. His English had been good but he had more often than not forgotten and jabbered on in his kraut language. *Vier* Four. She did not want to believe anything she had heard that morning, but Trisha's evasive attitude was not helping to convince her.

Sitting up straight and snapping her eyes open; eyes that flashed with alarm, Trisha in a gush of protest cried. "What is there to find out? I went clubbing."

Finally having her daughter's full attention, in particular, her visual attention, Doreen reached for a cigarette from the new packet on the table.

"Look babe, I don't want to ruin your holiday I know you think you are so grown up now you're seventeen, but I don't want you showing us up. I was seventeen once."

Staring at her mother and stifling the urge to laugh out loud, Trisha wondered what planet her mother was on? Not wanting to go down that ancient road of her mother being seventeen, she watched as a cream coloured butterfly fluttered in front of her, then in an indignant tone scoffed. "You are so unreal, I'm not *just* grown up. Seventeen is seriously adult these days. We are so now out of the dark ages." She rolled her eyes in exasperation.

Lighting up her cigarette, the memory of Trisha's birth flooded back to Doreen. She had not been much older than Trisha when she'd had to accept her name would also include *mum*. Puffing on her cigarette, she gazed at Trisha through the thin smoke, her heart overflowed with love for her baby who was so grown up and had more confidence than she would ever have if she lived until she was a hundred and seventeen! Even the lip she was getting was undaunted by her daughter's response.

As the cigarette smoke corkscrewed through the warm morning air she said. "If you ask me, a bit too adult sometimes, because I heard some gossip this morning that made me blood run cold. Not to mention how I felt, as me knees knocked and me hand trembled when the maid and manager came in to see me."

Trisha stared down at her feet her toenails were painted with black nail polish. The right big toe was chipped. She would have to re-do them. She would laugh if she was not so nervous at being found out. The thought of her mother discovering that she had been *enjoying* herself had her heart beating a little faster.

Swallowing down a lump of bile that had risen into her mouth at what she was hearing, it took just a nano second to realise her mother was not the fool she liked to think she was. She knew she must steer the conversation away from whatever her mother had heard and believed. Shrugging; she had not lived on that rough Council estate without learning to think fast. Taking a deep breath, Trisha stared down at her fingers, her long polished nails, painted black and knew which words would work. Confident, she lifted her head; a picture of innocence and whispered. "That's so not possible….."

Ignoring her daughter, Doreen continued. "As you well know I ain't one for eavesdropping, but it was impossible not to hear. I want to think I not only heard it all wrong, and I ain't jumping to the wrong conclusion." Fiercely adding, "And we ain't gonna be the talk of the place!"

Noting the switch from defiance to innocence on her daughter's face, Doreen repeated firm and harsh. "That you ain't been misbehaving or that we're being talked about?"

"Chill Mama, you've got to realise that you are so seriously rich that some people freak. They can't help it. They gossip and wag, it is seriously gross, but you must just ignore it."

Cocking an eyebrow, unconvinced, Doreen gazed at her daughter. She knew how good Trisha was at convincing, hence why she was called *mama*. The snotty little girl who had once lived next door in the Council flats had used the name *mama*. The mother, thought she was a cut above the rest, had told her, *"I'm destined for a better place, the gypsy told me, so best me girl sounds like she might have had some breeding. I let her call me Mama."*

Trisha, liking the sound and had convinced her it was nicer and more loving. All these years later, she was still trying to convince her *mama* of something.

Stifling a giggle at what her daughter had said then letting the memory slip away, Doreen said, "Mmm, I ain't so sure, but just as long as *they* ain't *freaking* over us behaving badly, that's all I'm gonna say for the time being."

Relaxed, Trisha settled back into the chair and smiled as she looked up at the cloudless deep blue sky. A flock of sparrows darted over head. “You know, Mama, this is such a cool place to have fun.”

Stubbing out her cigarette, Doreen rubbed her hands together to remove any residue from the tobacco and watched the smile that crossed her daughter’s face; she wanted to believe her, it was better than believing the other. “And that’s what we are here for, so promise me girl, you won’t do nothing daft. I want this to be the best holiday ever. It’s the beginning of a whole new life for us. And I want nobody to spoil it.”

Reaching forward, Trisha took hold of her mother’s hand, squeezing it jubilantly cried. “So right Mama! Just so right! We are so in agreement. Loves you. Loves you loads!”

Leaning over, Doreen hugged her daughter. “You know girl, I’m so proud of you. You are me special babe, even if you talk posh with lots of odd words these days. Most I ain’t able to understand, but I only want you to have a good life.” Smiling, she kissed the top of Trisha’s head, adding. “Ain’t nobody gonna say different.”

Relieved that her quick thinking had worked, Trisha pulled herself up from the chair. “Want another drink?”

Nodding a yes, Doreen stood up, moved her chair into a patch of sunlight nearer to the dividing hedge of the villa next door where laughter erupted floating from an open window.

“Cor blimey Trish, can you hear them fella’s next door? Do you think they’re *gay*? And this place being so posh and all! Blimey, you never know who you’re gonna meet do you?”

Collecting her mother’s empty glass, Trisha snorted. “Right Mama! As you say, you never know, these days, *who* is staying in *posh* places. Just look at us!” Rolling her eyes heaven wards in an exaggerated, exasperation, groaned, “Mama you are just so seriously priceless.”

Alone, settling herself comfortably in the sun, Doreen reflected on the last few minutes. She was not the fool Trisha took her for. She was very aware of her daughter's little ploy to divert her questions and had played along. The excited voices coming from the villa next door highlighted everything that was changing in her life, and all of it at such a dizzy speed, making her head spin. Even her Trisha was changing, growing up, and like it or not she would have to accept that too.

The unexpected shrill of the phone ringing pierced her thoughts. Jumping up Doreen dashed into the villa. "God where is the bleeding phone?" she cried, frantically searching, pausing she listened then located the ringing, "Blimey even the phone has a posh ring tone!" She spied it on the unit near the drinks cabinet. "Who the bleeding hell would be calling me out here?" She cried, grabbing the receiver. "Hello? Who is it?"

Listening, nodding in a couple of places, the giggle gone, Doreen's face turned chalk white. It was a short, one sided conversation. The line went dead. She tottered to the nearest chair and sank into it before her knees gave way.

"Who was on the phone?" Curious, Trisha walked from the kitchen, a bowl of ice in her hand. She put it down quickly, hurried across the room. "Mama? Ma? What's wrong? You look like you've seen a ghost."

Doreen fumbled weakly for her daughter's hand. "I can't believe it," her voice was wobbling with shock. "It ain't true. It bleeding can't be true."

Trisha knelt beside her mother, her thumb rubbing over Doreen's cold hands. The skin was chapped and wrinkled from years of scrubbing floors and doing dishes and laundry. No amount of expensive cream would put them right.

"Mama? What's happened? Tell me. Have we lost the money? Has the bank gone bust? Was it all a wind up? It is all a big mistake? Mama, please I'm freaking!"

Stunned, Doreen stared at her daughter. "I think I need a drink, girl. A bleeding big strong one."

Trisha jumped to her feet, ran to the drinks cabinet and snatched the brandy. She poured a hefty measure for her mother and a smaller one for herself; coughed as the heat burnt her throat.

"Strike a light, and knock me down with a feather," Doreen whispered as the liquid began to revive her. "I can't believe it. I can't bleeding believe it."

Chapter EIGHT

Standing at the end of her private pathway, Frau Hecks rummaged in her handbag to find her front door key. Snapping the bag's clasp shut, the sound of someone running caught her attention. She looked around, surprised, saw Cissie the maid heading, at an alarming speed, towards Judge Denbie's villa. Tutting, she wondered what the girl was up to.

Cissie was kind and good hearted but a dizzy thing, her head always in the clouds. Frau Hecks tutted again; what had she forgotten to do this time?

Walking down the path she admired how the sun's light created a dazzling effect as it reflected through the palm fronds on to the white walls. She squeezed her eyes to slits to reduce the glare despite wearing her sunglasses. Smiling as she looked around her, everything was beautiful. She loved so much about Villas Bonitas: the rich well tendered gardens, staff buzzing around the place keeping it in order. The high security, she felt safe.

"A perfect place to live," she murmured. Then remembering the earlier incident, her smile fading as she muttered, "Tsk. Ja *it should* be perfect!"

Gripping the plastic bag holding the medication she had collected from the little Chemist in the village, briskly headed to her font door. Pushing the key into the lock she heard the telephone ring from the villa next door, immediately followed by the hurried padding of feet. The phone stopped.

"Huh, they already in demand," she scoffed as her door swung open and she stepped into the cool interior.

Pulling the packet of tablets from the plastic bag, Frau Hecks screwed her eyes tight trying to read the instructions. "Pah, where my glasses?" She clicked her tongue with irritation as she scanned the room. Spying her blue pair next to the phone, reached for them, then remembered something she had forgotten to do.

"Damn," she spat, "I forget Carmen!"

She put the tablet packet down, and sighed with annoyance. "Damn that stupid man." Because of Bob Preston she had spent too much time writing in her diary and had almost missed her appointment at the clinic. Though she now realised that writing her diary had not been the best thing to do before having her blood pressure and heart checked. She smiled, a rueful smile; she had at least vented her feelings in words; a few in bold and others underlined, though so far, it had not improved her mood. If anything, it had only fuelled her impatience.

Picking up her glasses she hesitated a moment; she needed to telephone Carmen to complain, but she also needed to take one of her tablets. The doctor had told her to start this new prescription immediately she got home. Taking hold of the box and at the same time placing her glasses on her nose, she squinted at the instructions. Why did they use such stupid small print? She felt the stiffness in her neck from sitting earlier at her table writing. Now, on top of a sore neck her heart rate and blood pressure was up and all because of people behaving badly. Speaking to that foolish man, Preston had been the final straw. "*Dummkopf,*" she growled.

Pouring a glass of water from her drinking tap, she popped a tablet into her mouth and gulped it down with the entire contents of the glass. Bending down, placed the glass into the dishwasher. She felt low and dispirited of late, or was it loneliness? An unexpected tear escaped, ran down her face. Irritably she wiped it away as she huffed. "Lonely! What am I thinking? I have no time for zis loneliness. I am too busy." She was German, strong and proud. Using the surface top for support, she stood up straight and made her way back to the phone. *Ja*, she would ring Carmen and teach that Bob Preston he could not get away with being rude. Angrily, she snatched up the cordless phone and with unnecessary force punched in the three digit number.

Snorting with disdain Frau Hecks listened to the ringing tone, a malevolent smile creasing her lips. Staring through her patio doors, glimpsed Bob marching along the pathway towards the main entrance in his chauffeur uniform; her lip curled. An answer machine clicked in. Impatiently, listened to the cheerful message, hearing the beeps, curtly announced; "Carmen; Frau Hecks, I speak with you. You call me. It is very important and do not you forget it is me. *Auf wiedersehen*."

Irritated, she roughly replaced the phone into its rechargeable stand. Why was that wretched woman never in her office? Not hearing the *beeping* to confirm it was correctly positioned, she jiggled the phone, nodded satisfaction as she heard the correct sound and looked up sharply as a high pitched, excited scream sounded from Judge Denbie's villa. Alarmed, she bustled out onto her terrace, the bright sunlight stabbing into her eyes as she stared across the hedging toward villa number five, but saw nothing.

What is it those two men do to make such noise? This is too much," she snapped. "Much too much. There is no peace. No quiet anymore."

Hearing his mistress's voice, a fat ginger cat crawled from underneath a yellow oleander bush and brushed eagerly against her legs, his back arching, his green eyes closed as he purred wildly.

Bending down, Frau Hecks carefully picked him up, snuggling her precious pet into her arms. "What is happening? Not only do filthy things happen, Wolfgang, now they disturbing the peace with screaming and unpleasant noises. Even though I make the complaints and write in my diary, things do not improve, they get worse, much worse."

Chapter NINE

Wrapped in white towelling robes, hair dishevelled and damp, Simon and Chicky stepped through the open patio doors back into their villa.

"I don't think I have ever been in such a warm pool, I've had cooler baths," Simon said laughing. "But the *piece de résistance* was that Jacuzzi, My my, I feel every muscle in my body is tingling."

Grinning, Chicky snorted. "My muscles tingled. Or was it they tensed when I witnessed your so called dive? I should imagine the whole of Villas Bonitas heard that splash." Laughing he threw his wet towel on to the bar stool as he stepped past Simon.

"You cheeky boy," Simon said grabbing hold of Chicky's hand as he tried to slip past him, pulling him close. Leaning forward he kissed Chicky on the lips, tasting the salty wetness as their mouths met, then pulled away. He looked into his lover's eyes, about to add that he loved this handsome man standing barely millimetres away, but a sound, a faint, unfamiliar sound, distracted him.

Puzzled, Simon and Chicky let their hands drop to their sides and stepped a little away from each other.

"We left the doors open, what were we thinking?" Chicky whispered alarmed.

"It's not Beirut," Simon countered keeping the mood light and his ear cocked for more sounds. He was not disappointed. Again, the same faint sound. Eyebrows furrowing into deep grooves of wariness both men walked into the hall from where the noise appeared to come from.

"What on earth…?" Simon murmured, ignoring their reflections in the startling floor to ceiling mirror that filled the entire opposite wall as he stood and listened intently.

Nothing!

Chicky sidled up to him, the only sound, their breathing.

"Maybe it was outside?" Chicky whispered, indicating towards the door to his right.

"Let's check here first, you never know if any one saw the doors open and walked in: An opportunist or petty thief."

Nodding in agreement, Chicky crept over to the nearest door, slowly pushed down the handle and nudged the door open. As he stepped into the room, concealed lighting flashed on, revealing a magnificent marbled bathroom. Relaxing pan pipe music immediately started to play from unseen speakers. Feeling foolish, he checked behind the walk in shower and inside the linen cupboard: Nothing, except a tiny spider running along the edge of the shelf. Leaning forward he asked, "Did you make that noise?" Watching the spider run off, added, "No, I guess not!"

Simon opened the bedroom door. He frowned, he did not remember closing it when they had rushed out to have a quick, first swim. Inside, suitcases were flung open, clothes were scattered on the floor and bed. Ah, he did remember unpacking in a hurry to find their bathing trunks. Then a stifled sound of a sneeze. "What the…?" Simon exclaimed, walking round the large bed to the far side, "What the devil is going on?"

Hearing Simon's loud cry, Chicky rushed into the room,

"Damn…" a disembodied female voice floated from beneath the bed, the protruding trouser clad legs and buttocks wriggled backwards, then the torso, scrabbling arms and finally the tousled haired head of a young woman.

On all fours, mortified and burning with embarrassment, Cissie Palmer swore silently as she scrambled to her feet, her hands automatically smoothing her maid's uniform. She sneezed again, cursing herself for not taking more care over vacuuming beneath the bed. If she had, the layer of dust would not have got up her nose.

Chicky burst into laughter. Simon remained looking gruff.

Feeling the heat on her face shading to a deep red, Cissie had no idea what to say. "Um. I can explain," she finally spluttered.

"I'm sure you can," Simon retorted, digging Chicky in the ribs with his elbow to stop the snorts of laughter.

"Well?" he added, folding his arms, and looking every inch the formidable barrister that he was. All he needed to complete the picture was his gown and wig.

"Innocent until proven guilty," Chicky reminded him, stifling a grin. "Give her a chance to explain. We can only hang a culprit once for crawling around on all fours under our bed."

Rooted to the spot with humiliation and looking down at her feet, Cissie only managed a flow of incoherent words. "I'm, I'm, er, er look… was, um, looking for my earring!" Looking up at Simon, her eyes pleading she added, "I promise you it's not what you think…"

Interrupting, hands going to his hips Simon retorted in his sternest courtroom voice. "You can say *that* again!"

"Off with her head, I say," Chicky suggested.

Spreading her hands in supplication, Cissie cried, "I'm your maid, I lost my earring." She pointed to her left ear as evidence, indicating a small hole the size of a pin pick, but no earring. "It's gold with two diamonds." She bit her lip, the redness returning to face. "It's not how much it is worth that is important, but it's very precious to me. It must have fallen out when I was cleaning earlier. I'd checked the blinds were positioned correctly." She pointed at the floor to ceiling blinds that hung in front of patio windows. "I heard it drop, roll off somewhere. I had a quick look, but couldn't see it. I was so busy I forgot all about it, then when I remembered I came back in my tea break." Hastily added, "I saw you in the swimming pool and thought I'd be able to have a quick look before you returned. I'm sorry I didn't hear you come back." She studied her feet again. "I feel such a fool, what must you think of me?"

Relenting the teasing, Simon placed his hand on her arm. “Of course we believe you. Why wouldn’t we? If we find your earring, I promise we’ll keep it safe for you.”

Relief flooded across Cissie’s face, a grateful smile touching her mouth she exclaimed, “Thank you.” She hurried to the door and said in a rush. “I shall be back again tomorrow to clean and change your linens. And…” she hesitated, “And please, you will not tell the manager will you?”

“As long as you stay standing on your feet and don’t attempt any more under bed expeditions your secret is safe with us.” Simon assured her. “We’ll hang you for certain a second time though.”

“Poor thing, I think we scared her almost to death,” Chicky laughed as

they heard the front door close.

The two barristers stood silent for a moment, taking in their surroundings, the luxury of the room, the size of the bed, their suitcases open and clothes scattered everywhere reminding them of their eager rush to the pool.

A breeze rustled the blinds and the scent of honeysuckle wafted in.

A muscle twitched at the side of Chicky’s mouth and suddenly he was laughing.

Collapsing with laughter, they both fell on the bed hugging each other.

Chapter TEN

"Cor blimey what a shock. I'm all a tremble, best you fill this up again girl." Doreen handed the empty glass to her daughter. Stood up, her legs feeling wobbly she stumbled over to the patio doors. Breathing heavily, the fresh air made her feel woozy. She giggled, a nervous giggle with not much amusement behind it, "Bleeding hell," she mumbled under her breath, "what a turn up for the books, what the hell do I do?" Resting her head on the door frame, she could hear Trisha muttering incoherently behind her.

Handing the filled glass to her mother, her voice an octave higher with alarm, Trisha cried. "I can not believe this. Will you *just* tell me what is going on?"

With a glazed look Doreen stared at her daughter. "I tell you girl, you really don't want to know. I can't take it in myself."

"Mama, you are seriously freaking me. Please, just tell me what could have been so scary on that phone?"

Doreen half shrugged, glanced at the filled glass of brandy in her trembling hand, her throat felt too constricted with the shock to drink it. In a quivering voice said, "To tell yer the truth babe, I not sure myself."

Grabbing her mother's arm Trisha steered her back inside to the leather sofa, pushed her down gently. Tightening the belt on her robe, she ordered; "Mama, spill. You'll feel so much better. I know I will." She hunkered down. Her uncombed hair fell across her face. Pushing it back irritably, her mind ran wild as she muttered. "*Oh My God! There's been a seriously mega error. We're not lottery winners! Oh my God I feel* sick."

Bewildered at her daughter's behaviour Doreen answered in a weak voice, "I tell you girl, I'm all jellified, that geezer on the phone's taken the wind right out of me sails."

Sails? Jellified? Tears of frustrated anger and disappointment started to flow down Trisha's face. With the sleeve of her robe she wiped her eyes and wondered how on earth she would survive the humiliation. Her life was over. She would be laughed at, ostracised or worse! How could anything be worse? *Oh my God, no money. No money! Nada! Nothing!* She thought. More tears spilt. *I'll be a laughing stock. Those bitchy girls at that stupid school will be a hundred times worse, please God tell me It's not true? Please!*

"What are you crying for?" Doreen asked suddenly aware of the tears. "God, did I frighten you? Sorry babe, it's just a bit of a shock, that's all. We'll be all right. You see if we ain't."

Trisha stared at her mother, her cheeks glistening wet, her eyes red rimmed. Very quietly, with a couple of false starts and more than one gulp she stated, "We are poor again aren't we? It was all a hoax wasn't it? There was no money was there?"

Doreen stared in astonishment at her daughter, then giggled and reached out a hand to brush away the tears and hook her daughter's hair back.

"What? Good God girl, this isn't nothing to do with our money." She patted the sofa, inviting her girl to sit beside her. "Trish, you are not going to believe this. That geezer on the phone I knew him years ago, before you were born. We were together for a long time, we had such a laugh. Still can't believe it. God knows how he knew I was here."

Aghast Trisha jumped to her feet. "What? What are you saying? You are so not real. There is me on serious melt down, in free fall panic believing we have lost everything. Wondering how I am going to tell my friends what a gross mistake it was. And you sit there telling me you went all pale and shaky with that scary look on your face because of someone you used to know? All this fuss had nothing to do with your lottery win? I don't believe it. You are spaced out on a memory!" Shocked, annoyed, Trisha dropped to the cool floor and lying flat on her back stared at the tiny lights fitted into the ceiling. In a piqued tone, added. "So Mama, no pressure, just what *is* going on?"

Looking dreamily at her sprawled out daughter, she really did not understand her half the time, Doreen shook her head, the untouched brandy spilling over the side of the glass. "Trish you don't know the half. Not sure where to begin, but you might have heard me twittering on about those days before you were born. Yonks ago me and Pat were an item. You know I loved him back then. The things we did in those days you just wouldn't believe; right cocky monkey he was. Don't sound like he's changed much neither." She giggled at the memory, her self confidence returning as rapidly as it had diminished. "So much I can remember and all of it from that call. Who'd believe it eh?"

With a steely gaze mixed with disgust and relief Trisha mentally posted, a *do no*t *go there* sign in her mind. The last thing she needed to hear was what her mother had got up to back in the dark ages. Her tears dried, she snapped. "I can not believe you are giggling about the long ago past. Old men are just gross!" In an attempt to bring her mother back to reality, continued. "So I can take it, we are definitely still rich?"

"God babe, you don't think I'm old do you? I ain't no spring chicken I grant, but I ain't no gerry-attic either. I assure you if he's like he was, he ain't old." She giggled at her naughty thoughts.

Taking her mother's words as positive confirmation about the money, nauseating as what she was talking about sounded, Trisha stood up, relief flooding her face. The millions were not lost, though it seemed likely that her mother's marbles may well be! With a look of disdain she plonked herself on the sofa. "Ugh! That is so too much information. So how is it possible that *he* knows you are here?"

A puzzled frown crossed Doreen's face. She had been wondering that too. "I ain't got a clue, but he's asked me to go out with him tonight. Can you believe it?"

Horrified, her mother *had* lost the plot, Trisha squealed. "That is simply a no go situation."

Raising a well shaped eyebrow in amusement, Doreen queried, "Blimey, why ever not?"

Glaring at her mother in disbelief Trisha retorted, "Excuse me, but this is seriously out of order. For all you know he could be your first gold digger."

Laughing loudly Doreen noted her daughter's concerned face. "He isn't like that. Mind, I like the idea of having a gold digger chasing me. Blimey what a scream!" Seeing the black look on her daughter's face, she grinned adding. "I'm only joking, I ain't no fool. No matter what you think, so for old times sake I'm off out with him." With a flash of memory, added, "I've nothing to loose. I lost *that* with him a long time ago."

In disbelief Trisha opened her mouth to add a further comment, changed her mind and remained silent. The room was suffocating despite the air-conditioning pumping out cool air. Disgusted, she headed towards her room. Stopped, smiled and sauntered back. "Right! You know Mama…" a devious smile making her eyes sparkle. "I just want you to enjoy yourself. After all, that's what we are here for. It is cool with me if you must see him, but I take it you will be out until late?"

Not registering the quick change of attitude Doreen answered without thinking. "I never thought you would miss your dear old mum. But, don't you worry about me, you go and enjoy yourself clubbing."

Overjoyed at how things had unexpectedly turned out, Trisha trilled; "You are so right my mummsy. Clubbing is where it will be happening for me."

Gulping at the brandy, licking her lips Doreen added, "You know? I'm so excited I feel sixteen again. That's how old I was, when me and him were an item."

Cringing at the thought Trisha headed for her room, this time she did not stop until her door was firmly closed.

Chapter ELEVEN

Antonio Perez checked his watch as he walked through the security gates into Villas Bonitas. He noted the date displayed and smiled. He had been running the cocktail bar for five years to the day. Where had the time gone? Reminiscing, he thought about how many cocktails he had mixed, how many bottles of wine he had opened and champagne corks that had been popped. Enough, he thought to fill an ocean!

Born and bred in Yorkshire, christened Barry Ramsbottom, after leaving school at sixteen he went to work in the village garage. But a holiday to *sunnier climes* changed his view on what he wanted out of life. He had packed his bags, reinvented himself as Antonio Perez and headed for the sun. After years of work in bars and hotels, he had landed the manager's job to run the cocktail bar at Villas Bonitas. He had never looked back.

Making his way along the sun drenched paths, Antonio cocked his ear at the beguiling sound of a bird singing and admired the expensive and immaculate surroundings. Antonio smiled. He had fallen on his feet the day he had been appointed, Bar Manager. Villas Bonitas had a reputation second to none. He loved it: Loved everything about the place.

Passing the terrace of villa number four he noticed Doreen Wilkinson sitting alone, a cigarette in one hand, a glass in the other. Gin and tonic, he guessed. She'd had a few at the bar the previous night, her first night here. Giggling with her 'fink' and 'fought' accent, a breath of fresh air, he had thought, he had enjoyed her company. Usually, he was surrounded by the pretend posh and the so called *real* posh! Over the years he had learnt that was how it was at Villas Bonitas: The rich came in all guises. But after a few moments in Doreen Wilkinson's company he knew she was not posh, just rich. Very Rich!

He had seen her picture splashed all over the UK Dailies. It would take a lot more than money to change her cheeky little manner and voice. Secretly he hoped, despite her sudden wealth that would never happen. He had met too many people who had lost their true selves once they became rich. Last night, talking to her, watching her sip at her drink followed by a pull on her cigarette, he had seen that she was genuine: the real thing. Unlike some of the people who came to Villas Bonitas. He pulled a face at the hypocrisy and waved to her as he passed by. She was stunning to look at. Money was not needed for *that*.

Crooning, "Buenos dias Dor…rreen" - he over emphasised her name.

She glared at him, a startled expression. "Ooha I was miles away, just had the shock of me life." Giggling, Doreen added "Sorry, what did you say?"

"I say, you looka more beautiful today, than even yesterday. Impossible I knowa." He raised his eyes and hands to the blue sky. "It musta be our beautiful sun that makie your cheekies glow"' Bowing his head slightly, he blew her a kiss. "*Adiós*, Dorreen, I sees you later? It is possible?"

"Oooooha…. You're a one." Giggling, Doreen raised her right hand, touched her lips and blew a kiss back.

Antonio could still hear the giggle as he walked towards the bar, he chuckled. If only all the people who came to Villas Bonitas could be like Doreen Wilkinson then his life would be filled with sunshine. He sighed, he was not that lucky!

Raising a small hinged section of the grey granite counter, Antonio stepped through into his octagonal shaped bar. Lowering the hatch back into place he surveyed his little domain, he might not own the bar, but it felt like his and he was proud of it. Flicking his fingers across the grey marble counter a fine layer of dust rose up. The bar open to the warm days and sultry nights, the dust was a permanent feature. Taking a bunch of keys from his pocket he moved to the closed section of the octagon, unlocked the padlocks and pushed open the security shutters. Clattering and squeaking, they rolled up, revealing bottles of alcohol and soft drinks; shelves filled with glasses of different shapes and sizes.

"Antonio, now you are open, pour me a large stiff drink," Carmen called, emerging from the shade.

Turning abruptly, dropping his false accent, "You are not serious?"

Walking over to the bar, her step heavy Carmen admitted, "No, I really could do with one, but you had better make it a strong coffee. I've a mountain of things to get through. I shouldn't be standing here asking for coffee, but I really need it. There are times when I wish I had never heard of Villas Bonitas. Today is one of them."

Moving to the coffee machine, Antonio checked the water level and flicked the switch to 'on'; the red light glowed. Picking up a clean cloth from under the counter he strode back to Carmen, frowning, creases appeared across his forehead. Wiping down the counter, he observed. "You mean to say you have woken up to this place not being paradise?"

A sardonic smile flashed across Carmen's mouth. "Paradise in hell, it's hot here. Some of the owners breath fire. The rest are either devils or angels, and Hell's angels at that."

Raising an eyebrow and tossing a look of surprise at her, he said. "So who has been plucking their harp too loudly?"

Casting a rueful look at her bar manager, Carmen knew only Antonio would try and make light of the situation, "You'll only laugh if I told you."

"Why would I do that? I don't know who's upset you."

"Why do you think it's *someone?*"

"Because it normally is!" Hearing a hissing sound from the coffee machine he walked over and placed two cups under the jets in readiness and asked, "Black or white?"

Carmen laughed. “Black. I’ve been doing this just a tad too long. Secrets and deceptions, even if they are not going to hurt anyone, are hard to keep.”

Stepping back to the counter Antonio shrugged and carried on wiping down. “When it comes to saying the right thing, you’re perfect.”

“Not sure that is true,” she added, giving him a sceptical look.

“You always talk firmly, friendly and make people feel at ease, no matter who they are or what is going on. It’s a compliment, that’s why everything runs so well here.” Turning his attention to the coffee machine, added. “The water should be hot enough now, let me get your coffee and I’ll join you.”

Over the noise of the machine, Carmen called. “Do you think that Doreen Wilkinson and I are in any way alike?”

Antonio laughed, almost spilt the coffee. “If you don’t mind me being honest, you are two very attractive women, but what a crazy question?” He set the two cups on to saucers, brought them to the front of the counter, pushing Carmen’s towards her. He went to the fridge, fetched the milk and poured it from the carton straight into his own. Tearing open three packets of sugar added that as well. “Mind you, now you mention it, I’ve noticed you’ve started to giggle and say *fink and fought* instead of think and thought.”

Carmen laughed. “Very funny, I guess I deserved that.”

Despite hearing the laughter, Antonio clearly saw the strain on Carmen’s face, noticed the sparkle in her eyes was not there either. The tired look, he knew was down to the heavy workload. Her responsibilities were not for the faint hearted. Today was a busy one, Carmen would be in the front line if bullets flew, and there would be one or two fired across her bows. Though concerned, he had kept his response to her question light. She had laughed, but he knew she must be very tired to think about asking it in the first place. Over the years they had become good friends, she had been there when he had needed her, he had needed a good friend at times. They had never been lovers but even though their backgrounds differed, he would have liked it to have been a possibility. One day, maybe.

Stirring sugar into her coffee, Carmen noted the concern on Antonio's face, today was not a day for indulging in self pity she had to snap out of it. Wanting to reassure her bar manager; her good friend, that all was okay she smiled, said in a voice more positive than she felt, "Don't worry I'll get over it. Keeping busy and some time away eventually, will sort it all out."

She took a sip from her coffee. "To add to everything else, our dear Frau Hecks is on the war path *again*. She left one of her cryptic angry message on my answer machine. I grow sick and tired of her constant complaining. I don't know what has got into her. She's like a bear with a sore head these days." Sighing, continued. "Bob said she was on about something in the pool house. Perhaps I'd better speak to him first."

"You won't find him here, love, he was in his chauffeur's jacket and cap, left as I came in and was in a mighty hurry. He said something about Jeff Butler wasn't able to go to the airport, Bob was stepping in. You know who he's collecting?"

Pressing her fingers to her forehead, Carmen grimaced. "Can this day get any worse?"

Chapter TWELVE

"I could have died,' Simon moaned leaning on his elbow, raking his fingers through the fine hairs on Chicky's chest. "I could have been ruined. Shock can have some terrible side effects."

Chicky gazed at his partner, a satisfied smile lighting his face, his heart still racing; their lovemaking had been so beautiful. He had never known Simon so relaxed, so stress free and tender. Turning over, his damp body clung to the satin sheets, taking hold of Simon's wrist, his thumb moved up and down the clammy skin until he detected the throbbing of a pulse. Amused and in a mocking tone scoffed. "Mmmm, just as I thought, you are very much alive and your pulse has slowed just a teeny weenie bit. My verdict; you have spent far too many hours in court. It clearly has turned your head and your conduct into an Oscar winning performance!"

"I'm glad you are satisfied," Simon teased, "but I was referring to the incident with the maid."

Chicky laughed. "Were you indeed? Well, if you ask me that poor girl had a bigger shock, looking up at our ugly mugs."

Stabbing his index finger into Chicky's chest, indignant, Simon countered, "Speak for yourself. There's nothing wrong with my handsome visage. It will resume its youthful look when the shock lines disappear."

"Shock lines? I hope you are talking about the poor girl. I can only see old age creeping in on yours"

"Very funny,' Simon scoffed leaning over to the bedside table where a bottle of champagne cooled in a bucket of ice. "The only way to calm my nerves and stop my pulse from racing further will be to open this bottle of bubbly." Swinging his legs off the bed he lifted the chilled bottle from the ice bucket, expertly removed the foil before releasing the cork which shot out of the bottle omitting a loud *pop* as it flew across the room.

"A fine sound. I can think of nothing more beautiful than popping a cork with the person you love." Chicky grinned as he stretched out, his head resting on his hands as he watched the golden liquid flow into the champagne flutes. As the bubbles rose to the top of the glass, he was reminded of the first time they had drank champagne together. A moment he would never forget. They had won an important libel case: One that had hit the news headlines, creating too much publicity for anyone's good. After the verdict a toast had been made in the privacy of Chambers. Throughout the court hearing, he had admired Simon. The look he had received as he had surreptitiously peered over his glass, wig removed, but still gowned, had made his heart skip. Eyes sparkling with excitement and desire had shone back.

Leaning over the crumpled sheets, Simon caught the faraway look in Chicky's eyes as he handed over the filled glass of champagne, grinned. Feeling a surge of warmth flow through his veins as he guessed where his partner's thoughts had drifted too; his own had remembered that moment as he had poured the champagne.

"I know exactly what you are thinking," he said as his fingers grazed against Chicky's. "The day we drank champagne after the big court case win."

"Peeping into other people's private musings is an offence," Chicky scolded as they chinked their glasses together, but secretly was thrilled that Simon was thinking the same thoughts. Happiness coursed though him, it meant their relationship was important. To him it was very important. He did not want to make another mistake. With renewed desire he rested his naked back against the headboard, declared, "To popping corks, to you, me, and our week together in paradise."

Chapter THIRTEEN

"Bob, get those suitcases into our villa. And, be careful, they're expensive. Like everything we have." Jack Hoskins hollered as Bob rode off in the buggy with the porter and the Hoskins' luggage.

Swinging his arms as he strode towards the bar, his large frame clothed in expensive slacks, open neck, pure cotton shirt and a well tailored jacket, not a hair out of place or a crease in his attire despite the journey, Jack Hoskins hummed a cheerful tune. Then less than four yards from the bar, barked in a commanding voice. "Good Afternoon," staring down at his watch, "yes the sun is over the yard arm."

He grinned as he looked around inspecting the immaculate gardens, the perfect spherical shape of the fig topiaries. He took in the freshness of the white painted villas and finally looking down he nodded at the spotlessly clean tiles under his feet, snorted approval and strode to the bar.

"Perfect!" He announced resting his palms on the silver grey marble of the counter then surveyed the condition of the bar and snorted approval again.

Raising a hand, Jack waved towards Carmen who sat at the other end of the bar, jovially beckoned her to join him. "Carmen, the jewel in Villas Bonitas' beautiful crown, how wonderful to see you again. Come here, you're a sight for sore eyes." Extending his arms, added. "As always it's grand to see you."

Puffing his chest out, adding extra bulk to his large frame he grabbed hold of Carmen as she approached and placed his hand on her shoulder. A broad grin on his face, his eyes alight with pleasure he wrapped his arms around her and hugged the manager tightly.

Carmen flinched and silently swore under the pressure of Jack's arms hurting her ribs.

Releasing her, oblivious of her hostility, Jack stated. "You simply have no idea that when we are out in the big bad, greedy world, caught up in the cut and thrust of business, the boring meetings and endless phone calls how we think about being here." His hand thumped her shoulder again.

Cursing silently, he had only been here a few minutes and her nerves were already shot, Carmen winced and moved back a pace, extricating herself from his unwelcome grip. Jack Hoskins was a man full of bonhomie, but was also as irritating as a mosquito. Equally as annoying, his incessant use of '*we*' as if he and his wife, Sheila were royalty.

"It's a tough decision, Carmen, to drop everything and just walk away, but you have to every now and then, hence why it is so good to be back." Jack stepped forward and grasped her elbow. "No doubt you've been wondering what we have been up to since leaving this little paradise, eh?"

Noticing a stack of English newspapers to the left of the bar he stretched over and snatched one from the pile. Licking his thumb and index finger, flicked through the first few pages then stabbed at a headline. In a loud and excited voice instructed, "This is what you should be reading; '*Rich get Richer.*' Keeping abreast of movers and shakers will keep you up to date with where it is all happening."

Winking at Carmen he added with pride, "You'll see my name there from time to time. Life is not always for sitting around; it's for making money. And I for one do that extremely well. Wheeling and dealing. That's the name of the game."

Carmen formed a false, polite, smile. It was well known at Villas Bonitas and in the local town of Pelito, that the Hoskins' money was more down to ducking and diving than wheeling and dealing. As for checking the papers, the only things that shook and moved were the heads of those who knew Jack Hoskins as they checked to see if he had been rumbled and arrested.

Taking Carmen's silent smile as one of agreement, Jack carried on with his diatribe. "Having just arrived you can appreciate we've a great deal to catch up on as well as important people to entertain. The list, as you'd expect, is a long one, my good wife Sheila, the hostess goddess, has already booked caterers and the like for the parties and get togethers we're intending to have. It's our duty." He snorted. "Duty, ha, the burden of our lives."

"Well, yes. I must…" Carmen tried to interrupt and make her escape, but folding the newspaper up and tossing it carelessly back on the pile, Jack continued.

"Life in the fast lane, Carmen is as you know, not for the faint hearted. Me, I thrive on it. It's in my blood: The adrenalin rush. At the end of the day it's what makes my ticker beat with such passion." He thumped his chest with a beefy fist, and shouted across the bar. "Antonio my man get me a drink." The request resonated around the area making the glasses on the shelf jingle.

Carmen's lips twisted in irony, she knew *exactly* what made Jack Hoskins' ticker beat, or rather, *who*. He might have pulled the wool over his wife's eyes, she was far too busy preening and feeling important to notice, but he most certainly had not fooled her! Adrenalin and a racing heart had everything to do with him living in the fast lane, but not the fast lane he liked everyone to think he was speeding along. He was bullet proof, he had once told her. She wondered if there was *a use by date* on bullet proof vests; from what she had heard, she hoped there was not, for his sake.

"Well," she said briskly, "It's good to see you…"

Jack stared straight into Carmen's eyes, his face taking on a serious look. "Shouldn't you be getting along Carmen?" he interrupted. "Plenty to do and all that. Villas Bonitas won't run itself. Standing here gabbing with me is all right if you have the time and I know you haven't. So, I won't keep you a moment longer. Just long enough for me to say it's grand to be back. And despite the need to keep my finger firmly on the pulse, we're here for six weeks. You can't beat having quality time in your own sunshine home, especially when you're in the cut and thrust. I don't have to tell you, there's no rest for the wicked. God, I must be a serious demon." He chortled as he watched Carmen hurry away. "Don't you graft too hard and overdo it," he called after her. "I'll see you again later."

With an expansive grin Jack returned his attention to the bar.

"*Beinvenidos,* welcome, Jack, I ask that you have the same drink as always?"

Staring across at the impeccably dressed barman, Jack jeered, "Good God it's me, Antonio, you surely know we have our usual at this time of the day. How many years have we stood at this bar? Don't bother to answer, just get me a *Bucks Fizz* and make sure it's got plenty of the bucks. And, whilst you're at it, prepare one for when I've drank the first."

Bristling, Antonio selected a bottle of champagne and fresh orange juice from the chiller unit. With skilled practice he popped the cork, not wasting a drop of the precious liquid and plucking a large glass from the shelf mixed the two ingredients. He had his back to the large, irritating villa owner and mentally counted to ten, then one to ten again while calling out in a cheerful, pleasant manner, "*Si si*, you have perfect bucky fizzy. Mucho bucky!"

"You don't fool me Barry lad with your fake *si si* banter. Save it for the lasses. I've been coming here far too long. Just remember there's nowt wrong with being Yorkshire. You should be like me, proud."

Without saying a word, Antonio placed the frothing drink on the bar.

Raising the glass, slopping some of its contents down the side, Jack drank greedily. Wiping his lips with the back of his hand he set the empty glass down with a thud. "Not bad Antonio, less buck in the next one would improve it. Talking of which, you'd better bring that other one over here. I've a powerful thirst, spitting feathers!"

Antonio silently served the prepared drink.

Ignoring the barman, Jack stepped away from the bar and squinted through the prolific greenery of the gardens towards his villa. "Where the hell is that lass of mine?" he hissed as he strode to the edge of the paved bar area. Placing his hands over his mouth to form a cone, yelled, "Sheila where the hell are you?"

Startled, birds took to the air. A rush of feathers flapping, rattling of leaves and loud squawks and shrills. As the peace returned, the disturbed bird life re-settled, an uneasy hush hung over Villas Bonitas.

With a look teetering on despair Antonio reflected that by now he ought to be prepared for this regular routine, but he never was. The pantomime of the Hoskins' stay had begun. Nothing, if previous occasions were anything to go by, would be the same as long as they were in residence.

Chapter FOURTEEN

Bob Preston struggled through the opened front door of the Hoskins' villa, each arm straining with a heavy suitcase. Despite the cases having sturdy wheels, the weight inside had buckled them to the point they could barely rotate. Wheels or no wheels, Bob knew it would not have saved his arms, he had been given stern instructions from Mrs Hoskins; *on no account was he to wheel the cases across the marble floors*.

Grunting loudly with the exertion he set the cases down inside the spacious open plan living area. He was nearly 65, his birthday was in a few days' time. Maybe it was time to start thinking of packing this side of the job in? He rubbed his numb arms before bending down and resting his hands on his knees as he gasped for breath. Perspiration trickled down his face, the jacket of his chauffeur's uniform had damp patches under the arms. His heart thumped against his rib cage and he wondered if he was about to have a heart attack. "I'd not be that lucky," he grumbled in between his fight for breath. "And if I did she'd still have me unpack."

Straightening up, he dragged a handkerchief from his breast pocket, raised his cap and with his free hand mopped at his soaked brow. Setting his cap back on his head, he coughed, a choking sound emphasising the state he was in, sniffed and peered around for Mrs. Hoskins. Where had she gone? She had been a few steps ahead of him as he had struggled through the door.

Mmm…vanished into thin air? He could hope!

Clocking a straight back chair close by, tempted as he was to plonk himself down on it, he knew murder would be committed if he was found squatting on one of the Hoskins' much bragged about antiques. Instead, he slumped down on to one of the suitcases, sighed at the relief of taking the weight off of his feet. Barely half an hour past noon and already he was knackered. Glancing around the villa he shook his head at the furnishings and décor; heavy and dark colours clashed, nothing fitted in with the light and airy style of the building. Knick knacks were scattered everywhere, larger, tacky ones even on the floor. He stared at the pictures that hung on every wall, likely originals, set in ugly and gaudy frames. Nothing matched or coordinated. He mentally cringed, all that dosh and everything loud and tasteless!

Standing in front of the floor to ceiling mirror in her dressing room, Sheila Hoskins smiled admiring herself. She was buxom with a fresh complexion, teeth all her own, straight and pure white; breasts, despite childbirth, full and rounded. She twisted to get a side view; her bottom had enough meat on it to make a seductive wiggle. Placing the flat of her hand on to her stomach, preened, almost purring with pleasure; just enough there to remind her she was a woman and a mother. Sheila loved what she saw; attractive, very rich; a social diva, but honest and down to earth.

Reaching for her handbag she fetched out her lipstick and moving closer to the mirror carefully applied a new coat of colour. The expensive gloss shimmered in the glare from the ceiling micro spotlights. Poised to smack her lips together to even out the colour, to her annoyance, Bob Preston's rasping voice distracted her.

"Petal? Where do you want these crates put?"

Bristling at his undignified brazenness, Sheila tutted at her reflection, "How dare he call me *Petal*? The cheeky bugger!" She tossed her head indignantly, her highlights glimmering in her well cut style.

"Just as well I'm an easy going person or else I'd have had him sacked years ago," she said running the left palm of her hand over her perfectly conditioned hair. "Fancy describing my beautiful luggage as *crates*?"

Ignoring his exaggerated coughing and snorting she continued making her lips full and beautiful. Leaning forward, she placed her face close to the mirror, her breath creating a fine mist on the glass as she smoothed her lips together. With a stylish pout smiled at the result. Placing her lipstick back into her handbag she extracted a bottle and sprayed copious amounts of Chanel around her neck.

Feeling important and with a shimmy of her hips, she walked out of her dressing room, her high heels tapping on the marble as she left a perfume trail in her wake. Gasping in horror, shrieked: "Get up off of that suitcase! Have you any idea how much the set cost? They are not only designer label, but the best money can buy!" Teetering into a half run towards Bob, she waved her arms like lethal batons.

"Gawd, a suitcase is a suitcase ain't it?" Bob grumbled as he creaked to his feet, hips and knees protesting. "The weight in those *designer* cases nearly finished me off. I had to sit down to get me wind back."

Staring at him with utter distaste, Sheila flapped her hand as she saw how carelessly he had dumped her luggage. "It is hardly surprising you're known as *Bob The Bodger.* Good God man, have you no sense at all? Could you not put them down carefully and leave them alone?"

Striding over to her suitcases she ran the tips of her fingers over the leather exterior checking for scuff marks, silently chiding. *What is Villas Bonitas coming to?*

"If you're not up to the job, then I think it's high time someone younger took your place," she snapped. "I've only brought a few essential bits as most of my things remain here in the wardrobes." Huffing annoyance she headed back into the bedroom. "Just bring one at a time then. And mind the marble."

Bob stared down at the two bulging suitcases. "However did they pass baggage control?" he mumbled. "You say you've only brought bits? Blimey Petal, all I can say is thank Gawd for that, coz you certainly have some heavy bits!"

One hand on her hip, her head tilted to the side, Sheila stared pitifully at him from the bedroom doorway. "Shall I call Carmen and ask her to send someone younger and fitter?" she sneered. Losing her patience she strode back to him and ushered him to the front door. "Leave them, leave them alone. I'll sort them out myself. You'll probably only do more damage anyway."

How on earth was he still employed here, she wondered, but refrained from saying so. She would deal with him later, there was plenty of time whilst they were here to keep him firmly in his place.

Pointedly she went to the door and opened it wider. "You may go. I wish to say hello to Carmen and Antonio." Her face lit up at the thought of seeing Antonio. "He will be over the moon to see we are back. Jack and I bring the right amount of social elegance to Villas Bonitas. Our soirees match celebrity status."

Bob was half way through the door eager to be going, but Sheila stretched out a well manicured, immaculately nail polished hand and lightly rested it on his arm. "I am thought of as the official first lady of Villas Bonitas, a title close enough to be almost royalty. Remember that in future when you are squatting on my expensive luggage."

Staring at her in disbelief, Bob mockingly touched one hand to his cap in salute. He would have attempted a bow had his joints not seized up with all the lifting. He had heard it all before, but the arrogance still took him by surprise. He stepped out on to the pathway, halted as Madam Bonitas snapped a parting shot.

"Oh, another thing, keep that uniform of yours clean, crisp and well pressed and your cap squarely on your head. We have a busy social schedule planned, you will be needed now and then, if you think you can manage a few light duties, that is? People like us are constantly in demand." Looking Bob up and down Sheila wondered if he would make it through the six weeks they were here for. He looked so unfit. "Well, prattling with you won't get me my drink, so let's be having you. We don't pay you to sit in our homes and show disrespect, do we?"

Bob saluted again. "No Ma'am, that we don't Ma'am. Anything you say. Ma'am."

Under his breath as he walked away, Bob mumbled; "Three bloody bags full Madam Bonitas."

Chapter FIFTEEN

The afternoon sun blazed down through a cloudless sky creating heat shimmers across the resort's landscape. Beyond the pool and the cocktail bar the ground sloped away down through dense shrubberies and palm trees to a secluded sun terrace, which in turn led to the beach and the expanse of the ocean. The sparkle of silver and the occasional white seahorse a contrast against the deep, deep blue. Occasionally residents and guests of Villas Bonitas wandered down the meandering path to play beach volleyball or relax beneath the tent like sun canopies on the terrace, but as it was a trek back up the long slope, most stayed within the privacy of the grounds.

Villas Bonitas, nestling in its splendour of semi tropical gardens, basked in the sultry heat. Frau Hecks stretched back her shoulders and felt her muscles ease as she stepped out onto her terrace. Her afternoon siesta had left her feeling refreshed, the ache in her neck eased and her mood calmer. The new prescription tablets she had taken that morning had made her sleepy and more relaxed. She sat down under her large sun parasol, the sun too intense at this time of the day, and settled herself comfortable on the yellow sun lounger. Her view of the gardens and the sound of the sparkling waterfall that cascaded down into the ornamental area of the pool were restful and calming. Villas Bonitas was beautiful, truly a paradise on earth, she needed to try and enjoy it again. The position of her lounger gave a vantage point for watching the comings and goings of her neighbours. Picking up her book from the cushion she flicked to her book mark, read the first paragraph, but hearing a scratching noise, smiled then snapped the book shut.

Standing outside the open door of the pool house, Bob made a fuss of closing and locking the door. Pulling it almost to a close, he then yanked at it, shutting it with a bang. With an exaggerated rattle of the key in the lock, producing a loud scratching noise he turned the key and the lock clicked home. Testing the door was secure he rattled it then dropped the bunch of keys into his trouser pocket. Chuckling, he guessed the old bat, Frau Hecks, would be watching his every move. He did not want to disappoint her.

Satisfied, he swaggered along the wide pathway, turned right and walked briskly through the cactus garden. Glimpsing a cluster of delicate yellow flowers on the crown of two large pumpkin cactus, he slowed and admired their beauty before continuing to the swimming pool. Several owners, and their various guests, were sprawled out on the large cushioned recliners. With a sly look he ogled at the semi naked bodies of the women, his dark sunglasses hiding his eyes. He sniggered, he might be the wrong side of sixty, but beautiful bodies were still beautiful bodies: Especially when topless. Not wanting to be accused of being a dirty old man he hastily averted his gaze and headed to edge of the pool. Peering down into the crystal clear water nodded with approval. He had tested the correct chemical balance earlier and the water sparkled like diamonds, but nonetheless he liked to check it glistened brightly before he left for home.

Turning, he scratched at a cut on his elbow and realised no matter which path he took to the gates, he would have to go past Frau Hecks' terrace. The cut now bleeding, he licked his finger, wiped away a tiny drop of blood, licking his finger again to remove the excess blood. With his finger still in his mouth, wondered what he was fretting about? He had locked the door hadn't he? What more would the old battleaxe find to moan about? Making his way slowly along one of the paths he whistled, a nervous, tuneless sound, but no sooner had he taken a few steps on to the main pathway then he spied Frau Hecks strutting across her terrace. In an attempt to avoid another confrontation he hastened his pace and lengthened his stride. Head up he focused his attention on the gates and escape to freedom.

"You leave early. You finished everything today, eh?" Frau Hecks called. "I talk with you, you listen. I only ask *ein* question."

Frau Hecks' voice was loud and dominating. Her question caught the attention of the people around the pool; inquisitive, a couple of the sunbathers sat up and looked towards the indignant woman standing on her terrace, more than one of them relieved it was Bob about to get it in the neck, not themselves.

With an exasperated expression of weariness, Bob walked onward, as he neared Frau Hecks, enquired politely, "Flawline, what can I do for you?"

Stifling a smile he thought: *Wring your neck? Stick Ductape over your mouth? Fetch a couple of lizards and a blind bat? Slip arsenic in your cauldron?* "I am off home for a few hours. It's been a long, trying morning and the day isn't finished yet. I want to put me feet up, have a bite to eat then get cleaned up and changed. I've some chauffeuring to do this evening."

Frau Hecks stared down her nose at him, then switching her gaze to the pool, glared at one of the girls bathing on a lounger. With her eyes focused on Trisha, she said. "I know you leave. I not stupid, but you make sure you lock that door good. You hear what I saying? I know what went on there this morning. I know much more than you imagine: Too much!"

Keeping her narrowed eyes locked on Trisha, she emphasised her point. "Nothing, I tell you, nothing I miss. Don't you ever forget."

He was beginning to get a bit tired of kowtowing to these women. Sheila lick-her-boots Hoskins, or was it now Madams Bonitas? And this German biddy. Lifting his right hand as if to pull at his forelock, Bob touched the peak of his baseball cap, opening his mouth to speak hesitated as Frau Hecks shifted her penetrating stare to concentrate back on him. He shivered. Realised he could be in serious trouble with this particular villa owner. He had half an idea who had been in the pool room, at least an idea as to one of them, and he would sort it, but in his own time. When his rough guess was more inclined towards absolute certainty.

In a reassuring tone, one he hoped would calm her ruffled feathers, he quietly said, “Rest assured Flawline it’s all locked and safe. You’ve got my word.” Not waiting for a response, he strode away.

Chapter SIXTEEN

The fragrance of coconut oil drifted in the air, Doreen had slathered her body in the sweet aromatic sun protection lotion. Not that she wanted to protect too much, she was here to get the real thing she had reminded herself as she had smoothed the milky oil over her fake tan. She felt relaxed and comfortable sitting around the pool, laying on the comfortable sun lounger and soaking up the sun. It was as close to heaven as she could ever imagine.

Hearing the sound of a voice, a voice she had heard earlier that day, the smell of the rich and expensive cream lost its tropical allure. Sitting bolt upright, swinging her legs to the side she perched on the edge of the sun lounger, her earlier tension returned. Picking up her packet of cigarettes from the little table at the side, shook one out, pushed it between her lips and lit up. She could hear that old witch rabbiting on about doors being locked. Turning she saw the German woman staring across at the pool area, she did not need twenty-twenty vision to realise that woman's beady eyes were focused on her Trisha.

Why is the old bat still harping on about a door? she thought. *Bleeding hell what is wrong with her?* Closing her eyes, she wished she could disappear. "Who would've thought having money could be such bleeding hard work?" she muttered as she took a puff on her cigarette. Tears pricking her eyes, she bit her lip. *Gawd give me strength because at this rate, I'm going to need it,* she silently cursed.

Looking through her dark, designer sunglasses her mind drifted to her old life, the opulence around her disappeared she could see the water dripping off the metal framed windows in her old Council flat: A 60's built hovel, cramped and cold with its damp rooms and mouldy walls. Out in the street there had been more cars perched up on bricks than on wheels, and at night the shadows had been particularly scary, gangs and louts hung around looking for trouble.

Despite the desperation of the place, it had been her home and she had known the rules; everybody had. She could have handled the situation there, not like now. Here, people did not come right up and yell at you, give you a chance to get whatever it was off your chest with a few choice words, and, if necessary, the odd slap. No, here they look, mutter and nod and you have to try and work out what is bothering them as if you are a mind reader.

All this giving of the evil eye was doing her head in. On the Council estate she would have stood up and confronted the old battle axe. She would have shouted and screamed at her like that time when that old busy body of a neighbour had pulled Trisha's hair out in clumps all because the little girl had refused to get out of the way. Her poor Trisha, only seven at the time, had howled the street down.

Doreen exhaled cigarette smoke, remembered clearly running out of the flat as if the place was on fire when she had heard the yelling. Pulling herself to her full height of 5ft she had stood in front of Mrs Gardner and screamed at the top of her voice saying should she ever lay a finger on her baby again, she would kill her. Of course she had shook with fright.

Sniffing, she let the past melt away and watched the gardener-handyman touching his cap and walking off, the German woman, she noticed, did not move. She was still glaring towards the pool. Doreen transferred her tension to biting her nails. She would have to say something. Of course, she would not scream or carry on like she had done back then on the estate. She would say what was on her mind in a friendly manner and leave it at that.

Guiltily checking that her lovely false nails were still intact, she felt better; she had thought through a plan. Smiling, puffed on the stub of her cigarette then nipped it out with her thumb and forefinger before dropping it into the ashtray.

"Best to get it off me chest, then I can get on with me hols," she told herself as she slipped her arms through her wrap. Standing up she pulled it around her as she fastened the belt, keeping her eyes down to ignore the other people sitting around the pool. With a step lighter than she felt, forced herself to walk towards Frau Hecks' terrace. Her heart beating nineteen to the dozen her legs feeling as if they were going to collapse under her she made it to the bottom of the German woman's terrace.

In a voice that sounded like a squeak, called, "Excuse me!" She cleared her throat, said firmer, "I hope you aren't talking about me girl? Because she's a good girl and I don't want to hear you suggesting nothing different. We're decent people and we don't want any bother. So if you've got something to say, best you say it now to me."

Frau Hecks stared straight down her nose at Doreen and with a sour glare, her thin lips emitted a loud, "Tut Tut" She turned abruptly away and strutted back into her villa without uttering a single word.

Her legs about to give way Doreen was shaking like a jelly, but the outrageous snub turned her anxiety to anger. Not wanting to show herself up by shouting out, but inside she screamed with rage.

Bleeding hell, I'll get me revenge, so don't hang around just you wait and see! Her eyes filling with tears, she felt so much out of her depth that she could easily drown. Humiliation pouring out through every pore, she felt the eyes of the people around the pool burning into her back. Knowing she must turn around and return to her sun lounger, she took a deep breath. It shuddered down to her lungs, she promised herself she would find a way to get back at the old bitch. But for now she had to save face. What could she do? Adjusting her sunglasses and with all the dignity she could muster, she called out in a loud, pleasant cheery tone to Frau Hecks departing back, "Thank you! Most kind!"

Smiling and over exaggerating the swing of her hips she strolled over to her daughter laying with her eyes closed listening to her iPod. Everyone else, Doreen noted, was suddenly busy with their magazines or drinks or pretending to be asleep. Hypocritical bleeders!

Poking Trisha's ribs, Doreen hissed. "Take them things out of your ears, and listen to me."

Startled, Trisha snapped open her eyes and removed her ear plugs. "That is just so dangerous. You can't go poking people when their eyes are closed and their brain is overloading with music!"

With neither a smile nor a sneer Doreen focused her eyes on her cheeky daughter, "Gordon Bennett girl, just you listen to me for a minute. I'll be having a word with you when we get back in our villa. That foreign biddy's been insinuating things again and giving us a very nasty look. And, I can tell you for nothing, we ain't putting up with it. Savvy?"

Trisha, half asleep, snorted. "You mean to tell me I nearly died of shock because you got the evil eye from some old woman? You are just *so* weird."

Annoyed, Doreen looked around and noticed a woman sitting a short distance away pretending to read a book. She knew the nosey parker had been listening intently to everything that has been said. She smiled and waved. She was not going to run away and let them gossip, instead she called over. "What do you do with them? At this age, you can't do nothing can you?"

Chapter SEVENTEEN

Sheila Hoskins grimaced, peeking over her paperback book at Doreen. What was Villas Bonitas coming too, letting such riff raff in? Good God, how on earth did they get in here? Laying her book on her chest, she stated, “Are you talking to me?”

Doreen, bare foot, skipped across the hot tiles and winced, she had not expected them to be so hot. Plonking herself down on the chair next to Sheila’s sun lounger, she lifted her feet up, “Blimey didn’t expect that.”

With a smug look, Sheila eyed Doreen. “You and me both!”

Her feet dangling inches from the ground, Doreen blurted out. “I’m at the end of me tether with that old woman over there,” she indicated Frau Hecks’ terrace. “She’s really got it in for us. Blimey we’re here on our holidays. What is her problem?”

Studying Doreen, her nose wrinkling as she took in the bright coloured bikini and wrap, she uttered. “Good God!” Then in a haughty tone said, “Don’t you think I should introduce myself before *we* begin a conversation? I am Sheila Hoskins and this is my husband Jack.” She pointed a finger at her husband sitting in the next sun lounger reading a newspaper, he ignored her. “You do not need to tell me who you are. I believe it is Doreen Wilkinson?”

Astonished Doreen placed her feet on to a shady tile and in a voice louder than she intended replied, “Yes, that’s right, but how on earth did you know?”

Lifting her sunglasses onto her head, revealing steely grey eyes, a sly grin curving her lips, Sheila announced, “Having noted you on our arrival I made enquires. Put it like this, I know you have not been here before because if you had you would know who Jack and I are, and you do not.

But that is by the by for the moment. You would also know that to cross Frau Hecks would be to invite trouble." Sheila smiled with self importance, dropped her sunglasses back onto her nose and lifted her book, an obvious act of dismissal.

Giggling, not to be snubbed a second time, Doreen squealed, "Blimey, not much gets past you does it? You're right it's our first visit. First holiday in fact for yonks."

"Mrs Wilkinson, I know *everyone* who comes here. And up until now I did not know you." Snapping her paperback shut Sheila looked directly into Doreen's face. "My husband and I spend a lot of the year here in between our commitments. You would never believe how many functions we have to attend and give. Coming here is still business as normal. Functions to attend, deals to close, people to organise, friends to catch up with, the list is endless and…" tilting her head towards Doreen, added, "…at times daunting. Of course, there are those who are a little jealous, naturally, of our lifestyle but that is their cross to bear." Pausing, she took a deep breath. "Well I think that is enough about me for the moment, it would be useful to know something about you. We are a very exclusive club. So tell me where are you from?"

"You mean you don't know? We're from London, not a bad place to be from. What about yourselves?"

Cringing, Sheila replied with pride. "Harrogate."

"*Oh* 'Aringey? Blimey, that's not all that far from me, Straight up the North

Circular, we are almost neighbours!"

Choking on her spittle, Sheila gulped then cried, "*Harrogate* in beautiful Yorkshire."

Clicking her fingers and giggling, Doreen squealed, "Gordon Bennet what must you think of me? Course I've heard of it. Me mate went there had some lovely food at that famous Harry Ramsbottoms, said it was like going to the ends of the earth just to the chippy!"

Sheila gasped and silently sobbed, *Bloody hell*!

The quiet relaxation of the pool terrace was suddenly interrupted by a loud melodious ringing. Almost falling off his recliner in haste to get to his mobile phone, Jack grabbed the leather case.

"God damn it," he cursed, almost upending his sun lounger as he managed to wrestle the phone from its captivity. With unnecessary force punched a random key, the musical jingle stopped. "Hello, Jack Hoskins speaking." Listening, a sly look crossing his face, "No, definitely no. You have the wrong number. Goodbye." Flushed, Jack punched the end call button.

Her attention diverted to her husband, Sheila snapped. "Why don't you leave that thing in the villa? You could have broken that bed with all that cavorting. Important as we are, whoever it was could leave a message."

A devious smile on his face Jack eagerly agreed. "You are quite right, my dear I'll take it back to our little homestead." He stood up and flicked his newspaper under her arm.

Smiling up at her husband, Sheila added, "I think it is best. We do not want to be disturbed during our relaxing personal time do we?"

Jack grinned and happily walked away.

Catching sight of Doreen standing up, Sheila commanded, "Hang on a minute, Mrs Wilkinson, we have lots to talk about, sit down." Watching Jack walk away, Sheila smiled and turned to Doreen, pleased to see she had sat down again.

"Sorry about that, but you know what it is like." Her eyes hidden behind her sunglasses she stared at Doreen. "Well of course you do not, but never mind. To be perfectly frank, what I do not know is how you have managed to be staying here? Villas Bonitas is an exclusive and very, *very* expensive private complex. I would not have thought it was your kind of… "about to say *class*, hesitated, "er, thing."

She indicated to where Trisha was sprawled out, earplugs deep in her ears, "Especially as you have a *teenager*." She said the word as if it was an obscenity.

Doreen glared at Sheila. She might be a little lost in this fancy world of riches, and sounded common compared to these swanky accents, but she was not dumb nor naïve. And as for that so called wrong number phone call that was about as likely as her being the Queen! She giggled. She would play along for the moment.

A shiver of confidence trickled through her veins, cheekily she answered, "Seems after all you don't know everything then. But you are right about one thing, it is a bit pricey here, but so what? I've been saving me benefits. Bit of moonlighting here and there and all, plus what me old man put aside after that last job of his, before he went off on his holidays" She winked, "If you know what I mean?"

A look of horror on Sheila's face made Doreen laugh outright. Winding up people like Sheila Hoskins, thinking they own the bleeding world, was too easy to be fun. "No of course I'm fooling you. I won the lottery, millions. It was in all the papers: famous as well as rich. To tell you the truth, me adviser organised all this. Never heard of the place myself, but she said it was the bees knees. Seems she's right." For the first time since arriving she was enjoying herself.

"Who *exactly* is your advisor?" Sheila demanded.

Wanting to laugh at the snooty cow and tell her what she really thought, Doreen said instead, "Lovely girl called Stephanie Rawlinson, you must know her? She knows everything about this place and everyone."

Baffled, Sheila had no idea who this Rawlinson woman was, but she would certainly be finding out. "Of course, Stephanie, I should have guessed. So much going on in my head, the name did not spring immediately to mind."

A black cat appeared from under the sun lounger. Sheila turned her attention to the cat as it stretched before ambling off down the pathway. Thankful of the distraction, the last thing she wanted to talk about was someone she had no idea about. "How strange, we have seen nothing about your win and fame. Although having said this, we have never been ones for reading the red tops. You can't believe a word they print. The *Financial Times* and *Guardian* are our newspapers. I don't suppose you were in there?"

Ignoring the question, Doreen happily trilled. "Well you can take it from me, it's true alright." Silently adding, *seems to me there's a few things you don't know about or can't believe*!

A short distance away, Simon had heard enough. He detested bigotry in any form. Rising from his sun lounger he walked over to where Sheila and Doreen sat. His body casting a shadow, he raised his sunglasses above his eyes and looked down at the two women, gave a small half bow towards Doreen.

Sheila looked him up and down, impressed by what she saw in his lithe, lean body. "You are a deceptive one aren't you?" she said with a silken seductive voice. "Taller than I thought you would be seeing you laying down on your sun bed."

"Deceptive. Aren't we all at times?" Turning to Doreen, a genuine smile creasing his face, Simon offered an invitation. "Mrs Wilkinson, seeing as I too am a newcomer to Villas Bonitas I think it is high time we become acquainted. May I get you something to drink?"

Looking up at Simon, Doreen giggled. "Thanks, that's nice of you. I think with all the *hoo ha* I'm having with everything, I need something strong."

Graciously he also gave a small bow towards Sheila. "And for you Mrs, er, Hoskins? What would your poison be?"

Sheila simpered, adjusted her costume straps, drawing attention to her well rounded breasts. "Please do call me Sheila. I'll give you this you are nicely built as well as tall and good looking. As you're asking, I'll have a glass of champagne."

"Ooooah! I could murder a glass of champas," Doreen cried, clapping her hands with delight. "I so love it when those bubbles tickle your nose!"

Raising a blond eyebrow, Simon laughed, "If you don't mind, with one thing and another and seeing as I too am on holiday, I think it best if we try and avoid murder!"

Doreen giggled. "You are a one!"

As Simon left to order the drinks, Sheila called. "I do not want Antonio pouring any old rubbish in my glass. Tell him it is for me and he will know better than to send you back with anything short of the best."

"Indeed I will. I will make sure only the best is popped for you." Leaning towards Chicky, who, resting on his elbow was watching him, said. "I don't need to ask you, as I know the answer; a large one with lots of bubbles."

A ringing tone, *Who wants to be a millionaire?* shrilled from Doreen's handbag beneath her sun lounger.

"It's for me," she cried as she skipped across the hot tiles and grabbed her bag. Rummaging inside, moaned, "Maybe these mobile phones shouldn't have been invented." Snapping it to her ear, yelled. "Hello? Dorry here. Who is this?"

She frowned as she listened to the voice on the other end, the frown deepening. "Gordon Bennett, how did you get this number as well? You have already scared me half to death once today." She listened again as she sat on her lounger, giggled. "You ain't changed have you?"

Simon returned glanced over at Doreen, then settled on his own lounger, one eyebrow raised as he exchanged a glance with Chicky.

"What? Of course I ain't changed me mind. Tonight. Eight thirty. I'll be ready." She switched the phone off and shoved it back in her bag, her hand trembling.

"Secret admirer?" Simon asked with a chuckle.

"Sort of," Doreen answered, "though more of an old flame popped back to life it seems."

Balancing a tray holding four filled champagne glasses in his left hand, Antonio negotiated the head of the pool. "*Hola, amigos*, this is a-perfect for keeping the blood a-cool."

Approaching Doreen he handed her a glass and smiled as she nodded her gratitude.

Antonio headed for Sheila.

"I hope this *is* well chilled, Antonio, and I mean *well* chilled. In these temperatures you should have brought it in a cool glass holder. Never mind, it will have to do, but remember next time."

Accustomed to Sheila's cutting remarks Antonio was prepared. "La champagne I have it-a so cold it could-a freeze off-a your tongue. Be very careful laydee." Aware he was skating on thin ice he briskly served the two men and returned to his bar.

Simon winked at Chicky and raised his glass. "Cheers me dears, bottoms up, I think this is going to be one very different kind of holiday for all of us!"

Chapter EIGHTEEN

With the memory of the afternoon still fresh in his mind and on his skin, Jack smiled as he strolled through Villas Bonitas opening security gates. Casting his gaze around the luxurious complex, noted the pool area devoid of bathers, the recliners placed back in their tidy position, the Jacuzzi silent. On the air the sound of chatter as voices drifted from the bar. Antonio's false accent ringing out, Jack chuckled to himself. "How we can fool others so easily!" A salacious smirk replaced his chuckle as he marvelled at how he had spent the last hour; sixty long minutes of heart pounding, mouth watering and skin tingling passion. God, he could not get enough of her! Satisfaction softening his face, a lighter step to his gait, he marched towards his villa.

Aglow with deceit he sauntered across his terrace and through the open patio doors into the lounge. The coolness of the room made him shiver. Glimpsing Sheila talking on the phone, he grinned that she was distracted from his arrival. Nodding at her, mouthed, "Hello, I'm back."

With no intention of stopping he headed straight to his bathroom. Pushing open the door he stepped inside, about to close it, heard Sheila calling to him. "Damn and blast," he spat. Ignored her and shut the door, but could still hear her pretentious voice echoing through the villa. He frowned, whipped his clothes off, tossed them on to the marble floor and stepped into the shower. Turning the gold plated knob to full power let the warm water jets massage his shoulders and back, conveniently drowning out Sheila's words.

Pushing the door open, Sheila shouted testily, "And where've you been? Have you seen the time?" Not waiting for an answer, pulled the door closed and wandered back into the lounge continuing her phone conversation.

"Your daddy's just walked in. I've no idea where he's been." Frowning and agitatedly waving her free hand about listened to her daughter on the other end of the line. "No, we were sitting by the pool and I told him to do something about his wretched mobile. He said he'd take it indoors and well I've not set eyes on him since. He's having a shower now, so I'd better get off the line for when he eventually emerges, then I can find out what's he's been up to. Now you take care, darling and I'll talk to you again tomorrow. No, don't worry, I love calling you when we are away. No don't think it's a nuisance, because it's not. I'd better be off as daddy will appear shortly, just take care. Love you! Tat ta." Stretching over the silver framed photograph, taken last year of Jack, Michelle and herself, Sheila placed the telephone into its charger, her heart squeezed with affection for her daughter. She loved chatting with Michelle. Jack however was a different matter. She strutted towards the bathroom door. "Jack, where the devil have you been?"

Having taken what must have been the fastest shower on record Jack dried himself off. Tossed the wet towel onto the unit top next to the double sink and stepping over his clothes, reached for his comb and raked it through his wet hair. Staring at his reflection in the mirror he looked down and gloated. "Nothing wrong with you my man, nothing wrong at all."

Hearing Sheila's voice, grabbed his towelling robe from the hook behind the door, slipped into it and as he tied the belt around his, not too thickened waist, opened the door. Smiling asked. "What's all the fuss about? You know full well where I've been. Exercising! Power walking that's what I've been doing. And a damn good session it was." He grinned at the memory of the afternoon's activities that had made his pulse race madly. "You know, I always feel invigorated when I've had such an energetic session."

Stepping round Sheila, he padded, bare foot, into the open lounge area. The sun was far enough to the west to cast its glow across the floor, picking out the light gold flecks in the marble creating a sparkling effect.

Watching him stride away, her face puckered, Sheila cried. "Well I'm glad to hear it, but surely it is a bit much when we've just arrived? There's no point in overdoing it on our first day especially in this heat. Jack, you ought to have more sense at your age."

Casting a sly look at his wife, in an indignant tone said, "I'm not as past it as you think."

Giving him a once over she nodded, despite their active social life he was in good condition. *Belly could do with toning up a little, but then that's what he's doing with his power trots,* she mused and smiled at the fact he was making an effort with his physique.

Striding over towards the drinks cabinet and trying to keep the excitement from his voice, Jack said. "Don't you worry, I took it steady. No need to rush these things, what I did this afternoon was enough for any man my age."

Walking over to her husband Sheila leant against the breakfast bar, folding her arms, smiled. "Glad you've got some sense."

Pulling two glasses from the shelf, Jack placed them on the unit top. "Now, let me get us a drink and then I'll tell you what I've *really* been up to, okay?" Grabbing the gin bottle from the cabinet, twisting the cap removed it and poured the translucent liquid into the glasses then added a dash of tonic. With both glasses obscenely filled, he picked them up, clutching them tightly, made his way out to the terrace. Putting the glasses down on to the table he looked behind him and called. "Well if you want this drink and to find out more about what I've been doing, best you get yourself out here."

Preening at such consideration from the man she had been married to for thirty years, Sheila sashayed out onto the terrace.

Handing his wife her glass, Jack sat down and took a greedy gulp from his own. With more gin than tonic flowing down his throat, he coughed. "Bloody hell, I've made this a bit strong." He coughed again, took a smaller sip. "You know me Sheila, despite being out sweating buckets, pulse racing, heart beating madly, I've checked up on that other business ordered before we left Harrogate. Well I can confirm it is all organised."

A screech from a parrot sliced through Jack's words as if laughing at him. Looking up, he swore, "'Bloody thing, better not crap on this terrace."

Pulling a face at his profanity, Sheila winced.

"As I was saying, our little surprise is all organised. So we're off to Amigo's restaurant tonight and everything's in place, so no need for you to mither. I've even got Bob running us there."

Beaming, Sheila trilled, "What can I say? I should make a fuss about you disappearing like that, worrying me, but I'll leave it as it's our first night." Reaching over she stroked his hand. "You're a good man, Jack. How else could I have stayed married to you all these years?"

Looking over the top of his glass, Jack watched as his wife drank her gin and tonic, though it was not her face he saw, he was picturing that other face the one as familiar as Sheila's. *Oh what a tangled web we weave,* he silently recited, but knew nothing would stop him having his cake and eating it. After all, he was a greedy bugger. He sniggered with pleasure.

Chapter NINETEEN

"What am I going to wear?" Doreen cried panic rising as she stared at the chaos in her dressing room. Dresses, skirts and trousers scattered all over the floor. Tops and shawls draped over the drawer units. Shoes and sandals littered everywhere. The cavernous wardrobes looking depleted.

"Gordon Bennett," she sobbed stooping down to pick up the black dress she had tried on earlier. Inspecting, the low cut, sleeveless dress, groaned. "It ain't all that bright is it?" Sighing threw it on the chair in despair. Stepping over garments piled on the floor she walked into one of the open wardrobes, rummaged around and pulled out a box filled with jewellery. Clasping the box in her hand, she pushed a top to one side, making space on the drawer unit top, opened the lid and giggled. "Blimey that's more like it," she cried plucking out a purple necklace. Offering it to her throat, stared in the mirror and smiled. "Phew think I'm going to be saved!"

Clutching the necklace she peered back into the box, rooted around and found a pair of matching earrings. Placing the purple jewellery down on the unit top, she moved to the chair, picked up the black dress, this time slipping it on, it fitted like a glove. The neckline, carefully fashioned to show of her slender shoulders and the tops of her rounded breasts at the same time highlighting her small waist. The hemline, sitting just above her knees, Doreen looked stunning.

She fastened the necklace around her neck. It hung low enough to sit on the top of her breasts then she popped the matching earrings into each pierced ear.

Admiring herself in the mirror, Doreen smiled. "Now isn't that better?" Giggling, added, "Don't want to scare him off with all me bright colours." She did a twirl in front of the long mirror and nodded. "Not bad girl. Not bad at all!"

Having applied her makeup earlier, she pouted her lips, studying her choice of lip gloss colour, frowned. "Mmm, I think red would be best. Pink isn't me." Snatching a tissue from the box, partially hidden under the array of strewn clothes she wiped the pink lipstick off. Grabbing her makeup bag Doreen searched through and fished out a deep red lipstick. Staring into the mirror, applied the shimmering gloss to her lips and smiled. She had worn red lipstick when she had gone out with him all those years ago. Funny, she thought, that she should remember that one thing.

Admiring herself again she wondered what *he* would look like after all this time. He had not sounded any different. Then sniffing loudly squealed, "Blimey

what am I thinking?" Reflected in the mirror she could see the mess she had made trying on all the different outfits, but why had she bothered? Her excitement evaporating as she realised the truth of things. She had not seen him in over sixteen years. So why did he want to see her now? She puckered her brow, maybe her Trisha was right and he was only after the money. It was no secret she was rich.

Feeling deflated she sighed loudly. "I need a ciggie." Stepping over the piles of clothes, she stumbled to her bedroom. A new packet lay on her bedside table. Tearing off the cellophane she opened the box and took out a cigarette. Irritably she stubbed its end on the box. "Strewth, what should I do, because I'm not in the mood to be made a fool of? And why does he want to see me now after all these years?"

Picking up her lighter she flicked it to life. The flame flashed, she let it burn, then without lighting up her cigarette, snapped the lighter shut. Throwing the cigarette away, she sat down heavily on the edge of her bed. Should she go? Should she stay? The question was nagging at her. Catching a glimpse of herself in the mirror Doreen giggled. "You're a silly cow Doreen Wilkinson, what were you thinking? Pull yourself together, you have now got yer glad rags on, so get out and enjoy yourself. Just what have you got to loose?

Nothing girl, nothing!" She giggled again as she stood up, straightening her dress, added, "What am I like?"

Strutting back through to her dressing room, ignoring the mess she

selected a bottle of expensive perfume. Spraying the sensual fragrance liberally all over her, she sneezed then plonked the bottle down and randomly selecting a bright purple wrap from the scattered pile she sashayed out, heading to the open lounge.

Sprawled across the sofa Trisha, with nimble fingers, was busy texting on her mobile phone. She wiped her hand across her nose which irritated and had begun twitching at an alarming rate. She looked up as her mother glided into the room, sniffed the air, smelling a mixture of expensive perfume and pungent cigarette fumes, cried. "Ozone Mama…," and at the same time punched buttons on her phone. "Breathe and die, don't breathe and die. This is a seriously unhealthy pad."

A puzzled expression masked Doreen's face as she strode over to where her daughter sprawled out. "Good word to use girl, *die*. Talking of which, I don't want to be dying of embarrassment again. I'm going out for the evening and I want you to promise me you'll behave whilst me back's turned. I don't want to come home and have that German witch giving me another nasty stare or anything else."

Amused, Trisha looked up at her mother. "Chill Mama. We simply freeze out the evil eye. By the way, black is such a cool colour these days. Take it from me, you look just so fab. I seriously hope the blast from the past is worth it."

Bewildered, Doreen really did not understand her daughter sometimes, she shook her head, but the words about her choice of dress colour made her smile. She decided to ignore the other barbed remark. Leaning down she kissed the top of her daughter's head. "Thanks Trish, that's nice of you to say that. I'm in bits with me nerves, but I admit I'm curious and best I look the part." Aware her daughter was not paying her any attention, added. “You sure you’re going to be okay with me out?”

Trisha laughed, waved her mother away. “Mama, behave be good and be gone. Bye bye!”

Giggling, Doreen shook her head. “You’re a one.” Satisfied her daughter would be fine Doreen made her way towards the front door. Reaching out for the door handle she pulled the door open and turning looked around the room and across at her daughter playing on her phone. Her heart filled to overflowing with love for her only offspring, stepping through the open door, called. “You call me if you need me. See you later alligator.”

Her stiletto heals clicked on the tiles as she walked down the path, her heart racing, Doreen reminded herself, that she was going on a date not a death sentence and giggled nervously. Making her way along the wide pathway that snaked through the gardens to the main entrance, the swaying fronds of the palm trees, the rich colours of the bougainvillea and the flaming reds of the hibiscus were a blur to her. Her mind swirled like a kaleidoscope; a mixture of curiosity, happiness and apprehension mingled together on what might happen when she met him and what had happened all those years ago.

Chapter TWENTY

With most guests and owners of Villas Bonitas preparing for an evening out, Frau Hecks was not one of them. Preferring her own company these days, she sat content in her lounge. The evening, sultry and still, her patio doors wide open, music played quietly from a CD. Wolfgang, curled, asleep on her lap, her novel opened midway through the book laid face down on the low table next to her chair.

Gently stroking Wolfgang, her ears were cocked to the outside sounds as the little world she lived in went about its business. Hearing the chatter of voices as people meandered through the gardens, the tip tap of heels as footsteps echoed along the tiled pathways; the distant clinking of glasses as toasts were made, all familiar sounds drifting on the night air, she sighed; it was a resigned sound. Of late she had felt grumpy and wanted to keep herself as private as was possible. Living in a transitional community was irritating at times and more so of late. People came and went, staying for a week or up to several months at a time. Few, like herself lived permanently at Villas Bonitas. She used to enjoy seeing different people, she knew the insufferable ones left eventually, went back home. Slowly she swept her hand across her cat's smooth fur, a tear trickled down her cheek; her memories were close to the surface. Why was that she asked herself? Tired? The new medication? The date? Maybe all three? She did not know. Another tear splashed onto her hand and another.

They were sixty when Hans and she had bought the villa. They had bought off plan, the price was high the specification even higher. They had not been disappointed when at last contracts were signed, keys ceremoniously handed over. Everything had been carried out to perfection.

Their luxury villa set in the exclusive complex of Villas Bonitas, nestling on the fringes of the old town of Pelito was simply perfect. The gardens from the start appeared to have been there for years. The palm trees mature, the shrubbery; bushy, green and flowering, filled with nose twitching fragrances: A heaven on earth. They had enjoyed three years of regular visits. The relaxing atmosphere and tranquillity should have made for a long and healthy retirement. But three years to the day after they had opened the door as new owners, Hans Hecks had been diagnosed with cancer. Six weeks later Frau Hecks with her daughter, her son-in-law and two little grandchildren had stood at the graveside of a beloved husband, father and grandfather and with tears streaming down their faces they bid him a last goodbye.

His life cut short. Sixty three was no age to be taken so cruelly from them. The shock of losing Hans was all consuming and she had decided, not only to keep the villa, but move in and live permanently in the paradise she and her husband had chosen for themselves. She had felt closer to her Hans in the villa than she had in their large old family house in their adopted England. Paradise had not been all it had seemed, though. As she had settled into her life without Hans, instead of embracing the friendship of other owners, over time she had grown resentful. And resentment was an unpleasant companion.

Blowing her nose and wiping her face, she heard a giggle followed by the clicking of heals on the ceramic tiled pathway she craned her neck to see who was walking past and tutted as the phone suddenly shrilled. Clutching Wolfgang hurried to answer it.

"Frau Hecks… Oh it is you Carmen. What now? You come earlier and tell me all is fine, so why you calling me?" Wolfgang wriggled and she held him tighter. "*Ja, danke schoen* Carmen, I fine. What that you say? *Nein*, I have the touch of hay fever. I am quite well. Good *nacht*."

Placing the phone down, struggling with Wolfgang tucked under her arm, Frau Hecks pulled a handkerchief from her cardigan sleeve and blew her nose. With a silent sob she ambled to her chair, sat down and hugged Wolfgang close to her chest. His responsive purring was a comfort.

"Pah," she sobbed into her handkerchief. Carmen asking how she was feeling, coupled with the rush of sad memories overwhelmed her, she wept freely.

Chapter TWENTY ONE

Dressed in trendy casuals, Simon and Chicky strolled along the wide quayside admiring the expensive cruisers and sailing yachts moored in Pelito's exclusive Marina. Size appeared to be of importance, nothing as insignificant as a dinghy could be seen among the display of such astonishing wealth. As if this was not enough of an appetizer, the air pungent with contrasting aromas of grilled fish, meats sizzling on flamed griddles, fresh fruits flambéed in spirits assailed their nostrils and taste buds from the plethora of smart bars and stylish restaurants. Pelito's Marina Plaza buzzed as the well heeled, smartly dressed and rich dined at white linen covered tables waited on by attentive staff.

In the centre of the Plaza a beautifully sculptured life size yacht cast from bronze, resplendent with crew, drew their attention.

"An amazing eye for detail and presence," Chicky observed. "The designer carefully thought out how his work would sit here amongst all this opulence."

"It's beautiful," Simon agreed comparing the sculpture to the reality of the rows of slick, stylish vessels moored mere yards away. "I wonder how many mega fortunes are made legitimately in our modern world?"

"It is easy to be lost in all of this," Chicky gazed in awe at a vessel larger than his London apartment and likely cost several times more. "It's so unreal and yet it is. It's surreal."

Simon, his mind wandering to the main reason why *he* was here, stared past Chicky and metaphorically pinched himself, *surreal*, he said silently *is a good description.* Returning his thoughts back to Chicky smiled and agreed. "It *all* seems surreal to me too!" Not wanting to be distracted by his thoughts and certainly with no intentions of sharing them, added. "Pains me as it does my dear Chicky, but I must bring us back to our *real* life. We need to make tracks for the restaurant, our table's booked and I'm famished. Admiring these floating gin palaces, expensive and flash as they are, won't change life for us." He would like to have added, *just yet*, but knew better, instead said. "We can't afford one." He grinned. "But dinner we can!"

Sharing the pleasure of the moment, Chicky wanted to reach out, take hold of Simon's hand, hold it tight and tell everyone how much he loved this man, but he could not. They were not Romeo and Juliet, man and woman, they were two *men* in love. And men in love were not as readily accepted as young, star-crossed lovers. He linked arms with Simon, that, surely, was acceptable in public, smiled, he laughed lightly. "Sea air and bubbling champagne always gives me an appetite!"

In the middle of the Plaza, opposite the bronze scene, *Amigos Restaurant* stood elegantly, its name engraved in bold script style letters into the large picture window. Simon pointed to the blue and yellow painted facia.

"It would appear our table is in that rather splendid restaurant over there. "Once again it seems Paul's tastes have excelled our expectation. Not only a villa, but also a first night restaurant recommendation."

As they entered the restaurant, a waiter advanced to great them, a wide smile spilling across his face. Confirming their reservation he escorted Simon and Chicky to a front table overlooking the bronze yacht sculpture. With the exception of three empty tables which had reserved cards placed neatly on the linen tablecloth, the restaurant was full. The ambience appeared tranquil and relaxing; the murmur of soft voices, the muted clinking of cutlery against crockery, created a sophisticated, intimate atmosphere. Simon and Chicky seated, the waiter placed the wine menu and the restaurant menu onto the table, nodded cheerfully. "At your leisure gentlemen." With a cursory bow he left the two men.

Simon casually rested his hand on the edge of the table and surreptitiously glanced around, catching Chicky's look, he winked, "I think we should be safe in here, discerning clientele I note. After this afternoon's carry on with that dreadful woman, I was beginning to wonder what Paul had been thinking when he bought a holiday home at Villas Bonitas."

Looking down the menu Chicky nodded. "It takes all sorts, I suppose, but I know exactly what you mean. I quite like the sound of this fish, or maybe the lamb?"

Simon leant forward to see what his partner was pointing at on the menu and glimpsed two people approaching the door. He exchanged a resigned grimace with Chicky and suppressed a groan.

Warm air rushed in as the door flew open, mixing with the cool air-conditioned interior. The patter of hasty steps sliced through the conviviality of the dining area as a waiter hurried to snatch the handle in order to steady the door before it banged against the nearest table.

Jack Hoskins stepped inside, his wife behind him. Glancing quickly around he raised his arms in bewilderment and cried, "Carlos, my man where the heck are you?"

Astonished faces stared back at him. "Where's the master of the house?" he added as he dropped his arms and with a sheepish grin, nodded amiably to the other customers as they returned to their meals.

Pulsating with importance, Sheila moved next to her husband casting her gaze at who was dining. With a superior twist to her lips she smiled benignly at Chicky and Simon, then linked her arm into Jack's. Together, they glided down the wide space between tables, like A list celebrities walking along the red carpet on Oscar night, towards the bar at the rear.

Appearing from behind a beaded curtain, Carlos hurried to greet them.

"Señor 'Oskins! Madam Sheila! 'Ow delightful to see you! 'Ow beautiful you look tonight, Lady!"

A broad smile fixed on his face, Carlos extended his hand. Grabbing it, Jack pulled the small, swarthy restaurant owner towards him and embraced him in an over exuberant hug and proceeded to pat him on the back. "Good evening Carlos. There is nothing more heart warming than the welcome we always receive here at Amigos. It's what brings us back time and time again."

Carlos freed himself from the vice like grip and embraced Sheila, making the motions of air kissing her on both cheeks. "I have, of course, reserved your usual special table. But first, you like a complimentary drink at my bar, *si*?" Grandly he escorted them to the bar, the smile fixed, the generous welcome convincing. The thought of why these two wretched people should always choose to target his restaurant when there were plenty of other restaurateurs to annoy, safely hidden from public view.

Sheila perched herself on the edge of a chrome bar stool. "You know Carlos it is the fact that you treat us how we expect to be treated that brings us back time and time again. You understand and, wisely, appreciate your more important clientele."

"*Claro si*, indeed!" Carlos said as he swiftly moved to the other side of the bar. With his back to them grimaced, poured two drinks. He had not bothered to ask what they would like; he knew. They always had the same; the best and the most expensive. He shrugged. Business was business, despite who the customer was. All the same, he wished that, just once, he could tell these two exactly what he really thought of them.

"Glad to see business is brisk," Jack observed, "and you're keeping the place up to scratch. We are here for six whole long weeks this trip, so don't forget to keep our area reserved eh?"

Jack's words hit Carlos like a physical blow. Could he cope, or worse, would his business survive their regular visits? Maybe, after all, some business was not always the best business? Swinging round to face the Hoskins, the smile on his face as false as the snow in his restaurant at Christmas, handed each a glass of champagne. "Six weeks? You are almost a native these days."

Taking the drink and resting his other arm on the rich dark wood bar, Jack sniffed loudly. "If things go to plan, you might find us actually turning native. We're toying with staying: Becoming full time residents." Raising his glass to his lips, added, "Chin chin!" He slurped the expensive champagne. "And of course, Carlos, I know what you are thinking. In your shoes, I'd be thinking the same. You're saying to yourself, I'm about to make so much money in the next six weeks, I'll be able to retire early. Well don't worry Carlos, because we *will* make it all happen."

With a snort that almost turned into hysteria Carlos replied. "Indeed Mr Hoskins, you will make it happen, everyone they say so."

"So right, so right," Jack lustily cried out, "and I have it from good authority that it's your birthday today, eh?"

Alarm flashed like lightning in the swarthy restaurant owner's eyes. "No! no Mr Hoskins! No birthday today!" The memory of last year's birthday present from the Hoskins brought him out in a sweat.

"Well I know for a fact I've not got it wrong." Facing towards the entrance door, Jack beckoned wildly then clapped his hands; several diners dropped their cutlery in alarm clattering on to crockery and the floor. As waiters scrambled to replace knives and forks, a rush of warm air wafted through the restaurant as the door flew open. Bob Preston, dressed in his chauffeur's uniform, carrying a large wicker basket, trudged up to Jack.

"I thought you were never going to give the signal; I've had my eye cocked at the door that long I was beginning to think you'd hopped it."

Ignoring the chauffeur, Jack swung round to face Carlos, "We do not forget our friends' birthdays. You are a special friend and our gift reflects this."

Carlos eyed the large basket and wondered what hell was about to be let loose in his precious restaurant. A shiver raced down his spine. He wished the ground would open up and swallow him instantly.

"Never mind gawping at it. Get yourself round this side of the bar and open it!" Jack demanded.

Tentatively, Carlos did as he was told. Hesitant, cautiously, he raised the lid. Taking a surreptitious look inside, he gulped and slammed the lid firmly back down. Bob plonked the basket on the floor and the lid flew open and out jumped a large, fluffy black and white rabbit, immediately followed by another almost identical. The pair bolted off in fright, leaping and weaving beneath the tables.

Gasps echoed around the restaurant, one woman half screamed.

Laughing, despite his size, Jack moved swiftly, grabbing at one of the furry escapees.

"Excuse me," cried an indignant lady as Jack grappled with the fur. "Leave my handbag alone." Inspecting the bundle, realising his mistake, Jack apologised and backed away.

Five minutes later, the two rabbits safely returned to their basket, Bob told to remove it and its cargo and not return. Carlos, nerves in tatters, desperately tried to take control of his business. Apologising to his customers, sending his waiters round to take orders for drinks on the house, it was going to cost him a fortune to placate everyone, insisted Jack and Sheila should be seated at their table. Maybe with their meal served, some sort of sanity would return to his precious restaurant?

Opening the menu, Jack, crestfallen, stated. "Those animals are for you to eat, Carlos, not play with. You have said, countless times, that rabbit is a speciality that's why we ordered them. Never mind, Bob will deliver them to your home tomorrow. And before you protest, it's a done deal, so say no more. I'll not be thanked. They are a gift."

Simon dared not look up from the menu he was studying. Tears of laughter brimmed in his eyes. Chicky had his attention firmly buried in the wine list.

"I think I'll have the steak," Simon said. He sucked his cheeks to stem the explosion of laughter. "What are you going to have? Not made your mind up? Come on, hop to it!"

Chicky masked the spluttered guffaw by pretending to cough.

Chapter TWENTY TWO

The loud knock on the door startled Trisha, her eyeliner pen poised under her left eyes skittered across her face leaving a black smudge. “Damn,” she cursed snatching a tissue; black eyelashes and eyeliner was one thing, smudges were definitely a no no. Concentrating, she frowned as she wiped away the mess. The black mark removed, she tossed the tissue to one side. With practised deftness redrew the line under her eye. Inspecting the result, grinned into the mirror; she knew exactly who was knocking at the door. Checking her appearance she smiled,

“I just love black.” She added black gloss with glitter to her lips. “You are seriously cool Trisha Wilkinson,” she said and blew a kiss to her reflection, pleased with the Goth look she had created. Everything was dramatic black, even her outfit; a short, sleeveless top which sparkled with hundreds of silver sequins. Her shorts, tailored and tight, matched the glittering top. Twirling in black patent pumps, Trisha skipped out of her bathroom, tossing her head her black hair shimmered in the villa’s artificial light, headed to the front door. Yes, she thought my holiday is so back on target!

She had survived an incredibly boring day, surrounded by seriously weird people checking up on everything said and done by anyone on their radar. If it had not been for her music and the thought of seeing Ben to go clubbing and maybe repeat what they had so naughtily done in that cool pool lounge, she was certain she would have gone gaga! Giggling, she pulled open the door. The sight of the designer stubble face beaming a flirtatious smile, made the butterflies in her stomach flutter wildly. She took a quick breath and with mock surprise, cried, “Wow you *were* serious about tonight!”

Bemused, Ben leant against one of the porch's white pillars clutching a box of chocolates; he ran his free hand through his highlighted short hair and frowned. "I thought we'd agreed that I'd be here and we'd go out. I've even brought these for you."

Keeping her face straight, Trisha chuckled; she knew exactly what had been agreed, be it hastily said as they had parted that morning, but she was not about to let Ben realise that; not yet at any rate. Reaching for the dark coloured box of chocolates, amused, smiled. "Mmm interesting, I hadn't you down as old fashioned."

Taking hold of the gift she read the manufacturer's name on the box. Silently giggled, Lordy lordy, she was not in the slightest interested in who made chocolate, or what fillings were designed to tempt you. In fact who cared anyway? But she needed to hide her pleasure of his arrival, reading the small print created a distraction. After all, she didn't want him thinking that she had been waiting for him! She cooed at her deceitfulness.

Relieved Trisha had taken the box, Ben's pleasure turned into a broad smile. Her initial coolness had made him feel that maybe he had misunderstood all the signals from the morning. He had thought of nothing else all day except for the wonderful Trisha Wilkinson. He shoved his hand into his left trouser pocket, his pleasure at what he saw in front of him about to betray him; Trisha so seductive, so attractive, so in control. She looked amazing in all that black. He had never met anyone like her. She was a serious chick, exciting, alluring, sexy, and a tiny bit dangerous.

Waving the chocolate box like a flag in front of her, Trisha chuckled as she observed the changing expressions on Ben's face. She surmised he had expected her not to see him, to send him away,Tom and Jerry, cat and mouse, she laughed, a silent laugh. She most certainly was going to be the cat. Eyeing up his sexy body, had noted his left hand push down into his pocket. Betraying none of her inner excitement, she said in a matter of fact tone. "Right, now I think about it, I do remember saying something about a maybe."

Knowing he should play cool, Ben pulled his hand out of his pocket and took hold of Trisha's. In a calm voice that surprised even himself stated. "Well then, I'm glad I decided to knock on the door and better still, that you remembered me."

Had her heart not been beating so fast and had she not been so excited at the sight of Ben, she might have laughed or worse, giggled like her mother; instead exclaimed. "Remember you? From what has been going on in this freaky place, I'm not all that sure if you are better known than I dare to guess. Evil glares, sniping, insinuations. No names mentioned, but I knew what it was all about."

Raising an eyebrow Ben said nothing. If his grandfather got wind of what had happened that morning, he would lynch him. Pulling her close, Ben put on a brave front. "I'm popular, babe, but not that popular."

Trisha burst out laughing. "Seriously, I am just so glad to see you. Nobody here is remotely on this planet; weirdoes everyone."

Wrapping his arms around her, his mouth close to Trisha's, he whispered, "Then it was fate that meant us spending your entire holiday together. I hope you've got the stamina."

"Depends on what you have in mind, but whatever it is, I'm sure I'll outpace you."

Ben grinned. He had already had a taste of Trisha's energy, and if it was anything to go by, come the end of the week he would be exhausted. He shuddered with pleasure and excited at the thought. Placing his lips on hers he hungrily kissed her. He needed to make up for the wasted moments of talking nonsense. The box of chocolate, crushed against their entwined bodies. Minutes passed, Ben pulled away, this was not right, not now at least. The taste of Trisha in his mouth and on his lips, he must take the lead. He had promised clubbing.

Stepping back very slightly, his voice quivering, said. “So my dark, midnight, princess, I think it is time we hit the town, because if not, all that beautiful makeup will get smudged, not to mention what will happen to all those silver sequins.”

Clasping the crushed box of chocolates, her lips slightly parted, her eyes sparkling, she reached up and with the fingers of her right hand, wiped the gloss of her lipstick from Ben’s lips, then staring at the mangled chocolate box in her other hand, tossed it onto the floor inside the front door and laughed. “Control is my middle name. Let’s go.”

Outside, in the dark, sweet scented night, she took hold of Ben’s hand and gazed into his excited eyes. Frissons of passion sparked between them. Their bodies touching, their hands held in each others they walked slowly along the pathway that would take them away from Villas Bonitas and out towards the town.

Chapter TWENTY THREE

One of the few customers still seated in the restaurant, Simon and Chicky relaxed, enjoyed a cognac. Chicky swirling the golden liquid around the large balloon glass, grinned. "I am doing my best to keep my eyes averted."

Amusement lifting the sides of his mouth, laughter lines visible, Simon chaffed, "I know, from the corner of my eye I see we're getting the beady eye glare. With good fortune, we will slip away without being hallooed!"

Grinning, "We can but hope. It's certainly been an evening we'll not forget for a long time: value for money in every sense." Sipping the remains of his cognac, Chicky set the empty glass on to the linen covered table, continued. "Though unsure who should take the honours for tonight's spectacular; the chef for providing exquisite cuisine? Or do we consider, the Hoskins for the unscheduled entertainment, which verged on the ridiculous and the unbelievable, even if it did have us howling in our gourmet soup?"

Feigning seriousness, Simon considered. "Indeed my learned friend, the evidence points to both sides being guilty. It appears we have a hung jury. For a majority verdict I press that we have a retrial. In other words, we book a table when we know the Hoskins are dining again."

Decision agreed Simon stole a glance towards the Hoskins' table. "I suggest enough is enough, pay the bill and glide away into the balmy night." Turning to attract the waiter's attention, a familiar voice carried across the restaurant.

"From where I'm sitting, it looks like you two have finished. Not wanting to intrude earlier, please come and join us for a night cap." Sheila beamed and would like to have added, *we want to get to know you and find out what makes boys like you tick,* but was not that tactless. Gesturing with her index finger, like a hook to reel the handsome chaps in, carried on, "We don't bite. We've just eaten."

Jack guffawed at his wife's humour. He had made an effort to be considerate and attentive to her all evening. He needed his power walks.

Dismay etched on their faces, Simon politely responded. "Thank you, but another time." He patted his stomach. "A good walk is needed. With such excellent food you do overdo it."

Not to be given the brush off, Sheila rose, strode across the restaurant. Standing next to Simon, resting her hand on his shoulder she removed a hair lodged in the fabric of his jacket. "We've hardly met properly. Sitting around half naked on a swimming pool terrace is not the best way to get to know new guests. Now is a perfect opportunity. Come join us. Goodness, we're here to enjoy ourselves!" With a coy expression, added. "We don't take no for an answer. No such word in our vocabulary."

"Put like that, we must accept," Simon answered looking up at Sheila's face. Defeated, though not deflated, Simon and Chicky followed Mrs Hoskins as she glided back to her table; almost tripping over her feet in victory.

In a whisper Chicky quipped. "Our chance of escape is about as good as Houdini's in his last act." Simon snorted. "It could be worse, though at the moment, I can't think how."

As Simon held her chair, Sheila nodded her thanks. "Do sit down," she crooned as her blue mascara eyes stared up at the two good looking men and pointed at two empty chairs. "It is lovely to have someone join us who has never been here before." Her intent gaze darted around the restaurant. "We've been here that many times, we almost own the place." Placing her hand at the base of throat she stroked the heavy gold chain, "The restaurant I mean, not Pelito. Though if Jack had a mind with his business dealings, I'm sure we'd own that too."

Sitting opposite, Jack snapped his fingers. Within seconds a waiter appeared brandishing four brandy balloons and a bottle of fine cognac. Carefully, the waiter placed the glasses onto the table, but before he could do more, Jack scooped the bottle from the tray and sloshed copious amount of the expensive liquid into each glass before slapping the bottle down onto the table. He was not best pleased at Sheila for inviting the fellows over, but in light of what he was up to these days, decided to stay quiet.

"Now lads, get one of these down you." He snatched his own glass and drank the entire content in one swig. "That is good stuff.' With a thud, put the brandy balloon down and turned to Simon. "Now what did you think of the food? Before you utter a word, I can tell you you'll have to go a long way to enjoy better. And, believe you me I know what I'm talking about. I've eaten all over the world, Melbourne to Manchester, Deli to Doncaster, Lisbon to London, Boston to Brighton. More places than you can shake a stick at." He swung his arms out drawing a circle in the air. "Intrepid globe trotters and entrepreneurs personified, that's the Hoskins."

Simon sipped at his cognac, the fiery liquid burning his throat, coughed. Jack, like a coil, swung round and with a heavy hand slapped him on the back. "That will help. In future just pour it down in one go, stops all this choking malarkey." *Bloody Nancy boys*, he silently uttered.

Dumbstruck, Chicky poised to speak, noticed Sheila staring at him. Shaking her head, her eyes moved from one barrister to the other. Unable to stay silent blurted, "It is a shame. Such beauty wasted. Do your mothers weep? I know I would."

Jack glowered. He had not been too keen on inviting their sort to his table in the first place: Bad enough having to put up with unnatural behaviour at Villas Bonitas, but over dinner as well? What was the world coming to? And now Sheila adding her two penneth. "What are you talking about woman?"

Sheila stared at her husband, repeated in staccato. "I simply said. What a shame: Such attractive men. Many an educated girl would be glad for one of them. Never mind, I suppose it can't be helped."

With a look of embarrassment, not a feeling he normally suffered, Jack scowled at his wife: he might think what Sheila had said, but he certainly would not say it out loud. Turning his stare to Chicky and Simon, "I'm sorry about this, unfortunately Sheila speaks her mind. God alone knows where she gets it from."

Ignoring her husband, Sheila continued. "I've been thinking. It's no good me talking about you as a couple because that's not strictly what you are. The thing is what should I call you? I can't exactly say *that gay pair* because it's not polite, but…"

Unabashed, Simon stared straight into Sheila's mean, calculating eyes. In a slight camp voice, retorted. "Well you've certainly got me thinking. Let me see." Resting his right elbow on the table, raising his index finger he placed it on his cheek. "Yes of course, there are those who call us *those nice boys*. And our special friends," he smiled a sardonic smile, "call us *darlings*."

Not as amused as Simon and on the verge of getting up and walking out at Sheila's open insult, Chicky choked down his indignation. He felt Simon's foot nudge his own. Ah! Word games! Simon was good at that. Coyly he joined in,

"There are other terms, but they are not so flattering; though personally I like pansies. Cute little faces, don't you think?"

With a skin of a rhinoceros, unaware she was being mocked, Sheila peered into Simon's laughing eyes, placing well manicured fingers on his hand, chirped. "Darlings? Oh no, we would not presume to know you *that* well."

How vulgar, she thought. "So, *the boys* it is. I'll drop the *nice* for the time being." Patting Simon's hand in a motherly fashion, continued. "You can tell I'm a liberal woman. It takes all sorts to make this world go round and I like to think my open mindedness helps it to spin more smoothly." She lifted her fingers from Simon's hand, unaware that she had left the three men, for different reasons, speechless.

Chapter TWENTY FOUR

In the distance a clock chimed, three strikes announcing the new hour. "Blimey it can't be that time already?" Doreen, cried as she staggered along the pathway towards her villa then squealed, "*Eins, zwei, drei*. It's me bit of kraut lingo, I know it best when I'm piddled." Tottering precariously on her high heels, asked, "We haven't been out that long have we?"

Pat Greenwood, stocky, tanned with a shock of mousy coloured hair, lightened by years of living in the sun held Doreen's hand, keeping her close to him in an attempt to stop her tilting over. "Doll you haven't stopped talking since I picked you up, it was only the restaurant locking the doors that stopped you talking then. If not we would still be there." He smiled, he had tipped the owner to close the place up for the night or they would still be sitting at that table. The owner knew who he was and was grateful. Grinning as Doreen tried to keep upright, Pat was relieved that she had not changed after all these years.

"You would think I'd know why you took me out tonight, because it's been years since you did, but I haven't a clue. Remind me again, what you told me earlier."

"Tomorrow Doll, for now, I think we need to get you home."

"We've had a laugh though." Stopping dead in her tracks, Doreen looked down and cried. "Me feet are killing me. I got to get these things off." Gripping Pat's arm tight Doreen unsteadily bent down, with her left hand yanked at the thin strap holding the shoe to her foot. "Blimey what are these fixed with?" Pulling and tugging, she managed to flick the strap over her heel the shoe fell to the ground and she repeated the performance for her other foot. Her bare feet now planted on the pathway, she sighed. "Such a relief."

Standing up straight, noting her shoes were still on the ground, yelled. "What am I like?" Then bending down, her dress riding up revealing silky underwear she snatched at her shoes.

"Bloody hell Doll," Pat hissed, "bending down like that will get us into serious trouble at a place like this." Surreptitiously, he glanced around the gardens, shadows cast by the solar lights created pools of darkness. The vibrant colours in daylight, now dark silhouettes; the night was still, not even a leaf moved. His gaze followed to the nearby private terraces, no one to be seen, and apart from Doreen's giggling and the crickets chirping, Villas Bonitas was silent. Taking hold of Doreen he steered her towards her villa; thankfully close by.

"Come on Doll let's get you inside before it's too late and we're arrested by the Villas Bonitas police," Pat added with amusement.

Hiccupping and giggling, wriggling her hips as one hand tugged on her hemline in an attempt to pull her dress back down, her other hand clinging on tightly to Pat.

Pat soberly aware Doreen was tipsy struggled to keep her upright. He could think of nothing worse than anyone of these rich snoots glimpsing Doreen's worse for wear state. With these thoughts tumbling around his head, he again checked to make sure he had missed nothing or no one.

Standing outside the villa's front door, Pat begged, "Give me the key Doll and I'll get you inside."

Doreen dropped her shoes, the stiletto heals hitting the tiles first, making a loud *clunk* in the silent night. Leaning against one of the white columned pillars on the porch she rummaged through her bag.

"Me key," she wailed, "I need me key, because if not we can't get in. Gordon Bennett, where's me key? It can't be far, it's such a likkle bag."

Cursing under his breath Pat looked on in disbelief as the woman he had gone to endless trouble to meet fumbled in her clutch bag.

"Doll let me take a look."

Hiccupping loudly, handing the bag to Pat, Doreen slithered down the pillar, aghast, Pat grabbed her before she reached the ground. An inebriated smile lit her face. "Think I've had a bit more to drink then I thought."

"You haven't changed one bit. Thank God!" Pat laughed. Bending down, he kissed the top of her head. Leaving Doreen hanging on to his leg he extracted the key, unlocked the door and pushed it open. Taking a firm grip round Doreen's waist hauled her inside. Holding her in his arms, he stepped into the spacious open plan room and without a backward glance kicked the door closed. His face creased with pleasure, everything so far had gone to plan. It had all happened smoothly and rapidly. Looking at the lady in his arms he knew it was the right thing to have done.

The villa and the exclusive Villas Bonitas were perfect for her first multi-millionaire holiday. Familiar with the villa's layout he carefully carried Doreen through to her bedroom. He knew exactly where the two bedrooms were situated. He also knew the one Doreen would have taken: Trisha would be sleeping in the other room. He smiled. What made everything exciting for him was the fact that Doreen knew nothing of what he had organised. He had told her a few things, the rest could wait. He needed to be sure. Standing outside Doreen's bedroom, seeing it ajar, he nudged it with his foot. Doreen's eyes snapped open and in a loud whisper cried. "Shhh! We mustn't wake me girl."

"Shhh yourself you'll wake the dead with all your noise. Time, I think, to get you to bed."

With a happy smile, a slur to her voice, "Now you're talking."

Laying Doreen on her bed, Pat could not believe how little she had changed. Despite her breathtaking wealth, she was still the same Doreen he knew. Back then, they were penniless, silly and young. Seeing her tonight after all these years brought the crazy times flooding back. They had wanted fun, they had messed around and he had loved her.

After tonight, he wanted the chance to love her again, but properly this time.

Seeing her flopped out on the bed, hiccupping nineteen to the dozen, he grinned. Everything he had done, not only these last few months, but the last few years, had been for her and Trisha. Taking off his shoes, he settled himself next to her.

Chapter TWENTY FIVE

Opening her eyes, Doreen blinked several times, tried to focus as the room moved in and out. The spots she could make out on the ceiling must be mildew at 67 Wentworth House because she could not think what else they could be. Her head was spinning faster than a Catherine wheel. Blimey, she had drunk far too much cheap gin. She cursed, flung her arms out, her right arm hitting something solid and warm; she froze.

Rolling over, saw a man. "Blimey, I must have sank a few," she gasped, seeing a bloke on her bed fully dressed, the shock bringing her back to reality. She was not in Wentworth House, she had not drunk cheap gin, she was on holiday and the bloke was Pat Greenwood. She giggled with relief. *Thank God for that!*

Jumping at the sudden smack, Pat, half awake turned over and with a beaming smile, asked. "You're with us then Doll?"

Sheepishly, Doreen answered. "What must you think of me? Out for the count, I put it down to shock, seeing you again," she giggled and ran her fingers down his shirted chest.

Pat shivered and wrapped his arms around her kissing her lips, then her face, her eyes. Moving he pulled down the zip on the back of her dress; Doreen's breathing grew heavy as he slipped her dress from her shoulders, kissing her skin, he pushed the dress further down. Unhooking the fastener on her bra, his lips traced the contours of her breasts before moving down to her belly. Shuddering and with trembling fingers, Doreen tried to unbutton Pat's shirt. As his lips reached her silken knickers, she cried out as he removed them, sliding them down her legs, then removing his own clothes, hungrily laid on top of her. Greedily they made love.

As the light of dawn filtered through the vertical blinds, bringing brightness to the room, Pat, covered in perspiration, rested on his elbows, taking his weight as he lay over Doreen. "My God, I'd forgotten how beautiful you are."

Sated and spent, her eyes shining, Doreen giggled, "You've not forgotten everything that's for sure, because I've lost count how many times we've done it since you ripped my threads off."

Raising her head, she kissed the tip of his nose and at the same time placed the palms of her hands on to his buttocks. "Loved it, let's do it one more time."

Not wanting to admit he needed a breather, Pat lifted himself, swivelled his body and a bolt of pain shot up his back and down his leg. He gasped, the pain rendering him immobile. He dropped on to Doreen. "Oh my God, it's my back."

Doreen, pinned underneath, unable to move, cried out, "Pat get up you squashing me."

His face, contorted in agony, Pat lay smothered in the pillow, mumbling. "I can't Doll, my backs gone. Christ, I can't move."

"Good grief it was only a bit of hows your father! Come on Pat stop messing around."

Cautiously, he turned his head so he could breath. "Jesus," he gasped again as another bolt of pain shot through him. Waiting for the piercing pain to subside, he silently cursed before imploring, "Doll, try and move very *very* slowly from underneath me. Try not to jolt my body."

Sucking her breath in, Doreen heard Pat muffle a cry and gingerly inched herself from under him, their bodies damp from their passion made her movements slow and laborious. "I'm almost there, so you can stop worrying" she said, relieved that at last her body was freed.

Lifting her head she stared down at Pat's sprawled, naked body, his bottom twitching. She giggled. Only moments ago her bed was a cauldron of passion and high jinx. "Think you should have come with a health warning. I can't believe it. Best I get some clobber on, because you're in no fit state to ravish me again."

Doreen threw on a silky gown, slipping her arms through the soft fabric she pulled the belt around here and tied it loosely. Placing a hand on his sweating face, said, "Must be something I can do? What about Asprin?"

Pat winced, if he had not been in such pain he would be laughing. "Doll, in my jacket pocket," he stopped to let the pain ease, "you'll find some tablets, bring them here with a glass of water." How the hell he was going to drink water with his head buried in a feather pillow he had no idea, but at least it gave him a moment to think whilst Doreen did something other than giggle.

Returning with the water and packet of tablets, Doreen twittered, "You know I still can't believe how you found me. What a shock hearing your voice after all this time, seems it's been a shock for you too."

Flinching, he thought only Doreen could carry on like this as he lay in agony. "Doll, stop giggling. I need to get off this bed, swallow those tablets and get myself out of here. Come here and help. It won't be easy, but we can do it."

Bending down, Doreen grinned at Pat. "What a state you've got yourself in."

Ignoring her latest quip, precariously he placed the flat of his hands on to the mattress, took a deep breath, his eyes glazed with pain, looked at Doreen. "I'm going to push myself up, can you try and hold me so when I turn over, I'll not fall too hard on my back."

"Mmmm what should I be getting hold of then?"

Speechless with pain Pat wanted to laugh but knew he must concentrate. Heaving himself up on to his hands, carefully he rotated his body, Doreen's hand slipped round his waist as he dropped on to his back. "Thanks Doll for your help, I couldn't have done it without you."

Kneeling at the side of the bed, seeing the pain wrinkling Pat's face, Doreen wanted to hug him and take the pain away. Grasping hold of his hand, murmured. "Let me help you try and sit up. I'm not Hercules, but I think I can manage and then you can take your pills."

Squeezing Doreen's hand, "Thanks, but if you don't mind, I'll take it slowly." Adding, "That will teach us to try and catch up on sixteen years."

Giggling, "Seems to me, your main springs gone, but thank God your sense of humour hasn't."

Grinning, he took hold of her hands, "I'm going to try and sit up." Ignoring another giggle from Doreen, swung his legs to the edge of the bed, sat up, sweat poured from him. Taking a deep breath, "Not sure I'll be able to get much further at the moment, hand me the water and pills and my mobile over there on the bedside table. I need my man to collect me."

Doreen picked up his phone, handed it to him as he swallowed the pain killers and at the same time threw down a towelling robe. "I haven't a clue what to do to help you, but put this on because I don't think you'll manage much else." Seeing the pain in his face, added, "I know I keep giggling and it isn't really something to laugh about, but what else can I do?"

Taking his phone from her, Pat attempted a wry smile. "When I'm not in pain I'll laugh too, for now there's not much you can do. I've got to get myself back home. It's not your fault; we shouldn't have been so greedy."

"Speak for yourself," Doreen retorted, as Pat grimaced as another spasm of pain shot through him.

"Whilst you call your man, I'm going to have a ciggie. It'll help steady my nerves. Mind a G and T would do that, but it's a bit early and I think enough is enough of the booze for now."

Pulling the blinds open, Doreen walked out through the open patio door, blinked at the bright dawn light. Looking up at the cloudless blue sky saw the white shape of a crescent moon. On the small patio table sat an opened packet of cigarettes, she took one out as she heard Pat talking on his mobile. He had told her last night he was rich, had a man who looked after his house. He had also said the expensive chauffeur driven car he had collected her in also belonged to him. He had told her many things as they had sat in the restaurant sipping vintage champagne and eating like kings. But the question going around in her head…. was it true? The coincidence of him turning up now after all these years was strange, very strange. She wanted to believe all he had told her. She wanted to believe her wealth was not the reason he had come looking for her. She wanted to believe lots of things, but from where she stood she was not sure. Her cigarette finished, she stepped back into her bedroom. Pat was wearing the towelling robe she had left on the bed.

"Funny world isn't it when you boil it down? Me with me lottery win and you so rich an all. I know you are in a bit of pain, but when you're up to it, I hope you will still show me that fancy floating gin palace of yours?" She felt the need to remind him of what he had promised last night. It would be one way of confirming if he was really the wealthy man he had said he was. Though she realised no matter what she thought, for now she would have to wait, whether he owned a big boat or not, she was not about to find out just yet. A thought ran through her mind. Maybe with him incapacitated for a while she could discreetly find out? Check up on a few things?

With pain shooting down his leg Pat only managed a chuckle. "Here's me in agony and all you can think of is gallivanting." He had noted her scepticism, it spoke volumes: *Why now?* it said. He had seen questions crossing her face many times during last night and he would eventually tell her the truth, but now was not the time. "It's a date Doll, just need to be back on my feet and we'll christen it….but very carefully next time!"

Doreen giggled, reached up and carefully placed a kiss on his cheek. "Better not rock the boat then."

"It's not a boat, it's a luxury cruiser."

"Right," she answered a sceptical lilt in her voice. "Whatever floats your boat!"

“I promise, in a couple of days I’ll be back to normal.” He ignored the uncertainty in her voice as a knock on the entrance door resounded through the villa. Thank God, his man was here. He shuddered at how he must look, sweaty, unshaved, naked, wrapped in a towelling robe, not to mention being in agony.

Giggling at what had caused Pat’s back to go Doreen hurried to open the door, “Am I glad to see you, come on in. He’s in a right two and eight with his back. It happened all of a sudden, scared me half to death.”

At the sight of his man, Pat almost cried with relief. “Thank God you’re here Brian. Just get me home. I’m fragile, so let’s take it easy.”

Brian could clearly see the pain in his boss’s eyes. He had seen it before, though he had never collected him from a bedroom! Without preamble wrapping his muscled arms around Pat he lifted him off the bed and onto his feet. Half holding and half carrying, Brian had his employer firmly in his grip as they headed out of Doreen’s villa.

“Sorry about this, Doll,” Pat said, “I must have forgotten what a little devil you are. I’ll call you later. I just need a quiet moment to get this back right for you. I can’t have my mainspring going every time I look at you.

Giggling, Doreen answered. “I’ll be more gentle with you next time.”

Chapter TWENTY SIX

Closing the front door, Doreen could still taste Pat's kisses on her lips. "God what a night," she giggled, stuffing her hands into her robe's pockets and dancing to the kitchen. She needed a coffee, strong and sweet. Filling a jug from the drinking tap, she poured the water into the coffee machine, her mind racing with all that had happened in the last twelve hours. Watching as the water reached the two cup marker she stopped pouring and closed the lid. Putting the jug down, she laughed then frowned making her forehead crease. What was she to make of all Pat had told her; he had said he had money, a big house, butler cum chauffeur. He even had her going about a big boat. Was it all dreams to be realised on her winnings? Or should she believe him?

She picked up the coffee packet and pulled the seal open. A rush of aroma filled her nostrils. Adding coffee to the machine she scoffed, a long way from drinking supermarket instant, but then, she reminded herself; everything was a long way from what she had been used to including Pat Greenwood. She took two cups from the cupboard, pulled the filled jug from the coffee machine and poured the dark liquid into each cup then added milk and two spoonfuls of sugar to both. Stirring vigorously she thought about Pat. She wanted to see him again, wanted to know all about him, wanted to know the truth. Being with him for those short hours had made the last sixteen years melt away, it was if they were young again. Grinning, she could not remember laughing so much. She'd had far too much to drink, she'd giggled and hiccupped loudly. They had made love so many times in her big bed, she had lost count. Dropping the teaspoon onto the kitchen top again giggled at the memory of being squashed underneath his body.

"What a finale!" Picking up one of the cups, headed for Trisha's room.

Knocking, Doreen opened the door, "Trish, I thought you might……Cor blimey, what are you doing here?" The coffee still in her hand she pulled the door shut and marched back to the kitchen.

Eyes bulging with shock at the woman in the doorway Ben had instantly dropped his hands over his privates. "Aaaargh, Mrs Wilkinson…" he yelped as the door slammed shut. Trembling, his breath coming in short bursts, he did not know what to do.

"Trisha! Your mother, it's your mother. My God this is not how I was supposed to meet her! Get up Trisha, just get up."

Leaping off the bed, in a frenzy he scrabbled around searching for his clothes scattered all over the floor.

Sitting up, pulling the sheet over her naked body, Trisha cooed. "Ben chill, I will talk to Mama. No doubt I'll get a lecture, she'll scream at me, stop my pocket money, have me arrested, pack me off to a children's home. Very likely have you castrated or worse, have you march me down the aisle." Laughing at Ben's panic, continued, "I think not. But whatever, believe me, I can handle her."

Trisha knew she was in trouble, but she also knew which buttons to press to keep her mother from blowing a gasket. Especially after hearing the groaning and moaning and the creaking bed coming from her mother's bedroom.

Ignoring Trisha, Ben groaned, "What am I going to say? What kind of a guy must she think I am?" Spying his boxer shorts, grabbed them, in his haste, struggled to put them on, not realising they were inside out.

Tricia laughed. "Mmmm, it is just so scary watching you put on your clothes like this. It was only hours ago you were manic ripping them off."

Standing up half dressed and totally dishevelled. "Did you not hear me? Your mother is out there, she's seen me.

She's seen *all* of me. Everything! Oh my God I cannot believe this is happening." Ben snatched his shirt from the heap on the floor.

"Don't worry. You are sexily normal. Everything is in perfect working order, so stop having a breakdown."

"My God, this is a repeat performance of yesterday, how on earth did this happen?" He checked his flies, they were still undone. He fastened them. Looking around the palatial room, what was he thinking? So posh, so up market, so out of his depth! Directing his gaze back to Trisha, "I'm sorry this is not what I was expecting to happen. I need to apologise to your mother, it's the least I can do."

Jumping off the bed, Trisha pulled a silk wrap around her, taking hold of Ben's hand, smiled. "You really are old fashioned. Come on we'll go together and maybe you will stop shaking."

Squeezing his hand she pulled a wry face, "You are so uncool at times!"

Her coffee finished, hearing footsteps and whispers Doreen added more water to the coffee machine and extracted another mug from the cupboard. She swung round and saw two people sheepishly peering at her from the other side of the breakfast bar.

"Mrs Wilkinson, please," stammered Ben, his face turning crimson.

"Think it's Ben isn't it? Let's talk later, for now I just hope you've both been sensible and used something safe. Go on sit yourselves down." Glancing at her daughter, added, "I've got the coffee brewing for you." Moving back to the counter, she took two slices of bread from the packet and dropped them into the toaster, stifling a giggle at Ben who was shaking like a jelly.

Oh to be that age again, she reflected. She knew nothing about this Ben, but he seemed to have a few manners and was decent enough to be embarrassed. From over her shoulder she glanced at her daughter and wished she could not see so much of herself in her at that age. Taking the butter and marmalade out of the fridge, offered, “Help yourselves, there’s no rush. I’m off to have me shower.” Stepping out of the kitchen added, “And Ben, after your breakfast best get yourself dressed proper. Your shirt buttons are all skew-whiff.”

Chapter TWENTY SEVEN

Finishing their second cup of coffee, Simon and Chicky sat on their terrace and watched in fascination as two men staggered from the villa next door, one dressed in only a towelling robe, barely able to walk. The other, with surprising dignity, virtually carried his companion. Simon grinned. He recognised both of them and wondered what had happened to Mr Greenwood. From the corner of his eye saw Chicky giggle.

"This place just gets better," Chicky said finishing the last of the cereal in his bowl. "If last night's fiasco was not enough to amuse us, we now have guests being virtually carried out in bathrobes. With what has taken place these last twenty four hours, it now has me wondering if we have been duped and our invitation was not to Paul's villa, but we are in fact on a TV Reality Show; the location is exotic and so far there has been nothing but drama and hilarity." He bent down and peered under the patio table, sat up again. "No hidden microphones as far as I can see, but," he pointed at one of the bushes behind them and mouthed "*there's probably one in the shrubbery.*"

Simon smiled, he had no idea what had happened next door, but he knew they were not in any show. Though for now, he had no intentions of letting Chicky know the real reason why they were staying at Villas Bonitas. He dare not, for he had a big decision to make, one that could be the end of their relationship for ever. He knew he ought to tell Chicky the truth, but he could not bring himself to risk spoiling everything.

"Talking about humour," relieved to be distracted Simon pointed towards the cleaner pushing her trolley along the pathway, "It appears *Guzunderthebed* is on her way."

“Pardon?” Chicky asked in a baffled tone, turning his attention to where Simon’s finger indicated.

“I wonder what our *maid on her knees* has mislaid, forgotten, or lost today?” Simon added as he smiled and waved to Cissie. “I only hope that whatever befalls her, she stays on her feet.” He grinned. “I take it you will hand over your find?”

Dropping his spoon into the empty cereal bowl, Chicky extracted an earring from his shirt pocket, the tiny piece of jewellery sparkled in the sunlight. “I will, with pleasure.”

Seeing one of the men from Judge Denbie’s villa wave at her, Cissie felt a flush rise up her neck and into her face, nervously, she waved back. Parking her cleaning trolley on the pathway she selected a bundle of fresh linen and headed towards the front door. Perspiring with the morning heat, but more with embarrassment at being caught yesterday, she knocked on the carved hardwood door. Immediately the door swung open and Chicky, smiling jubilantly cried. “Good morning. I am glad to see you.”

Expecting a frosty reception after yesterday’s fiasco, Cissie was taken by surprise at such a welcoming cheerfulness. Relieved, she opened her mouth to speak, but her words never reached her lips as Chicky snatched the bundle of linen from her arms and stacked it on to the hall table.

“You are never going to believe what I am about to tell you.” Noting the maid rooted to the spot, added, “And standing there won’t get you the answer.” Chicky slid hold of Cissie’s hand and pulled her into the villa, propelling her into the lounge area sat her down on one of the cream leather sofas. Standing in front of her, his face fused with pleasure, extending his arm and very slowly he unclenched his fist. “Surprise!”

Cissie’s face lit up as she focused on the tiny object and squealing with delight, cried, “Thank you! My earring, you found it? You’ve no idea how much you have made my day.” Plucking the piece of jewellery from Chicky’s palm, she jumped up and forgetting who she was, reached up and gave Chicky a kiss on his cheek. Realising what she had done, stepped back. "Oh, I'm sorry. How embarrassing."

Placing his hand on her arm, Chicky smiled, "Don't worry, we are already getting used to your *faux pas*."

Fastening the earring into the hole in her ear, Cissie questioned. "Was it under the bed after all?"

Chicky patted his bottom and wiggled it slightly. "Having recovered after witnessing such a *délicieux*," took a deep breath for added effect. "It turned out you were absolutely right. It was in the bedroom, not under the bed, but jammed between the skirting and the floor."

Ensuring her precious earring was secure. "Whatever made you look there?"

"The gold sparkled against the white walls and the diamonds created a prism as the sunlight filtered through the patio doors this morning. It made a rather beautiful rainbow along the wall."

Cissie smiled, realised not all the people who came to Villas Bonitas were too rich to be polite or kind. "I can't thank you enough. I appreciate the trouble you have taken. I shouldn't wear them all the time but it seems pointless leaving them in a box. Wearing them keeps him close to me."

Chicky cocked his head to one side. He wanted to ask more, but caught the glimpse of a shadow as it fleetingly cast itself across Cissie's face when she had said *him*. Sorrow flashed in her eyes. He sensed there was something sad about the young maid and as much as he would like to understand, he did not want to pry.

Changing the mood and placing his hand on his chest, in a teasing tone, declared. "It was worth the shock of seeing a *derriere* wriggling beneath the bed to see your happy face this morning. My startled heart has recovered."

Cissie blushed, apologised. "I didn't mean to inconvenience you and your friend. I am sorry." Through the patio doors she glimpsed Simon sitting on the terrace talking into his mobile phone, he was writing something on a card, then looked at his watch and nodded his head.

Stepping away from Chicky, Cissie walked to the hall area, picked up the clean sheets and towels. “Thank you again Mr Wentworth, I’ve taken enough of your time I must get on with looking after your villa. And as promised, I’ll stay on my feet,” she laughed.

Watching her bustle down the hall, Chicky shook his head, Villas Bonitas was full of entertaining surprises, he wondered if Paul Denbie had any idea what he had invested in.

Chapter TWENTY EIGHT

No sooner had Carmen removed the set of keys from her handbag to open the office door then she noticed two men leave Mrs Wilkinson's villa. She smiled. Pat Greenwood had clearly caught up on some of the past!

"You really should take more care of that back of yours," she murmured with an amused smile as she placed the key into the lock. Opening the office she turned on the air-conditioning unit and fired up her computer. Staring out of her window she could see several terraces and villas at this end of the complex. She wished she could be sitting on a terrace drinking coffee, relaxing, reading a book or thinking about nothing. Instead she had a full day ahead, more people arriving and the weekly barbeque to organise. Turning her attention back to the computer, she entered her password, clicked onto her email folder and groaned. Twenty five emails. Flicking through each one she relaxed, nothing to worry about, all routine.

Hitting the 'send' button on the last email, Carmen felt relieved it had taken her no more than half an hour to answer them all. Satisfied, she pressed the log out button, rolled her shoulders in an attempt to free the tension and sat back in her chair. Her attention straying to the window she saw Ben Preston leave the Wilkinson's villa via the front door. He was walking jauntily, turned to wave as he reached the path. Carmen raised one eyebrow. Pat Greenwood *and* Ben Preston had spent the night there? She shrugged. It was nobody's business, including her own how Mrs Wilkinson and her daughter intended spending their holiday, but she knew there were owners who would take great delight in making a scandal out of indiscretions.

Watching Ben hightail it towards the gates, Carmen wondered what he was getting involved in. He was a good looking young man and despite his ad-hoc upbringing he was turning out to be a decent chap. Even if he did have a penchant for pretty rich girls. A bright light flashed through the window pane as the sun's rays reflected on an object out in the garden. Shading her eyes Carmen caught a glimpse of Bob half way up a ladder sawing at one of the palm tree fronds, the sun glinting and shining on the blade of the saw as it moved backwards and forwards. Watching as the branch gave way, tumbling to the ground, despite her years at Villas Bonitas she could never get over the alarming rate at which everything grew: It almost seemed possible to see the plants multiply. She gazed on as another branch fell to the ground.

The Bobs of this world did not come much more down to earth than Bob Preston. His grandson clearly wanted more from his life than being at the beck and call of others, but whether dating rich girls was the answer, Carmen had no idea. One thing she did know, Bob's attitude appeared cavalier at times but without him, the gardens and the chauffeuring would be a very different kettle of fish. Her *Jack of all trades*, put up with far more than he should and to his credit, always took whatever was thrown at him in good spirit. He was no fool, his sense of humour and wit provided him with the necessary resilience to ensure he coped. Although his sixty fifth birthday was mere days away, neither he nor Carmen had talked of retirement. He would be impossible to replace; Carmen only wished some of the more difficult owners realised that too.

The ringing of the phone reminded her that day dreaming was not part of her job description. Accepting her responsibilities with a heavy sigh she answered the call. After several attempts to engage in the one sided conversation, Carmen gave up and allowed the caller to continue ranting, adding an occasional "Mmm." and "I see," where appropriate.

Stepping off the bottom rung of his ladder Bob heard Carmen calling to him. He pulled off his leather gloves as she approached and wiped the sweat from his brow with his sleeve. Not yet long into the morning and the temperature was already hotting up. To his dismay he saw that Carmen was frowning. That did not bode well. Cheerfully he called, "Mornin' Pressy. What can I be doing for you?"

Carmen winced at Bob's nickname reference to her, but made no comment. "At some point I need to talk to you about your grandson, Bob, but for now it is important that you take Frau Hecks to the shopping centre." Carmen did not add that Frau Hecks had got herself into a state having forgotten to buy a birthday present for one of her grandchildren. The phone call had been painful enough without having to repeat it.

Grimacing, Bob started folding the ladder away. "What have I done to deserve this? What with them Hoskins moaning about this, that an' the other, and the Flawline on me back all the time, I'm on me knees." Kicking a palm branch to one side continued, "Now she needs me to take her shopping? I ain't her slave you know?"

Understanding and silently sympathising with Bob's situation, Carmen had no intention of openly agreeing with him though. "Please, go and change into your chauffeur's suit and take Frau Hecks shopping. I know these are difficult people, Bob, but they *are* owners who pay your wages. Please remember that."

Bob shrugged his shoulders and swung his tree sword elaborately round once, muttered, "I should have been a musketeer, not a dogsbody." He sniffed loudly, lifted the ladder to his shoulder and saw in hand, shuffled away.

With Frau Hecks and Bob organised, Carmen's next job was to discuss the arrangements for the evening with Antonio. It was still early in the morning, but a delivery was due at the bar and Antonio would be there to sign for it. As she headed in the bar's direction she could clearly hear Sheila Hoskins' shrill voice giving Jack a lecture about his mobile phone. Did the woman shut up when she was sleeping? Chuckling, Carmen pictured Sheila in bed, rollers in her hair, rolling pin in hand, sound asleep but a lecture still pouring from her open mouth.

"What are you grinning at?" Antonio asked looking up from the order form he was checking as he saw Carmen approaching. "You look like you've lost a penny and found a pound."

"Good morning Antonio, let's just say the sun is shining and everything so far, seems well with the world. Is everything okay here with you?"

Antonio laid his pen down and turned his attention to Carmen. "Everything is tickety-boo here too. Last night was quiet, apart from a few who came in for drinks before going out for dinner. And before you ask, tonight's barbeque is sorted."

Smiling cheerfully, Carmen said, "It would be rather silly of me to think it could be any other way. I'm assuming Raymond is chef as usual?"

"Yes, that he is and as usual he's sending a lad to sort out the grill, lighting it etcetera well before he arrives."

Carmen had made sure there had been a barbeque every week since Villas Bonitas had opened. Their popularity had never waned. Even the rich enjoyed the simple taste of charcoal smoked food.

"Let's hope all goes reasonably okay tonight," she said. "I don't think we can expect much more than other weeks, but with the eclectic mix we have here at the moment, heaven only knows what little dramas will take place."

Antonio laughed and returned to checking his order. Carmen wandered back to the dreariness of her office. They were a rum bunch, this group of owners and guests; some more difficult to tolerate than others, but in her own way Carmen was fond of them all. Well, most of them.

Chapter TWENTY NINE

The sun's rays reflected on the droplets of moisture creating rainbows as the water cascaded down a long, stone column before splashing over the white pebbles into the pool at the base of the fountain. Erected in the middle of the Old Square, it was not only a focal point but had, of latter years, become a place to make a wish with coins tossed into the clear water in the hope that dreams would come true.

Sitting at her favourite table in Solos café, Ginny looked on as a good looking well dressed man flipped a coin into the water as he walked by. He saw her looking, smiled, then sat at another table, obviously waiting for someone. A few minutes later, an older man joined him. The smile of the young man's face was quite lovely. She wondered what he had wished for. Maybe she should drop in a coin, who knew what might happen then?

Transferring her attention to the archway that served as the main entrance to the famous Old Square she watched dreamily as smartly dressed tourists sauntered around the stylish shops, drank coffee at the chic cafes and greeted each other with embraces. Though her eyes followed the activity around her, her mind wrestled with the decision she knew she must make; everything was about to change and she had to tell him. The question was, should she tell him a lie and walk away, or the truth and see what happened? She fiddled with her ring as if by doing so, the right answer would materialize. She began to count the times over the last four years that she had waited for him, laughed with him, lain in his arms after sex and in the end, to her surprise, had fallen in love with him. The latter causing her more pain than she cared to admit.

Falling in love was not part of the deal of their torrid little affair. Their relationship, shrouded in secrecy, lies and deception and originally built on lust, meant she had benefited extremely well: a luxury apartment a stone's throw from where she sat, a couple of five star holidays and a nice bank balance. Ginny Solomon was aware that they had both benefited nicely out of the affair; he had always got what he had wanted and she had never once regretted being involved with him.

The clinking of crockery on a tray carried by the waiter brought her mind back to the present. As two cups of coffee were placed on to the table, she saw her lover walk through the wide arch into the Square. Her heart lurched at the decision she had to make. Ambling towards her, his face aglow with what he was expecting, she knew she could not tell him today; she would talk to him tomorrow. And knowing everything was on the brink of change all the things she loved about him snapped into focus; he was attractive, slightly overweight for his age, but very desirable. His piercing blue eyes, devilish, naughty and wicked, his smile and sense of humour kept her laughing and happy. He was married. He was rich and bragged about it. He was loud, over the top, but he had always treated her well. The other, well, she grinned, the obvious one, was good; very good.

She pushed her worrying thoughts to the back of her mind as he arrived at the table, and gave him a cheeky smile.

"So you managed to escape? It still surprises me that she has no idea what you are up to. Though she did give me a fright following you that last time you were out here. She seemed a nice lady."

Sitting down in the chair opposite, Jack leant over the table and placed his hand on hers. "I can't stay long. Let's just say, for both of our sakes, it is best Sheila never finds out. Believe you me, neither of us would want to know just how *nice* she can be. Anyway, I've not come here to prattle about her and as I've not got more than an hour we can either sit and talk or…" he chuckled, "we can do what we are best at together."

Ginny pointed to the two cups of coffee, “Drink your coffee first and get your breath back. You’re puffing like an old steam train.”

With a cheesy grin Jack pulled his stomach muscles in tight. “I’ll have you know, this is not the panting of an old engine, it’s the enthusiastic pace of a greedy man; so get that coffee down and we will be seeing who *puffs* out first.”

Gulping his coffee down in one mouthful, Jack stood up and threw half a dozen coins on the table, leaving an over generous tip, and jested. “I’d chase you back to your pad, but you’d probably run too fast and then I’d be buggered for what I need my heart to race for.”

Ginny stood up and stepped toward him, linked her arm into his and looking up into his sun kissed face stated, “In your dreams lover.”

Despite her joviality, the decision she needed to make sat heavy on her shoulders. Squeezing his hand, she forced a laugh from her tight throat, and walked with him to her expensive mistress’s apartment.

Chapter THIRTY

Jack Hoskins plonked himself down onto one of the high stools in front of the bar and chortled loudly. It had been a productive morning and he was feeling particularly pleased with himself. His latest financial dealings were going extremely well and more importantly, the other little business that he had set up here kept his finger nicely on the pulse. He nodded his head with self satisfaction. He knew there were aspects of his business that never should be discussed with Sheila and that particular deal was one of them. He grinned. Aye, it had been a most *satisfying* morning!

Slapping the palm of his hand onto the cold granite bar, bellowed, "Antonio, jump to it and get my usual sorted, make it large, in fact very large. Better make that two."

Swivelling round on the stool, to Jack's delight Lindsey Palmer-Brown jogged through the bougainvillea archway, her blonde ponytail swinging like a pendulum through the back of her baseball cap as she headed towards the bar. He sucked his cheeks in, there was something about Lindsey that made him shiver with anticipation; she oozed fitness, was attractive and a tad bossy. The combination made him wish he was twenty years younger. Not that his age stopped him *enjoying* himself!

Lindsey Palmer-Brown, manager of the *Well Being Centre* at Villas Bonitas was always affable to her rich and famous clients. Their egos were often larger than their bank balance and like their bodies, had to be massaged. Hearing Jack Hoskins coarse voice long before she clapped eyes on him, she slowed her pace. She had met enough Jack Hoskins' with their exuberant behaviour, loud voices and extra marital behaviour to handle and if necessary, crush. Arriving at the bar, her breathing steady and even, she needed to stretch her calf muscles. Removing her sunglasses saw the lecherous glint in Jack's calculating eyes and decided cramp would be a lesser pain than having him drool. Ignoring him, called. "Good afternoon Antonio."

In response Jack warbled, "Lindsey, looking at you always makes me feel I need to lose a pound of two. No doubt with some help from you and one of your jiggy-jerk classes I could look svelte again."

Lindsey shivered at the thought of Jack Hoskins in her gym/fitness centre and in an attempt to erase the image of the unappealing prospect, removed the light towel from around her neck and dabbed at her perspiring face. Her back half turned towards Jack, but setting the towel down on the bar became aware that Jack was sidling nearer.

"You get bonnier every time I see you," Jack declared as he closed the intervening gap and placed his hands on either side of her face to drop a wet kiss on her lips. Squeezing her shoulders he beamed, "There's no meat on your bones. What the hell do you eat? No doubt the odd lettuce leaf? I can tell you, there's no protein in that. A decent steak would do you good." Reaching for his drink he sank onto the nearest stool. "Good God woman a puff of wind would have you over. I've seen more flesh on bones after the dogs have picked at them."

Both feet firmly on the ground Lindsey wiped her lips with the back of her hand. "You know, Jack, I now feel as limp as that lettuce leaf." With a sardonic twist to her lips nodded towards Jack's belly. "A little less flesh might do you some good."

Grinning, Jack poked his middle. "This is real living my girl, though I admit it's mainly in the fast lane not jigging about in latex and drinking biotex."

"Lycra, Jack, its lycra and bio yogurt…and, it's called lifestyle!"

Shaking his head as if Lindsey had spoken in a foreign tongue Jack retorted, "If you say so love. I take it you'll have a drink with me?"

Not really wanting to stay, but intending to have one anyway, she answered, "If you insist. I'll have a sparkling water, please."

Pulling a face of total disgust, Jack snorted. "*Good grief!* Go on Antonio give the lady a glass of duck's wine. You'd not catch my Sheila drinking that stuff."

"Did I hear my name being mentioned?" Sheila called, ambling towards the bar, wearing a pair of white shorts with a strapless blue and white top. Her healed sandals made her legs appear long and shapely.

Looking over his shoulder, Jack chortled. "Ah, Sheila, I've got a Bucks Fizz all ready for you."

Ignoring her husband, Sheila glided over to Lindsey. "Hello Lindsey, sorry I didn't see you standing there at first. Mind, hardly surprising, you're like a blade of grass that's been over trimmed."

Lindsey had heard enough from the Hoskins over the years not to take offence. "Hello Sheila, welcome back. Maybe this time you'll find a slot in your busy schedule for some tips on body shaping? Taking care of bottoms and hips is so important in mid life." *Touche!* Not waiting for a response, she picked up the bottle of water and glass that Antonio had served, and moved to a table.

"Pity she doesn't look in the mirror more often," Sheila said loudly. "My body shape is of more interest than that broom handle look she prefers."

Chapter THIRTY ONE

Talking to the men in the villa next door had endorsed Doreen's determination to have a go at the gym. In fact they had persuaded her to join them that afternoon, though Doreen was not too sure about going so soon, but over excited at being treated as an equal, had giggled and said yes. Now standing in her dressing room, all neat and tidy thanks to the maid, she had slipped the girl a few bob for her help. Having pots of money did, after all, have its advantages. Pulling out the Lycra outfit she had brought with her in anticipation of giving the fitness lark a go, she giggled.

"Blimey I didn't think I'd actually wear these weird togs, but me system needs a bit of a sort out after Pat squashing it." She laughed at last night's antics and hoped Pat was getting himself sorted. Stepping into the shiny purple, body hugging shorts, she pulled them up to avoid the crotch hanging around her knees before struggling into the tight top. "Phew, I think I know what a straight jacket might feel like," she cried, trying to catch her breath.

Slipping her feet into trainers, she pushed her hair behind her ears, admired herself in the mirror. "You know girl your not looking too bad, even if I say so myself. Being a scrubber helped with me curves." She chuckled at what she and her mates had called each other when they were cleaners. She had read in the glossy magazines how celebrities bragged about how often they went to the gym. She was not sure what all the fuss was about, but now being like them, rich, she was going to find out. Her kit had cost a bomb but she did not care, she was going to look the part. Waltzing through the villa she paused to call goodbye to Trisha, then remembered her daughter had said something about going to sunbathe by the pool. Opening the front door she waved to Chicky and Simon waiting on the path and stepped out into the heat to join them, unaware a tag was hanging from the tight top down her back.

Simon and Chicky patiently waiting, watched as Doreen wiggled her hips ambling towards them. Delight in his voice, Simon beamed, "Mrs W, you most certainly look the part. Are you sure you've not done this before?"

Giggling, "Thanks, but I haven't done none of this kind of thing before, so not sure what I should be doing."

"You need worry not one iota, because Miss Palmer-Brown will give you a thorough check over and will not allow you to do anything without being supervised." Taking hold of her arm, Simon added. "I had a long chat with her this morning, so nothing for you to worry about. We have all afternoon to tone and enjoy."

"Phew that's a relief," Doreen said looking up at Simon. "Thank goodness you two are here to help me."

Chicky had fallen silent for a moment remembering that Simon had gone into town on his own earlier. He had only been gone a short while, but he had not said why or where he had gone. He had a secret, Chicky was sure and it worried him. Glancing towards Simon, he smiled and wondered what was going on and has he stepped towards Doreen he pushed the nagging doubt to one side and chuckled. "Looks like you are already advertising yourself." He tugged at the tag hanging down from Doreen's top. "Hold fire for a moment."

Not waiting for a response, he sprinted back to their villa. He remembered Simon using some nail scissors earlier and was sure he had left them on the dressing table. Dashing into the bedroom, he spied them, "Ah yes, there they are!" He grabbed them quickly and in his haste knocked Simon's wallet off the side. It fell open on the floor. Bending down Chicky picked it up, paused. He knew he should not look, but plain to see was a telephone number written on the back of one of Simon's personal business cards, beside it Simon had doodled, *So exciting! Can't wait to meet him again!* Underneath were the words. *Coffee. 10.45, Pelito.* Chicky shoved the card back in the wallet and biting his lip hurried back out into the sunshine. So that was where Simon had disappeared to this morning for an hour! To meet someone! Who? Why? Why had he not said?

Now he forced a laugh as he snipped the tag off Doreen's top. "Can't have people seeing how much you cost can we?" he quipped. Popping the tag and scissors into his sports bag, he added, "Now we are all set for a good workout."

"If you say so," Doreen muttered her voice now less confident.

Sandwiched between Simon and Chicky, all three strolled towards the bar area. Doreen spotting Sheila waved, but was ignored. Doreen sniffed, it was clear the snooty cow had seen her.

"You spent a long while talking to this Lindsey this morning?" Chicky said to Simon as they walked together, a slight question in his voice.

"Yes," Simon answered, "there was a lot to sort out."

Chicky said nothing more. He was a barrister: A good one. He knew a lie when he heard one.

Chapter THIRTY TWO

Ambling into the pool area, Trisha was surprised, but very pleased that no one else was there. Those awful Hoskins people were seated at the bar, but that was far enough away to not concern her. It was early afternoon and despite trying to chill on her own terrace she was seriously stressed out. Her mother had spent most of the morning oscillating between castigating her for her night with Ben and giggling about the past and that man, Pat Greenwood. And if that was not enough, she had been twittering about going to the gym because she had giggled about it with the gay men next door. How embarrassing was this holiday going to be?

Dropping her beach bag down next to two sun loungers she wondered if her mother was on the verge of a breakdown because the thought of her working out in a gym was ridiculous. Although, at this moment, desperate for peace and the need to revitalise her energy cells, Trisha did not care if her mother wanted to sit in mud, do spinning, whatever that was, have fish nibble her toes or giggle with gay men. All she wanted was to crash out beside the pool. Looking around at the empty sun loungers, she sighed and flopped down on to the deep soft cushion. Closing her eyes thought of Ben.

His morning business over and his lunchtime Bucks Fizz drunk, Jack decided to take a dip in the pool. He also needed to catch up on what the press was printing today. Hopefully, there might be a mention about what he had been up to and his latest coup. Nobody was safe when he flashed his wallet he tittered to himself as he turned a deaf ear to Sheila's voice prattling on at Antonio. Grabbing a newspaper from the pile on the bar, he then programmed his mobile phone for vibrate only before pushing it into his pocket, then turning broke into his wife's diatribe.

"Sheila, you'll find me on my back if you need me." Grinning, "Swimming, that is." Not hanging around for Sheila to make a remark, he threaded his way to the pool.

Jack was surprised to see only the young Wilkinson girl laid out on a sun lounger. Where was everyone? Pulling a face at the lack of bathers he decided to take a recliner close by the pretty lass. Putting his paper and phone on the table, he divested himself of shorts and top. Clad only in swimming shorts he strolled to the side of the pool. His tanned body covered in fine fair hair made him appear vulnerable and youthful. Tugging at the baggy swim shorts, he stared down into the crystal blue water and cautiously dipped in a toe to test the temperature. Satisfied it was warm, took a deep breath and slowly swung his arms back and forth.

Lindsay had once told him that before making any dive he should ensure his limps were free and relaxed. He did not often listen to her silly athletic mumbo-jumbo but that particular suggestion made sense. More vigorously he swung his arms round and round like a windmill, then slowed down and stopped. He could feel his joints were lithe and free. With a furtive glance towards Trisha, he stood straight, pointing his arms forwards, his bottom up he launched himself off the side of the pool. He hit the water hard. His intended Olympic style dive, designed to impress the young girl, had turned into a spectacular belly flop. Water splashed over the side of the pool creating a localised rain shower.

Shrieking and soaked through, Trisha leapt up. Oblivious of the mini tsunami he had created Jack swam to the far side and climbed out of the water. Standing at the top of the steps he fiercely shook his head to rid his hair of the water.

Trisha stormed round the edge of the pool and stood in front of him dripping wet in her tiny black bikini. "You are so out of order. You have ruined my new bikini."

Shaking his head in an attempt to dislodge the water in his ears, Jack questioned. "Eh? What did you say?"

With disbelief written over her face, Trisha snapped. "You are simply so unreal."

Looking her up and down, Jack frowned. "Now, now, if you don't like getting wet you shouldn't sit that close to the edge. I suggest you find somewhere else if you don't like water."

Pointing to her bikini, Trisha complained again, "This is seriously priceless, and is now totally destroyed by *your* out of orbit belly flop!" Through slit eyes she had watched his arm twirling and his ultimate flop in the pool and wondered how such grossness could show itself in public.

Standing in a puddle of water, indignant, Jack scowled. "I'll have you know that was my finest dive yet. Anyway, I thought bikinis were supposed to get wet."

Giving Jack a look as black as her bikini Trisha turned and stalked back to her damp sun lounger, retrieved her things and marched off.

With his towel wrapped around his dripping body and watching the rapidly disappearing back of Trisha Wilkinson, Jack moved to his sun lounger and picked up his mobile phone, punched a button from his address book. Hearing the call connect, to his delight it was answered after two rings.

"Hello it's me…no there is no problem. Wanted to check that subject to nothing going wild here, I'll see you at four, usual place. No need to worry. But should there be any problems I'll just walk straight past. See you soon… yes of course I do you know that. Bye for now."

Jack stabbed the end call button and to his dismay saw Sheila heading towards him. She had no idea what he was up to and he had every intention of it staying that way, although she was driving him wild with her constant checking on his calls. Quickly he slipped the phone under his pile of clothes on the table and picked up the newspaper. With luck, she would not have noticed anything amiss. He grinned at the thought of his meeting later that afternoon and realised, despite the risk, it was all worth it.

"You'll never guess who I've just seen, Jack. No you can't guess can you? You were once again on your phone."

Jack scowled at his wife, she had missed nothing then. Trying to think of an excuse, found himself saved as she continued loudly. "That Doreen Wilkinson is something else. Her and those *nice* boys are dressed to the death in their gym kit. I saw them all tottering towards the health club. Mind you, those boys are fine looking specimens. It's a shame such good bodies are wasted on the likes of their kind, don't you think Jack?"

Staring at his wife, Jack was staggered at what she found to prattle on about. And like so many times of late, he wondered how they had managed to stay married as long as they had, then reminded himself that he would lose far too much financially if they were to part. She would take half of everything. Half, and the rest!

Scowling, Sheila shook her head. "Are you listening to me Jack?"

Jack nodded, "Of course I am love. Anyway, I must pop back to the villa. I need to visit to the little boy's room." Getting up from his sun lounger, he collected his things and without another word walked away.

Chapter THIRTY THREE

Perspiration dripping off the end of her nose Doreen glared at the big clock on the wall in the gym and could not believe sixty minutes could last so long.

"Gordon Bennett, I'm cream crackered," she gasped, clinging onto Lindsey. All the talk about the gym being good for your body had proved to her that it was absolute rubbish. The last hour had been the longest sixty minutes of her life. Never could she have imagined that something that caused such pain and had you fighting for breath could be remotely good for you.

"Mrs Wilkinson, sit down for a minute and drink this." Lindsey said as she sat Doreen onto a chair and handed her an orange coloured drink. "This will give you more energy," she added.

Glaring at the piddle coloured liquid, Doreen groaned then greedily drank it down. Burping, flashed her hand over her mouth. "Oops sorry about that," she squeaked, handing the glass back to Lindsey.

Lindsey sucked in a quick breath to stifle the mirth rising. "No problem. Sit here and I'll get your workout card and sort out your next session." She moved away towards her table.

Horror crossing her flushed face, Doreen cried, "Thanks and all that, but I'll not be doing this again. Mud baths, a bit of gentle massage, even fish nibbling me tootsies I'll be back for, but not this."

Raising an eyebrow, Lindsey handed Doreen her workout card, the added. "I am sure you will enjoy our pampering programme more, but with time you might enjoy coming back to the gym. And, Mrs Wilkinson, I will always be here to help you. You have done very well this afternoon."

Gripping a paper towel, Doreen wiped it across her face and neck. “Thanks again, but no offence, this lark isn’t for me, I’ll be better off with being pampered.” Clutching her card she saw Chicky and Simon bounding towards her. “Don’t worry about me Lindsey, these lovely boys will see me back to me villa. “I’ll see you another day.”

“If you are sure,” Lindsey said, before turning and walking away.

Twisting round to Simon and Chicky, Doreen cried, “Am I glad to see you.” At the same time she caught a glimpse of her face in the wall mirrors and slapped her hands to her cheeks. “Blimey me face is the same colour as me kit.”

Catching Doreen’s expression, Chicky and Simon laughed.

“Mrs W, you are looking rather hot and bothered if you don’t mind me saying.” Simon said.

“Glad you think it’s funny, even my legs won’t hold me up.” Doreen tried to stand, wobbled, and sat back down.

Chicky tried to hide his amusement. “It might be a good idea if Simon and I carry you to the bar for a reviving tipple.”

With a loud sigh, Doreen answered, “That’s the best thing I’ve heard yet, but I’ll take your arm to help me totter there. Me being wrapped in your arms being carried back would give some of them owners more to squawk about. I think I’ve heard enough being said since we arrived.” She giggled and grabbing hold of Simon’s arm pulled herself up. Standing she hooked her other arm through Chicky’s then looking up at their laughing faces, giggled again.

“I’ve never seen anything like this,” Simon chortled as Doreen rested her head against his shoulder.

Lifting her head, her voice thin, “I don’t think I’ll ever recover. It isn’t normal to do this sort of thing, is it? I can only think those rich girls are lying about all this gym malarkey.”

Simon and Chicky’s eyes met, sparkled with amusement.

"Let's get you to the bar and something to invigorate you," Simon suggested. "And before you know it you will be back to your old self and feeling great."

Hanging on to Doreen, Chicky and Simon chuckled.

"I'm glad you think it's funny. I could be damaged for life."

Antonio grinned at the sight heading towards him. "You Englis' 'ave very strange-a ways."

Grinning Chicky called, "Don't ask please just serve three very large glasses of champagne."

"Make mine a very large G and T because it could be me last," Doreen amended, finding her breath.

Approaching a table with four chairs, the two barristers carefully lowered Doreen down onto one, then lifting her legs propped them on the chair opposite. Doreen sighed with relief

Recalling the deliberate snub earlier, Doreen looked across at Sheila Hoskins who was stretched out on a recliner at the far side of the pool, a sun hat pulled firmly over her face. *Snooty cow*, she thought, then turning her attention to her own aches and pains cried, "What a way to spend an afternoon. Now I think I know how my poor Pat felt with his back going this morning. Mind, I think I'm in a worse state. I ache all over."

"I promise you Doreen," Simon said, sitting down next to her, "you will recover. You simply need to do this more often and then your stamina will improve."

Visibly paling at his words, Doreen squealed, "You don't mean…*do it again!*"

"We do this three times a week," Simon said.

"That's all well and good, but I am not doing it again."

"Let me see the card Lindsey gave you, it will have recorded everything you did in your session." Simon picked up her workout card and studied what Lindsey had written

At the sight of Antonio approaching Doreen's eyes lit up, "A life saver," she purred as he handed her a large gin and tonic. Grasping the full glass, she took a drink, happiness spreading over her face. “Thanks.”

Placing the other two glasses on the table Antonio laid a light hand on Doreen’s shoulder. “I hope it makey you wobble no muchy on your feet, then no needy for biggy men to carry eh?”

Antonio winked at Simon and Chicky.

”Just check what’s recorded here is what I think it is,” Simon said as he handed the workout card to Chicky, then toasted, “Good health.” Chicky glanced at the card, raised an eyebrow, glared at Doreen. “It’s just as we thought.” He paused to add drama and shook his head, “Your workout consisted of a cycle ride of five hundred metres and then you did another five hundred metres on the running machine.”

Gasping, ‘It’s hardly surprising I’m cream crackered. That Lindsey has nearly killed me. I should have had a gentle session.”

“But you did okay,” reassured Simon. “It is less than half a mile.”

Reaching out her hand, Doreen snatched back her card. I think you’ll find it was more than that. You can keep all this. As I’ve said, it isn’t for me!”

“Nice to hear people are having a good time,” Sheila remarked scathingly from beneath her sun hat. “But could you be a little less giggly, if you please?”

Forgetting her pain and indignation Doreen was about to retort with a cutting response, but bit her tongue. For some strange reason she felt sorry for the snooty cow. Her husband, Jack, was an odd man. She did not know him from Adam, but there was something about his behaviour that made the hairs on her arms stand on end. Holding her drink to her lips, she took a mouthful. Nothing and nobody were anything like she had expected. Even Pat had not seemed real. Why now, of all times, and here of all places, had he contacted her again after so many years?

“Excuse me are you with us?” Simon asked as he watched Doreen stare vacantly at Sheila Hoskins.

Turning, Doreen looked at the two men, she had never had anything to do with gay men before, but these two were kind, very kind. She giggled. “Just thinking if I’ll ever recover,” she lied then giggled again. She knew she giggled far too much, but it helped her cope with being in a world that was as alien to her as living on the moon.

Chapter THIRTY FOUR

Wearing black trousers and a silk top, heels a little too high Sheila, with her arm slipped through her husband's, walked into the entertainment area situated between the bar and the pool. Going past one of the tables she assessed the standard of presentation, ensuring the cleanliness of the white, crisp, tablecloth with its matching napkins set perkily in exquisite silver napkin rings. The silver bread knife, knife, fork, dessert fork and spoon were laid out correctly.

She snorted. "I trust Carmen Santana has brought everyone into line this time. On the last occasion when we frequented one of these hip-hop barbeques, the evening fell well short of the standards we expect."

The live band was setting up to one side of the small dance square. Sheila turned her scrutiny on the three musicians. "Let's hope these have the right volume and taste tonight." She pulled a face of dissatisfaction at the memory of the previous band, then added in a barbed tone, "The last lot sounded more like a country bumpkin village bash than an exclusive social event."

Jack rolled his eyes and with great effort held his tongue. He had heard it all before. Different words, different places, but the same sentiment. He had been cursed the day he had met Sheila, and even more so the day he had wed her. Everything, he reminded himself, had a price and the one he was paying was high. But then he mollified himself with the thought that he made up for his suffering in other ways. He laughed silently at his years of satisfying deceit and smiled at his late afternoon activities.

With her critical gaze roving across the festivities, Sheila was halted before any further reference could slip from her lips as a cool glass of champagne was thrust into her hand from one of the waitresses.

Not waiting to be handed a glass Jack grabbed one from the tray and drank it down in one long gulp before taking another. He needed something to keep him going tonight, Sheila was out to impress and he knew that usually meant trouble.

"Thanks love," he winked at the waitress. Placing his glass back on the tray, the young girl smiled then turned away.

Spying Antonio behind the bar Sheila hurried over to him. "Good evening Antonio. I know we are early but it is imperative that I check the arrangement to make sure they are correct. And, most important, to ensure the champagne is well chilled. This…" she handed her almost empty glass to Antonio, "is a tad warm for my palate. Deal with it."

Not giving him the opportunity to respond, Sheila turned away. She paused, frowned. Who was that clinging to Doreen Wilkinson's arm? Walking away, she called to Antonio over her shoulder. "I do not wish to find that I need repeat myself, Antonio. See to the champagne immediately. I have more important things to do, people to see." And with a tip tap of her heels, headed towards the person she had been planning all afternoon to ensnare.

Holding his annoyance in check Antonio watched as Sheila Hoskins, with focused purpose made her way towards Doreen who was helping a gentleman friend to sit at one of the tables. Antonio had a feeling Mrs Wilkinson could more than handle the likes of Sheila H. This thought, as he went to get more ice, cheered him. Someone needed to pull Madam down a peg or two. Or three or four!

Trying to ignore the pain that was not only in his back, but shooting down his left leg as well, Pat Greenwood gingerly lowered himself into a chair, grateful for using Doreen's proffered arm to balance himself. He pointed to the chair beside him and suggested Doreen make herself comfortable. "Come on Doll, sit down or you'll fall off those high heels and do yourself some real damage. Then we'll both be a pair of old crocks."

Looking down at the sparkling red shoes, Doreen groaned. “It’s got nothing to do with me shoes. The aches are to do with overdoing all that gym malarkey this afternoon. It was more like a torture chamber!”

Amusement lighting up his face, Pat grinned at Doreen. “If you say so Doll, but do sit down, it’s giving me a crick in my neck looking up at you. I’m in enough pain without adding any more.”

As Doreen sat, Sheila Hoskins sailed upto the table like a Spanish Galleon under full sail. To Doreen’s surprise she offered a greeting as if they were the dearest of friends.

“How lovely to see you have made it to our *charbon de bois cuisine* Doreen. It is one of the many informal little get togethers we have here. So wonderful when new people, like yourself, support Carmen’s efforts. Of course, it is all about us getting to know each other better and I admit to looking forward to hearing more about you.” Glancing at Pat, added, “And your friend?” Graciously she leaned across the table offering her hand. “Good evening. I am Mrs Sheila Hoskins. You are….?”

Pat carefully reached forward and touched the tips of her fingers. “Pat Greenwood, forgive me for not getting up, I’ve a back problem.”

Taken aback at the show of friendliness and despite knowing Sheila Hoskins could be so stuck up, Doreen leapt up from her chair, in her excitement forgot she was wearing high heels and tottered slightly losing her balance. She grabbed at Sheila’s outstretched arm to save herself from falling and giggled.

“Oh my giddy aunt, I nearly went a pearler, just as well you were there to save me!” Straightening her short dress back to decency, Doreen dropped back into her chair. She wanted to believe that they were on the same social scale, but seeing the enforced smile on Sheila’s face was not convinced.

Sheila dabbed at an imaginary speck on the expensive silk of her top. She ignored Doreen and spoke to Pat. “Are you from round here? Of course, any guest of anyone residing here at Villas Bonitas is more than welcome."

Doreen was not going to be brushed off so easily. "You might not believe it Sheila, ducks," she said in a lowered, confessional tone, "but I've never been to anything like this, what did you call it? Charbum de boys something? I've been to a few knicker parties, but that's not the same is it?" Giggling silently and keeping a dead pan face she watched as Sheila cringed with disgust: perfect! "I bought sum frilly knicks for a quid last time. Not real silk of course, but they were gorgeous, all lacy, but blimey there was hardly nothing to them when I pulled them on. Came right up me bum they did. Thank goodness we don't have to flash our drawers here is all I can say!" Doreen could not contain her mirth; she giggled loudly.

Scandalised, Sheila stared, askance, her features as taut as a drum, a muscle ticked in her cheek. That lottery was vulgar, had a lot to answer for; it encouraged gambling for one thing and was a bad influence on the lower classes. Either the prize money should be lowered, or poorer people banned from buying a ticket. Look at the results!

God, I am a martyr to the human race, Sheila thought. *I make the effort to befriend even the lowest of the low. No one could accuse me of being aloof, with my reputation I should be given a mention in the Queen's honours list.*

With a calculating twist to her mouth that represented a half smile, Sheila reminded herself that she had not got where she was today without being a little devious. Despite having to suffer such coarseness she was determined to maintain her appearance as a thoughtful lady; you never knew what opportunities were waiting to be taken. And as much as she was interested in *Miss Fink Fought's* background, she wanted to know who this man was. Doreen Wilkinson had arrived at Villas Bonitas with just the daughter. Now here she was with a rather good looking stranger, the same man, Sheila was certain, she had caught a glimpse of that morning tottering to his car half naked and clinging to some younger man. What was he up to? Oh yes, she knew all about the sort of men who conned widows out of their fortunes. Well, he was not going to get his grubby little hands on her money, married widowed or otherwise, though she had no idea of Doreen's marital status: Divorced probably. *Knicker parties?* Good God!

With a forced look of camaraderie, Sheila cleared her throat and realised she had to make some sort of dignified response and to change the subject. "Really? How fascinating? This evening's little gathering will be nothing compared to the Al fresco Soirees we will be having in a few days. Of course you are invited Doreen dear, and you too Mr Greenwood? You will be more than welcome to escort this lovely lady."

"I am sure we will be delighted," Pat responded carefully, "assuming my back has eased out of its present uncomfortable spasm."

Sheila touched his arm, concern flooding her face. "Oh poor you, backs are so *de rigour*, don't you think? Have you a chiropractor? I am sure Lindsey could recommend someone suitable."

So, she thought, is this his game*?* Pretend to have a bad back and gain sympathy*?* Oh yes, she knew all about how con men lied their way into gaining a vulnerable woman's trust then disappeared without trace. Well, he could fleece Doreen out of her last penny, but he would get nowhere with herself! She smiled and returned her attention to Doreen. "Of course it is not *just* any invitation. No, I want you to be my guest of honour, Doreen. I have never met a lottery winner before." Sheila pronounced the word *lottery* as if it was a killer disease. "It will be *so* good for you to be seen in *proper* circles, and meet *proper* people." She did not add that her friends would take great delight in meeting a genuine gutter bred trollop.

"An al frecko sworray?" Doreen queried. "The paper gave me a big flash do after me winnings. It was at some posh place up town. The Savoy, God it was a laugh, all them men in their penguin suits, and their posh floosies with their bits bulging out over their skimpy tops." She laughed and looked down at her own low cut dress. "Mind you, I can talk!"

Despite his pain, Pat would like to have grabbed Doreen and gagged her, carrying on about knicker parties, floosies and bits bulging out. Did she not realise she was adding fuel to Sheila Hoskins' raging fire? That was the last thing Doreen needed, let alone an invitation to a highfaluting shindig where she would be ridiculed and out of her depth. He knew enough about all the owners at the Villas Bonitas and was more than aware that Sheila Hoskins was a nasty sort. As much as he wanted to say something, he remained silent. Too much at stake to show his hand yet, but he mentally marked the woman's card.

Passing the table where Doreen and her man were sitting, Antonio overheard the snide comments Sheila Hoskins was making. He hurried to the bar and quickly returned with a tray of drinks. He liked Doreen Wilkinson and she did not deserve to be on the receiving end of such venomous spite.

"I trust the champagne is to your satisfaction now, Mrs 'Oskins?" he said, with a small bow, handing her a champagne flute with a delicate pattern of frosting on the glass. "Mrs Wilkinson? Sir?" He served their drinks and placed a bowl of mixed nuts on the table.

"Who is that fellow over there?" Pat asked Antonio, pointing at Jack. "I reckon he's downed a whole bottle already. I hope we're not in for any rowdy drunkenness this evening. I was under the impression Villas Bonitas was a respectable place." He smiled, he knew perfectly well who Jack Hoskins was, but he needed to pull the wife down a peg or two.

Antonio sucked in his cheeks to stop himself from grinning. Exaggerating the slowness, he turned to look direct at Jack Hoskins. "Zat fellow? 'E is the 'usband of Mrs 'Oskins 'ere." He smiled at Sheila. "Do I fetch your 'usband another drink, Madam?"

"No, Antonio. You do not. See to your other customers and is it not about time we had some food served?" Sheila pointed towards some other people arriving at the far end of the pool and turning on her heels stalked towards her husband, a look of thunder on her face.

Pat chuckled. He raised his glass and chinked it against Doreen's. "I know that fellow, I've seen him several times." He lowered his voice, "With someone who is *not* Mrs Hoskins."

Doreen's eyes rounded. "Ooh, I say! Tell me more!"

Pat grinned. "Later maybe if I think you've behaved yourself enough to hear more."

Chapter THIRTY FIVE

Simon and Chicky, strolling close together, arms touching, arrived behind a group of people who had villas on the far side of the lavish complex. Within seconds they were offered a glass of champagne by a young waitress. As they helped themselves to a drink, to their dismay, they heard the now familiar dulcet tones of Mrs Hoskins cooing in their direction.

"Hello boys. Do come on over to our table. I insist you join us."

Exchanging glances, Simon whispered, "Repeat performance comes to mind." He placed a hand on Chicky's shoulder and slightly shook his head. "Surely there should be easier challenges for us to face than having to survive another evening at the Hoskins table? I could jump through burning hoops without burns, swim with sharks and still have all my limbs, even stick my head inside a lion's mouth and survive, but I am not sure I will come out unscathed from sitting with that woman again."

Patting Simon's hand, Chicky soothed, "It could be worse, I grant you, but once the band gets going we'll limber up over there." He nodded to where soft music was playing. "Come on, if we don't join them, ever likely they will make a fuss and *we* will end up being tonight's entertainment."

Shrugging, resignation shadowing his face, Simon agreed but slowed Chicky to almost a funeral march pace.

"Coo-ee! Are you coming to sit with us?" Doreen's voice rang out. "Ooh Pat, these are me neighbours, Simon and Chicky, a lovely pair of boys."

Grinning, feeling saved by the bell, Simon lengthened his stride and towing Chicky, all but ran to join Doreen.

Chicky spread both hands towards the Hoskins, "Sorry, it seems we're in demand!"

Pat again apologised for not getting to his feet. "My back has somewhat incapacitated me," he explained, holding his hand out first to Chicky then Simon.

As he shook Simon's hand he said, "It's good to meet you at last, I've heard a lot about you."

Simon blushed slightly. "All good I trust?" he stammered.

Pat smiled as the two men sat down. "Oh I think so," he said, "I think so."

To change the subject, Simon grinned at Doreen. "Mrs W, you look stunning, a picture of health and beauty. The gym did you proud!"

Doreen giggled, "Don't remind me! Pat, these are the two so and so's who nearly killed me." She wagged a finger at Simon, "You can be certain, I am not doing nothing like that again."

Chicky placed a kiss on her cheek. "The best sound of the night, that lovely giggle of yours, Doreen."

"These two…" Doreen continued taking Pat's hand and giving it a squeeze, "These two so and so's gave me such a hard time this afternoon I ache all over. It's all I could do to sit up after we'd finished." She paused, went bright red and clapped her hand to her mouth. "Oo er, that didn't come out right did it?" She giggled, "I meant, they made me do one of them work out regimes things. Half killed me." She leant forward and patted Simon's hand. "For all they are a wicked pair, they've looked after me proper, Pat. They're nice boys."

Trying to ignore the dull pain twitching in the base of his spine, reminding him to sit still, Pat gave Doreen a kiss on the cheek. "I know what you meant Doll, I wasn't born yesterday." Added 'Sit yourselves down lads. Anyone who likes my Doreen's lovely giggle is a friend of mine." He winked at Simon, who returned a sly grin.

Jack was sulking. Sheila did not much care. "You are on mineral water for the rest of the night," she hissed as she had joined him at the table he had chosen. "You're drunk."

Watching as the two barristers joined Doreen Wilkinson and that man friend of hers, she cringed at the fact that she had actually invited Doreen Wilkinson to her planned Soiree. What had come over her! Then grinned deviously; she would make sure beforehand that her other guests were aware of the woman's coarse vulgarity. They would be delighted at the unusual form of entertainment. With a sly look she glared at Pat Greenwood shaking hands with the two gay boys. *They might be homosexuals*, she thought, *but at least they are educated and know their station in life.* She watched as Greenwood leaned over and kissed Doreen Wilkinson's cheek and frowned. There was no doubt about it, the man unnerved her. The hairs bristled on the back of her neck just looking at him. Yes, there was something not quite right about him; too suave, too sophisticated. *Bad back, my foot!* She thought.

The appearance of two waitresses carrying large serving platters filled with aromatic char grilled meat halted Sheila's ruminations, bringing her mind back to the moment. Starring at what was laid out on the platters, she wrinkled her nose with distaste. "Whatever is this?" she sneered.

Jack was already tucking in; steak, chicken, sausage, a tiny portion of salad and a pile of chips. He squeezed a generous dollop of ketchup onto his plate. Mouth full of food he grinned at the waitress.

Sheila pushed her plate away and reached for her champagne glass, it was empty. She waved at Antonio, signalling for a refill. She had not come to eat the cremated food, but to see who was here.

Having selected several items, Doreen looked up at the young girl and with an appreciative smile said. "Thanks darling, that's really kind of you to bring it to me table."

The waitress smiled. “Thank you madam; it’s my pleasure.” She served Simon, Chicky and Pat then moved to another table.

Sheila heard and leaned across from her table then called loudly. “She is a waitress, Doreen dear. That is what waitresses do. Wait at table.”

She broke off to wave at Carmen and beckon her over, “Is there nothing more edible?” she asked as the young woman came nearer. “This really is not very palatable.”

Chicky exchanged a glance with Simon and cringed. Simon then beckoned Carmen and announced, “My dear lady, my compliments! As fine a repast I have not had in many a day.”

Several people within hearing began to applaud, Jack Hoskins included.

As dusk fell, the solar lights began to twinkle and Carmen had arranged for coloured lanterns to be hung around the barbeque area. It all looked very celebratory. Engorged, his belly feeling as if it were about to burst, Chicky watched Jack leave his table without exchanging a word with his wife. It appeared the two were not on speaking terms.

“You know,” Simon said, swallowing down a burp, “I don’t think I will be able to eat again for a week.”

“Good food weren’t it?” Doreen said as she watched Jack perch himself on a stool at the bar and noticed Sheila was now sitting on her own. “Do you think we ought to ask her to join us?” she whispered loudly to Pat.

Chicky heard and blanched. “Good grief, no!” He stood up abruptly. “I don’t know about you Doreen Wilkinson, but I’m going to try my hand, or should I say, my feet at dancing. Care to take my arm Mrs W?” Giggling, Doreen looked across at Pat as if needing permission.

“Go on Doll, I can tell you I won’t be tripping the light fantastic for some time.” He took Doreen’s hand and passed her into Chicky’s keeping. “Show this gentleman you are a stylish lady on the dance floor.” With a sly glance he peered across at Sheila as he spoke.

Jumping up, Doreen giggled. "Not sure if me feet remember the fox trot, I was a right diva once in me youth."

"Then let us go and youthfully find out." Chicky smiled, sweeping Doreen towards the dance square.

Simon, being the gentleman he was, got to his feet and asked Sheila if she would care to dance. Sheila smiled, delighted, tossed back the remains of her drink and accepted, under her breath sneered. "I'll show them. I'll certainly show all of them!"

"You know I haven't danced like that in yonks. I didn't think I could remember all those steps." Doreen plonked herself down on her chair and slipping her feet from her shoes, rubbed her sore feet.

"Well you most certainly danced the legs off me," Chicky laughed breathless. "Between Simon and me, I don't think you've missed a dance all evening. Hardly surprising Pat is in the way he is with all your energy," he added, and winked at Simon.

Doreen merely giggled and Pat grinned.

With an inebriated glaze to her eyes, Sheila tried to focus on Simon as the dance ended. She had danced with almost every man present, accepting their polite offers and spending a while between dances at each table, drinking champagne, making sure everyone was enjoying themselves. She swayed as Simon escorted her towards her seat and collided with him. "Ooh, I'm a lucky girl. It's a good job you were standing just there. I could have fallen right over on to my prize *posshession*."

Simon glared across at Chicky, disbelief flickering like a bright light. Sheila Hoskins was drunk.

Instead of sitting down, Sheila stumbled towards Chicky. "Now, where is that nimble partner of yours? It's his turn. You never know what people are capable of do you?" Her face was flushed with alcohol, "Come on Chicky Chicky," she called, then added, "Ginger Rogers and Fred Astair, who would have thought it, a gay barrister and a lottery winner here at Villas Bonitas?"

Swaying, grasped Chicky's arm and hauling him to his feet, cried, "Let me show you how to tango."

Not waiting for a response, Sheila lashed her free arm around Chicky's waist, pushed their arms forward and hurtled towards the dance area where she stopped, stepped back, stepped forward, and stopped again. Releasing her grip from Chicky's waist, she pushed damp hair off of her face. Chicky stood there looking around desperately while Sheila carolled, "Once more! *Olez*!" Making a grab for Chicky, misjudged her step and as Chicky stepped back trying to avoid her, Sheila plunged forward hurtling past him under the force of her own momentum.

A scream pierced the night.

The band stopped playing: a moment of silence. People began to stand up. Someone started laughing.

Jack, at the bar, several drinks inside him, but not drunk, marched to where everyone was gathering.

Standing stock still he gazed down at his wife. "Good God woman, what are you playing at? Get out of the pool before you drown and soak everyone into the bargain."

Bedraggled, her clothes making movement difficult, Sheila struggled through the water making her way to the steps. She spluttered loudly as she dragged herself up the underwater lit steps, aware her trousers and top were ruined and her hair a mess.

Glowering at Jack who was not making the slightest effort to help her, she stepped onto the tiles beside the pool. "Give me your jacket," she hissed, trying to snap her wet fingers at him.

He removed it slowly, scowled as she draped it around her shoulders.

Sheila walked a few paces, realised she only had one shoe on. The other bobbed towards the centre of the pool. Calmly, she stated, "I have told Carmen time and time again about that loose tile, now I have tripped on it." Her voice now steely added, "I suggest Jack, that you ensure she loses her job for this incompetence."

She bent down, removed her remaining shoe and walked with dignity towards her villa, Jack trudging behind her in the wake of dripping water.

Neither of them turned round as the silence was interrupted by a few sniggers, which turned to louder chortles and then a full burst of laughter.

Chapter THIRTY SIX

Hands held tightly, Trisha and Ben weaved their way through the gardens of Villas Bonitas. Above, stars twinkled brightly and the moon, full and round lifted the darkness. The gardens gave off their nightly fragrances which hung heavy in the air. From near the pool area a cacophony of sound, voices rang with laughter and chatter mingling with the sound of guitars strumming and singers crooning.

Hearing the music, Trisha scoffed. "How sad is that noise? Just tell me our taste in music will not slip to such scary levels when we are as old as the people here?"

Before Ben could respond, a scream immediately followed by a splashing sound filled the night air.

"Lordy Lordy," Trisha tittered. "Late night swim or someone fallen in? Ben laughed and at the same time listened to make sure help was not needed. After all, he was a lifeguard when not studying. Hearing nothing more, said, "Likely they're just larking about."

With no further interest in the antics going on around the pool, Ben pulled

Trisha close to him, kissed her. "Thanks for seeing me again, I thought after this morning you would be grounded and I would be banned from coming anywhere near you."

"Did you indeed? Well you thought wrong." Squeezing Ben's hand, Trisha had no intention of repeating all that her mother had said after he had left that morning. Doreen had given her hell, before reminding her that there was more to life than being stupid and careless. She had wagged her finger, repeated the facts of life and given a beady eye glare, then to Trisha's surprise, had hugged her. She silently thanked this Pat Greenwood because it seemed his appearance into her mother's life had made her soft and forgiving.

“If I was you I’d stay well away from thinking or thoughts, it has a lot to do with things going wrong.” She said cryptically.

Confused, Ben grinned. “Right.”

Trisha silenced him as she placed her mouth on his and twined her arms around his neck.

“Ahem.”

At the sound of the discreet cough, Ben opened his eyes and to his alarm saw Trisha’s mother and her man friend standing a few yards away. He pulled away from Trisha’s hungry mouth and backing into the bushes with her in tow, yelped, “Oh my God, it’s your mother.”

Not realising his panic was genuine Trisha wriggled her body closer to his. “Panic not. They are so more interested in rewinding and checking out the past, than bothering about us.”

Doreen coughed again.

A moment’s pause.

Trisha disentangled herself from her boyfriend, turned and smiled sweetly. “Mama!”

Staring at her daughter’s face, Doreen caught her breath. A shiver ran down her spine. It was not the cheeky words she had overheard that had given her a jolt. Nor was it the fact that Trisha was with Ben, because her daughter had that morning assured her she was being sensible. No, if it was any one of these, she would merely giggle and walk away. Something else, something other than cuddles and kisses had taken the wind out of her sails.

Seeing her daughter in the soft glow of the lanterns that lit the pathways and gardens showed her something she had not realised until this moment. Standing close to her offspring, her arm linked with Pat’s she could seen her daughter’s features beautifully emphasised in the artificial light. The face of the child she had brought into the world: the one she had conceived, given birth too and brought up for over seventeen years. If she was blind, she would have said that she would know every inch of her daughter’s face, it was as familiar to her as the back of her own hand: The oval shape with its small straight nose, the dimple in the middle of her chin. The beautiful hazel coloured eyes with their long lashes and her mouth, which Trisha called, *my wonky mouth*, because the right side of her upper lip curled slightly when she smiled

Doreen shivered involuntary. The mistake she had made all those years ago was suddenly there before her, mocking her like some grinning devil come to haunt her. The curl of that lip was the same as the little quirk to the side of Trisha's father's mouth. Exactly the same! Why had she not realised it before now?

Doreen's mind went into free fall and raced down the years at an alarming speed. Memories slammed into her mind as if all those years ago had happened yesterday.

She had been a bit of a girl back then, carefree, a laugh a giggle. Her and Pat had had been an item, but one night they had argued, an argument that had turned into a full rampage corker of a row. She had screamed at him and he had stormed out. They had both been in the wrong, but that had not stopped the foul words, the accusations. He had been seeing Tracey Brooks, her best friend and she had been carrying on with Jimmy Fuller. Not on a regular basis, but in those days they were all having fun, except she was the one who got caught, got pregnant.

At three months gone, the bitter row not healed, Pat had suddenly announced that he was engaged to her friend. No one knew Doreen was *in the club* so she was left with Jimmy. He could have been Trisha's father just as Pat could have been, so although Jimmy was not impressed by the prospect of fatherhood, he had found a Council flat and stood by her.

They had never talked about marriage, Doreen had kept her maiden name of Wilkinson, but when Trisha was born his name had been put on the birth certificate as the father. In less than a year he had gone, buggered off somewhere. Pat had married, was living abroad, something to do with oil rigs. Life as a single mum had been hard and tough and she had never found anyone she could trust. She had blown away the only person she'd had feelings for, Pat Greenwood. And here she was in paradise with the truth of her stupid mistake in front of her. Pat was Trisha's father, not Jimmy Fuller.

Doreen's head was spinning. She forced a cheerful smile at her daughter's quizzical expression and relieved, received a smile back, a bright little smile with the corner of the mouth tipping upward. How could she tell Pat? There was no way they could put the clock back. No way to put the mistake right, not after all these years. What a mess.

"We were about to go clubbing." Trisha announced, 'Just having, you know, a little peck."

Giggling to restore some level of normality, Doreen told a lie. "I was just thinking about what happened at the pool. It was a bit of a laugh. That Sheila Hoskins fell in. Three sheets to the wind, what a dark horse she's turned out to be!"

Not amused, Trisha snorted. "I should have guessed it would be something just so incredibly trivial." Turning to Ben, hissed. "We are going. Let's just leave these weirdoes alone."

Trisha did not wait for a response, but took hold of Ben's hand and headed at a fast pace towards the entrance gates.

Pat, having said nothing turned to Doreen who was crying, tears trickling down her cheeks.

"Doll, what on earth is the matter?" he asked concern in his voice. "She's only going clubbing and as for the lad, well she's just having some fun."

Letting Pat hug her to him, Doreen looked up into his eyes. "Oh Pat, if only it was that simple."

Chapter THIRTY SEVEN

Given the opportunity, she could sleep all day but night time was not that easy, of late any time after midnight her eyes snapped open and her brain went into overdrive. Ginny was exhausted with the weight of her dilemma and trying to keep up as normal an appearance as possible with Jack now he had officially arrived back at Villas Bonitas with his wife. Life was so much easier when he came on his little *business trips* on his own. He did not stay at the Villa, but booked a hotel to cover appearances. He rarely actually stayed with her in the one bedroom apartment that he provided for her. Why was that? she suddenly wondered. Because it would tie him down? Commit him? A quick tumble in bed was all he wanted not responsibilities. But then, that was all she had wanted. Or so she had thought.

She had resolved to tell him, only to then immediately convince herself that it was not a good idea. Whichever way she jumped, she had far too much to lose. Just what should she do? she asked herself for the hundredth time as she sat drinking a cup of tea at four o'clock in the morning. Even the television was rubbish at that hour. As insane as it was, it occurred to her that a wander around Villas Bonitas might help. Maybe seeing Jack in his own environment would help clear her thoughts.

She looked at the clock that sat on the glass unit. As silent as the grave it did not tick, just displayed the time, a modern case stuffed with two batteries, soundless, but accurately showing her the hour, the minute, the second and the date. She sighed, the date was critical, time was running out.

Until of late she had never thought about clocks, time and dates, now they seemed to be everywhere reminding her of what she must do. It was far too early to be sneaking around anywhere at the moment, let alone Villas Bonitas. The phrase *cake and eat it* sprang to mind. She laughed. Her merriment echoed through the quiet apartment, reverberating off the ceramic tiled floor and paperless walls.

"God how many times has Jack said that?" she muttered aloud. If she was honest, that was exactly what she wanted: her cake and eat it. Finishing her tea, she made up her mind to go to Villas Bonitas, what had she to lose? Ever likely it was all about to be lost anyway, but not without having a nose around first. She smiled at her decision and wished her other decision was as easy to make.

As daylight broke, awakening the birds, their morning calls rapidly turning to song which gathered momentum and turned into a beautiful chorus, Ginny pushed open her balcony doors and listened to the twittering and thought how innocent the world seemed when the birds sang. Her courage had evaporated a little, but not enough to change her mind. From the balcony she had a glorious view towards the beach and the shimmering sea that was not yet its deep sapphire blue colour. She noted there were already a few people walking along the shore, several exercising their dogs and a young couple strolling hand in hand. The girl had black hair, slim and probably pretty. Ginny could not tell from this distance. They stopped, kissed, strolled on then kissed again. Young love. Ah, what it was to be young.

A little further along the ground rose steeply covered in lush vegetation. Between those trees and shrubs Ginny knew there were steps in the hillside which led to the private beach and terrace that was exclusive to the residents of Villas Bonitas. Would it harm if she were to slip in that back way? She would not be anywhere near the main gates or the office. Would anyone see her?

She decided to shower, dress and have breakfast then leisurely walk the short distance along the beach. No one would notice her strolling there this early in the day.

An hour later, she was at the bottom of the paved steps that led up to the Villas Bonitas terrace. She hesitated. It would be possible to climb over the fence at the top of the steps, but what if she was seen? Then she smiled and hurried up the slope her feet, in comfortable trainers, making no sound. Ahead were the young couple, arms wound around each other stopping every few yards to kiss, if they were going up the steps they must come from the Villas!

She loitered back a little, pretending to retie her shoe lace, as the black haired girl punched the security code into the electric gate and watched as it swung open. Ginny's smile broadened. She was in luck! The couple were so engrossed in each other they would not notice if an entire army slipped in behind them through the slow closing gate.

Apart from the couple wandering along the pathway, no one else seemed to be around. It was too early for the office staff and even the cleaners would not be about yet. Ginny had carefully selected a smart jogging suit as no one would pay attention to a resident out for an early morning run. Jack himself often pretended to go for a morning jog along the beach, part of his *power walking* fitness repertoire.

It was not her intention to draw attention to herself, her mission, to look, observe, weigh up and hopefully decide. She wanted to give the impression that her jogging exercise was finished, so she loosened the lightweight top, unzipping it and strolled along, running her hand through her hair, then pretending to search for something in her pocket: A picture of innocence.

Her step slow, but purposeful, her gaze took in the opulence that surrounded her. She had been to Villas Bonitas once before when Jack had been there on his own for a few days to oversee some interior decorating or something, but still the magnificence of it all caught her breath. She had forgotten how luxurious the millionaires' complex was. Pathways peeled off in several directions, the place was a maze! She turned to her left and found herself staring at a sparkling swimming pool. She walked past the closed and shuttered bar, noted the tables and chairs and folded up sun umbrellas. The sun loungers, their cushions stacked in a little attractive alcove away from any night damp air. Where now?

Unsure of her bearings, she hesitated, considered where to go next, then chose to retrace her steps to her right she recognised a cluster of white villas. Ginny knew exactly which one was Jack's; the heavy, rather ugly terrace furniture, large over ornate garden pots filled with flowering plants. She recognised his holiday home straight away.

She lengthened her stride. Walked quicker, reached the pathway to the front door and then her nerve failed her. What was she doing here?

Then she heard a sound. She swivelled her head, alarmed. A man was walking towards her, his head down, deep in thought by the look of it. Her instinct was to run, but that would only draw attention to herself. Instead, she walked calmly away and took the first left hand turn. The black haired girl and the boy were standing on the same path, arms entwined, kissing. Should she just jog past, she wondered?

There was a little building on the far side of the grass, perhaps she could hide in there?

Coming here to Villas Bonitas had been a terrible mistake. How had this helped her reach a decision? If anything it had only made things more complicated.

Chapter THIRTY EIGHT

Alone, tossing and turning in the large bed, Doreen had not slept a wink. The previous night's escapades around the pool had slipped from her mind as she had spent the last few hours fighting with her conscience on how to come to terms with what she had, after all these years, realised. Now sitting in the lounge, the blinds open, the early morning sun starting to pour in, its bright light creating a cheerfulness that was not there, Doreen sat with a large cup of coffee in one hand and a cigarette in the other. Already she had drunk four cups and smoked an entire packet. Chain smoking was something she had not done for a long time. But then, she had never been in such a state as this for a long time.

She had spent the night beating herself up on the mistake she had made about Trisha's father, but how was she to have known? Pat and Jimmy had been part of her life and her bed.

"God." she sobbed. "Why is me life not only turning upside down, but spinning out of control?"

She had won the lottery, taken a holiday, not robbed a bank or committed an evil crime and yet she was finding life, at the moment, to be a frightening challenge.

All night she had asked herself, why had she not seen the resemblance before? She should have, but she had not. A tear escaped from eyes still puffy from crying. Doreen ignored it, took a mouthful of cold coffee. Maybe if she explained everything to Pat all would come right in the end? Blimey! How could it? Apart from anything else, why would Pat believe her and worse what would he want with a seventeen year old daughter?

Standing up, she shuffled to the patio doors, opened them. Waved her arm around to circulate the air, the place looked like the *Smoke* with so much smog from her cigarettes. Taking a lungful of fresh morning air she thought the best thing she could do now was simply pack their bags and get out of here; leave without a trace and go back home. She had more than enough money to run away from everything and everyone if she wanted to. And right now, she wanted to. If she legged it she would not have to speak to Pat again.

Raising her gaze to the early morning blue sky she swallowed down a sob that threatened to choke her and realised the sky had been this colour every day since they had arrived. Doreen smiled for the first time in hours. She stared at the terrace, the comfortable furniture, she sniffed the air and felt its fragrance tickle her nose. She sneezed. Wiping her nose with the back of her hand, she knew deep down, that leaving was the last thing she wanted to do.

This place was lovely and the thought of never speaking to Pat again would be the worst thing she could imagine.

"Almost," she sobbed as she stepped back into the villa. Though, she reasoned, he might not want to speak to her again after she had sent him home last night. He had stood, expectantly at the door after the barbeque had ended. She had told him that it would be best if he did not stay, using his poorly back as the excuse. She had even managed a giggle as she had spoken. Her head had been in a mess and she knew she needed to be on her own to sort out all that she had learnt.

"What a nightmare it all is," she cried to an empty villa. Even Trisha had not come home from clubbing. Here she was a multi millionaire, surrounded by luxury she could never have imagined, home alone and scared witless because she did not know what to do.

Picking up the overflowing ashtray, she headed towards the kitchen and the waste bin. Tipping the contents in with the rubbish she heard a tap on the front door. Looking up, she noted the time from the wall clock, sniffing she could not imagine who would want to knock on her door at such an early hour and decided to ignore it.

The tap came again, this time a little louder. Leaving the kitchen, she shuffled with weary steps to the door, her face set to send the caller away. Pulling the door open expecting to see a maid she was shocked to see Pat standing there unshaven, his hair ruffled and his hand placed at the base of his back. Her face softened, she wanted to cry, ask him to hold her and tell him everything so that he could put it right, but she knew how wrong that would be.

Standing on the doorstep Pat took in the woman he had spent years following and to his sadness saw how wretched she looked. Ignoring the dull pain in his lower back he wanted to take hold of her, kiss her and tell her how much he loved her. But somehow he did not think that was the right thing to do and instead said. "I couldn't sleep Doll, missed you already."

He caught a weak smile on Doreen's lips, but it did not reach her eyes. "Just tell me what's going on. We had a great night at the barbeque and then something happened. I thought…" His voiced trailed away because he had thought so many things during the last few hours.

Staring down at her bare feet, Doreen could not trust herself to answer him. Instead opened the door wider, inviting him into her villa. She did not shut the door.

Close to tears she took a deep breath to steady her voice and with more conviction than she felt answered. "I had to send you home. I needed some space to think. Everything is going a bit quick. I needed to get me head around it all. You turning up after all this time has got me head spinning."

Pat stood motionless, looking on at the lady he had hoped would love him again and all he could think was had she found out about him and was this her way of brushing him away? Perhaps he should come clean and tell her everything?

He took hold of her hand. It was clammy.

"I've seen you for just a few days and I can't think of what I could have done to make you look so unhappy. Do you think I am lying to you? Because I can assure you I am not. Tell me what you want to know and I will not only explain, but prove it to you."

Letting go Pat sighed a deep sigh, he could see there was a problem, but which problem was it? He was tired and Doreen was emotional, now was not the best time to open a can of worms. He'd had little sleep, his mind had thought of nothing other than Doreen refusing him into her villa after their wonderful evening. His back had ached all evening and he knew she had used that as an excuse to send him home. Her mood had changed as they had walked away from laughing at the Hoskins' woman falling in the pool. They had stopped and Doreen had spoken to her daughter. Surely, he asked himself, that was not it?

"You know you can tell me anything Doll, we go back a long way." He had hoped these few words would be enough for her to tell him what was making her so sad and at least give him a clue on how to answer. "If it is me, just say and I'll get out of your hair." He smiled it was a strained smile, because leaving was the last thing he wanted to do.

Through troubled eyes Doreen stared at up at him, shuddered. She could see it so clear now how his upper lip curled as he smiled, just like Trisha's. Seeing him smile with her Trisha's *wonky mouth* added more weight to the terrible thing she had done.

"For God sake Doll, it can't be all that bad." But as the words left his mouth he saw tears slip down Doreen's cheek. "Please can I stay and then we can talk?"

Unable to speak, Doreen shook her head she needed to sort this out by herself and then maybe she could talk to him. Between sobs, said. "Give me time, but not now."

Seeing Pat lift his arms to hold her, she stepped back.

Emotion making his voice hoarse and sharper than was intended, Pat said. "You've got my number. Call me. Please…" his voice trailed off, he did not trust himself to say anymore and stepped through the open door and walked away.

Leaning against the varnished wood, heavy tears cascaded down her face. Whatever she had done wrong she knew she must try and put it right, because she really did not want to lose him again.

Brushing her arm across her face to wipe at her tears she straightened herself up and making her way to her bathroom, sobbed. “There must be an answer.”

Hearing the front door open and not wanting her daughter to see her in such a state, she quickly stepped into her bathroom and closed the door.

Chapter THIRTY NINE

The sun's increasing heat was already making the early morning air sultry, but Sheila Hoskins still had the blinds shut in her bedroom. The room, like her face, was sombre and grey. Sitting propped against two pillows resting on the high headboard, Sheila watched as Jack crept into their bedroom. In his hands he held a tray with teapot, cups and saucers. Her nostrils picked up the fragrant aroma of the tea, she gagged. Covering her mouth with her hand, she winced as her headache throbbed in her temples.

Placing the tray on the side table next to Sheila, Jack grinned at the memory of the previous night's escapade. He stifled a chuckle. Sheila had brought the party to a shuddering halt. The silence that had followed her scream and the splash had meant that a pin dropping would have sounded like thunder. He would bet money that there were a few still laughing this morning over the drama. He certainly was.

"You mentioned yesterday," he said, pouring tea from the pot, "that you wanted an early start today. Things to do and such. I've a meeting in town a little later on, so I'll be going out."

Holding a tissue over her nose, Sheila looked at her husband, to her annoyance saw amusement in his eyes.

"I'm glad you've found something to entertain you this morning, but I can tell you for nothing, I will sue."

Jerking his head up from adding milk to the poured tea, Jack snapped. "What?"

Contempt, like saliva, dripped from Sheila's tongue. "You heard what I said and if you had anything about you, you'd be on to our lawyers this very moment. Good God the place is a death trap."

Not sure where Sheila was coming from, but knew it spelt trouble, Jack felt a knot tighten in his stomach. He picked up a cup and saucer as Sheila continued, her tone aggressive.

"If those tiles were inspected every day then I would *never* have tripped and fell. It is clear as the nose on my face that the terraces and paths are dangerous. It's been an accident waiting to happen and to Villas Bonitas big mistake, I *was* that accident!" Huffing, added. "What happened last night made a laughing stock of me, but as sure as eggs are eggs, I will be the one that has the last laugh. Mark my words, just you wait and see."

Handing Sheila the hot tea, his features changing from amused to concerned, Jack asked cautiously, "What tiles are we talking about Shelia? From what I heard and saw, you fell in."

Choking on her tea, Sheila glared at Jack, scorn replacing aggression. "I sincerely hope I am not hearing what you are saying. I tripped. End of story." Sipping her tea, Sheila glared over at Jack, she would listen to no more arguments on the matter, her head was splitting and the last thing she needed to admit to was a hangover. In a calmer voice, added. "Thanks for the tea and in my special cup and all. You can be kind, I know that, but you have to accept that we don't do falling into swimming pools. We are respectable owners. Now, before you go gallivanting this morning, because I take it that is what you will be doing, get that Carmen Santana and Bob *the bloody Bodger* to check those tiles. I want a report on their state by the end of today."

Dismayed and not wanting to delay getting out of the villa as soon as possible because he had a genuine business meeting before his *other* meeting, Jack felt duty bound to get through to his wife that she fell into the swimming pool because of her own fault.

"Sheila, please tell me, do you seriously believe that you tripped over some imaginary broken tile? I can tell you, no one else will. Let's put it down to a good night and that be the end of the matter."

Banging her cup down onto the saucer, tea spraying up, indignant, Sheila snapped. "I can't believe you've just said what you just did. What kind of mind do you think I have to imagine such a thing?" Bristling she carried on. "You of all people know how slapdash that Bob Preston is. I was wearing those lovely new shoes. You remember? I got them in the Caribbean. They were very expensive. No, you are wrong and I can tell you I will get this sorted."

Jack knew better than anyone that arguing with Sheila was a waste of breath and time. In a compliant tone reluctantly agreed. "If you say so, I'll speak with Carmen when she comes in." He intended to do so, but only to warn her that Madam was on the warpath and bullets would fly.

Slouching out of the bedroom, resigned to having to avert a drunken slip into a swimming pool turning into a fiasco, Jack shouted, "I'm off. Don't want to be late for my meeting. Time is brass you know. I'll see you later."

"What about Carmen?" Sheila shouted crossly.

"I'll leave a note to say I want to see her."

Hearing the front door close, Sheila put her cup and saucer onto the bedside cabinet, a sickening feeling rising in her throat from the strong tea. She slithered under the sheet. Her head throbbed and felt like it would explode at any moment. She grimaced at her state, but there was no way she was not going to let Jack know that she had a hangover.

Chapter FORTY

Enjoying the splashing of the water on their bodies, Simon and Chicky sat on two of the round tiled stools positioned behind the spectacular waterfall. The water stools, cleverly arranged in the pool at the rear of the cascading water between the high volcanic wall and the large swimming pool, created a secret grotto effect. The occupants could see out, but no one could see in.

Peering through the curtain of water, Chicky sighed. “It is hard to believe it is cold back home, everyone wrapped up with gloves and scarves and here we are sitting here, very early in the morning, naked under a waterfall. This place is paradise. I don’t really want to go home.”

The two had been awoken by the trilling of the dawn chorus and had both had the same idea, to go for an early morning swim. Only it had been so quiet, so still, that they had ducked under the waterfall, divested their bathing trunks and made love behind the shrouding curtain of water. It had been an exhilarating experience.

Grinning, his own satisfied excitement now fading, but the excitement about Pelito and Villas Bonitos building, Simon wanted to say so much, but knew it would be unwise, instead said, “Indeed and to match this wonderful climate we have entertainment by the most unlikely. I’m glad to see Mrs Hoskins' shoe has been fished out of the pool.” He laughed at the memory of last night, but more so to hide his own thoughts.

“For my part,” Chicky observed, ‘I’ll try and keep a low profile. No doubt I will be accused of tripping her up. If only I’d had the nerve.”

“Hello, who’s that?” Simon pointed to a woman in a jogging suit standing on the far side of the pool, near the bar.

Chicky leant forward and peered through the rush of cascading water. "Never seen her before."

"I think I have," Simon said slowly. "I don't think she belongs here at Villas Bonita."

"Ah," Chicky quipped, "an intruder, eh?" He leaned further forward, his face almost next to the curtain of water and watched her walk confidently off down the path, said, only half serious, "Ought we to call the police? Though she seems to know where she's going in my opinion."

Simon was frowning. "I've seen her somewhere." He was picturing in his mind the girl he had seen yesterday morning. She had watched him toss that coin in the fountain and he had smiled at her. He grinned.

"I know who she is! She's the *girlfriend*: The girlfriend of Jack Hoskins."

"How on earth do you know that?" Chicky asked surprised, looking back at the gorgeous man sitting without a stitch of clothing on beside him.

Suddenly aware he had said too much, Simon realised he would have to back pedal so not to alarm Chicky.

He looked wistfully at his partner. He needed to think everything through before he took the decision that could end their partnership for good. End this love that he felt for Chicky for good, but sometimes, love was not strong enough to survive the other things that life threw at you. Things happened. This holiday was paradise, but it would soon come to an end and then things would change. It was imperative that Simon should choose the right moment to explain to Chicky that his life had come to a turning point. That he did not know if he was going to take that turn or stay on the straight, boring road with Chicky. But now was most certainly not that moment. Least of all because he was not certain yet *what* road he wanted to follow. The road with Chicky back home in London, or….

Chicky was sensitive, unsure of himself at times, Simon realised that he would need to select his words carefully, once he had decided what to do, and with whom he wanted to do it with. Those thoughts swirling round in his head, he suddenly grinned. A diversion tactic had presented itself. Jack Hoskins was striding up to the pool, obviously totally unaware that his mistress had been standing there moments before.

"What the blazes is he doing?" Simon said, also leaning forward, his body brushing against Chicky. He pointed at Jack, who was shuffling his feet around the edge of the pool.

Trying to appear nonchalant in case anyone unexpectedly came along, Jack slithered his right foot along the smooth surface of the tiles. "Hells bells," he muttered as he stepped to one side and repeated the performance several times. "I must be bloody insane doing this." He growled and at the same time checked to see if anyone was appearing along the pathways. He had to be quick, Carmen sometimes came in early.

"Bloody woman has me behaving like a half wit," he hissed as he bent down and ran his fingers along a few more of the tiles. "Nothing bloody there," he snapped, as he tapped with his knuckles on a couple more of the ceramic tiles.

His patience at an end, he stood up. Rubbing his hands together to wipe away any dust, he headed for Carmen's office. There was a little book she kept in a box on the windowsill where anyone could leave notes and messages for her when she was not there. In case Sheila decided to telephone the manager herself, he needed to put Carmen in the picture and make it crystal clear that he was not part of any suggestion that tiles, loose broken or otherwise had been the cause of Sheila dipping into the water. The silly bitch had been three sheets to the wind, not that he would be mentioning that in his note to Carmen.

There was no doubt in his mind that his wife was getting worse. Next she would be announcing she was the bloody Queen of Villas Bonitas. He had to find a way to stop her, but had no idea how. A runaway train, he mused, would be easier to halt than Sheila.

He looked at his watch. God he would be late! The taxi would be outside the gates by now. Then he had a thought. Maybe the sexy Ginny would have a suggestion about how to handle Sheila? He thrust the notebook and pen back into their box and walked quickly towards the main entrance. No, best keep wives and sweethearts separate. Ginny need not know there was *trouble at mill.*

Simon looked at Chicky and Chicky looked back at Simon. "What on earth was all that about?" Chicky said. His instinct told him that he ought to lean forward and kiss Simon, maybe even suggest that they made love again here in this quiet, secret place, but instead he said, "And what has that woman to do with it all? Did you see where she went?"

"No I didn't but, take it from me," Simon said getting off his stool and reaching for his bathing trunks that were discarded on the floor. "She is potential trouble and trouble is brewing." Simon wished that he had not mentioned her in the first place. If he told Chicky how he had seen Jack meet her at the coffee bar in the Old Square yesterday his secret indecision would be out of the bag.

The bathing trunks were cold and wet and difficult to pull on. He wondered if he would make it back to the villa naked, decided not and wriggling pulled them up over his bottom. He was anxious to create a little space between him and Chicky to save having to explain further, said, "I'm hungry. I'm heading back to the villa for breakfast and a cup of coffee. Coming?"

Chicky nodded, but remained silent as Simon ducked out under the waterfall and made his way back to their villa. Why would Simon not tell him the truth? And more worrying, what was he up to? He had made secretive phone calls, had disappeared without so much as a goodbye. What was this holiday about? Why had they come here? What was the meaning of that telephone number and scribbled message?

Staring out through the curtain of water, reluctant to move, Chicky could only think of one explanation. Simon had found someone else. He was not certain whether the moisture on his face was from the cascade of the waterfall or his own tears.

Chapter FORTY ONE

Keeping to the shelter of the bushes Ginny walked to the pool house, tried the handle and found it was locked. *Damn,* she thought. She stood there, panic rising.

Through the trees and gardens, she caught a glimpse of a man walking away his back towards the main gate! Thank God!

Trying to look like she was a resident, she started jogging along one of the paths that she hoped headed back towards the pool and beyond that, the beach. The place was a maze! Ahead of her she saw another group of villas. She turned right, jogged a little way then turned left. Thoroughly disorientated she felt like crying. Why on earth had she thought up this stupid idea?

A woman was coming towards her, also wearing a jogging suit, she sighed it was too late to hide and realised she would have to brazen it out.

"Good morning," Lindsey chirruped as she slowed slightly. "You look a bit lost. Can I help?"

"Um, yes," Ginny said, sticking to the truth as much as possible. "I'm new here, I thought I was on the right path, but I must have taken a wrong turn."

Lindsey laughed. "Yes, we often find starved to death skeletons under the bushes! Where do you need to get to?"

"The pool." Ginny answered tentatively, hoping that was not where this young woman was heading for. The last thing she wanted was the offer to jog together!

To her relief, Lindsey said brightly, "Go down that path over there and turn right at the next little group of villas. You can't miss it from there. Bye!" She ran off in a different direction.

Ginny's heart was pounding she had to get out of here. Following the directed route she rounded a corner and to her horror saw Jack about to walk through the opened entrance gates to leave Villas Bonitas then turn and look down the pathway.

Panic gripped her as she pressed herself into the shelter of the bushes and wanting to burst into tears, crouched down as low and as inconspicuously as she could.

Chapter FORTY TWO

Having stood under the tingling shower jets for the last twenty minutes, refreshed, Doreen finally knew exactly what she must do, the past could not be changed, but she needed to put right the error she had innocently made. She only hoped that it would not create too much pain. Dressed, she went in search of her mobile phone and tapped in the speed dial number. Her call was answered immediately. In a tone that held none of her usual sparkle, she simple said, "I've got to talk to you."

She listened, adding nothing more than, "Thanks, later then," she stabbed the end call button, relief flooded through her. She smiled. The empty hours of the night tossing and turning, worrying and fretting had not been wasted, she would sort it out. What happened all those years ago had to be put back where it all belonged; in the past, but not before she put the record straight. She was tired, but happy, everything would come right in the end.

Placing her mobile on the unit, in a loud whisper she spoke to the empty room. "It'll get sorted because things have to be put straight for everyone's sake."

"You are getting seriously worse talking to yourself is simply gross," Trisha called from her en-suite bathroom making Doreen jump out of her skin.

"Blimey girl, what are you doing scaring me to death?"

Draped in a towel, Trisha sauntered over to her mother and saw that her eyes were puffy. Without saying a word she wrapped her arms around her mother and hugged her tight

"What's brought this on?"

Releasing her grip, Trisha grinned. "Maybe I've just realised that I've a seriously scary mama, but no matter, loves you loads. Now I shall go and get some sleep. The clubs stay open far too long."

Doreen, trying not to cry, watched as Trisha ambled to her room, she could smell her daughter's perfume on her skin, she sniffed her arm again. She loved her girl. How was she ever going to explain to her and Pat she had no idea, but she had to. She loved them both too much not to.

Biting her lip Doreen looked at the clock. It was too early for a glass of something nice, tempted as she was with all that was going round and round in her head, instead, she went to the kitchen and switched the coffee machine on. If she was not careful she would rapidly turn into an alcoholic. As the coffee aroma filled the room, replacing the smell from all the cigarettes she had smoked, she wondered where Trisha got the energy to dance all night. At her age, she was working in Woolies, pregnant, tired and growing up fast.

She smiled, thankfully, that was all they had in common from when she was seventeen and that was growing up fast. At the same time, she was pleased that her daughter was being careful. Ben seemed okay, but the last thing she wanted to hear was the patter of tiny feet, well not for another few years yet.

With her cup of coffee, Doreen picked up a packet of cigarettes, read the health warning and dropped them back down on the counter top. Strolling through to the lounge she grabbed a magazine. She liked *Hello!* It gave her lots of ideas. Feeling relaxed with the weight of her decision sorted for the moment, she wandered out to the terrace. Seeing Simon walked past wearing only a skimpy pair of bathing trunks, she smiled, he was a good looking young man. Very good looking. She waved and called "Coo-ee," but he did not hear. "Things on his mind, I suspect," she told herself and managed to giggle at the short revealing wet trunks.

Funny, she thought, as she sat down in one of the comfortable chairs, with all that had been going on in her head she had forgotten about last night. She giggled at the memory of Sheila Hoskins flapping around in the water.

Picking up her cup of coffee and taking a mouthful she saw Carmen walk by. She waved, but received no response from her either. *Too busy that girl,* she thought. *Too many people expecting her to do too much.* She took another sip of coffee then spluttered dregs over herself as she put the cup hastily down, its contents spilling out with the impact.

"For Heaven's sake! That's Ginny Solomon. I'm certain of it!"

She jumped up, waving her arms furiously and almost running made her way to the bottom of her terrace. "It can't be?" she gasped, the hairs on the back of her neck rising. "Ginny," she shouted, "Ginny, it is you isn't it?" she called louder. "Blimey, it is!" Her mouth dropped open, her eyes wide Doreen stared straight at her old friend.

Ginny blinked rapidly, surely it could not be? On legs that had suddenly turned to jelly she made her way over to Doreen's terrace shaking her head in utter disbelief.

She had crouched in the bushes for what had seemed an age, peering cautiously out in case Jack had seen her, but it seemed he had not then a good looking man had walked by wearing only bathing trunks. His face had appeared familiar, but Ginny had not really been looking that far up. She had briefly wondered why he only had wet trunks on. Had he been in the pool when she had arrived? She didn't think so, she was sure it had been empty. Perhaps there was another one somewhere, or he had been down to the beach? Then a woman had hurried past. Ginny knew her, Carmen, the manager. They had often exchanged greetings in the town, although rarely more than a quick *hello*.

Judging it quiet at last, she had decided to get to the main gate as fast and as dignified as she could. Then she heard her name being called, turned round and there, right in front of her was Doreen. Doreen Wilkinson!

Stunned, forgetting where she was, she cried, "Never! This can't be! What on earth are you doing here?"

Disbelief written on her face, Doreen stared at the woman who had once been one of her best friends before Trisha had been born. "I might ask you the same question. Hell girl, you can knock me down with a feather seeing you standing there. And if you don't mind me saying you look like you've seen a ghost."

Not sure whether to laugh or cry at the ludicrousness of the situation, here she was with the stupid idea of spying on her lover, hiding in bushes and whatnot and now here was Doreen Wilkinson standing as large as life in front of her. The shock made Ginny laugh out loud and on legs that threatened to give way, she walked onto Doreen's terrace to immediately be enveloped in Doreen's arms.

Releasing her Doreen squealed, "What are you doing here? Been jogging have you? Guess you have. Blimey O'Reilly I can't believe this!"

Not waiting for an answer, Doreen steered Ginny towards a chair. "Ginny, I don't know about you, but I need a drink."

Taking a deep breath, Ginny watched as her old friend ran indoors, then slyly glanced across to Jack's villa afraid that the commotion had attracted attention. Seeing nothing to alarm her she sat down and wondered what she had been thinking about to come here. The last thing she needed was being made a fuss of and her name being shouted out for all to hear. But equally she wondered what Doreen Wilkinson was doing in a five star villa and here of all places? Sitting uncomfortable in her seat, Ginny watched as Doreen hurried back onto the terrace clutching two large glasses of champagne and suddenly Ginny didn't care anymore about whys and hows and where's. Doreen had been a good, very good friend and at this moment, all Ginny wanted was a very good friend.

Giggling loudly Doreen handed an overflowing glass to Ginny. "Best get this down you girl it'll help with the shock."

Her hand shaking, Ginny took the glass from Doreen and sipped the sweet content to stop it from spilling and tried not to show her displeasure at the taste. Nothing tasted decent anymore.

To hide her grimace, she said, "You've certainly taken my breath away Dor. What are you doing here?"

With half of her champagne already drunk, Doreen, looked over at Ginny, "We're supposed to be on our hols, me and me girl, Trisha, but I'm getting too scared to move with all the things that's happened to me this last week. Now you turning up, I tell you it's the strangest holiday you could have."

Ginny had no idea what Doreen was talking about, as if her own life was not complicated enough without finding an old friend living close to the man she was having an affair with. How weird could fate be?

"You know Ginny you haven't changed. I still can't believe that you've walked in here." In the old days, Doreen knew Ginny was a girl wanting a good time and too often with someone else's bloke, jokingly she added. "Don't tell me you're chasing some poor old girls hubby, because if you're after a flash life, this place is dripping with dosh."

Ginny picked up her glass to hide her face. "Seems I could say the same about you Dor. You haven't changed much yourself. Why don't you tell me why you are here? It is probably far more exciting than my story."

Aware her old mate had avoided the question, Doreen thought, *No change there, always one for avoiding saying what she was up to.* Said, "You'll never believe me, I won the lottery. Big time."

And hens have teeth, Ginny thought. It seemed neither of them had changed much. Doreen had lived in cloud cuckoo land back then, thinking everything was laughs and giggles. "If you say so, seriously what are you doing here?"

Looking hurt, Doreen said. "I won the lottery."

Laughing to keep herself from giggling hysterically at the ludicrous situation, Ginny said. "If you've won enough to give you and your daughter a good time, then I am pleased for you. I know how you struggled when we were young. You deserve it if anyone does."

She did not add that she knew another old friend, Pat Greenwood had hit the big time financially. That would be too cruel, probably Doreen never thought about him now anyway, but she wished Doreen luck, whatever or whoever had fallen at her feet. She smiled. It seemed both her and Doreen were a million miles from Wentworth House even if they had met each other in the most, unlikeliest of places. If her own life was not such a problem, she would be keen to sit here all day, laugh, drink champagne and learn more about her old friend, but she ought to be going, she had already outstayed her welcome as far as Villas Bonitas was concerned.

Opening her mouth to speak, to her horror saw Jack stride along the pathway from the main gate. Before he reached his terrace, he turned and looked across the gardens and despite the distance his eyes locked onto Ginny's. The shock on his face was tangible.

Doreen saw her friend's face pale and her eyes widen at the sight of Jack Hoskins, she instantly felt the electric charge that surged between the two of them. She knew instinctively why Ginny Solomon was out, supposedly jogging, at Vilas Bonitas.

Chapter FORTY THREE

Sheila had crawled from her bed soon after Jack had left. All she really wanted to do was curl up in bed and die, but she was too proud. A cool shower had revived her a little and she decided that fresh air and chilled orange juice was the antidote she needed.

Wearing her darkest sunglasses Sheila sat on her terrace, a glossy magazine open. The pictures and print that normally kept her up to date on celebrity gossip appeared blurred. Flicking the pages she swallowed down a couple of heavy duty pain killers. She would like to think it had been the shock of tripping and falling into the water that had given her such a pounding head, but even she knew it was a result of far too much alcohol. What had possessed her to drink so much she had no idea, but knew she was paying for it now.

It's no good, she thought, *I need a coffee.* Getting up she noticed a pretty woman sitting chatting with Miss Fink Fought. She ignored them both and shuffled back into her villa, the kitchen her destination. The coffee machine filled, Sheila stood against her counter top letting the marble surface take her weight. The marching band strutting around in her head appeared to be on full parade. She was so very tempted to go back to bed. Pouring herself a coffee she heard footsteps clop across the marble floor. In too much pain to swing round called, "Is that you Jack? I thought you'd gone to a meeting."

Breathless, sweating profusely, Jack silently swore. Bloody hell what was Ginny doing? Gasping for breath he answered his wife half truthfully. "Bloody meeting has been cancelled. The guy's got a bad back or something. He could have bloody informed me." He had gone to Ginny's instead.

Found her not there. Found her here at Villas Bonitas instead drinking champagne with the Wilkinson woman next door!

Falling down into a chair, he puffed. "As I'm here, I'll have a cup of that coffee you've made." The shock of seeing Ginny on Doreen's terrace had him in a lather. He screwed his eyes up tight at the thought of Sheila and Ginny coming face to face. *What the blazes was Ginny doing here? Jesus, this was far too close to home!*

Perspiring with fright he pulled a cloth off the table and mopped his face then realised it was one of Sheila's ornamental mats. He shoved it into his pocket. Bloody hell what kind of life was he leading walking on eggs shells even with a linen mat?

Pouring a large coffee for Jack, Sheila swiped the sunglasses off her face. There was no need to advertise her head was splitting, but she was annoyed he was back so soon. It was the last thing she wanted him hanging around until she was back to her sharp self. Carrying the cup and saucer over to Jack who was flopped down on the sofa, she glared at him through puffy, but suspicious eyes.

"You are out of breath, what the heck have you been doing?" She asked and handed him his coffee. "Have you spoken to Carmen?" she snapped.

Jack nodded. He did not want to go through all that silly nonsense about the tiles again. On the other hand, he did need a distraction. "Has she not responded to my message then?" he asked. "I told her to telephone you."

Sheila vaguely remembered hearing the phone ring while she was in the shower. She looked at the answer machine. Yes, the light was flashing.

She walked over to it, pressed 'play' and Carmen's slightly irritated voice floated into the room asking Jack to come to her office any time after 11.30.

Sheila nodded with satisfaction. "Perhaps we will go together." She added as she stood by the window looking out and saw a woman in a jogging suit waving to Miss Fink Fought. "I hope to goodness that woman next door is not inviting more of her riff raff into the area. We don't want those sorts of tarts here at Villas Bonitas."

Taking a firm grip of his coffee mug Jack sipped the cooling liquid.

How he would love to bellow at her that she was a stupid woman, that she did not know just how very wrong she was about that young woman who had been with Mrs Wilkinson. But suicide was not a good option

Not getting an answer, Sheila considered going back onto the terrace, but the beep of Jack's mobile phone cut into her head like a knife. Irritably she snapped, "It's a pity folk have nothing better to do with their time than send messages to important people when they're on holiday."

Jack looked quickly at the text message, fresh sweat breaking out on his forehead. What could he say to her? He thought quickly, smiled and got up from the sofa. "The meeting is on after all! Good, good."

"We are supposed to be on holiday," Sheila pointed out. "We are not supposed to be going off to meetings that get scheduled, unscheduled then scheduled again."

"I know my pet," Jack said, "but the man I want to meet lives here in town. He is a good contact for the business. I'll not be long. An hour at the most." He could not believe his luck at thinking up such a plausible excuse to get out of the house so quickly.

Chapter FOURTY FOUR

Trying to understand how Ginny had ended up sitting on Doreen Wilkinson's terrace was a question that rattled round and round in Jack's head as he waited outside the main gates for a taxi. It was only a short walk into town, but he was sweating in his suit and he was supposed to be going to a business meeting. Sheila would be suspicious if he walked. The suit was part of the ploy too of course. Climbing into the taxi as it arrived, he supposed he could at least take his jacket and tie off now he was out of the house.

Meet me at the café in fifteen minutes was all that the text had said.

It had taken him about twenty, would she still be there? He paid the taxi and slinging his jacket over his shoulder marched along the pedestrian Avenue that led to the Old Square in Pelito

"Hell's bells," he muttered feeling the sweat run down the side of his temples as he wound his way through groups of people meandering along the wide walkway. In a hurry he dodged round them as they wandered along gazing out at the blue ocean where yachts and small cruisers sailed by. Twice he bumped into someone and cursed.

There she was just as she had said in her text, relief flooded through him, now he might get to the bottom of what is going on.

As he sat down opposite her, to his surprise instead of looking sheepish Ginny looked troubled. Normally he would be concerned, but after this morning he was too angry to care. If he was honest, he was pleased that she looked upset. Serve her right. She had changed out of that jogging suit and had a light summery dress on now. Her hair was still wet though. She must have had a very quick shower.

The waiter came over with two coffees. Jack fished out a handkerchief and dabbed at his sweating, florid face.

As if to contradict what he saw, in an amused calm tone Ginny trilled, "I see you are still having your hot flushes then."

He should snap at her, ask her what the hell she was playing at, instead he sniffed. "After your little shocker this morning is it hardly surprising? Christ what were you thinking of?"

Ginny could see he was flustered, expected she thought, but what she had to be flustered about made his concern pale by comparison.

She had not yet quite decided whether to drop her bombshell on him or not. Seeing Doreen Wilkinson out of the blue had unnerved her, yet in another way it had strengthened her resolve. All this excitement no wonder her hormones were playing havoc with her moods! "You are never going to believe me," she said, "you've heard of strange sightings: chance in a million. Well, Doreen Wilkinson happens to be staying at Villas Bonitas and I know her. We were good friends years ago, you needed good friends living where we did. So when I heard she was here," Ginny sucked in her cheeks at the unexpectedness at seeing Doreen and the lie she was about to impart, "I thought it was only proper that I call and see her. What a shock she got when she saw me. And what a shock I got when I realised your villa was right next door to hers!"

Furrowing his brow, Jack grumbled, "It must be catching then, your antics have had the same effect on me!" He was not happy, but what she said sounded plausible. But why had Ginny never mentioned anything about an old friend staying at Villas Bonitas before now? Because she had not, in fact he realised suddenly, she had told him nothing about herself or her past. In all the years he had known her, he had never asked.

Satisfied that she had come up with an acceptable excuse she was thinking straight again. Taking hold of Jack's hand she said, "I know it was a bit hairy for both of us, but what could I do? No way could I ignore popping along to say hello to her."

Seeing a flicker of panic flash in Jack's eyes, she added. "To put your mind at rest, I never mentioned anything about you and me. Doreen and I go back a long way, but we haven't seen each other for a very long time. We have a lot to catch up on, but I'm not stupid." Staring at his worried face she asked, "Friends again?"

"When you look like that and say it so tantalizingly how can we not be? Come on let's be off to your place. I've got an hour madam thinks I am at an important meeting." He grinned. "And I am. I've had enough of the outdoors for one morning."

But despite his outward lightness to the situation, he was disturbed. Their affair could be blown wide open so easily. Pat Greenwood was sniffing around this Doreen woman and therefore the Villas and now Ginny's old friend turned out to be the same woman? He was not happy. Where would it all end?

Chapter FORTY FIVE

Standing on her terrace, the heat from the sun burning her arms, Doreen rubbed her red skin. She should move to the shade but she was enjoying the warmth as the sun soaked into her bones. Drinking champagne with her old mate, coupled with her shock of knowing who her daughter's father was had left her lethargic and stressed. Stepping back into the dappled shaded area of her terrace she sat down on the edge of the yellow stripped cushioned recliner. She stroked the fabric and snorted as she realised Ginny had not changed. Still chasing someone else's bloke, but turning up here was something else. What was going on? First Pat now Ginny? At this rate half the Council estate would be knocking on her door.

Her head was spinning, she knew she needed to relax, stop her mind thinking and ease her aching muscles from her workout at the gym yesterday.

Standing up she strolled to the end of her terrace and looked towards the pool area. With a weary smile she knew what would help bring her back to her bouncing self. She could just about make out that someone was sitting in the Jacuzzi. Not that she wanted any company, but thinking about the water whooshing around made her feel calm. Jacuzzis were a new experience for her, one she absolutely loved.

Her towel dangling over her shoulder, a sarong draped elegantly to hide her bikini, Doreen strolled towards the Jacuzzi, her flip flops tapping on the tiles. Lindsey was at the bar and several people were sitting around on sun loungers reading or chatting with each other. In the swimming pool were a couple of children splashing each other, she smiled and waved to one of them, her thoughts straying to what she would have been doing this time last year. She giggled. It most certainly was not heading for a soak in a spa!

Stopping on the edge of the large bubbling pool, her mind brought back to the moment as she saw who the person in the Jacuzzi was. Sheila! She sighed. Asked herself did she want to spend time with the snotty cow? Answer, not really, but seeing Sheila wave, her hand dripping water, "There's plenty of room if you want to get in. It would be nice to have some company." How could she refuse?

With a weak smile, Doreen slipped off her sarong and shuffled out of her flip flops. Dropping her bag, towel and wrap onto the covered lounger next to the Jacuzzi, grimaced. All she wanted was to relax in the water and slow her mind down, but with Sheila there, it would be difficult.

Stepping into the warm, swirling water she squealed with delight. "This is alright isn't? Perfect!' Just what I need to get my head round a few things."

Sheila had also not been pleased at having her peace and quiet shattered. Once Jack had disappeared, she had decided that the Jacuzzi was the perfect place to relax, now watching Doreen slip into the pool, her headache almost disappeared, Sheila crooned, "I can tell you there is nothing more therapeutic than sitting in a pool of warm water that massages all your little areas. I know from years of experience it really does help with everything. And I do mean everything."

Surreptitiously she touched her temples. With a calculating smile and a false caring tone, added, "There's nothing worse than bottling everything up until you explode. I've done it too many times. After all that's what friends are for, helping each other out, a troubled mind is a troubled shared. I'm all ears if you want to get, whatever it is, off your chest."

More than anything Sheila wanted to stay away from any reference to the previous night. Better to keep the conversation to something she could control.

Peering at Sheila as a mist rose from the warm water, Doreen wanted to believe every word that poured out of the woman's mouth. But she had already cottoned on to her. There was more than fag smoke between her ears and Sheila Hoskins was the last person she would want to tell her business to. Though she would like to mention Sheila's nautical dance last night and Jack's carrying on, but decided it would be best to have a bit of fun. Keep the real stuff for later. She giggled. She knew what Sheila would rather talk about.

"Thanks, that's kind of you, but for somebody like yourself it's nothing, it's just getting used to having all this money, but you'd know all about it."

Preening, the words were like music to Sheila's ears. She could never have imagined that this dizzy thing could be so intuitive. Perhaps after all she had been a little unfair in her first opinion? With a sickly sweet smile, said. "I more than understand your situation. Wealth is a huge responsibility: broad shoulders, thick skin and an ability to command will hold you in good stead until you get used to being able to cope with having everything you want."

With a blank expression, Doreen stifled a giggle. "Thanks for that. You know you're right, you never know when it'll be best to use those kinds of things." She giggled silently.

Confused, Sheila blinked trying to understanding what Miss Fink Fought spluttered because it most certainly had eluded her. Deciding that common sense was not a natural to Doreen, Sheila changed the subject. "That friend of yours, Pat is it? I'll certainly be hanging on to my purse, I suggest you do too."

Relaxed, the massage jets seeking out her aching muscles, her body tingling, Doreen smiled at the mention of Pat's name. She needed to try and find out a bit about him herself but Sheila was the last person she was going to let on to about that. In a reassuring voice said. "I don't need to worry about anything like that. He's got plenty, no need to pinch mine. I knew him when we were kids, we had some good times, but he's come good and with a few bob."

Sceptical, Sheila frowned. "Mmm, I've heard all that before, but you'd do best to keep your distance until you are certain."

"He tells me he's got one of those fancy big boats and said he's taking me to one of his places just a couple of weeks after me and Trish get back home."

Opening her eyes wider, Sheila scoffed. "And you believe him?"

Giggling, Doreen was enjoying taking the wind out of Sheila Hoskins sails. She had no idea how much money Pat had, if any at all, but she could easily make the information up. "Course, we go back too far for that sort of fib. If he says he's rich, then I believe him."

Still unsure Doreen had any idea what she was taking about, Sheila enquired. "So what kind of place has he got that he needs to show off?"

"Now you are asking," pulling a face, Doreen added. "Something to do with holiday camps: Chalet lets at the beach or something."

Smirking, Sheila cautioned. "Some people have a caravan and think they're in the holiday business so just watch out, he could still be after your money. Trust no one and then you cannot get hurt."

Giggling at Sheila's concern, "I appreciate you telling me these things and I know you got to look after yourself, but Pat isn't like that. I just know."

Delighted at Doreen's gratitude Sheila felt important and decided that Doreen, a bit dim and unbelievably common, though in a lower class way was tolerable. "So tell me where are these holiday camp places supposed to be? Bognor? Southend? Canvey Island?"

Not missing the snide remark, Doreen slithered further down in the water, pulled a face to add a little more dramatics to her reply. "I think everywhere that people want to go on holiday. You know, them sort of self catering holiday camp places. Nice bar; healthy activities, entertainments, plenty of things so you have a good time and a laugh."

Sheila shuddered at the memories resurfacing of a miserable childhood with two weeks at Butlins in the pouring rain.

"The one he's taking me to," Doreen continued, not noticing Sheila's grimace, "is a big place; garden, swimming pool, even got some maids. Calls it his second real home."

"I must say we've travelled all over the world, nowhere we haven't seen. Mind, we always do it in style, luxury and top class no matter where we go. So where is this place you are going to?" asked Sheila, disbelieve in her voice.

"Blimey, you've been about!"

Accepting Doreen's words as a statement of envy, rather than a derogatory remark Sheila waited for the next words to tumble out of Doreen's mouth.

"It's got one of those funny names. Sounds a bit like you've hurt yourself badly." Shaking her head to help concentrate, the water splashed over her face, she cried, "It's a long word and everyone's heard of it….now what is it called?"

"Let us try and narrow it down. Which country is it in?"

Giggling with relief, Doreen squealed, "Now Shelia, I can tell you that. It's Spain. That's the place people with money go to. I'm going to buy myself a place there now."

"Good God," Sheila gasped twisting around to another set of jets. "Spain! That narrows it down a lot," then sniffed, silently adding, "It had to be somewhere common."

"Got it! I said it sounded like an injury, it's Torn-me-knee-off."

Sheila looked at Doreen and this time laughed out loud. "Good grief, you are a one Doreen Wilkinson. *Torremolinos*!"

Chapter FORTY SIX

Standing at the open door of her office Carmen heard the distinct giggle of Doreen Wilkinson. Turning her gaze to where the sound came from she was surprised to see Sheila and Doreen laughing in the Jacuzzi. She shook her head in amused disbelief. They were the last two people she had expected to befriend each other. She hoped Doreen was not about to fall under the interfering spell of Sheila Hoskins, though. Sheila was cunning and manipulative, encouraging others to tell all their business and then cleverly using it when the time suited her.

Admiring the exotic surroundings, as she did every spare moment, Carmen reminded herself how beautiful everything was at Villas Bonitas. Even the birds' song was a symphony to rival any high class orchestra. She smiled as if seeing everything for the first time. She loved not only her job, but Villas Bonitas. The decisions she had made years earlier had been the right ones. Hearing Sheila's false high pitched laugh reminded her it was only the behaviour of some owners that, at times, clouded her appreciation of all that she had. She chided herself that she must ignore those who spoilt her mood and appreciation of Villas Bonitas. Turning her attention to the pathway that lead from the entrance gates, her pleasant expression changed to a scowl, her resolve to ignore swiftly evaporating as she saw Bob, his arms laden with heavy bags of shopping. Frau Hecks was taking advantage and she would need to do something about it. Bob was supposed to have driven Frau Hecks to the clinic, not on another shopping expedition.

With the door unlocked and opened, Frau Hecks with a wide smile, turned to Bob and in an unusual cheery voice said,

"Bob, when you put all bags in my home, I give you small beer. *Danke schön*, you been most helpful, you deserves it."

She had slept soundly all night, not waking until gone nine o'clock, very unusual for her, and she felt better for it. Bob had arrived on time to take her to the clinic to have her monthly pedicure and then she had decided to do some shopping. She had bought something for her grandchild's birthday the other day when Bob had taken her into town, but she had wanted to get something else for him as well.

Placing her handbag on the floor to the side of the hall table she removed her sun hat and sunglasses and placed both on the table top. Gazing into the mirror above, she straightened her hair then picked up the photograph frame that sat to one side. She ran a finger across the clean glass that held the photograph of her and Hans.

"I miss you Hans, even shopping is lonely without you," she whispered to the smiling face staring back at her.

"That your hubby then? The mine hair?" Bob asked, as he set the heavy shopping down and peered over her shoulder at the photograph.

"*Ja*, this is my Hans. He long dead now." With a rueful smile she placed the frame back onto the table then bustled towards her kitchen.

"Bring ze bags here, then I gets you a small beer," she ordered, Han's memory slipping to the back of her mind as she cleared a space on her counter top.

Bob muttered under his breath, "I'll not only bring them to you, I'll empty them, stack the contents in the cupboard, cook your dinner…grrr."

Roughly grabbing the bags, one of the packages fell out. Bob bent to pick it up: A remote control car. He looked at the picture of the car on the box and smiled. Frau Hecks had wanted something for her grandson and had asked his advice. He had suggested the car, saying that he had always wanted one. "Never got one though," he muttered.

"Ze small beer if you wants it is in here. Where my shopping should be, *nein*?"

Bob sighed heavily. "I'm just coming. That's very kind of you, a *small* beer would be perfect," adding under his breath, "for hours of lifting and carrying, not to mention all me driving and hanging around."

Frowning and in an exasperated tone Frau Hecks cried, "One day Bob, I know you will learn to speak good English like me, and then I understand all your words. Now put ze bags on my counter."

Rolling his eyes, he clicked his heels and silently snapped, *Ja vull!*

Checking everything was emptied from the bags and positioned the correct way up in her cupboards, Frau Hecks, with a critical eye stood to one side of the counter top. "I know you should not drink when at work, but today I think you earned a little extras treat. It is what I do for my Wolfgang when he been very good, I give him treat." Frau Hecks reached into the fridge and pulled out a small bottle of beer, then handing it to Bob, clucked, "You take it away and drink only when you have finished all your work. When you have no driving."

With a slight nod of the head and in a mocking tone Bob grovelled. "Flawline, you're just to kind to us humble workers. Thanks. Life would be miserable with out a treat. So I'll say good day to you." Clutching his gift and leaving Frau Hecks with her shopping, Bob marched out of the villa.

"You are welcome, hard work must be given reward," Frau Hecks called after him.

As Bob strode past the bar area he heard Antonio's voice. "Looks like you're in favour today. Do I note a bottle of German brand beer?"

"Very funny," Bob grumbled turning back and heading towards Antonio. "I've nearly ruptured myself for her and she rewards me with a *small* bottle of beer."

Sneering added. "To top it all she compared me to her cat." Bob mimicked Frau Hecks' voice: "*Vhen he been very goods, I gives him treat, you also good so you now gets a treat.*" He patted his head with his hand and tickled himself under the chin. "*Meow!*"

Handing the bottle over to Antonio, he sighed. "Open it for me, will you? I'm parched." Sitting down on a stool Bob removed his chauffeur's cap, laid it on the next stool then loosened his tie. The bottle opened and handed back to him, he placed it to his mouth, took a deep swig then placing the bottle on the bar, added. "That's wet me whistle. Mind, I'm surprised I'm not choking to death, Flawline probably cursed it." He laughed. "Frau Hex!"

"I think you needed that. Have one on me?" Antonio felt it was the least he could offer. He admired Bob for his joviality no matter what he had to put up with.

Nodding his appreciation, Bob regretfully declined. "I'd love one, but better make it a shandy, emphasis on the lemonade. You never know when I'll be expected to drive someone around," he cast his gaze towards Frau Hecks' villa.

Using her mouse, Carmen clicked the X in the top right hand corner of her screen and closed the file. She pushed back her chair, glanced through the window and noticed Bob having a drink at the bar. She frowned. She needed him away from Villas Bonitas. Her plan had gone awry thanks to Frau Hecks and her shopping trip.

"Why is everything so difficult?" she muttered through clenched teeth. Ben was expected shortly to finalise the details of their surprise preparations for Bob's approaching 65th birthday; her grimace turning to a smile at what they had organised in secrecy. Though she would like to mention the other issue with Ben regarding the alleged pool room incident, but at the end of the day she reminded herself, what young people, or older people come to that, got up to was not her business. Picking up her document case she left the office. Making her way to the bar she felt the band on her skirt pinch at her waist and groaned. She should be stick thin the kilometres she walked in a day.

The bar was surprisingly quiet, there was a middle aged couple sitting at a table at the far side of the seating area and apart from Bob perched on a stool the place was deserted. Positioning herself next to Bob, Carmen realised it was too early to send him home, but was necessary. He should have been at the airport collecting the owners of villa twenty two, but his unscheduled shopping trip with Frau Hecks had meant Jeff Butler had been organised to do the chauffeuring. The last thing she wanted was Bob here at Villas Bonitas when Ben arrived or for him to have any idea of what was being arranged.

"Bob," she said, placing her hand on his shoulder, "Once again thank you for looking after Frau Hecks. I realise she has taken much of your time of late and I feel responsible. We have everything under control here, so let me suggest you take the rest of the day off. I'm conscious you spend many long hours working and I think we can manage until tomorrow without you. So drink up and be off home."

Gratitude spread across Bob's face. Gulping down his drink he chuckled. "Well Pressy, seems me birthdays come early. Second unexpected treat, but one I'm happy to take. Thank you. Much appreciated. I just might sit and watch the football on the telly when I get back home."

Placing his empty glass on the bar he grabbed his cap from the stool and rakishly placed it on his head. Nodded, "Thanks again, sees you all tomorrow."

Carmen watched as Bob headed to his pool room to lock up. She smiled; everything should go to plan.

Chapter FORTY SEVEN

Looking for the telephone, Sheila dressed in a black evening dress, tutted loudly as her gaze roamed around the room.

"It should be on its pod," she muttered. "Jack what have you done with the phone?" she called towards his bathroom. Seeing her reflection in the hall mirror, reminded herself that she was amazing for fifty two. "Appearances are so important," she said with a satisfied smile. She had little time for women who just let it all hang out and flop, but then she reminded herself that she tried to avoid those kinds of people. And should they happen to waddle into her world she told them in no uncertain terms what they looked like and to get it sorted.

Placing her hands under her breasts she pushed them up and smiled, firm and rounded. From the mirror's reflection she caught sight of the phone laying on the table top, letting her breasts settle back into her, personally fitted bra, picked up the black handset.

"I've found the phone Jack, where *you* left it," she growled and stared at the closed bathroom door.

Punching in the memory code, she placed the phone to her ear and listened to the ringing tone. After five rings she heard the cheerful voice of her daughter's answer machine. Perching on the edge of the leather sofa, exasperated at not being able to talk to Michelle, Sheila sighed.

"Michelle it is Mummy, our Soiree is tomorrow so can you fly down?"

Ending the call with a heavy press on the button, Sheila threw the phone onto the table. At the sound of footsteps she caught sight of Jack heading towards the drinks cabinet.

"What a day it has proved to be, I can't get hold of Michelle and you letting me down with those broken tiles."

With a heavy sigh, Jack glared at his wife. "Sheila, I have not let you down you were drunk and tripped the light fantastic into the pool. I am not going to talk about it anymore. Can we not just have a nice evening without all this bloody argy bargy?" He snatched a glass, filled it with whisky and gulped it down.

With a steely stare Sheila watched as Jack downed his drink. "You'll be turning into an alcoholic with what you are drinking. Anyway, our driver should be here any moment and it won't be Bob Preston. And despite your swearing, I'm suspicious that *Miss I'm in charge* sent him home because she feels guilty about what happened."

Jack rolled his eyes, pulled at his shirt cuffs to ensure his cufflinks showed. Satisfied, looked over to his wife, snorted and wished she had stayed in the pool, preferably at the bottom. Hearing the doorbell ring he smiled. "It must be our carriage," he quipped, knowing he had to keep calm and try and make the best of life with Mrs Hoskins. Walking towards the front door he stopped, crooked his arm. "Come on Sheila, let's go and enjoy ourselves."

As Sheila linked her arm into his, he patted her hand. "There are worse things to worry about than tiles."

Sheila looked at Jack, her face lighting up, she would deal with the tiles herself and changed the subject. "I think our Soiree tomorrow is going to be another one of our many great successes. It's a pity we can't get *Hello!* magazine to run a feature on me."

Jack sighed heavily, but made no comment.

Chapter FORTY EIGHT

Pouring herself another drink, Doreen fretted how on earth she was going to get through the evening? She stared at her hands, they were shaking. "God, I'm a mess," she said trying to stop her drink sloshing over the top of the glass. Thank goodness Trisha had seen Ben earlier when he was talking to Antonio. At least she would be out of the way when Pat arrived. Pacing up and down the room, the marble cool on the soles of her feet, she could not imagine how so much could happen in a just a few short days.

In the old days when she was a bag of nerves she would get Trisha sorted and then curl up with her designer wrap, bought from the charity shop and with a drink would watch the telly. And just like then, she was wearing something that made her feel good. Tonight, she had made a special effort. She knew she had gone mad, but she needed courage. Holding her glass tight she walked over to the open patio doors. Listening to the noises outside; a mixture of sounds, voices, bird song, leaves rustling in the breeze, the strange hum of the electric luggage cars, all creating an exotic melody in the air. She stared down at her bright white dress with its big red poppy flowers filled with gold and silver sequins and realised compared to what surrounded her, her outfit was the loudest thing in Villas Bonitas, but she did not care. Stepping outside and leaning against the cane sofa she saw Sheila and Jack Hoskins, arm in arm stroll past. A strange couple, she thought remembering the shock of seeing Ginny that morning.

Although Ginny had said nothing, a blind man could have seen what passed between her and Jack. An affair that would end in tears, but which of the two would be crying? she asked herself.

She grinned at the memory of the Jacuzzi and Sheila Hoskins, aware that Mrs H had no idea her husband was a cheating bastard.

"God what would Sheila do if she found out it was me old mate from the Council estate?" Doreen giggled. Even though her own troubles raced around in her head, she had to laugh. And despite Sheila being incredibly nosey and a first class snob, she had enjoyed playing her at her own game. She had not exactly told lies, just not told the truth, but only because she had no idea what the truth was.

Finishing her drink, she padded back to her villa, Sheila and Ginny had distracted her from fretting about what she was about to reveal, but now it was time to face the music. Stepping back into the cool room, cried, "God what a holiday this is turning out to be."

Her glass empty, she strode over to the table and picking up the bottle of gin, was about to pour when the door bell rang. Its *bing bong* shattering the silence. Her stomach muscles knotted. Putting the bottle down she stood stock still, felt her heart thump heavily and tried breathing evenly. With feet that felt like the weight of lead and a heart not much lighter, she went to answer the door.

Clutching an armful of red roses wrapped in clear cellophane tied with a huge purple bow, Pat stood on the doorstep.

"Hello Doll, you're looking gorgeous. I can't tell you how pleased I am to be seeing you again. I've spent all day wondering what I've said or done to upset you."

A broad smile lit his face as he handed the roses to Doreen. Holding her arms out to take the blooms, tears pricked the back of her eyes and a lump rose in her throat, she nodded. Averting her eyes from Pat's face, admiring the fragrant bouquet, sniffed loudly her emotions about to spill over.

"Well Doll, are you going to let me come in?"

Silently stepping back, Doreen nodded. A memory had flashed into her mind. A memory of that last night before they had rowed and they had parted forever. Pat had rung her doorbell and brought her roses, half a dozen plastic ones from Woolworths. An hour later she had never seen him again until three days ago. God she had been a bloody fool!

As Pat brushed past her she felt the heat from his body, shivered and knew the burden she had shouldered since the previous night was too much, her resolve to keep control was about to be lost. Tears slipped down her cheeks. Closing the door and with her free hand tried to wipe her anguish away, but it was impossible, the tears flowed freely. She swallowed a sob, her emotions, like everything around her were out of control and Pat bringing her red roses was the final straw.

Chapter FORTY NINE

Removing the bouquet from Doreen's arm, Pat laid the roses down on the hall table then silently wrapped his arms around her and held her tight. He could feel her sobs vibrate on his chest.

"Doll, what can be so terrible that every time I look at you, you cry?" Stroking her hair, he lifted her head and looked into her face, now streaked with mascara runs and for the second time in twelve hours, asked. "Is it me Doll? Because if it is, just tell me and I will go. As I said this morning, I don't want to hurt you."

Laughter filtered in from outside through the open patio doors, followed by cheerful voices and more laughter: A contrast to the emotional atmosphere inside the villa. Doreen sniffed as she looked up at Pat's face and swallowed another lump of emotion, then in a strained voice said, "It's terrible, I don't think you will ever forgive me when I tell you."

Grinning and in an attempt to lighten the situation, Pat said, "You've not won the lottery. You mean to say you've tricked me into being here so you can steal my money?"

With an attempt at a smile and in a tone calmer than she felt, Doreen whispered, "If that was it, I'd been leading yer a dance, not sobbing me heart out."

Wiping the tears from her face with a clean white linen handkerchief Pat chortled, "That's more like it. Come on Doll let's get to the bottom of whatever's making you cry instead of giggle."

Taking hold of Doreen's arm he steered her towards the sofa. "And as for forgiving, for the moment, let me be the judge of who will or will not forgive. Come on Doll get it of your chest, please."

Sitting upright on the edge of the sofa, Doreen looked into Pat's face and saw care and love in his eyes. Realising there was no easy way to tell him she blurted it all out in a rush.

"It's Trisha. I now know she's your girl. I made a mistake back then, but seeing you again it's all there. Pat she's your girl. I'm sorry I never knew." The relief of spitting it out lifted the weight that had threatened to crush her. Wiping her eyes, a nervous giggle escaped as she added. "What a mess I've made of everything."

Squeezing Doreen's hand, Pat quietly said. "I know Doll, for a long time now I have known."

The colour drained from Doreen's face, in a shaky voice cried. "What are you're saying? You never could have known because I never. There's me thinking all sorts of things and you sit there smiling. Pat, I'm in bits. Is that what you're doing here trying to pinch me girl?" Her anxiety now turning to caution.

Shaking his head at Doreen, Pat said, "The timing was right, but you seemed certain that Jimmy Fuller was her dad, even though he once told me he was certain he wasn't. Who was I to step in and say different? You'd put his name on the birth certificate and you were living together. And I was engaged, what was I supposed to do?"

"But I'd struggled all those years and you thought me baby might be your girl, why didn't you come back when you were free?"

Letting go of her hand, he brushed his hair back from his forehead. "I've just told you. I had no rights and why should I upset the apple cart? But despite that, I could see, like you can now, that she's a chip off the old block."

Despite her anger, which had replaced upset, Doreen giggled. "God help her then." She knew she should not have giggled, this was a mess and far from funny. Her mind raced with questions, not sure where to begin, she snapped. "So tell me then, what year was it when you made up your mind she was yours? Because I haven't seen hide nor hair of you since before Trisha was born." She was not finished, but needed to take a deep breath before adding, "And more importantly, is that why you are sniffing around again to make up for lost time now that we've got a bob or two to spare?"

Feeling the force from Doreen's words Pat winced, though he had no intention of answering her questions yet, he needed to explain a few other things first. Looking Doreen squarely in the eye, asked. "Tell me this, how did Trisha manage to get to that posh school if you had no money?"

Not appreciating the implication of Pat's question, Doreen smiled as she remembered the day her girl started at the grammar school instead of the local comprehensive like the rest of her friends were going to. She had felt so proud. And so she answered Pat's question.

"She's a clever girl, passed the entry level because she was the brightest girl in her school. She won a place and got a grant. It was the proudest day of my life. She was going to do better than I ever could. No scrubbing and cleaning for my girl." Having answered Pat, Doreen suddenly realised the question he had asked. How could he know about Trisha at the posh school? In a voice that held fear, she hissed, "So how do you know my Trisha has gone to that school then?"

Seeing suspicion flicker in Doreen's eyes Pat realised he should not have mentioned the school, but as he had, he had to see it through.

"Doll, once I'd made some money I wanted to give Trisha a better start than we'd had and the school fees were, and still are, paid for by me."

Shock gripped Doreen, what was happening, was anything in her life real? Her anger boiling over she glared at Pat as she snapped, "So she never passed her exam and got a grant? You cheated her of that, making a fool out of both of us." She knew she was shouting.

"Hold your horses. I never cheated her of anything. She did take a genuine exam. She passed all the questions with top marks, the brightest girl in the school, but there was no Council grant. There was only a private scholarship. And before you say anything else, I just wanted to give her a bit of a head start if it ever came out she might be mine, though I was always certain and I always hoped she would be."

Doreen's head pounded, it was as if she would wake up soon and everything would be normal again. She tried to understand what Pat had said, nothing could have prepared her for such a revelation as she had lain awake all night worrying. As Pat's voice broke through her thoughts she looked at him, his face aglow with happiness, she sniffed. How different they both were reacting to such an announcement.

Grabbing Doreen's hand, his eyes moist, Pat said in a voice that verged on begging, "Maybe you'll think about everything because I'd love to be her proper dad. That's if you'll both have me."

It was all too much, Doreen realised she could not take any more and dissolved into tears again. She sobbed as Pat hugged her tight.

Chapter FIFTY

Their dinner jackets slung over their shoulders, a five o'clock shadow darkening their faces Simon and Chicky strolled along the path towards their villa, the sun already giving off warm rays promising another hot day.

Slackening off his red bow tie Chicky reflected on the night out. "That had to be the best Legal Convention I've been to," he said. "For the first time we were not totally outnumbered by the older generation. The sight of youth and our open ideas had them turning various shades of colours that are not good for the heart. Though, I fear we turned a few heads when I announced you as my *personal* partner, not my Chambers partner."

Simon felt his heart lurch as Chicky said the word *partner*. For how much longer would that be the case? He had made his decision at the convention. Now all he had to do was break the news to Chicky. Even being in close discussion with Miles for half of the evening, the secret remained intact.

Chicky smiled. "I heard a few sudden intakes of breath, of course, but I think the real turn up for the books was when Jeremy Gillespie sidled over, shook our hands and said how delighted he was that we were open about our relationship."

Despite his smile, Chicky felt a cloud hover over him and wondered just how *open* their relationship was. Simon had spent far too much time with that damn upstart Miles Griffin. They had been talking for a long while and Chicky had clearly seen Griffin put his hand on Simon's arm, even gently stroked it a couple of times. He had seen Griffin's' eyes meet Simon's. They had both smiled. The same smile that Simon used for *him*. He had thought it was *his* special smile. *Their* special smile. The animation in Griffin's eyes and body language had made it plain that he fancied Simon.

But did Simon fancy him back? He had made no attempt to get away from the scoundrel and had been most eager to chat to him in a more than friendly manner for quite a while.

It was clear to Chicky that Griffin had set his eye on Simon from the moment they had arrived at the Conference and that they knew each other well.

Simon had not made an answer to his comment.

"What do you think?" Chicky asked.

"Mm?" Simon's mind was miles away on what and how to tell Chicky in fact. He jerked back to the present. "Think about what?"

"Jerry Gillespie?"

"Mmm? Yes, nice man."

The suspicion was dawning on Chicky that maybe Griffin was the one Simon was secretly seeing. He wanted to speak to Simon about it, ask for the truth, but knew it would sound petulant and childish. He wanted to scream, *Are you having an affair with Griffin? Is that why we came here?*

His face now glowing in rising anger from the recollections and the assumption that there was something not quite adding up here he unthreaded his arm from Simon's and stepped a little to one side. As far as he knew they had come to Villas Bonitas for a holiday and to attend this Conference on behalf of their London legal partners. Not for Simon to have a fling with someone else! He felt his jealously rising higher at how Simon had appeared to be enthralled with *that* man. Chicky was certain something was going on, something he was not part of. Something he did not like!

Unaware of Chicky's insecure, worried feelings and wrapped up in his own thoughts, Simon wandered on along the path.

"It's beautiful here," he said after a while. He stopped as he realised Chicky had fallen a few paces behind and held his hand out. "I'd like to stay here forever. What do you think? Would you want to stay here in Paradise?"

"With you?" Chicky asked, wanting to add, *or without you because you've gone off to be with Griffin?*

"Of course with me," Simon said softly, a hint of sadness cracking his voice. Things were about to change, for better or worse he did not yet know. He should tell Chicky! Have it out in the open, but he could not, not here, not like this!

Chicky was suddenly confused. Had he got everything wrong then? Attempting to push the jealous thoughts from his mind he endeavoured to feel positive because they had left the Conference together and were back here at their villa, still a couple. Still together. He watched a small lizard dart across the path and scuttle into the garden before disappearing under a rock. Turning his attention to Simon, desperate not to show his insecurity, more cheerful than he felt, said, "Pity there is not a Conference Centre here at Villa Bonitas. The entertainment has been spectacular. Maybe we could suggest it and come back and have another fantastic holiday together next year. If you wanted me to come with you that is?"

Simon felt his heart lurch and suddenly realised what Chicky was alluding to: The secretiveness and Miles Griffin's keen attention. He inwardly groaned. He would have to tell Chicky, have to sort it all out, but until Miles gave him the official agreement to go public with their secret he could not say a word. Even to Chicky. Miles might change his mind, then where would Simon be? No. He had to keep quiet for now. He wanted them to enjoy the rest of this holiday, maybe their last one like this together.

Hearing quickening footsteps, he swung round and to his dismay saw Sheila Hoskins heading in their direction, hissed, "It's the Hoskins woman. Move fast."

Sheila's cooing voice, told him it was to late for escape.

"I can see you are so like ourselves you enjoy a good night out. Good morning Boys!" There was no trace of yesterday's hangover. Folding her arms across her breasts Sheila looked them over as if they were two mannequins standing in a shop window.

"By the look of you, you've been somewhere rather important." With a knowing smile, continued, "Dress code is so essential when attending social functions." Unfolding her arms she pointed to Chicky's red cummerbund. "Very stylish, I like coordination," she added as she took in the untied red bow. "No doubt you'll want a fresh cup of coffee to pick you up after being out all night."

His tone polite, Chicky replied, "Thank you Mrs Hoskins, another time we just want to get out of all of this." He pulled at his loose bow tie. "It's been a long, long night."

Interrupting, Sheila stated. "I've made a fresh pot. So no excuses, consider it poured."

"On this occasion we must refuse," Simon said firmly. "We need to freshen ourselves. Another time maybe?"

"In that case," Sheila retorted, a hurt look crossing her face, "you cannot miss our Soiree this evening. There will be no need to come in formal attire, smart casual will suffice." Seeing the two barristers smile, added. "We are hospitality personified. It will be an evening you will not forget. Anytime after seven thirty."

"Consider our acceptance," chirped Chicky, relieved they had escaped the coffee. Looking at Simon, added, "We are already looking forward to your Soiree."

Turning towards their villa and hearing the trill of Sheila's voice reminding someone else about her Soiree, Simon laughed, "A lucky escape for now."

Chicky smiled back at Simon and linked his arm through his and hoped the only escape on Simon's mind was from Sheila and not from their relationship.

Chapter FIFTY ONE

Having slept wrapped in Pat's arms, Doreen opened her eyes, smiled. She loved this man more than she could ever have imagined. What she had told him last night had given her more than a headache, but putting the record straight turned out better than she could ever have imagined.

"Penny for them Doll?" Pat asked as he gazed at Doreen snuggled down in his arms and wondered what she was worrying about now. Her face puckered in a frown, he saw a tear slip down her face. Brushing the wetness from Doreen's face, grinned, "Looks like I've lost my Barbie Doll and found a new one called Tiny Tears."

Doreen giggled.

"Now that's better." He pushed a stray hair from her face. "It's a good job my super strong pills have worked my back is feeling much better." He added pulling her on top of him before caressing her and kissing every inch of her face before making love again.

Sighing with satisfaction Doreen spent, exhausted and happy lay at Pat's side. "You know, I thought you'd scarper when I told you about Trish, but you didn't, why?"

Stroking her soft skin, moist with perspiration, he said, "Because I love you. I always have. I never thought for one minute you'd want to see me again. Let's face it we haven't seen each other for years. Well, let me say you haven't seen me for years."

Frowning, puzzled, Doreen pushed herself up, rested on her elbow and looked at Pat. "You've lost me. We haven't seen each other: Full stop."

Smiling, sitting up, Pat lent over and kissed Doreen on the lips. "Mmm you taste all naughty."

Giggling, "And what do you think you taste like eh? Anyway, stop this. I think we need to sort a few things out because you're scaring me. And let me tell you, I've had enough scares of late."

Swinging his leg across the bed Pat stood up, naked, his warm feet tacky against the cold marble floor. He padded over to Doreen's bathroom, a moment later returned wearing a white towelling robe. Tying the belt around his thickening waist he sat down on Doreen's side of the bed. His hands stuffed in the robe's pockets asked. "What are you scared about Doll?"

Picking at the sleeve of Pat's bathrobe, she answered sceptically in a voice that had lost its earlier sexy excitement. "Where do you think I should begin? For a start, you just said you had seen me, I don't think that's funny. Next, how did you know about me being here because that's really scared me? Also, finding out about you being my Trisha's dad and if all that isn't enough to scare me witless, I see Ginny Solomon." Looking up, she stared into Pat's eyes, "Pat, I won the lottery, not a part in a scary movie." She patted the bed, "We've romped around in this bed like sex is going out of fashion and still I'm not sure what you want."

Turning his gaze to his lap, Pat removed his hand from the robe pocket and silently took hold of Doreen's as she continued.

"I don't want to believe you're only here for me dosh." She stared at him, her eyes pleading, "But I don't know what else to think."

Wrapping his arms around her, Pat hugged her. Releasing her he held both her hands as he gathered his courage. "I should have told you the first day I saw you. I'm not after your money, I've more than enough of my own. When I knew you were coming to Villas Bonitas, I couldn't wait to see you.."

Interrupting, Doreen cried, "But how did you know I was coming? It scares me because I don't understand any of it. And you knew my telephone numbers. Don't you think that's odd too? Because, I think it is very odd and very scary!"

"None of it is odd, Doll. I knew all about you coming because I organised it for you to be staying here in this villa. I *own* this villa."

Stunned, Doreen paled and then giggled, a nervous giggle. "What are you saying?"

"I'm saying I own this villa and quite a few more. Carmen is my business partner here at Villas Bonitas."

Doreen shook her head confused, "I thought it was organised with my advisor. And even that Carmen never told me anything about this when she came to see me. Is nothing what it seems?"

Looking at Doreen's face Pat, asked himself how could he not love this gorgeous woman?

"Stephanie did organise your holiday, but I was the one who suggested this place to her. I know it all sounds crazy, but I promise you there is nothing scary about me. A few years ago I made a lot of money, that's how I got involved with Trisha's education. Then one or two things went wrong, I didn't lose everything though and to try and work my way back I took a risk, a big risk, it worked and I made a killing. On one of my rare visits when I went back to the UK I would call at the school to make sure everything was okay with the fees and Trisha's *grant*. I wanted to talk to you. I saw you once at the school, nearly had a heart attack. I thought if you saw me you'd tell me to bugger off. Then a little while ago I read in the papers that you'd won the lottery. I got in touch with Stephanie Rawlinson and the rest you know. I never meant to scare you. I just wanted to see if we could have some time together. I love you Doreen. I always have. I just hope you feel you can keep seeing me."

Crying and giggling at the same time Doreen spluttered, "Pat, what's a girl suppose to do? I tell you even *Eastenders* couldn't come up with lines like this." Pulling at Pat's belt, added, 'Best you get back into bed, we've a few more things to talk about."

Chapter FIFTY TWO

Clutching a clipboard with several sheets of paper attached, a stern look on her face, Sheila stood at the foot of the pathway to her villa. She gazed across the pathways and saw people in light clothing milling around. From the swimming pool area raucous laughter filled the air. She tutted loudly, disapproval etched on her face. She had enough to occupy her mind without the disruption of noise. The catering company was due any moment and it was imperative that she checked everything ordered was not only delivered without damage, but perfectly presented.

As two men, sporting light brown aprons over black trousers and a crisp white shirt, each pushing a sack barrow laden with boxes strode towards her, in an authoritative tone she called, "I hope you have brought enough of those coolly containers to keep this lot in." She pointed to the sky and blazing sun, "You might not have noticed, but it's hot here." With disdain she glared at the delivery men who were sweating profusely.

The two delivery men stopped in front of Sheila both ignoring her caustic remark and with a friendly smile in unison said, "Good afternoon Mrs Hoskins."

Andy, one of the delivery men, was perfectly aware that Mrs Hoskins was a nightmare client to his company and he wished that he did not have to deliver the order.

With a curled lip Sheila retorted, "Yes, good afternoon, so to my question, have you brought enough containers?"

Opening his A4 red book, Andy read the neatly written order list, turning to his colleague, in a matter of fact tone asked. "Danny, check what is on that list and how many boxes we have brought. We need to be container perfect."

Methodically, Danny read the list and on his fingers counted the containers. Confirmed, "Six."

Turning to Sheila, Andy repeated, “Mrs Hoskins we have brought six, you need five and half, we don’t do halves so we have provided six.”

Sheila read her own duplicate list, “Is that so?” Turning, she walked back down her pathway and just before stepping into her villa, beckoned the caterers to follow. Leaving their trolleys outside, they carried the boxes into the villa and placed each in the kitchen as per instructions. As each one was opened and inspected, Sheila ticked at her list.

Satisfied, she waited for the two men to bring in more boxes. Addressing Andy, her eyes taking in the latest arrivals, said. “Let me see what bubbly you have brought because I made it clear I did not want the expensive stuff for the main drink and before I discuss the matter of the decent champagne, let me see just what you have delivered.” She had followed her tradition of having bubbly on the terrace table and the finer, palatable champagne was to be at the drinks bar on the far side of the terrace where Antonio was to preside. The bar carried a moderate fee; this was a Soiree not a free drink up at her expense. Although any profit, once costs were deducted, would be given to the local hospice. It all added to her superior and generous position in Pelito.

Having placed the boxes down, with deftness Andy pulled at the sealed lid and revealed twelve bottles. “This is very popular, we call it C*hambueolic!”*

Sheila eyed the label and confidently chirped, “Looks good enough to me, now is it cold?”

Not answering the question Andy placed the bottle against Sheila’s arm.

“Bloody hell!” She squealed.

“I’ll take that as a yes,” Andy responded, holding his humour in check, but slyly grinning. “Now where do you want them? Your fridge or leave them in the coolly boxes?”

“I think it would be best for you to leave it all in the coolly boxes. My fridges are bursting at the seams.”

Looking into the boxes, she cried, “Don’t forget to keep the bubbly and champagne separate. I do not want my staff getting confused." She did not add, *and hand out the good stuff for free*.

As Danny brought in more boxes, noting the labels Sheila called, "Now, just make sure you leave all the glasses, plates, napkins and cutlery over there."

She quick stepped through the villa and on to the terrace, pointed to a large table under a larger parasol at the far side. "Place this lot there. The maids will lay it out properly later." She smiled as she stepped back into the villa. Her Soiree was going to be a show stopper.

Sitting at the Villas Bonitas' bar safely out of Sheila's way, Jack could hear his wife barking her orders. With one large beer already in his hand he asked Antonio for another. "I need to prepare myself for tonight and whilst you are at it, have one yourself."

No sooner had the drink been placed on the bar than Jack drank it swiftly down. Looking over to his villa, winced, he had no intentions of going there just yet. Turning his attention back to Antonio announced, "I'll see you later, I'm off power walking."

Antonio watched Jack stride off down the pathway. He wondered how the Hoskins managed to cope with reality, because they both had a way of deceiving not only themselves, but everyone else.

Chapter FIFTY THREE

Hurrying down the pathway and away from his villa, Jack could hear his bossy wife and with years of practice he had learnt to shut his mind to her voice. The only voice in his head now was Ginny's and he smiled. He should be helping with the organisation for this evening, but nine out of ten times he was in the way, so a quick romp with Ginny would put him in the right mood to cope with the approaching fiasco.

At a brisk pace he headed into Pelito. He was not due to see Ginny, but he needed to get away. He had forgiven her for her silly stunt at turning up at Villas Bonitas. Taking his mobile phone from his pocket he called her, best to let her know he was on his way. He chuckled as he hit the call button. It rang twice before he heard her sexy voice.

"I hope you are home as I'm on my way, thought I'd sneak a special moment or two with you before the *do* tonight.... What did you just say?" Raising his eyebrows he grinned. "Oh good, I like surprises."

Chortling, he ended the call and increased his stride, wondering what Ginny had waiting for him.

The phone call was unexpected, but it had not changed her mind, if anything it had strengthened her resolve. Now was as good a time as any. Sitting on her terrace Ginny stared down at her nails, they were immaculate. Had she not spent a small fortune on them the previous day she would sit and chew them to the quick. Her nerves were in shreds. Gazing through the balcony railings she watched as Jack approached the entrance to her apartment and despite her inner turmoil she was glad he had rung. His unexpected visit was well timed. She had planned on telling him tomorrow, but would much rather get it over with. She giggled at his words of a moment ago, *I like surprises* well he might, but she was certain shocks were not on his list.

Hearing the entrance door open she walked through the open French windows into the high ceilinged lounge as Jack strode towards her.

A wicked smile on his face, he chuckled, "I've no idea how I'd get through my life without you being here for my little needs. Why didn't I meet you before her?" Noting her sombre expression, added, "Enough of my twittering, what is this surprise you have for me?" He pulled her towards him, "Come here so I can give you an experience you'll never forget."

She ambled over to him and let him hug her then pushed him away.

Hurt, Jack asked. "Now what's all that about? I thought you were up for my visit this afternoon?"

"Not this afternoon Jack, we need to talk."

"Sounds serious and we don't do serious do we? We do fun!" But even to his ears his words sounded flat. The look on Ginny's face was beginning to worry him. "Sorry, I'm my usual greedy piggish self, can't help it with you barely a whisker away from my arms."

She smiled, because despite her dilemma she loved him. He believed he was God's gift to women and he had all the chat to go with it, but that was her Jack.

"You have all the patter Jack Hoskins, but at this moment it isn't going to work, so get yourself a stiff drink then we can talk."

Apprehensive Jack went to the drinks cabinet and meaning to sound jovial, twittered, "You want me drunk so you can be more wicked than usual, eh?"

"In your dreams lover, just get a drink." She giggled, her voice sounding as false as Jack's. She smiled a weak smile, her nerves were frayed and all his silly patter was not making it easy. She felt perspiration trickle down her spine.

His glass filled with whisky Jack sat himself down on the sofa next to her. Raising his glass, grinned, "Now the torment of my life, what is so serious that I need this?" He nodded at his filled glass. Looking back at Ginny saw eyes that held no laugher and for the first time since he had walked into her apartment, realised there was trouble. He suddenly felt tense and nervous. "Something is wrong. I can see it in your face. I'd like to think the worst thing you are about to tell me is that you don't want to see me any more, but somehow I don't think that is it."

He closed his eyes and then whispered what he feared the most. "You're pregnant."

It was a statement, not a question. He did not need Ginny to confirm the answer, somehow he knew. Looking at her he wondered why it had not occurred to him earlier, he had noticed her mood swings and even a little weight gain. But it was the last thing on his mind when he was holding her and loving her with a passion he had never found in his wife.

Her head bent, her eyes staring down at her hands clasped tightly on her knee, very slowly she nodded.

Holding his glass, having not taken a drop of the whisky he asked. "I thought you were on the pill? You said we were safe? You said…"

Eyes swimming with tears Ginny looked up at him and snapped, "Safe? We've never been safe. We've been playing an unsafe game, you've been cheating and I let you cheat with me. What's safe about that?"

Jumping to his feet Jack strode towards the French doors, looked out towards the famous Old Square, but did not see the turrets on the building opposite, the pigeons cooing on the roof ridges. Instead, Jack saw everything he had worked for and everything he owned being grabbed by Sheila. If she ever found out about what he had been up to she would destroy him. Pushing his hands through his hair he turned towards Ginny and asked. "How far are you gone?"

"Fourteen weeks."

He gulped down his whisky, then sank down into the nearest chair and stared down at the floor.

"God, how did that happen?"

"If the situation wasn't so serious I'd laugh at that question. You know how it happened, *an over enthusiastic man*, as you frequently kept telling me."

"Who else knows?"

Through tear filled eyes, Ginny glared at Jack and with contempt spat, "Everybody, I shouted it from the rooftops like you do when you find yourself pregnant by a married man. Who do you think knows? Me and the doctor."

With his hair ruffled and a grey pallor to his face Jack realised that for once he was not in control of what he wanted to do and it frightened him. He whispered. "I can't marry you Ginny."

She burst into laughter.

Snapping his head up straight, shocked at her outburst he growled, "What's so bloody funny?"

Pulling a tissue from the box on the table next to the sofa, Ginny wiped her eyes. "Jack you are priceless. Arrogant to the end. I wouldn't marry you if you begged me."

His pride hurt, he barked, "Why ever not?"

Shaking with the relief at telling him and angry at his response, her tears stopped. "You don't understand do you? You've had your fun and now I'm the one with the consequences." Glaring across at him, her anger fuelled. "Call it a mistress thing, we are left to carry the can, or in this case, hold the baby."

She took a deep breath that shuddered down her throat and into her lungs. "And for the record, I want to keep this baby and should you ever be able to tear yourself away from the clutches of your *wife's'* apron strings and purse, I'd like you to be part of its life, if only for maintenance payments."

Standing up he strode to the entrance door. "Ginny, I'm leaving because no way can I get my head around this. What is Sheila going to say when she finds out? Have you thought of that?"

Twisting round Ginny looked on as Jack opened the door and walked out of her apartment. The sound of the door closing brought on fresh tears.

“Walk out on me, go on!” she called. She should have guessed that was exactly what he would do because despite the dire situation all he could think of was his bloody wife and himself. She was angry. Very angry, but had loved him, and still did. She wiped her eyes, it seemed her bed was made and she would lay in it alone.

Chapter FIFTY FOUR

As the sun slowly slipped lower Doreen watched as the sky turned from blue to deep pink. In the stillness of the early dusk the sound she heard made her slowly click her heels against the hard ceramic tiles and tap her feet to the music coming from the Hoskins' terrace now all aglow with soft lighting. She had received an invitation and been told she was a special guest at Sheila's party, and for the first time since arriving at Villas Bonitas felt comfortable. This feeling, she knew was nothing to do with her lottery win. It was down to Pat turning up in her life again. In the last few days he had made her feel special and very happy. And, despite the shock of not realising before now that he was the father of her daughter, she wanted him. There was a lot about him she needed to learn, but he wanted her and loved her and that was enough for now. More important, he was not interested in her money. Gazing across to the Hoskins' villa she did not feel frightened, there was only one thing that scared her and that was telling her daughter about Pat. Trisha appeared to be in control for someone of seventeen, but nonetheless, the right words were necessary.

"You are such a scary sight when you are so spaced out. It seems you live in a different orbit to the rest of us."

Startled, Doreen swung round as Trisha's voice sliced through her worries. A surprised expression puckering her face, Doreen noticed her daughter was wearing her black wrap. It made her look beautiful against her newly tanned skin and also very young. Shifting her expression to a smile, she whispered. "I've got something on me mind, so taking five mins to sort it out."

Looking her mother up and down Trisha grinned. "If you are scaring yourself on just how fab you look, then stop, check yourself in the mirror. It seems you are wasting serious energy, you will not only be *the* babe at that show," she nodded to where the music drifted from, "but they will all crash with envy."

Laughing at the words that tumbled out of her daughter's mouth, Doreen wondered where she learnt them all from. "Come girl, let's take a pew."

Wrapping her arm around her daughter's shoulders, added, "You say some of the nicest things, not that I understand what you're saying most of the time." Sitting down together on the terrace sofa Doreen sighed. "If only I'd got my threads to worry about things would be simple."

Sliding her hand into her mother's Trisha was suddenly aware how vulnerable this beautiful lady, who giggled far too much, could be. To her surprise and delight she had seen a change in mother since she had met up with Pat and for the first time, knew her special mother was having fun, something she had not had much of in her life. "So spill Mama, what can be so absorbing that you are not thinking about how you look?"

Reaching over Doreen kissed her daughter's soft hair. "Nothing, things aren't always as you expect them to be. Sometimes you've got to work out what's best."

Hearing a resigned tone in her mother's voice, concerned, Trisha asked. "Is it to do with Pat?"

Doreen nodded, adding, "Yes, but it's not what you think."

"Think? No Mama, I'm not thinking. I watch, check out and listen. And, it's cool. I know. I guess since he turned up I've been wondering myself."

Alarm flashed across Doreen's face, her eyes snapped wide open as she stared at her daughter. "You might be clever, but you aren't psychic."

Laughing, "No, but I'm your girl, as you like to tell everyone and I take it from your pensive look that you think Pat is my biological father."

Doreen whispered, "How on earth do you know?"

"I guess, I began to add everything up that I'd not realised I'd actually seen."

A tear slipped down Doreen's cheek, she felt ashamed and bowed her head as Trisha continued.

"I guess his wonky mouth gave me a clue when I saw him that first time he came to the villa. I have never seen one quite like mine and of course you had told me you were together before I was born. It took my breath away at first and that is when the other things I had not even realised I had noticed sprung to mind. One of them was that I had seen him at my school. Funny, how you take things in without realising, because after that I remembered the Head and Pat having a serious chat. I had entered the Head's office and was immediately dismissed. Looking back it must have been about me. Now seeing Pat here, all these crazy things came together and I realised he was very likely my father." Smiling and squeezing her mother's hand tightly, added. "Chill Mama, it's no big deal, someone had to father me and let's agree better someone who loves you than any old weirdo who is likely to turn up now that you are super rich."

As her daughter's words sank in, Doreen with a look that held a mixture of relief and shame, whispered, "I'm sorry, Trish, I never meant it to be like this. What must you think of me?"

Gripping her mother's hand Trisha smiled. "*I think*, simply the best."

Slipping her hand from her mother's she stood up, but not before kissing Doreen on the cheek. "Stop crying Mama, go out, enjoy. Show that uppity Hoskins woman just who you are and then when your head has stopped spinning, we can talk and get on with our lives. Oh, and yes, loves you. Loves you lots!"

With tears of pride streaming down her face, her makeup ruined, Doreen watched her daughter calmly wander back into the villa and wondered how she had managed to have such a beautiful girl.

A moment later, through blurred eyes Doreen saw Pat step through the open patio doors onto the terrace. Wiping her face with the back of her hand, black smudges streaking her skin she cried, “Trish knows and she isn’t even upset.” She swallowed down another sob.

“I know, she calmly said ‘Papa take Mama out, make her giggle a lot tonight, tomorrow we chill, spill and trill.’ I wanted to hug her, but she went into her bedroom.”

“Seems that things aren’t all that bad after all,” Doreen sniffed, rubbing her hands together to remove the black marks.

Pulling Doreen gently to her feet Pat hugged her tight. “Come on Doll, there’s nothing we can change now, let’s do as our daughter said and make an impression at the circus over at the Hoskins. Go fix your face. You look like a panda,” he added, chuckling.

Wiping her tears away Doreen tottered on her high heels towards the bathroom.

“Doll,” Pat called after her. “What does, ‘spill and trill’ mean?”

Giggling, Doreen answered. “God knows!”

Chapter FIFTY FIVE

With so much to organise Sheila had not noticed Jack's unusual quietness. Though she had observed he was sweating heavily when he returned from his power walking, having told her he had been more vigorous than normal before locking himself in his bathroom. She was not happy, but she had far too many things to worry about than Jack tip toeing around the streets at speed. Now dressed in her themed outfit, a rumba-style black dress with gold and a red frill dancing at her calf, brandishing a black lace fan, she glided out onto her terrace. Stopped at the sight of Jack brandishing a large glass of whisky, her attention distracted she did not see the sun setting below the palm trees casting an orange glow across the sky to the west. Her steely eyes focused on her husband. "It is my Soiree Jack, not a stag do to get drunk quick. I need you sober."

A lock of hair already plastered to his head through perspiration, Jack glared at his wife contempt oozing out of every pore. His head was all over the place after what Ginny had announced. How in God's name was he going to sort it out? he asked himself as he turned and saw the solar lights in the garden flicker on at the rapidly darkening sky. He wiped a hand over his brow, he could not stop sweating. Knocking back his drink he walked past Sheila and back into the villa, he needed a refill.

Sheila could see there was something wrong, but now was not the time to be finding out, she thought as Jack brushed past her rustling the frill on her dress. Her attention was needed to survey the food tables because it was clear Jack was of no help. Glaring over to the food section of her terrace, grimaced as the two maids she had engaged were fiddling around with cutlery and napkins. She sighed. The girls should be standing with welcoming smiles ready to greet and serve her guests on arrival.

Positioned in front of the tables, Sheila admired the extensive and varied tapas dishes; every combination she could think of had been ordered, along with a wide selection of continental breads and spicy and sweet sauces. She smiled with satisfaction. Her Soiree was a Spanish flavoured banquet even the music was typical Latin. Waving her open fan below her chin she knew nobody could do better. Spinning round on her short heels, letting her dress flounce gracefully, she saw Jack holding a large drink and tutted loudly at his greed. Distracted at hearing the now familiar giggle, Sheila watched as Doreen and Pat strolled hand in hand onto her terrace.

Waiting to welcome them Sheila took in every minute detail of Doreen's beautifully fitted dress. "Welcome, to what is your first taste of our famous Soirees." As she spoke her eyes slowly travelled up and down Doreen before adding. "A bright splash of colour does make one stand out in a crowd. And of course as guest of honour you need to be noticed."

Looking at Sheila, Doreen amused, giggled. "Thanks, I knew I needed to look me best for your do. Me and purple do look good together." Staring at Sheila's dress she bit her lip in amusement, added, "I hadn't realised it was fancy dress though." Looking around she pouted, "I expected they'd be loads more people."

Swallowing down a retort, Sheila flicked her fan and wafted it rapidly, then cooed, "Rather early yet for some of my guests, but rest assured we are very popular as you will see. Of course, I will introduce you to all our guests very shortly." Turning her attention to Pat trilled, "Glad you've brought your man friend. Do please remind me again of his name?"

Doreen did not miss the edge to Sheila's question, giggled. She had already worked out that giggling irritated Sheila and she so wanted to say more about who Pat really was, but he had told her not to breathe a word. Instead, grinning, she answered. “You remember you met my Pat when you went tumbling in the pool. What a scream that was.” She had wanted to bring the subject up in the Jacuzzi, now she had her chance.

A sneer forming, quickly turned to a strained smile, Sheila clucked, “Now I remember. Doreen told me you are in the holiday camp business, fascinating! You must find time to tell me how business is these days at those sort of mass holiday places, but for now do help yourselves to a glass of champagne.”

Touching Doreen’s well tanned arm, added. “Give me a moment and I will introduce you to everyone.” She grinned. She would show Miss Fink Fought, how dare she laugh!

Extending his hand Pat chuckled, “I believe people love to holiday here too.”

Sheila withdrew her hand and said with a false smile, “Not quite the same class of holiday though. Ah! Simon, Chicky! Come in, come in!” Glad of the excuse to move away, Sheila hurried to greet the latest arrivals and laughed over her shoulder, “I don’t need to introduce you to these two Doreen, they know you’re an East End lottery winner.”

Squeezing Doreen’s hand, Pat grinned. “That smug smile will be wiped off her face before much longer.”

Doreen giggled.

Chapter FIFTY SIX

The night air was balmy, guitar music played in the background as Pat watched Sheila glide across her terrace to preen over more guests who had arrived. He sneered, how he disliked that woman! Taking hold of Doreen's hand, they strolled over to the drinks table where several bottles of champagne rested in ice filled buckets. There was little evidence of any other choice of drinks on the table. Lifting a bottle from the melting ice and at the same time plucking a cloth covering another ice bucket, Pat wrapped it around the base of the dripping bottle. Inspecting the label, amusement sparkled in his eyes, letting go of the cloth Pat dropped the bottle back into the watery ice.

Disappointed, Doreen cried, "Are you not going to pour us a drink?"

Before Pat could respond, Sheila suddenly appeared at his side. Chuckling reached over to the ice bucket. "I can see you are confused, but as I said to Doreen only yesterday, you have to get used to the high life and champagne is part of it." Without hesitation Sheila poured two glasses, handed one to Doreen before thrusting the other into Pat's hand.

Flicking her fan open she fanned herself as she directed a question to Doreen. "Now tell me what do you think? No doubt it's a bit dry for your palate." Not waiting for a response turned to Pat and watched as he sipped the frothy liquid. As the cheap bubbly trickled down his throat, he swallowed rapidly. Then with a sardonic smile winked at Sheila and wondered who she was trying to fool.

"There's no doubt about it Mrs Hoskins, you've got unique taste."

Sheila's lace trimmed fan trembling with the rapid movement and smugly she answered, "I'm glad you are able to appreciate such luxury. It's why we're here, to enjoy the fine things of life. Now before you go and mingle with everyone, I need to do something of importance."

Shutting her fan with a snap, she deftly tucked it under her arm then clapped her hands. A silence descended across the terrace, only the rapid strumming of a guitar could be heard from the music player.

Clearing her throat Sheila raised her voice. "Ladies and gentlemen, my dear friends," she peered around her guests, a smile covering her face, "I would like you to give a warm welcome and round of applause to my special guest this evening, Doreen Wilkinson." She turned to Doreen, a wide grin on her face then returning her attention back to her guests, her voice a pitch higher, continued. "Doreen is a lottery winner no less. Now before you start clapping," she had noted hands poised to do so, "please let me finish. Do take some time to have a chat with her, I promise you she will be delightfully entertaining."

A crescendo of clapping filled the air.

With an embarrassed flush crimsoning her neck and face Doreen giggled nervously. "Blimey Sheila, I didn't think you were going to do that." She giggled again, adding in a louder voice as she looked on at the people staring at her, "Thanks, pleased to meet you all. I'm sure we'll have a natter. Nothing like a get together and a proper knees up with a glass or two of champers."

Through hooded eyelids Sheila checked the expressions of her guests' faces, surprise and amusement was clearly in evidence. Hugging Doreen, she pretended to be the best of friends. "Now Doreen my dear, enjoy your celebrity status, I know there are a few who are dying to meet you." She grinned slyly at Doreen, adding, "Do make sure you help yourself to plenty of my champagne, nervousness is all part of the game. I always find the bubbles relax me."

Doreen giggled at the memory of the Jacuzzi. "Yes right, *She,* bubbles always does it for me."

Catching her breath at being called *She* Sheila crowed. "And of course, my special delights are now being served, Tapas."

As Sheila glided away fanning herself, Pat threw the contents of his glass onto the garden. "Bloody hell Doll, what was all that about?" Snatching Doreen's glass added, "Don't drink that stuff let me find you something decent." Cursing under his breath that he would get even with that bitch sooner than later, what was she doing? She made Doreen sound like a leper

Confused Doreen sighed, "I'm the guest of honour. Though I thought she was kidding." She knew exactly was Mrs Sheila Hoskins was up to and she would try not to disappoint. Giggling loudly a few heads turned towards her as she cried, "You said she had taste."

Tipping his drink away, Pat leaned forward and kissed her gently on the lips. "My china Doll what am I to do with you? This is not only seriously dangerous stuff, but a bloody dangerous place to be."

Not wanting to say anymore on the announcement Sheila had made he could see Doreen was not upset and so he kept his comments to himself. "When I said she had taste, I meant *bad* taste, very bad taste! Now come on, let's see if there is anything decent at the bar. The least you *mingle* with her guests the better." He was sure Sheila was up to something, and making a fool of his Doreen was not going to happen if he had anything to do about it.

Giggling, Doreen had every intention to mingle and aware of the heads that were turning, Doreen asked, "What about the Tapas?"

She smiled at a pink lipped woman. "I ain't never had tapas, tampax, but never tapas," She laughed secretly. If Sheila was up for a laugh, then so was she. She giggled again, loudly.

"I know what I'm doing Pat," she confided as they headed for the bar. "I clocked her nasty little number right from the start."

Pat looked at her astonished, then hiding his mouth with his hand, smiled. He should have known that his Doll was no fool.

Chapter FIFTY SEVEN

Simon and Chicky recoiled as they sipped the awful champagne, "What is this?" Simon gasped as the liquid attempted to remove the inner lining on his throat.

Having watched Pat toss the drink into the garden, Chicky grinned. "Seems we are not the only ones struggling with Mrs H's well chilled champagne, Doreen's partner just tipped his away, sadly I think the palm tree will die."

Laughing, "In that case we will take heed, I see Antonio is serving at Mrs H's other bar, strange she should push everyone along to the table with this stuff and away from that area of the terrace. No matter, let us see if Antonio is serving something better than paint stripper." Simon slipped his arm under Chicky's as they headed across the terrace.

Chicky looked at Simon, the uncertainties he'd had after the conference had faded. Simon had been the perfect partner all day.

Moving through the throng of people, Simon and Chicky passed Jack who stood at the end of the terrace wrestling with his pocket.

"Mobile on the go again," Simon mouthed and looking at Chicky, laughter escaping as he heard Jack swear.

Chortling at Jack's inability to control his mobile phone, Chicky glanced through the silhouettes of the shrubbery then paused as he saw Frau Hecks sitting alone on her terrace. He nudged Simon's arm. "Let's see if we can encourage *Mrs Home Alone* to join us."

Startled as his mobile phone vibrated in his trouser pocket, Jack knocked over his glass of whisky and with exasperation saw the drink spill over plates and food. He swore as beads of perspiration covered his face, ignoring the mess, marched to the end of his terrace.

"Bloody hell," he cursed, pulling the phone from his pocket, looked up and to his horror saw Ginny waving to Doreen sitting at the bar. Panic rose like bile in his throat, he turned away to avoid any possibility of eye contact with either of them and collided with Sheila.

"Jack, so far you have let me down at every turn," she said acidly. "The ice is melting, Jack…"

Not from where I am, he thought gloomily, *you're as frozen as ever*

"…. Do something useful. Fetch more from the freezer."

At least, he thought it was an excuse not to acknowledge Ginny. Perhaps if he ignored her she would go away. Dejected, Jack disappeared into the kitchen. He had been ignoring Sheila for years and she was still here.

He took his time, as much time as he dared. When he came back, clutching a large drink in his unsteady hand his worst nightmare became suddenly even worse.

Their arms linked together, Ginny and Doreen were strolling together, deep in conversation, towards the bar.

"Bloody hell!" He turned away, headed back to the kitchen still clutching the ice bags.

Having kept an eye on Jack, Sheila wondered if he was ill or drunk or both, but decided it was most likely the latter and ignored his behaviour for the moment. She made a mental note to talk to him later about his carry on. For now, her attention was focused on the stranger with Doreen.

"Who is that?" she asked herself in a low whisper as the two women threaded their way through the throng of people.

Sheila was certain she had seen the woman before, but no matter how much she searched her mind, she could not place the attractive, if slightly overweight, woman. It nagged at her, but she would remember she told herself. Pushing the thought to the back of her mind she drifted over to Doreen, the frill on her dress swishing as she glided to greet the mystery woman.

"Hello, I see you are with my guest of honour, this is a private party, however."

“Sheila,” Doreen cried in shrill excitement, “you won’t believe this,” Doreen pointed at Ginny, “Ginny’s an old mate of mine. We go back yonks. Back to the days when we were scrubbers,” she said the word scrubbers loud enough to be heard by Sheila’s pretentious guests. Giggling at the looks aimed towards her, added. “I rather hoped you won’t mind if she joins us?”

Sheila tried to hide her disgust as she stared at Ginny. For reasons she could not explain she felt apprehension and shivered involuntarily. “Ginny lives here,” Doreen added, “In town that is. Don’t you Gin?”

Ginny smiled, held out her hand. “Hello Mrs Hoskins, I am glad to meet you, I’ve heard such a lot about you and now I am actually meeting you in person. How wonderful!” Ginny’s nervousness had vanished at the same time as Jack had marched out of her apartment shutting the door on her. Well this was her way of showing him, shutting doors and strutting off was not acceptable. He would face his responsibilities and the consequences one way or another.

Chapter FIFTY EIGHT

Frau Hecks sat on her terrace, a glass of sherry in her hand as she listened to the laughter and exotic Latin music drifting through the still night air. Reflecting, she thought she would have liked to have gone to the Hoskins' party. Pretentious as it was, everyone dressed in their best, laughing and making small talk on how wonderful their hostess was, no doubt eating and drinking far too much. Maybe she should break her golden rule and slip along? She had been invited, but had declined, now was wishing she had not. At least she would be with people.

She was aware that of late, the feeling of loneliness was becoming more and more like a cloak; it had begun to shroud her. Hearing a loud guffaw of laughter she frowned, reminding herself that she did not do *that* sort of silly nonsense, certainly not since she had lost her beloved Hans. But despite the heaviness in her heart, hearing the music playing she imagined flamenco dancers, their dresses swishing, castanet's clicking, heels from the *señors* tapping in rhythm on wooden floors. She smiled and thought about the wonderful parties she and Hans had attended when they were young, he had danced her off her feet. She had been nimble in those days.

Looking down at her chubby legs with their puffy ankles, she sniffed. They were a long way from when she had danced the tango shamelessly. Hans would glide her across the floor, both in perfect step as they performed the foxtrot, the tango, the quick step. He had held her tight when they had waltzed to Strauss and she could still feel his touch, she smiled at the memories. Feeling warm fur brush against her ankles she looked down, her memories melting away at the sight of her cat. Leaning forward she placed her half empty sherry glass onto the table then wrapped Wolfgang in her arms. He purred with happiness as she held him close.

Distracted at a noise, Wolfgang wriggled then leapt out of her arms and shot off under a bush. Retrieving her sherry and humming to the music, Frau Hecks sipped at the sweet tasting liquid, hearing Wolfgang rummaging around in the undergrowth, no doubt a lizard between his jaws she mused. There were many lizards with tails missing at Villas Bonitas, thanks to her naughty cat.

A polite voice at the edge of her terrace startled her.

"Good evening, we thought we saw you sitting alone," called Chicky. "Please come and join us. It is quite nice. There's exotic food and the company is not all that bad."

Frau Hecks smiled at Chicky's kind face and noted his partner sidling up to join him. A strange couple she thought, but nonetheless polite and pleasant.

"Thank you, I am best at home away from noise."

"What would you say if we take your arm and insist you join us? Of course we can make sure you sit away from the music," Simon added in a begging tone. He was saddened to see the old lady alone when everyone was enjoying the party.

Looking at the two handsome men at the foot of her terrace, Frau Hecks explained, "I am not dressed for such occasion. I think it best you return to party without me."

"Nonsense," Simon retorted. "If you have no problem we will wait here for you. I am sure a little touch of lipstick will have you perfect for Mrs Hoskins' Soiree." He winked at Frau Hecks as he emphasised the words *Mrs Hoskins*.

Frau Hecks did not miss the gesture and despite hesitating, smiled and then laughed. Looking up at Simon then Chicky, she cast her gaze over to the party. Maybe she ought to go. Surely with two handsome men escorting her she would not feel so out of place? Shifting her gaze from the Hoskins terrace, she looked up at the smiling faces and in a voice mixed with sadness and pleasure, added. "I will drag myself away from my peaceful home, but only because you bully me to go with you." A smile hovered on her lips, "But first I need my shawl."

Humming softly she turned and headed towards her villa, entering the open patio doors, called, "*Ein moment bitte*."

Chapter FIFTY NINE

Jack watched as Sheila mingled into the crowd, his mind turning somersaults as he walked over to where Doreen and Ginny stood talking together on the terrace. As he approached to his dismay he noted Ginny was not paying attention to Doreen, but stealthily watching Sheila.

Staring at Ginny he wanted to throttle her. Dear God was she not satisfied with the bombshell she had dropped that afternoon? They had rules and Ginny knew them; stay away from Sheila.

Deciding to put a stop to this nonsense, Ginny had to be told to leave, he approached the two women. Putting his hand to his head in a vain attempt to blot out the nightmare that was consuming him, his sweating not abating and his nerves in tatters, he turned to what he hoped was light humour.

"Hello Doreen, now that you're one of us, wealthy I mean, you've already slipped into our bad habits and forgotten to introduce me to this friend of yours." He forced a laugh.

Stifling a giggle, Doreen could not believe what Jack had said. He really must think she was dumber than dumb. It was clear he had no idea what she knew. As she glared at him, she wanted to giggle, he was shaking and sweating, his voice sounded false. She had never seen anyone shake that much and still be standing.

"Ooh, what am I thinking?" She giggled loudly as she took hold of Ginny's arm and with another exaggerated giggle cried, "Ginny this is Jack, it's his party that I'm guest of honour." She giggled at the farce of it all. "And Jack, this is my old mate Ginny. I can't believe she turned up out the blue to see me. Now what do you say to that eh?"

Jack took a deep breath, felt his shirt pool with dampness as it clung to his skin and silently cried, *you can't believe it? well bloody hell nor can I!*

Raising an eyebrow at the absurdity of it all and with tight lips he tried to smile. "Really an old friend?"

Before he could add anything else, Antonio appeared with a tray of drinks and winked at Jack. Jack stared back. *Christ, does he know?*

"*Lo siento*," Antonio said to Doreen, "I sorry to speak when you speak, Pat he ask me to bring these drinks for you, but he also say you go back to bar and see him."

Giggling with mischief at the little charade, Doreen grinned at the barman. "Thanks Antonio, my Pat is the best," then placing her hand on Jack's arm, stated. "Sorry Jack, but we'd best get back to me fella." Taking hold of Ginny's arm, Doreen, stifling her mirth, added, "We can catch up with old times and you can tell me what you're really doing here."

Doreen was eager to know why she was here, guessed it was all to do with Jacky boy and from the state of him, Ginny was not welcome. Pat had said he was carrying on with someone and it didn't take rocket science to work out who that someone was. Nor did it take much to work out why Ginny had a look of carrying extra weight. She was not a girl who looked dumpy, but her middle had a distinctive bulge. Had Sheila noticed, Doreen wondered. But maybe Sheila Hoskins had no idea that her husband was having a lot of rumpy pumpy how's yer father on the side

"Now now Doreen, let's not spoil my evening, surely I can get to talk to this lovely friend of yours? Don't you worry off you go to your Pat and I'll take good care of…. Ginny is it?"

Stifling a giggle, Doreen let go of Ginny's arm. "On one condition only and that is, Ginny you must come to my villa tomorrow and then we can have a proper chin wag and catch up."

Over zealous, Ginny agreed. "I only called by on the off chance. I'm not really dressed for a party. I'll come back tomorrow."

She smiled sweetly at Jack. "It was so nice to meet you Mr Hoskins. We must do this again some time."

Swinging her hips, not looking back, Ginny left well satisfied that she had given Jack Hoskins the fright of his life.

Chapter SIXTY

By rights Trisha realised she should be wracked with emotion after learning moments ago that Pat was not only her mother's past, present and future lover, but now her own father too! *How weird is that* Trisha thought, sprawled out on her bed still in her wrap. Instead of feeling shocked and angry, she felt happy, her mother was happy and she liked the idea of belonging to a family, be it an odd one.

Her bedroom patio doors open Trisha listened to the stillness of the villa, from outside she could hear music, the chink of glasses, popping of champagne corks, laughter; including her mother's giggle coming across from the Hoskins' villa. She could not imagine anything more scary then partying with the likes of the Hoskins, they were such an out of time couple. Though she was glad that her mother was adding her specialness to the mad rave up, her mother she knew needed to laugh more. Life had been such a freak time until she had won the lottery. The shock was an out of this world experience, one that had had them both floating in orbit. Even the neighbours came knocking on the door, but apart from a couple her mother quickly told them where to get off. They had never knocked before, so now was just too late. Trisha laughed at the memory at their faces when Doreen had told them to bugger off.

The new house, they had moved to just after the XXX's were converted into real money made all the difference. For a start: no more stinky steps to clamber up or the risk of getting hijacked in the stinking lift. Even school seemed easier, not that she had felt out of place there, though no one lived or admitted to living in the pits, but her mother being catapulted to fame seemed to open those creaky doors a tad wider. Life had simply turned from its darkest side to a brightness that needed several pairs of designer sunglasses to stop the glare from creating a burnout.

And if that was not enough, for the first time in years she knew she did not have to worry so much about her mother. Though she knew her mother would just freak if she had any idea she was wasting energy thinking and worrying about her. Having the chance of the best school had given Trisha a new focus and had helped her see things differently, which she knew would make her life so seriously better and of course, her mother's too one day.

Now everything had changed and the word worry could be stamped out of her mother's vocabulary. With Pat on the scene life had got seriously weird, but as long as he made everyone happy who was she to care if he was her father? Weirder things had happened.

This holiday and especially tonight had made Trisha realise just how much she loved her mother. In all her life she had never heard her giggle so much, which was such a scary sound, but what was even better it would make those pretentious snobs squirm.

Trisha giggled, said aloud, "Now that is cool!"

With a feeling of happiness she jumped of the bed, flung open her wardrobe and selected a tiny skirt and even tinier top. It was time to chill with fun time Ben.

"Wow," she squealed. How she would blow his mind with her latest spill on her weird and fabby life!

Chapter SIXTY ONE

As the cheap and the *special* champagne flowed and the food was delicately eaten at the Soiree, Frau Hecks sat on the Hoskins terrace thanks to the two kind gentlemen. She had implied they had bullied her to attend, but she had been delighted to have been escorted like a lady. She had enjoyed their attention, but was also enjoying the company, not everyone was rude like the hostess. In Frau Hecks opinion, Sheila Hoskins was ill mannered and uncouth. Jack Hoskins was as bad.

Peering through the throng of people her glare sought out Sheila and then she grinned as she turned her gaze to her glass; it was half full. She sipped at the now warm champagne. Sheila Hoskins deserved all she got with that awful sweaty man as a lazy, good for nothing husband. She tutted as the dry tasting liquid slid down her throat. She had no idea where the two handsome men had gone, but her glass was almost empty again. She stood up and looked towards the bar, saw Doreen and Pat talking, smiled and headed in their direction. She knew Mr Greenwood, had known him for a long time, in fact.

Placing her glass on the makeshift bar to her surprise Pat Greenwood filled it.

"Drink this Frau Hecks it is far better than the poor stuff being offered by the maids."

"*Danke*, you are kind." She smiled and raised her glass towards Pat, "*Prost.*" Taking a sip she smiled, "You are correct. Much better!" Turning to Doreen she asked, rather terse, "And where is the daughter?"

Bridling, expecting a tirade of words, Doreen was about to answer as tersely when the old lady patted her arm.

"She is beautiful? Ja? I too was beautiful once. It is hard for an old woman to remember when she was so young. Of course, I was much in love with my Hans, though we were discreet with our love when the dawn comes and the sun rises, *nein*?"

Doreen saw a glint of amusement in Frau Hecks' eyes and giggled. "Yes right, thanks."

Taking another sip of her champagne, Frau Hecks looked across at Pat and winked.

Nodding his head, Pat caught the joke.

Clutching her glass Frau Hecks beamed as she realised that these people were not that bad after all. "I leave you fine people, I talk with more guests."

Leaning forward, Pat topped up all three glasses. "Keep away from the maids and their bottles. There's plenty more here if you would like it."

Nodding her head with gratitude Frau Hecks thought she had not drunk this amount of champagne for years. Walking away she felt emotional and seeing a chair close by sat down. Placing the refilled glass to her mouth she felt the bubbles tingle her lips and at the same time a tear slipped down her face. Impatiently she brushed it away with her other hand. Swallowing a mouthful of champagne to push down a lump threatening to choke her, reminding herself she could not change the past, but wondered why it insisted on shadowing her these days. The pleasant couple she had talked earlier had told her how they had enjoyed a visit to Germany. They had even visited the town she had been born in, the same town her beloved Hans had also come from. All this talk had excited the shadows of the past making her feel even sadder. She took another sip to quell the emotions that were swimming close to the surface.

"Are you alright?" A rosy cheeked woman asked as she saw Frau Hecks wipe a tear away.

"I fine. I am being a silly old woman watching the couples enjoy the party." As if to dismiss the woman she took a drink from her glass. The last thing she wanted was people feeling sorry for her. With her glass almost empty, she sighed with relief as the woman drifted into the crowd.

She nodded as a couple sat down at the opposite side of the table and then promptly got back up and started to dance.

Looking around, she wondered where the two handsome men had gone, standing to see better she grabbed the arm of her chair; the terrace seemed uneven. Swaying slightly and through hazy vision she saw Carmen talking to her two escorts. Placing one foot in front of the other she realised that the Hoskins' terrace was not that well constructed and was making her sway. Trying to maintain her balance she held onto arms of the other guests as she gingerly threaded her way through the chatting groups until she stood in front of Carmen and the two men. A girlish smile spreading across her face she swayed, this time bumping into Simon and spilling the last drops of her champagne onto his shoes.

"*Entschuldigen, paardon*! dis terrace not correct."

Astonishment flashed across Simon's face.

Stooping down, Frau Hecks cried, "I clean shoes *nein* problem."

Before Simon could take hold of Frau Hecks, she tilted forward and as if in slow motion she slipped to the ground. Simon and Chicky swooped down swiftly lifting Frau Hecks back onto her feet.

Carmen grabbed a chair and in a concerned tone hissed. "Sit her down before everyone sees what is happening. How much has she had to drink?" Looking up at Simon and Chicky, explained, "She is on medication, new medication."

Lowering himself to look into Frau Hecks' eyes, her pupils dilated, Chicky gently enquired. "My, my, what have you been doing to get into this state? I turn my back for five minutes and you let your hair down."

Through bleary eyes, Frau Hecks stared at Chicky, "I eat something *schlect.*"

Patting Frau Hecks' hand, in an understanding tone he answered, "Of course you did."

Standing up he grimaced as he turned to Carmen and Simon and in a conspirator tone, whispered. "Ever likely she's been drinking that dreadful champagne. We need a glass of water."

“Leave it to me,” Simon said striding towards a maid.

Carmen turned to Chicky. “We should get her discreetly home the last person we want to see Frau Hecks like this is Sheila Hoskins. That woman has an arsenal of ammunition we certainly do not want to add more.”

Chicky grinned, somehow he did not think Sheila would be concerned about Frau Hecks’ delicate state, he had seen Mr Hoskins behaving oddly ever since Doreen’s friend had turned up. Casting his gaze around the party he saw no sign of Mrs Hoskins, Jack or the other woman. Quietly he said, “From what I’ve seen this evening, I think our hostess will have more to distract her than a tipsy Frau Hecks.”

A knowing smile crossed Carmen’s face, but she passed no comment.

As Chicky took hold of Frau Hecks’ hand, she looked up at his face and snapped. “Who you are? Why you take my hand?” Snatching her hand away, Frau Hecks tried to stand, swayed and fell onto Chicky. Grabbing hold of Frau Hecks, Chicky turned to Carmen who was holding on to Frau Hecks other arm. “I have to say she is the last person I would have thought we’d be putting to bed in a drunken state.”

Carmen nodded, but was unhappy as to why Frau Hecks had drunk so much knowing she was on medication. “I will stay with her in her villa until I know she is settled and okay,” she said, concern edging her tone and at the same time made a mental note to give more time to Frau Hecks to find out what was the real problem.

Simon, clutching a glass of water, followed.

Chapter SIXTY TWO

Bidding the last of her guests good night, Sheila strolled back into her villa and headed straight to the drinks cabinet. From the small chiller unit pulled out a bottle of vintage champagne. Not a drop of alcohol had passed her lips all night she had been far too busy making sure everything ran as smooth as silk. She could hear Jack in his bathroom and she had not the patience to wait for him to open the bottle, instead deftly managed the cork herself. As it emitted a pleasing pop, she poured the frothy liquid into a glass. Taking a good drink of the dry champagne congratulated herself that she had organised another splendid event. Had she not been wealthy and had needed to earn a crust or two, she could have had a highly successful career in organising events for discerning people like themselves. She would have turned the entertaining at home world upside down. She smiled at what might have been.

Sitting on one of her leather sofas, her feet comfortably placed on the matching foot stool, she had no doubts that everyone would be talking about her Soiree for a very long time. Sipping her champagne she believed her Soirees were almost as famous as the Queen's garden parties. And with this warm feeling flowing through her veins she picked up the bottle and topped up her glass. At this point she remembered seeing Jack talking with that friend of Doreen's. It was not his talking, but his expression, his body language, his attitude that told her he was up to something. Jack has been behaving odd of late. Nothing she could put her finger on, but odd nonetheless. It was at this point a ludicrous thought flitted through her mind that Jack was having an affair with the woman. Then laughing out loud she reasoned, what would he want with another woman, he had her? Anyway, he would never have the stamina.

Smiling at such a ridiculous idea, she shut the door on these thoughts and took another sip of her drink. Then chuckled at the behaviour of Frau Hecks, she knew they thought she had not seen her, but she had. Maybe now she would stop being such a pain in the backside. Recalling the scene when the boys and Carmen carried the worse for wear Frau Hecks home, her mind returned to Doreen's friend, Ginny and what she had said about hearing a lot about her. For goodness sake, she laughed out loud, everyone had heard a lot about her! But before she could take this thought any further Jack appeared looking like death warmed up shuffling towards her.

Staring up at him, her face showing contempt, she snapped, "No doubt you've been poorly in your bathroom, hardly surprising after all that whisky I saw you pour down your throat, disgusting!"

Jack glared at Sheila, he wanted to snarl at her but in light of what had happened during the evening with Ginny, he forced a smile and cooed, "It was a good evening. You organised probably one of the best Soirees ever."

Sheila preened and feeling important, trilled, "Oh Jack you say the…." Sheila's words hung in the air, gagging, Jack ran to his bathroom.

Tutting loudly, a frown replacing her smile, she drained her glass. Looking around saw the detritus of her party, but made no attempt to clear it up. That was what maids were for. She hoped the girls would be early in the morning. Nothing worse than wading through party leftovers all day and knowing her Jack, he would be gallivanting on his so called power walk. There would be no help from him. "In fact, I might surprise him and power walk behind him," she said to the silent room. Smiling at the idea, she topped up her champagne. "It would be nice to know he was not sitting drinking coffee and eating cake instead of trying to lose weight."

Chapter SIXTY THREE

Staring at the mess on the terrace the next morning, Sheila sighed with exasperation. She had expected the maids not only to be here, but to have the place spick and span by now. "This simply won't do," she muttered, shifting items from one table on to another. The sun dipped behind a white fluffy cloud and looking up Sheila smiled at the temporary respite from the blistering heat. Sitting herself down with a cafeteria of coffee and a couple of slices of toast, thickly spread with unsalted butter, she mulled over the events of the previous night. As she bit into her toast she heard Jack as he ambled his way onto the terrace. She was under no illusion that he would be able to stomach breakfast, but to her surprise he greeted her with a little too much enthusiasm.

"Good morning, dear wife and what have we for breakfast?" He cast his eyes around the leftovers of last night and winced. What a bloody fiasco the whole evening had been. He thought back to Ginny's appearance before remembering he had far more to worry about than just her turning up at Sheila's Soiree: Her condition for one.

Looking up at Jack, Sheila scoffed. "I've little time to be thinking about a fancy breakfast with all this debris around me. What with this heat," she flicked a fly away with her napkin, continued, "and all these dirty glasses and plates littering the place, what am I to do? Just go and make yourself some toast and there's enough coffee in this pot for you." Not encouraging any further conversation, Sheila looked around at the mess and to her disgust spied Cissie sitting on Frau Hecks' terrace drinking coffee of all things with the old woman! Indignant, she leapt up catching the table with her foot and spilling her coffee. Ignoring the extra mess she marched to the end of her terrace, placed her hands on her hips and glared hoping it would galvanise the maid to her senses and come running to get on with the cleaning.

Hearing the rattle of crockery, Sheila turned and saw Jack sit down at the table. Stomping over saw his meagre breakfast and rounded on him. "This is simply not good enough. Do you know that Cissie is wasting valuable time over at Frau Hecks'? And would you believe it, she is drinking coffee?"

Jack smiled. Sheila's irritation was music to his ears, whilst she was fretting over the maids she was not mithering at him, he needed to think.

"That Cissie can see I'm standing here on my terrace, you'd think she'd have the decency to acknowledge that I'm waiting for her. If she is not here in five minutes I'll go and ask her what her game is." Sheila pointed to the mess. "This all needs clearing and cleaning. I take it you did tell that feckless girl that we needed her here first thing this morning?"

Exasperated at his wife's carping Jack suddenly realised that with everything going on he had completely forgotten to speak to Cissie. He closed his eyes to try to give him the valuable few seconds needed to come up with an answer, with false bravado, replied, "I did not, you did. You said you were going to tell her."

Aghast, Sheila barked, "You mean to tell me you have not organised the clean and clear up? Do I have to do everything? *I organised* the entire event and you…" She stopped in mid sentence, her anger momentarily leaving her breathless.

Despite his inner turmoil, in a calm voice Jack added. "For goodness sake Sheila, it's not the end of the world, we can manage it together." He felt defeated at every turn.

Sheila snarled. "End of the world you say, end of the world? Well let me remind you, I do not do clearing and cleaning. I am not Doreen Wilkinson or that other what's her name scrubber friend of hers. I will go over and if necessary drag that Cissie back here to clean."

Not waiting for a response Sheila left Jack at the table nibbling his toast and strode across to Frau Hecks' terrace.

Jack wiped his brow and wondered if his heart and sanity would cope.

Chapter SIXTY FOUR

Sitting on her terrace wearing a dressing robe and a pair of very dark sunglasses, Frau Hecks looked fragile. Cissie sat nervously next to the unusually quiet woman. She had been called upon by Carmen to help where necessary. Noting Frau Hecks' empty coffee cup, she refilled it.

Frau Hecks nodded her thanks and lifted the black coffee to her mouth and sipped at the warm liquid.

Cissie watched, a smile hovering on her lips, Carmen had explained briefly what had happened the previous night. Saddened that Frau Hecks was a little worse for wear, Cissie was secretly pleased that the old lady had attended the Hoskins' Soiree. And despite often being at the end of Frau Hecks' barbed tongue, she had seen a gradual change in her over the last few months, a change she now realised had not been for the better. Cissie felt Frau Hecks needed to get involved more and mix with people.

"*Danke* dear for coming to meine home, but I be okay after my coffee. You have many things to do." Frau Hecks smiled at Cissie, then turning her gaze towards the Hoskins terrace, snapped, "That woman with her parties make me sick, terrible food."

Patting Frau Hecks' hand, Cissie nodded thinking of a suitable response when Sheila Hoskins' brusque voice shattered the morning peace.

"Do you know what time it is?" Sheila barked as she strutted on to Frau Hecks' terrace.

Startled at the unexpected appearance, Frau Hecks bristled. "Missus Hoskins what is so urgent you need to rush without invite on my terrace when I drink coffee? You do enough damage. Now leave."

Ignoring Frau Hecks' terse instruction, Sheila glared at Cissie. She had already decided that she was going to play ignorant about Jack not asking the maid for help. Turning her eyes to Frau Hecks, tried not to gloat, *she must think I fell off a Christmas tree sitting there like butter would not melt in her mouth,* she thought. With tongue in cheek she trilled, "I take it you had an excellent evening at my Soiree."

Despite wearing dark glasses, Frau Hecks' eyes flashed menacingly at Sheila Hoskins, but was determined not be drawn into *this* particular conversation. "What is so urgent you need to dash to my terrace?"

"It is not you I need to speak with, but this maid." Turning and with a smile as false as her long manicured nails, gritting her teeth to keep her tone level, Sheila hissed. "Cissie are you not supposed to be clearing and cleaning my terrace not sitting here drinking coffee and gossiping with an owner?"

Flushed with embarrassment Cissie jumped up, almost upending the table and in a subservient manner whispered, "I am so sorry Mrs Hoskins, but I don't remember you asking me to help."

Outraged at Sheila's rudeness, Frau Hecks slowly rose from her chair and in a brusque tone stated. "*Frau 'Oskins* you on *my* terrace, I will not have you speak to Cissie in this rude voice. You will be polite or you will go." She did not add that Cissie was here to help at Carmen's instructions. She had no intentions of discussing her private arrangements with this insufferable woman.

Looking at Frau Hecks' shaded eyes, unflinching, Sheila smiled. "You misunderstand, I am talking to Cissie she is responsible for cleaning my villa. Now if you don't mind I would like…"

Ignoring her aching head, Frau Hecks snapped. "I mind. I mind much. You will leave my property now or I will telephone the owner of entire Villa Bonitas and get you removed from here."

Jack hearing raised voices, aware feathers would likely fly with Sheila over at Frau Hecks, dropped his toast onto his plate and strode over to Frau Hecks terrace. About to call over as he neared his neighbour's terrace he collided with Bob wheeling a bin filled with plant clippings who chortled.

"Cor blimey, there's gonna be fisticuffs in a minute, best you get yourself in there, it's far too dangerous for me." He nodded his head in amusement towards where Sheila was standing before marching away leaving Jack to deal with the debacle.

Standing on the terrace, Jack was confronted with three expressions: Cissie embarrassed, Frau Hecks pale, thin lipped and angry and his wife with her eyes blazing with annoyance.

In a placating tone he stuttered, "Good morning Frau Hecks, I am sorry Sheila has interrupted your breakfast with Cissie, but it seems there has been a little misunderstanding."

Looking Jack in the eye Frau Hecks sniffed, "Misunderstanding! Pah, you should know more than most."

Jack gulped as he glared at Frau Hecks not sure what to make of her comment, but decided to ignore it. He was here to sort out the maid business. Why was everything such a bloody mess? All he wanted was to get away. Preferably far away!

Fiddling with his handkerchief in his trouser pocket he turned to Cissie and in a pleading tone asked, "Cissie is there any possibility that you and one of your colleagues might have time to help with the cleaning up from our do last night? Of course, I will pay you a bonus." He pulled out his wallet and produced several notes. "Please take these." He laid the money on to the table and sighed inwardly. He wished Sheila had handled things better. If for nothing else then he would not be begging and bribing for help. Placing his index finger on the notes, added, "I for one would be very grateful."

Cissie embarrassed looked up at Jack then across at Sheila, in a gush of nerves replied, "Yes, of course I'll help. But you don't need to pay me all that money." She said as she stared down at the notes laying on the table.

Desperate to get away, Jack sucked through his teeth in an attempt to stay calm. Then smiling, "We want to pay you this extra, there's clearly a mix up with communications." He shot a glance at Sheila, "So please take it. And whenever you are free go on over and do what you can to make the place tidy." He would have liked to have added, the bonus is danger money for having to deal with our Sheila, but resisted.

Cissie almost curtseyed as she thanked Jack, "I'll be there as soon as I can."

"Perfect. Cissie. Perfect." Relieved he had sorted it all out without bloodshed he forgot himself, stepped forward and gave the young maid a bear style hug.

Cissie cringed as Jack released her. Thanking her once again, Jack turned to Frau Hecks, "Sorry for the intrusion. I really am."

He did not wait for a response, but turned on his heels and marched away.

With a look that could destroy an army Sheila glared at Frau Hecks then at Cissie before snapping, "I'd like to see you there in five minutes." Striding away, added, "I'm counting."

Watching Sheila leave, Frau Hecks snarled. "Pah. She is a despicable woman. Finish your coffee, she wait."

Chapter SIXTY FIVE

Smarting from Jack's outlandish show of extravagance at paying that silly maid such a large sum of money, Sheila headed back to her villa. Pulling a face she made the sinews in her neck expand. She muttered angrily, "At the end of the day, the girl is only going to clean, not rebuild the place. Jack is next to useless."

She stopped, placed her hands on her hips and with added annoyance watched as Jack marched off towards the main gates. A sardonic smile twisted her lips. She would definitely do what she had promised herself and follow him. She would catch him out. "Power walking my foot," she scoffed. "I'll fix his little games!" If he thinks he can pull the wool over my eyes, he has another think coming.

Striding towards the gates, comfortable trainers on her feet, a note left for Cissie to make sure she cleared and cleaned properly Sheila adjusted the peak on her sun visor and looked across at the blue calm ocean. She noted a few swimmers enjoying their morning dip, then turning left set her pace and headed down The Avenue. The route she guessed Jack would have taken. She nodded at the runners who passed her by, dodged a couple of cyclists and was almost mowed down by a woman motoring towards her on roller blades.

"Goodness," she cried almost losing her footing. Modern fangled things, she could never understand anyone in their right mind strapping wheels to their feet.

Approaching the Old Square she saw a limousine pull into a lay by a few metres ahead. To her surprise, Pat Greenwood alighted from the passenger side. Quickening her step she arrived at the passenger door at the same time as Pat stepped onto the pavement.

Cocking an eyebrow, she grinned, "Good grief what are you doing in that expensive car?"

Seeing Sheila Hoskins and with a proud smile lighting his face, Pat replied. "You noticed it then?"

Confused, but not about to miss this opportunity to unearth this fraudster who was surely after Doreen Wilkinson's money, Sheila added. "Noticed? How could anyone but notice a car of this quality? But my question is what are *you* doing in it?" She was not going to be put off with a friendly smile.

"Surprised you have I? Well here is another one.The car," he pointed at the long elegant white limousine, "belongs to me. And further more, I don't drive it, my chauffeur does!"

Sheila snorted, "If you say so, I believe you, though thousands wouldn't. But I tell you what I think. I think you are working some sort of con scam. Doreen Wilkinson might have fallen for it, but I have not."

Staring at Sheila, Pat could not make up his mind whether it was natural for her to be so incredibly rude or she had made an art out of it. But there was no doubt in his mind, whichever it was, he guessed she enjoyed every second of making people feel small and worthless.

"Well, we are all entitled to our silly opinions," Pat retorted. He turned his back on her, leant into the car and said, "I'll see you later, Brian. Give me about an hour?"

He shut the door and the car drove away.

Pat nodded ungraciously at Sheila. "If you would excuse me, I have important people to meet." He nodded again and walked off towards the pedestrian are of the Old Square. Inside he was furious! How dare she? How *dare* she!

Sheila stared after him, saw him stop at a table briefly, say something then move on to another unoccupied table at the far side of the Square.

Sheila's mouth dropped open at who she saw sitting at the table, it was that Ginny whatever her name was! She sauntered over, as if by surprise declared, "Ginny! Fancy seeing you here? We did not get much chance to say anything last night. May I join you?"

She did not wait for an answer. There was a coffee pot and two cups on the table. It had not taken Sheila long to work out that Ginny was waiting for a friend. And who was that friend? she asked herself.

"I was racking my brain last night," she said poring coffee into the empty cup. "May I? So kind.... as to where I had seen you before and of course, it is here." She obligingly topped up Ginny's coffee. "And I have been wondering about other things as well. I think I now have the full picture."

The colour drained from Ginny's face her mind falling into panic. Sheila knew!

It had been a mistake saying she would meet Jack here, but he had telephoned early this morning and insisted on seeing her. The last thing she wanted was him in her apartment. Now sitting here with two cups of coffee and listening to Sheila's silky, but sarcastic voice, Ginny wondered if the woman was playing a game with her saying nice and horrible things in the same sentence.

As these thoughts raced through her head she glimpsed Jack emerging from the toilet area behind Sheila. To her relief, he spun on his heel and all but ran away.

"Oh yes," Sheila went on, "I see what you are both up to. I was not born yesterday. I have seen you both here several times. You think between you that you can destroy someone's life by playing your evil little game of deception, but I assure you, you cannot." She put the cup down, pointed to it. "I have just seen him you see. I know perfectly well why you came to gate crash my Soiree last night and what he is doing! Oh yes, I have worked that out as well." She stood up and smirked at Ginny, "You will not get away with it you know. I will personally see to it that the both of you are stopped."

Sheila tossed her head and strode across the Square, stopped at Pat Greenwood's table. "I know," she said, I know exactly what you and that trollop are up to." She walked a few paces then strode back. "And perhaps you ought to know, or perhaps you already do, your girlfriend is pregnant. I can tell it a mile off." Nose in the air, she strutted away.

What the blazes is the woman on about? Pat Greenwood wondered. He had to set the puzzle aside, however, as the man he was meeting was coming towards him.

She knows, Ginny thought hearing Sheila snap at Pat. *How does she know? Has he told her*?

A look of disgust flashed across Sheila's face as she left the Square and headed back to the villa. Those two thieves had certainly taken Doreen for a ride between them! Old friends indeed! Huh! Poor Doreen what a snake Pat Greenwood was. It was obvious that the pair of them had planned this elaborate con trick between them. Pretend to meet by chance, Greenwood would get Doreen's attention, Ginny would get her sympathy. Sheila wondered if she had told Doreen about the baby yet. How long before they conned the silly woman out of all her money?

Seeing that clouds were gathering in the sky, Sheila quickened her pace. They were in for a storm, by the look of it and not only one up there, but down here too!

Nearing Villas Bonitas she broke into a sedate jog. The wind was getting up, the last thing she needed was to be caught in a rain squall. She smiled as she tapped the security code into the electronic gates. The squall she intended to stir between Miss Fink Fought and her so called friends was a different matter entirely!

Chapter SIXTY SIX

In the shadow of the arch that divided the open Square from the covered shopping areas, Jack had watched Sheila sitting with Ginny. Agitated he had wondered what they were talking about. Sheila was in control of the conversation. She always was. She tried to control everything and everyone. Had it not been for how much he would lose he would have left her years ago. Their love had started its decline at the same time as their bank balance had started to climb. It was as if the thousands, that very soon became millions, had stripped away the part of a couple that bound them together through thick or thin. Money had changed Sheila. She had always been a little full of herself, but nothing compared to what she had now become. He flinched at the way she talked to people and he had spent more time than he cared to add up apologising for her tongue. Meeting Ginny had made him feel like a new man. He'd had other affairs, but this one had lasted the longest. He had even bought her that apartment, a little gift two Christmas's ago. She had secretly joined him a couple of months ago when he had a week in Paris without Sheila in tow and she had visited him in the UK more than once over the last six months. Not once had Sheila suspected a thing so wrapped up in her world of keeping up her appearance.

Staring over at his wife and his mistress Jack could see all too clearly that all his nightmares had come at once. No amount of snapping his fingers or pinching his fat was going to wake him up him from this mess. Even as he stood in the shadows, he realised that the proverbial had hit the fan. If he was to survive and still have the use of his limbs and faculties at the end of it all he had better sort out a survival plan. Wiping his brow with his linen handkerchief, he knew he was in a mess.

As Sheila got up, he scuttled deeper into the shadows. Even from this distance he could see a look of disgust on her face as she left Ginny in tears. He caught his breath! Oh God she was coming his way! Where to hide…? Then Sheila paused at Pat Greenwood's table. It had amazed Jack that Sheila appeared to not know who the man was, but then why should she? She was always too busy with her own silly world to take notice of the real things.

To his relief, after she had said something to Greenwood she moved off head high and purposeful in a different direction. Jack watched her go until he lost sight of her. When he looked back at where Ginny had been sitting, saw that she had gone and caught sight of her about to enter her apartment door.

Seeing Ginny so upset disturbed him more than he could ever have imagined. Irrationally he reasoned if tears were all he would have to mop up then he would make amends to her. But even as he grinned at his own flippancy, he knew it was going to be his blood that would need mopping up. Sheila would not only take her pound of flesh, but bleed him dry into the bargain.

Moving out of the shadows, with a step that belied his inner turmoil, he thought he had better go to Ginny, start sorting things out once and for all.

As he passed Pat Greenwood's table, Pat stopped him.

"Hello Jack, you're here as well? I've just seen your wife. She's certainly one for surprises isn't she? I have no idea what she was talking about though, something to do with my girlfriend being pregnant? Is she drunk again maybe? Or maybe she's got her men muddled up?"

Pat chuckled to himself as Jack hurried away his words had Jack Hoskins turning as white as a sheet.

"That was Jack Hoskins, was it not?" the man sitting with Pat said.

"Yes Miles," Pat answered, "it was. One of the most stupid men I have ever met." He waved suddenly, smiled. "But here comes the exact opposite, one of the most intelligent. What do you think of him?"

Miles Griffin answered without hesitation. "Pat, if you want the honest truth, I think he is wonderful. I could not have found a better man to make my proposal to."

Simon smiled warmly as he held his hand out to Pat. "Mr Greenwood, thank you for arranging all this." He smiled at Miles and sat down.

"Have you decided?" Miles asked, leaning across the table and touching Simon's arm. "I will quite understand if you say no, but I so really hope you do not."

Simon took a deep breath. "The answer is yes. Yes I want to go ahead. It's the right thing for me. For my future." As he spoke the words, he was crying inside, the right thing for him, but what about for Chicky?

"Ginny!" Jack caught her up as she was half way up the stairs to the first floor. "Ginny, we've a few things to sort out."

Despite her tears, Ginny smiled. "Only you could understate the situation, Jack."

Shaking his head, he took in the tearful eyes and yet she still managed to smile at him. How could he let her go?

Saying nothing more, Ginny walked up the last few stairs, put the key in the lock and opened the door. Stepped inside, Jack close behind, the door safely shut, she said, "She knows about us and she also knows I'm pregnant."

Jack closed his eyes as if by doing so everything would disappear and Ginny would not exist, he would not be here and he would not have to go back and face Sheila. But that was not going to happen. He opened his eyes and looked at Ginny. She did not deserve this. He had always told himself that he had the best of everything, wealth, a wife, a daughter and a beautiful mistress, who could ask for more? But he could. He was always asking for more.

Peering down at Ginny, he asked himself how could he just let her go and loose her from his life for ever? They had been fantastic lovers, naughty and dangerous, but underneath all the excitement, he not only cared for her, but he now realised how much he loved her. And knowing what they were creating together, it was as if for the first time in their long relationship, he realised he could not live without her.

With these thoughts racing through his head he took hold of her cold, trembling hands.

"What a mess we've got ourselves in." He squeezed her hands and smiled. "You know I'm a married middle age man, thicker around the waist than I should be, a bit loud at times, well most of the time when I come to think of it."

Smiling, her nose running from her tears Ginny interrupted, "Jack, my world is falling apart and you stand there talking rubbish."

Chuckling, Jack winked, "No change there then."

Removing her hands from his hold, she wiped her face with a paper napkin then looking at him, asked herself, "*How on earth did I fall for this silly man*?"

"Ginny," Jack said, "It looks like Sheila knows everything so I'd better get back, but I promise you I will return later. Please, Ginny, don't worry about anything because no matter what, I intend to see you and our baby all right. I just hope you'll let me. Mind, I might not have as many millions to treat you with because Sheila will want it all and…" he looked down at her belly, "and you won't need to worry about another accident because Sheila will have my bits and bobs dangling from a lamp post before the day is out."

Despite the situation, they both laughed.

Chapter SIXTY SEVEN

The morning had the familiar pattern that he had come to expect these last few, blissful, days. The sun was shining, the air redolent with exotic fragrances and he was in love. Although this morning, Chicky realised there were clouds building in the sky and he had niggling doubts about Simon's feelings. One moment they would be making passionate love and then, like now, he would be alone as Simon went of on another mystery mission. Or was it a mystery lover?

An unhappy frown crossed his face, he did not want to entertain such a thought but he had felt the stirrings of jealousy too often since they had arrived here. Stepping back onto his terrace after visiting Frau Hecks to make sure she was okay, he had been delighted to find that she suffered from nothing more than a terrible headache. He half hoped to find Simon sitting there stretched out on a lounger in the sun. He was not. Where was he? Who was he with?

Hearing rapid footsteps approaching he swung round in the hope it was Simon, but to his disappointment saw Sheila panting and perspiring.

"Morning Mrs H are you walking off that wonderful Soiree of yours?"

Breathless with the exertion of her dash from the Old Square, Sheila puffed. "What a walk I've had this morning, you'll never believe just how beneficial brisk exercise can be." Throwing her head back she took a deep breath and let the air whistle through her lips before continuing. "Having organised such a successful Soiree last night you need to work it out of your system. And, believe you me," a sly smile reached her lips, "There's a lot to be worked out." She cast a knowing glance at Doreen Wilkinson's villa, nodding her head before returning her attention back to Chicky, cryptically said, "Surprises around every corner."

She would love to tell this handsome barrister all she had learnt because she was bursting to tell someone. But even she realised that she needed to talk to Doreen first. Dim and dizzy, Miss Fink Fought may be, but she deserved to be told straight from the horse's mouth that she was about to be made penniless. And, as she was the one to have unearthed Pat Greenwood and that Ginny's whatever her name was, little game, she deserved to see Doreen's face when she told her what she knew. She could not wait.

Praising herself for being so right with a self gratification blush to her cheeks, added. "Now I've got my breath back, I can get to work on what really needs to be done. I'm one of the best organisers you'll ever meet and I've got something very important to organise. So I'm not going to waste yours or my time in asking because I know you did, enjoy my Soiree that is. You're educated so it's a foregone conclusion." With this said she waved at Chicky and grinning like a cat who'd had the cream, marched off to her villa.

Chicky shook his head. "Whatever was she talking about?"

Chapter SIXTY EIGHT

To Sheila's great disappointment, Doreen was not in. Picking the phone up in her villa, bursting to talk to someone, she pressed the speed dial for her daughter's number. She had already been to Doreen's villa, but to her frustration was told she was out. She had not left any message, that Trisha girl had answered the door and for the life of her she could not understand a word she had uttered, something about her Mama kitting and fitting?

The sound of ringing at the other end stopped her thoughts and hearing Michelle's voice she cheerfully chirped, "Hello darling, it's mummy…Damn that blasted answer phone thing, it sounds so real," she muttered not too happily.

Impatiently she waited for the beeps, then left a message: "Hello Michelle, it's mummy again, I tried calling you yesterday, but got this confounded thing. Today I'm trying again as I do need to say hello and I've lots to tell you about last night's Soiree. On top of that we've got a lottery winner here. Can you believe it? Anyway you will remember I told you about her the other day. And I can tell you, what I'm about to reveal will shock... " *Beep*! The beep cut Sheila off in mid sentence.

"Damn it," she slammed the phone down onto the unit. She had so much to tell her daughter. "It's about time she put in a decent size tape," she growled, as Jack marched into the villa.

She glowered at him. "Jack, I cannot get hold of our daughter, I have so much to tell her." Seeing his expression was clearly flustered she ignored it and continued. "Can you imagine anyone having such a busy life that they cannot answer the phone? Just what does she do, I'd ring her on her mobile, but I can never hear what she is saying. Never mind, now that you're here, we need to talk."

With a cold stare, Jack looked at Sheila and despite feeling confident at how he was going to explain everything to her, decided a dash of extra courage would not be wasted, striding over to the drinks cabinet he poured a large whisky.

Far more interested in what she had to say than making a fuss over Jack's excessive drinking cooed. "You are never going to believe what I've learnt today Jack. Never!"

Jack opened his mouth to try and explain, but Sheila sailed on, "That Ginny whoever, the one who was uninvited to our Soiree last night, well I know why she was here. The little strumpet is trying to con Fink Fought next door out of her money and is having an affair and she's pregnant. Now what do you say to that."

It was a statement not a question, but Jack had not realised and opened his mouth to respond but Sheila cut him off.

"It gets better, I know who she's having her sordid affair with. Oh yes Jack. Little escapes me as you well know."

Jack gulped his whisky down in one shot.

"I knew from the moment I clapped my eyes on him he was no good, but would that madam lottery winner listen? No of course she wouldn't. But believe you me she will when I get hold of her because I saw him with my own two eyes. He must think I was born yesterday. She might be a bimbo, but …"

Jack poured himself another whisky. "What on earth are you talking about?" he managed to say.

"I'm telling you. That Pat Greenwood is having an affair with Ginny Strumpet. He has made her pregnant and they are going to con Miss F.F. out of all her money and…"

Jack stared at his wife. He could not believe the nonsense coming out of her mouth. No matter what happened, he was not having that poor Doreen or Pat Greenwood caught up in his mess. Because as sure as eggs were eggs, Sheila with her twisted facts would cause untold pain and sorrow, not to mention humiliation to all involved.

He braced himself. “Sheila, you are talking utter shite. Shut up and sit down.”

The shock of Jack’s loud voice stopped Sheila in mid sentence.

“Don’t you ever stop bad mouthing people?” He spat. “Let me tell you something you really don’t know. And maybe for once in your life you will actually listen.” He gulped at his whisky. “The only person Ginny Solomon is having an affair with and a baby with is me. And before you ask, it’s been going on for years. I happen to love her.”

He heard Sheila take a sudden intake of breath, but did not wait to hear her say anything. He plonked his glass on the nearest table, nodded his head once and stamped out of the villa.

Sheila stood there, speechless.

Chapter SIXTY NINE

Seeing Jack march down the pathway, Chicky decided rather than sit around watching life pass him by at Villas Bonitas he ought to take a walk himself. Simon had said he would not be back until one-ish. He had not answered beyond, "Just popping into town," when he had asked where he was going.

It was nearly noon, not a good time to be out walking, but the heat was sultry, the air cloying and there was a sharp wind blowing through the palm trees, making the fronds rattle and rustle. It would be cool on the beach, perhaps?

He had always liked the beach. The soft sand underfoot, the ripple of the sea as it gently crept along the shoreline. Maybe he would even take a swim in the surf and maybe, he would stop feeling he was about to lose the man he loved.

With his beach bag slung over his shoulder Chicky meandered through Villas Bonitas, his mind replaying the wonderful week they'd had at this amazing place. It had been an unbelievable experience and in two days they would be back on the plane to reality. And perhaps, he thought gloomily, solitary loneliness.

Negotiating the last few steps he stood on the beach and looked at the sea. He kicked at the sand feeling the sadness of leaving this wonderful paradise behind and the thought of what awaited him after the holiday.

"Excuse me?"

Chicky frowned, he had not seen the young man who had been taking Doreen's daughter out approach.

"May I come past?" the boy asked. "I need to go up."

"Sorry," cried Chicky as he stepped aside. "I was miles away. I've seen you at Villas Bonitas haven't I?"

"Not as an owner, my granddad, Bob Preston works there and I've had the pleasure of seeing one of the girls staying there." Ben thrust his hands into his baggy beach shorts' pockets. "She'll be leaving in a few days though. I don't want her to go." He paused, realised he should introduce himself. "I'm Ben by the way," but he did not extend his hand, just kicked at the sand.

Chicky did not miss the resigned tone. "I'm Christopher, but everyone calls me Chicky. I'm not an owner either." He half smiled, "I'm simply having a wonderful holiday. Well I think I am. I'm supposed to be." He shrugged. "Love isn't always easy is it?"

Ben gazed out to sea, the clouds were building on the horizon, they could be in for a bit of a storm, though it might not come to much, maybe a rumble or two of thunder, a sharp heavy downpour then the sun would be out again. He noted several people in the water. A couple had swam further out than he was comfortable about. "If that storm blows up worse," he said, nodding towards the blackening clouds, "the sea could get a bit rough. I'm a part time lifeguard. I'm off duty, but I ought to be offering to help warn those people." He made no move to do so though. Then with a shrug of the shoulders added, "Living here has its ups and downs. You can love them and leave them. You get the best of both worlds with holiday romances. Great fun, great..." He looked at Chicky, his expression far from indicating 'great'. "Let's just say there's plenty on offer. Nothing heavy, nothing serious, good old fashioned lust, they go home and another crowd arrive." Shoving his hands deeper into his pockets, added, "But sometimes it's different."

"Living here certainly has plenty going for it when you put it like that." Chicky looked around. The beach was not overcrowded, dotted around where sun loungers shaded with tropical style parasols. Several had couples sprawled on them, most of the women were topless. The wind was getting up, whipping the sand into tiny little whirlwinds. Further along the beach he noted the lifeguard station, a young man and girl stood with binoculars slung around their necks, their gaze fixed on the water. Turning his attention to the sparkling blue sea, he smiled. It looked inviting, maybe he would dip his toes in. "I can see why a young man would be happy living here," he said. "Plenty of freedom, no commitments, time to work out what you wanted or even who you wanted."

Ben shrugged, "Freedom, like everything, has a price but sometimes you meet someone who you *know* is the one you want to be with and not just for a holiday, but forever. I've found that person and I would give up my freedom, give up all this if I thought for one moment she would have me. I am so out of her league. I'm a student and a life guard, hardly holds a candle to what *she* has."

"I think you might be surprised," Chicky answered after a short, thoughtful silence. "Perhaps you should stop brooding and worrying and just come out with it. Propose. See what the answer is. What have you to lose, except for your dignity?"

Another silence. The wind ruffled through their hair then raced off up the beach to rattle at a few of the sunshades.

"You're right," Ben finally answered, "but it's not my dignity I'm bothered about. It's my heart."

"I know exactly what you mean." Chicky muttered. "I've found the best person in the world, but how do you let them know that without getting hurt if they don't feel the same?" Admitted, "Rejection is not something I'm good at."

"Well," Ben said, "I've got to go. I should be revising for my exams, I've done very little since meeting Trisha, but I promised to help Carmen with something first. If you stay on the beach, keep an eye on those clouds and thanks for the chat. Bye." Ben hurried on up the steps.

Taking off his sandals and slowly stepping through the sand towards the foaming surf, Chicky stopped as the water lapped against his toes. He glanced back at Ben who was almost at the top of the ascent now about to reach the gateway. "Good luck, mate," he murmured, "I hope it works out for you."

He paddled further into the water until the warm waves licked at his calves. *Come on Chicky pull yourself together,* he scolded himself. The scenery here was truly beautiful: The sand, sea, palm trees and lush green vegetation and brilliantly coloured exotic flowers. Over to the right he looked on at the town with its white walls, red tiled roofs and the turrets of the buildings in the Old Square. Behind him on the beach a family group were gathering their things together as the wind increased. Chicky laughed as the man let go of a towel and it was immediately snatched and blown away off up the beach. One of the little girls ran after it. There was a man walking along the beach, smart trousers rolled up, his jacket flung over his shoulder, shoes in his hand. Chicky would recognise him anywhere. Simon.

Simon saw Chicky paddling in the white foamed surf and waved, but received only a half wave back. "I love him so much," Simon whispered to the wind as he waved again. "How could I spoil it all because someone else tempted me?" Walking towards Chicky, his thoughts tumbling around his head, he silently cried, "I am going to have to tell him. Come clean. I can't go on like this, he deserves to know."

Chapter SEVENTY

She heard the knock on the door and at the same time her phone rang. Sheila could not believe it of all the times people wanted to talk to her, but at this moment she did not want to speak to anyone. Her mind was still trying to take in what Jack had told her before he had marched out of the villa. She needed time to digest everything, but the phone continued to ring and the knock came again. Looking at the phone then across towards the door, it was if by doing this she hoped they would answer themselves, but that was not going to happen and she had to answer one or both. As she reached out to pick up the phone, it stopped. The knock sounded again.

Wearily opening the door Sheila winced, her first reaction was how mean life could be.

"Sorry to disturb you, but my girl said something about you wanted a word? Well if it was to do with your do last night. We loved it, thanks."

Staring at Doreen, Sheila did not know whether to laugh or cry. Only someone as dizzy as Miss Fink Fought could stand on her doorstep giggling when she herself was on the brink of a breakdown: mentally, physically and matrimonially.

Feeling the outside hot air brush through into the cool villa, Sheila snapped, "I suppose you have come to gloat."

With a look of incomprehension, Doreen giggled nervously. "I suppose I have because I can tell you I could never organise a party like you did. It was the bees knees and everything."

As a tiny green butterfly hovered around Doreen's left shoulder; Sheila could not help wondering how Doreen Wilkinson had the wherewithal to count enough x's to scrawl on that winning lottery ticket. If she did not feel so devastated she would laugh out loud. Instead, against all her instincts said, "I think it best you come in and have a large drink with me."

Taken aback at the invitation Doreen hovered for a second, but as Sheila stood to one side, stepped into the Hoskins' cool villa.

"Thanks. I could do with a cup of tea actually, but they don't seem to do a good English cuppa over here do they. Don't suppose you've got any Rosie Lee have you? Me feet are killing me. I was out shopping when you came over. Things you've got to have on holiday. Pat says it's all part of the game. I'm never going to get used to it."

"I have only decaffeinated coffee. I am having a brandy, will that do?" She had no intention of sharing her Earl Grey tea and with heavy steps she padded over to her drinks cabinet and poured two obscenely large drinks, at the same time closed her ears to Doreen's scratchy voice. She was now wondering why she had invited her in and could only surmise it was because she did not want to be alone. But of all the people to knock on her door, how desperate she must be! Never mind, she sighed resignedly, the wretched woman was here now.

Carrying the drinks over to where Doreen had settled herself on one of her soft leather sofas, stared through her open patio doors and could just make out that Cissie was hob nobbing with some smartly dressed person from one of the other villas. The world had gone crazy; the common becoming rich, maids rubbing shoulders with the well heeled and worst of all, her Jack playing around with some tart. She wanted to scream and throw things, she even wanted to hurt someone, but to her utter shame she suddenly broke down and wept. Not a silent mewl, but a full sobbing wail that shook her body uncontrollably.

Embarrassed, Doreen had no idea what to do. She could never have imagined this sharp tongued woman, who appeared always to be in control, having any emotions beyond conceited arrogance, let alone sobbing like a fountain here in front of her.

Unsure whether to put her arm round Sheila's shoulder and comfort her in some way or just keep quiet, spying a box of tissues on one of the tables handed it to Sheila. "Here, use these things."

"Th…th…thank you," Sheila sniffed through the tears. "

It did occur to Doreen that maybe Sheila had found out about Jack and Ginny, but she didn't like to say anything in case this was all over something highly important like the wrong type of brandy in the glass. If it *was* Ginny…And all the time behaving like she was the cat's whiskers! It seemed Sheila Hoskins, after all, was no different to any one else. *Rich people*, she thought to herself, *are no different to poor people. Maybe all that money makes it easier to hide these things*.

Putting down her untouched drink onto the coffee table Doreen wrapped her arms around Sheila's shaking shoulder. "Come on girl, what ever it is it isn't worth getting in such a state about. I'm not being nosey, but if you want to talk, my ears are open and me mouth is shut."

Sniffing, blowing her nose on a tissue, Sheila looked at Doreen and could not believe that someone like Miss Fink Fought would be kind enough to say that to her. All the time she had been more than happy to show Doreen up and make her look ridiculous, and now, here she was offering genuine comfort and help. *Is nothing what it seems anymore,* she asked herself? "It's Jack and that friend of yours, Ginny…" More tears welled with a fresh sob.

Doreen squeezed Sheila's hand. "I wondered," she said truthfully. "I'm afraid Ginny always was one for the fellers. I suspected her of having a fling with my Pat once."

For some reason this statement renewed Sheila's sobbing.

The phone ringing startled both women. Thankful for the diversion, Doreen answered it. "Hello? Yes, this is Mrs 'Hoskins house. Yes she's here." she placed her hand over the mouth piece. "It's your daughter and wants to talk with you. Do you want me to explain or what?"

Sheila gulped, held out her hand for the telephone. “No, no I want to talk to her.”

Doreen handed the phone over and was uncertain whether to stay or not. She would help if Sheila wanted her to. She had helped countless neighbours and friends in the past when their men had either got their leg over the local tart or simply legged it. She had never got any thanks, not that she wanted them, but she did not want a thick lip either, especially as they often changed their minds and fell in love again. Sheila was not exactly the sort of person she wanted to help though.

“I’ll leave you to chat with her then. I’m only next door if you want me.” She patted Sheila’s arm compassionately.

“Yes. Yes thank you. You have been most kind.” She could barely comprehend that she was thanking the one person she would never have imagined would offer comfort.

“My pleasure. Things will sort themselves out. These things always do. Believe me. Ta rah then.”

Sheila heard the front door open, then her daughter’s voice from the telephone.

“Oh Michelle, you will never believe…. What? No that wasn’t the maid it was Miss Fink… the woman from next door… Yes the lottery woman. Oh Michelle, what am I to do? It’s Daddy. He’s having an affair and a baby.”

Chapter SEVENTY ONE

Carmen checked her list again. A smile ran across her face, everything had been covered. The surprise party for Bob's birthday was almost complete. The only thing remaining to do was to inform the residents and guests. This she had planned to do as soon as she had spoken with Antonio. She was aware it was short notice, but surprises, she reminded herself, had to be done at short notice. Bob Preston's life had been a long way from the privileged existence of the people who visited Villas Bonitas and Carmen knew many owners would be delighted at what had been organised.

Her worry was those gathering clouds which could turn into an unpleasant storm, although this time of year a downpour did not usually last long. Better to have the rain today rather than tomorrow evening. She would have to have the lounger cushions brought under cover in a minute and the sun umbrellas closed as the wind was getting strong. Antonio would probably shut the bar as well.

Hearing laughter coming from the swimming pool, she smiled. She would soon have to warn the bathers of the weather.

She had organised a catering company to supply fancy dress costumes for the party and they had agreed to personally deal with each guest. So far it had all proved to be straightforward. Of course the real test would be tomorrow night and how well the secret had been kept from Bob. She grimaced at how Bob might react, but dismissed any doubts. He liked a good laugh.

Striding away from her office, Carmen glimpsed Cissie talking to the dapper owner of twenty five. At the poolside, Bob with his reading glasses perched on the end of his nose was looking at a hand held electronic meter for checking the water quality. The meter was new. He loved gadgets and gismos. She smiled and was sure Bob had carried out the same check only an hour ago. She saw him look up and frown at the rapidly blackening sky and knew he would start battening down the hatches for her. She had yet to tell him that he would be on chauffeuring duty for most of tomorrow, the only way she could keep him away from Villas Bonitas. The afternoon was needed for the caterers and the costume company to have free rein around the place. Pat had agreed that he would take him as his driver, explaining his own was unable to drive due to personal commitments. She chuckled at her deceit. The plan was a simple one: a fancy dress party with plenty of food served buffet style. She had even ordered jellies, having heard him once moan about the lack of jelly as a boy. He would get his share at this party! Grinning, Carmen knew only too well Bob would be mortified if he had an idea of what was afoot, but Ben had assured her he would feel honoured that people cared. Ben was a good lad; he was young and youthful, but his heart was in the right place. He was in her office now checking the catering list.

She only wished everything else was that simple. Frau Hecks was not well, not just suffering a hangover. Her visit earlier had been unproductive though. Frau Hecks was adamant that Sheila Hoskins had poisoned her. Carmen had tried to explain that the new medication she was on was not compatible with alcohol of any sort. She should even be careful of a glass of sherry.

Bringing the Hoskins' name to mind, reminded Carmen that she had seen Doreen leave the Hoskins' villa a short while ago. She suspected trouble, because she had also seen Jack march out as if all the hounds of hell were on his heels. Which, knowing what he had been up to with Ginny Solomon, they probably were! But, the fact that Doreen appeared to be involved, was strange.

Hearing Antonio's voice, she turned and waved then smiled as he pointed that he was on the phone.

"Well that's about it, all done now," he said as he snapped his mobile shut. "The extra champagne is ordered and I've asked for a few bottles of the non alcoholic sparkling wine as well." He winked. "It was the good stuff you wanted? Not the Hoskins' Special Economy?"

"Don't go there" Carmen pleaded with a smile. "Ben's got his grandfather all sorted, so hopefully there will be nothing to worry about tomorrow."

"Careful," Antonio retorted, "you know what they say about famous last words."

With a sceptical look at the darkening sky Carmen nodded.

"Let's just have faith and keep everything crossed".

Chapter SEVENTY TWO

Strolling back into her villa, her mind distracted with Sheila's crisis, Doreen was surprised to find Trisha reading a brochure.

"My my things are looking up, you reading on holiday! Normally you've got them music things stuck in your ears."

"Gin Palace, Baby Doll."

"Beg your pardon, Trish?"

Blinking her large dark eyes, Trisha stared at her mother then laughed. "Mama, *Gin Palace*, and *Baby Doll* it's the name! I'm checking out on Pat's, *Papa's,* cool cruiser. It is a seriously scary floater. We are going to have such a brill time chilling on that deck or even decks. I think there is more than one! And it seems he's named it after you."

Doreen leaned over and looked at the brochure and smiled, but stayed silent, hearing her daughter talk about Pat in such a lovely way made her heart swell with pride. She now realised that she had won the real lottery all those years ago when she had given birth to her little girl. Nothing would change the way she loved her Trisha. She smiled at her good luck and happiness, so lost in thought she did not hear Pat step into the villa and creep up behind. Only when he placed his arms around her was she startled.

"A penny for them Doll?"

Giggling, Doreen turned her face aglow. "I was just thinking how lucky I am. A bit different to that Sheila, she's sobbing her socks off. Funny, I never thought she was able to cry, but she can. It seems you were dead right about them two: Ginny and Jack. They've been at it for years."

Removing his arms from Doreen's waist Pat strolled into the kitchen. "Mind if I make coffee?"

"I'll do it," Doreen offered and was staggered when Trisha interrupted.

"Neither of you will do it, I'll boil and toil. You two go chill and trill."

"Blimey," Doreen laughed, "What's come over you?"

Trisha didn't answer, just shooed the pair of them out of the kitchen by flapping her hands.

"You know Pat," Doreen confessed as they sat together on the sofa, "I haven't ever seen Trisha look so blooming happy."

Pat kissed her cheek. "Maybe she's in love?"

For a moment Doreen sat there silent. "She's a bit young for that!" she said at last.

Pat put his arm round her and held her close. "Is she?" he asked. "You sure? You were only her age."

Doreen changed the subject. "Funny, how things turn out. There's me thinking them Hoskins next door had everything, posh and all, but it isn't true. When you haven't got any money you think it would be so much better if you had lots, but it doesn't work like that. Look at this place, all these posh villas filled with expensive and fancy things and most of the people aren't that content." She giggled suddenly.

"What's so funny?" Pat asked, leaning over and kissing the top of her head.

"I was thinking how strange that it was me who held Sheila whilst she sobbed, I know she'd never have done that for me. She'd have been nasty and gossipy."

Hugging Doreen, Pat grinned. "Well Doll, now you know that being rich doesn't always make you a nice person."

Bringing in a tray with coffee and a pile of freshly made sandwiches, Trisha calmly asked, "So just when are we walking the plank?"

Setting the tray down on the table she retrieved the brochure from under the plates and flicked open the pages, "Because this looks fabby dabby."

Pat stared up at Trisha and could not believe that in the last week he had not only found his old time love, but had gained a beautiful daughter and the icing on the cake was that he was so welcome in their lives.

Watching Pat wrestle with his emotions, Doreen felt she had been left out on something important, but before she could speak, as if reading her mind, Trisha cooed; "Chill Mama, Pat and I have spilled and trilled about you both and it's cool."

Chuckling, Trisha hugged her mother then hugged Pat.

"We weigh anchor the day after tomorrow," Pat said trying to hide the tears of joy threatening to spill down his face as Trisha hugged him.

Squealing with delight, Trisha yelped. "Cool." Then pulling away from her parents'embrace began to sing, "*I am Sailing...* " as she headed out onto the terrace.

Watching their daughter skip out of sight, Pat took hold of Doreen's hand, "You know Doll, in less than a week you've turned my world upside down. You've got me in a real spin."

Giggling, Doreen looked at the man who had once again stolen her heart. "And you think you haven't done that to me and my girl? Because I can tell you, you have. You've scared me half to death and you know I haven't been so happy since we were in our teens. But for me, what is really important is my Trisha. Thankfully she isn't fazed by it at all. God knows why not, but I just want her to be happy."

Squeezing the hand that felt so right in is own, Pat smiled.

"As Trisha would say, *scary,* but from what I've seen so far she's like her mum; nobody's fool. I didn't expect her to like me, let alone anything else, but she took my breath away when she told me, she'd try to love me. She said she liked me. That's a start. And she also said it would be cool if she could call me Pat and Papa, then something about needing to 'check her vibes' as to what would be best at the time," he laughed. "If we only spent more time checking our vibes we might all be in better shape."

"Sounds like my girl. No, I mean *our* girl."

From the terrace Trisha called, “Parents have you seriously seen the colour of the sky out here? Looks like some seriously un-cool damage is going on up there!”

Chapter SEVENTY THREE

Several people were moving off the beach, hurriedly packing away sun umbrellas, beach towels, cool boxes and such. The surf was churning, making Chicky's shorts quite wet. He didn't notice. Didn't see any of what was going on around him all he could see was Simon standing there, looking so handsome with his tie loosened, shirt half unbuttoned and his jacket slung over his shoulder.

So handsome. So secretive. The anger suddenly boiled up inside Chicky. Anger as black as the clouds and as furious as the rising wind.

"How dare you!" He shouted suddenly. "How dare you do this to me! You bring me here pretending we are going to have such a fantastic holiday. Meet all sorts of interesting people at that bloody conference and all the time, all the bloody, sodding time you only wanted to come so you could have a fling with that Miles bloody Griffin!"

"What?" Simon's face creased into bewilderment. "I don't know what you're talking about."

"Huh! I put it to you my Lord," Chicky stood as if he was in Court, his fingers gripping each side of his open shirt, "that the witness is aware you have been disappearing to locations unknown. You have been making secret assignations. The witness is aware you are lying to him!"

Simon dropped his jacket and shoes onto the sand, went closer to Chicky so that he too was standing in the surf that was raging around Chicky's legs.

"Chicky. I plead guilty, but you are trying the wrong case. It's not what it seems."

"Oh isn't it? Chicky was almost screaming, his angry hurt voice tossed by the wind. "I know what I've seen, I know what is happening! You are going to leave me, shack up with bloody Griffin! Go on! I dare you to deny it?" Tears of anguish were streaking down his face, hidden by the spindrift that was blowing in the strengthening storm and the rain that was starting to fall.

People were running from the beach, hurrying to find shelter; a dog was barking somewhere, convinced his master was merely playing a game.

Simon said something, but a crash of thunder drowned his words. He strode further into the water not caring that his best trousers would be ruined.

"I said," he shouted, "I love you!"

"Well you have a damn funny way of showing it!" Chicky shouted back.

Simon grasped Chicky's hand. Chicky tried to pull away, but Simon held tight, refusing to let go and Chicky overbalanced.

He cried out and fell to his knees in the sea, Simon sinking down beside him, refusing to let go of the grasp to his hands. He had not missed the pain in Chicky's eyes. It had hurt him to do all he had behind Chicky's back, but he had needed to make sure everything would work out before he made his decision. Had to meet people, had to discuss things. Had to think about the past, present and alternative futures.

He held Chicky's hands tightly, brought them up to his chest and placed them above his heart. "Chicky, listen to me. I've been wanting to tell you, but I couldn't. I was sworn to secrecy until decisions and agreements were made. Our friendly Judge, Paul Denbie suggested it all. He suggested it, made the arrangements, talked to the people involved weeks ago. The conference was nothing more than a coincidence and a useful cover. I only made up my mind what to do this morning. Everything was only finalised, signed and sealed, verdict carried not more than half an hour ago. I promise you, I have not been cheating. I am not having a fling with Miles Griffin, he's a perfectly respectable married man, anyway with three children! Why would I fancy Griffin when I have you?"

Lightning streaked through the sky, closely followed by a clap of thunder.

"Then what have you been doing?" Chicky cried. "Why have you come close to breaking my heart?"

Simon had to lean close, had to put his arms around Chicky and speak directly into his ear because the roar of the sea and the wind and the thunder was too loud for his words to be heard otherwise.

The pair of them where soaked through by salt water and pouring rain, but they did not care, they knelt there, amidst the foaming breakers, holding each other tight, Simon kissing Chicky and Chicky kissing him back.

Chapter SEVENTY FOUR

Cameras flashed and several people were videoing. Bob stood amongst an array of famous film, TV and pantomime characters. He could not believe this wonderful party had been organised to celebrate his birthday. Never in his life had such an occasion been organised for him. As a nipper, he had shared the few jelly parties with the cry baby girl next door, both being the same age. Here he was at sixty five and he did not have the words to describe how he felt. Taking in all the costumes, the buffet food, Antonio at the bar, he felt to his embarrassment, emotional.

On an occasion like this he would normally be running around fetching and carrying, but tonight he was *the* guest. They had certainly been sneaky keeping him out of the way all day! He had not even thought it odd when asked to step in as Pat's driver. It had all seemed normal enough. Rubbing his hand across his chin, he nodded his head at how things turn out; *me and this party*, he thought, *Pat finding Doreen again after all these years and that girl, the one Ben's been taking out, being his daughter*. He could see the girl was a chip off the old block. Watching his grandson with Trisha Wilkinson, he smiled. The boy meant a great deal to him, he hoped he would not get hurt too badly.

A hand brushed his arm snapping him out of his reverie as Cinderella breezed to his side. To his surprise, realised it was Cissie.

"What a sight for sore eyes you look my girl, you couldn't have picked a more fetching costume."

Blushing, Cissie stood back to admire Bob's Mr Spock costume. "I never thought you'd be one for *Star Trek*."

Bob smiled. He had always been a fan. Spock, his favourite character, though Scottie being the 'maintenance man' of the Starship *Enterprise* came a close second. His grandson, it seemed had remembered having secretly ensured that this outfit had been ordered for him to wear. He had even secretly taken the measurements from Bob's chauffer uniform to obtain the right fit. "Seems there's a lot of things we're all learning about each other at the moment," he said to Cissie, then laughed out load at the sight of Batman and Robin approaching along the path hand in hand.

"Blimey, you two couldn't have picked more appropriate costumes," Bob laughed as they came up to him. "Fighters for justice, eh? And to think I thought the pair of you were on parole convicts when you first arrived, not barristers!"

"Zap! Pow! Wham! I think that is what we should say," laughed Batman - Simon.

"Congratulations Bob," Robin added, "what a way to celebrate a birthday. And I know I speak for both of us, we've had a fantastic time here. This place is only made in dreams."

Chicky winked at Cissie and whispered, "No pun meant with dreams and bedrooms."

Cissie felt the colour rise in her face, but giggled and seeing her co-worker, Tracey dressed as Bo beep made her excuses and skittered away, the memory of being caught under the bed still making her blush.

Laughing Bob grinned. "Dreams, more like a nightmare most of the time."

All three laughed.

Turning to Chicky, Simon smiled, "Sadly we are at the end of this amazing holiday and what a holiday it has turned out to be."

Bob leant close to Simon, whispered, "Believe you me, this is as normal as it gets, so should you ever be wanting a good time and a few laughs come back and see us again."

"Thanks Bob, hopefully we'll take you up on that."

Bob's attention was taken by someone dressed as a bear and he excused himself. "Must mingle. Help yourselves to drinks at the bar. Food over there, though lord knows how we'll manage to eat all that!"

"I'll get us some champagne," Chicky said, but Simon grasped his hand and held it tight. "Chicky, please, I need to know. Have you made your decision on what I asked you?"

Chicky looked at Simon standing there dressed as Batman. He looked seriously sexy with his lean, trim figure and those Lycra tights that did not do much to hide what was tucked underneath.

He stifled a giggle. "You are a chump. Do you think I'd be standing here looking as much a silly prat as you do if I wasn't going to agree?"

Simon grinned. "Let's get that champagne!"

Dressed as a witch, sitting at the edge of the party, Frau Hecks watched the festivities springing into life. She was glad Cissie had included her in the secret about the surprise party that morning, because it had given her time to think. She had come to the conclusion that she needed to think more before she acted or spoke. The last few months she had slipped further down into something close to despair. And now, for the first time in a long while, felt so much better. The new tablets appeared to be working. The sun had come out again, literally after that storm yesterday, on her grey grumpy world.

Her Hans would be mortified to know she had turned into a miserable old lady. She sniffed, she was going to put things right. It took a lot of courage to apologise to people, but she had always had courage. She smiled, she felt like smiling. Even her costume was meant to show she knew what people were thinking about her and she wanted to show them that she could laugh and have a joke too.

Turning her gaze to the gift wrapped box sitting on the table, she smiled with happiness. Everyone was enjoying themselves, although no one seemed to have noticed her sitting alone. Sighing, she realised that was her own fault; she had distanced herself from everyone, hardly surprising they were ignoring her now. Thinking about her Hans again, she knew he would be very upset seeing her so miserable and unhappy. She smiled because he would have taken her hand and hugged her tight telling her to stop being so silly. *"Meine liebling, what I to do with you when you frown like an unhappy jester?"* Hearing his voice in her memory made her feel his love again. "*Ja* Hans, I am a stupid old fool, but, it is time to stop being foolish," she whispered and standing up, straightened her pointed, star-studded hat, collected the parcel on the table and swishing her cloak, strode purposefully towards Trisha and Ben.

Their costumes dark and very odd and they had hardly stopped kissing since they had arrived.

"This is a decent place, you should keep your canoodlings to private," Frau Hecks announced from directly beside them.

Trisha stared, Ben blushed.

"Young people," Frau Hecks continued, "should…" she hesitated, smiled. "Young people should wear costumes that us old people recognise. What is it you wear?"

Trisha was too astonished to say anything. It was Ben who answered. "We are Gomez and Morticia Addams from the TV series The Addams Family.

"*Ja, ja*, that is all very well, but you have something missing from your costume young lady." Feeling into a pocket of her voluminous dress she produced a small gold pendant. "I like to give this to you."

Frau Hecks placed the star shaped pendent into Trisha's hand. "It is very old. My Hans gave it to me when I was a girl your age. He said it was a star of love and it brought me much love. I now give it to you to bring you much love because I have been the foolish old woman who has forgotten that love is the most important thing." She closed Trisha's fingers over the gift. "You must enjoy your life. It is too short already."

Turning to Ben she tapped his arm. "I talk to you also. You respect your young lady and treat her with the honour and courtesy. A lady should have a gentleman, so you make sure you are ze gentleman *nein*?"

To Trisha she added, "Be happy in love and you think about this young man. If he like his grandfather, he be a gentleman and you will be a foolish *fräulein* to let him go." She nodded once, as if casting a spell. You take my pendant and when you look at it, you remember what I say. *Ja?* You do not be a foolish old lady."

Not waiting for a response she turned away and headed directly towards Bob. He was talking to a gorilla, but Frau Hecks called out, "Bob! Bob, I talk with you now."

Bob muttered an expletive under his breath; it was a party, but still the old witch came after him. He excused himself from the gorilla and exasperated asked. "Flawline, what can I be doing for you? We are supposed to be partying."

"*Ja, ja*, I know a party."

She had a large box in her hand. *What's in there* Bob thought. *Frogs? Toads? Lizards? Bat's eyes?*

"*Danke schöne* Bob for speaking with me," she said, chuckling beneath her breath at Bob's look of distaste as he stared at her box. "I want to say, Happy Birthday Bob. I not wish to spoil your party, but please take this."

With both hands placed around the box she handed the gift to him. Smiling a smile that lit her face and made her eyes sparkle she instructed, "You open it now."

Bob stared at the gift wrapped in dark blue foil paper, then back at Frau Hecks. What had come over the old biddy, too much champagne again?

"Blimey Flawline, you've taken the wind right out of me sails."

Tearing the paper off the box his face lit into a broad grin when he saw it contained the remote control sports car. "Blimey Frau Hecks, you bought this for your grandson!"

"*Ja*, but I buy another when you next take me to the shops. You likes zis sort of thing, I watch you fiddle with things that are mechanical. You are young at hearts. You keep zat way."

"Fanks Flawline, I've always wanted one of these." He did not trust himself to say more, all he could manage was, "I don't know what to say."

Frau Hecks placed a hand on his sleeve, "You say nothing then. I have been the silly old fool. The wicked witch, but I change. Loneliness is bad thing. My Hans would never approve of me being stupid. So I stops being stupid. *Ja?*"

Bob grinned. Blimey what an evening this was turning out to be!

As much as he hated to admit it she was right though, she was right. Loneliness was a killer. He knew that all too well since he had lost his Missus a few years back. That was why he spent so much time here at Villas Bonitas, keeping himself busy. Keeping the loneliness at bay.

Tucking his splendid present under one arm, he offered the other to Frau Hecks.

"I think we need some of that lovely food I can smell drifting from the buffet. Let's see what we can over indulge in. I've heard there's even red jelly!"

Blinking to keep her tears at bay, Frau Hecks linked her arm into Bob's and looked up into his happy face.

"*Danke schöne* Bob, *danke schöne*."

Chapter SEVENTY FIVE

Dressed as Henry VIII and Elizabeth I, Jack and Sheila stood in their villa in silence. They had originally declined to dress up and join the party, they had enough charades to deal with, but Sheila had decided that appearances had to be kept up in public.

Swishing over to the coffee table, her face a picture of victory, Sheila picked up her glass of champagne and sipped as the bubbles rose to the top of the glass. She had told her daughter everything about her father and his affair on the phone, to her relief, Michelle had agreed to fly down at the weekend.

Sheila was determined to get Michelle on her side nothing would give her greater satisfaction than ostracising Jack and his daughter. He did not deserve a decent family.

Soon after she had ended her call, Jack had entered through the patio doors soaked to the skin from the rain his hair plastered around his face. He had looked like the drowned rat he was.

Sneering with satisfaction at his hang dog posture Sheila had been ready to throw him out on his backside with nothing but the wet clothes he stood in, but to her disgust he had grovelled and begged for forgiveness.

She did not believe a word of his promises that it was now all over, that Ginny had made a mistake about thinking she was pregnant. That is if she had been pregnant he was not even sure it was his.

"She conned me, Sheila. She seduced me; was after our money, just like you said she was. Only her target wasn't Doreen Wilkinson it was us!"

That had caught Sheila's attention and Jack knew from them on, that he was home and dry. There was nothing Sheila Hoskins liked more than being right.

“Jack,” she had said, “you are a bigger idiot than I took you to be. From now on I will run this family and most of the business.”

“Yes Sheila,” he had answered, half bowing, “what ever you say Sheila.” And thought, *over my dead body Sheila.*

Last night he had been made to sleep in the spare bed, was told that henceforth he would always be sleeping in the spare bed.

“Yes Sheila,” he had answered.

This morning, she had risen early and had started to pack. “We are leaving. I have telephoned Michelle, told her not to fly here after all. I am going to stay with her for a few days instead. You will fly back home to Harrogate and stay there until I decide to join you.”

“Yes Sheila.”

Discovering that she was unable to book a flight out until tomorrow, however, Sheila had then decided to accept Carmen’s invitation to the party. Although she had grumbled that it was impolite to issue such an invitation so close to the event. She believed that she should have had authority over the catering and how dare Carmen consider that she could not keep a secret!

The glass of champagne finished, Sheila headed for the front door. Appearances must be maintained.

“You,” she announced to Jack as he hurried to open the door for her, “will drink nothing but orange juice or mineral water tonight. Is that understood?”

“Yes Sheila,” he said, as she swept out into the night.

Neither Queen Elizabeth or Henry VIII, as they walked in silence, he one pace behind, noticed the young couple clinging together in a passionate embrace beneath a large palm tree.

Ben had kept a close eye on his granddad all day, eager to get the party going and then spend his last few hours with Trisha. Tomorrow she was leaving and though they had talked about seeing each other again, he was almost certain they never would. This week with Trisha had been amazing.

He kept telling himself it was nothing more than a holiday fling, but deep down he knew it was not. He loved her. Trisha had created a feeling no one else had ever done; she was too young, too rich and too far out of his league, but he had fallen in love with her. She was the real thing. And then the words Frau Hecks had said… he was almost close to tears as Trisha kissed him.

She stepped back, looked at him, her head cocked on one side with that funny little tilt to her mouth. "My, my, you are so spaced out. Come back to me Ben, this is serious stuff, I am away on the morrow, sailing. Can you believe that?" She laughed, but she noted Ben's sombre face.

She was pretending to be light and happy, but she did not really want to leave him. Her mother was deliriously happy now Pat was on the scene. Things had turned out good, but would she be that lucky?

For luck, she touched the star pendant that was now fastened around her neck. "Ben, chill, you are so not that wicked boy I met less than a week ago. Now, let me think what I must do to turn your naughty knob back to full on?"

She giggled as she put her arms around his neck again and despite his thoughts at her leaving, he laughed. She was so unlike anyone else he had met: confident, amusing and still very dangerous. What a combination!

"Know what I think?" Trisha said.

He shook his head. If he knew what this gorgeous girl was thinking even half the time he would be as brainy as Einstein!

"I think you should come with me. The cruiser is not large, it is enormous, we, that is you and me, could chill and do whatever we wanted. Mama and new Papa will be far to busy trying to catch up." She cringed at this thought.

Ben stared at her in stunned silence.

"Well say something? Same as me you're not back at your studies for a few weeks yet are you babe? We've both got studying to do of course, Mama made that plain to me, though I don't need telling what I already know. It would be fun to be at our books in between being at other things, don't you think?"

"I…."

But Trisha did not wait for Ben to say any more. "I take that as a yes then," and placed her lips on his.

Stopping to breath Ben gasped, "I'll need to pack."

"Ben, you are so seriously old fashioned, but I love you."

Chapter SEVENTY SIX

Watching as Sheila regally swished her way towards some unsuspecting costumed guest, Doreen could not believe the transformation in the woman; from sobbing to strutting. Turning to Pat she whispered, "Seems like the crisis is over and she's back to herself."

Spying Jack propping up the bar with a glass of orange juice in his hand, Pat grinned. "What's the betting there is a large splash of gin in that juice?"

He looked at his Cleopatra, his eyes sparkling with amusement. "My history is not all that great, but even I know that Henry VIII had several of his wives' head's chopped off, especially when a new piece tickled his fancy."

Cringing, Doreen giggled. "Oha! Sounds nasty."

"Very." Pat brought Doreen's hand to his mouth and kissed her fingers, one by one. "I also know that Mark Anthony loved his Cleo to bits."

Cocking his ear to the start of some lively music, said, "Doll, I believe I can hear our kind of music belting away, let's take to the floor and dance."

Wrapping his arm around Doreen's waist Mark Anthony fox trotted Cleopatra away to the dance area.

Sheila watched as Pat and Doreen danced; Doreen's giggle ringing out even above the band. She caught sight of Carmen standing next to Jack at the bar. It was about time she checked what her husband was drinking. Her layers of petticoats and ruffles rustled as she stalked over to him. Deliberately, she ignored him, talked to Carmen instead.

"An unlikely pair those two, especially here at Villas Bonitas."

Pat swung Doreen round in an exaggerated twirl, Doreen's loud giggle creating as much attention as her cavorting to the music.

"Is this Pat person really the sort we want here at villas Bonitas? Or even Madam Fink Fought come to think of it." Sheila stated. "Not really *our* class are they Carmen? In my mind they simply lower the tone. Common and loud! Standards are paramount."

Already she had forgotten Doreen's concern and kindness, though she would not forget Jack's indiscretion, but that was a different matter. Jack, she could control

Carmen's patience filled with loathing for this woman. How dare she so insult Doreen and Pat! There was no need to keep secrets anymore, no need to remain polite to the odious woman either. "Really Sheila, you don't know?"

"What is there *too* know?"

"Pat Greenwood specifically arranged for Doreen and Trisha to come here."

"That I find hard to believe. All these rumours of him owning a yacht and such. He is a holiday camp owner for goodness sake! Those sort of places that are all caravans, fish and chips and plastic tablecloths. Where the riff-raff go for two weeks to *Torna-my-knees-off'*. Doreen told me so herself!"

Carmen burst out laughing. Jack too guffawed.

"Yes, yes, I suppose you are right," Carmen spluttered. "He does own several holiday camps. Villa's Bonitas is one of them!"

Furious at being made a fool of, Sheila hissed, "That is utter nonsense. *We* own our villa!"

Jack finished his "orange" and ordered another. "That is your trouble. You think you know everything, but you never listen do you? Never. Ever. You're wrong, We own the leasehold, but not the freehold. All the land, the pool, the bar, the lot and other places is owned by Greentree Associates. Pat Greenwood.

Carmen laughed. "Dear me Sheila, it seems you don't know everything after all."

Not waiting for a response she walked away.

Spinning round, Sheila prodded a sharp finger nail into Jack's Henry VIII padded chest.

"You will do something about Carmen Santana. She is rude, insulting and a liar."

Jack thrust his face close to his wife's and poked her breast bone back with his index finger. "You are the one who insults people. You are the one who is rude. You are the one I should do something about"

Sheila sneered. "What? Divorce me? You haven't the nerve or the wit." She swivelled on her heel and stalked off along the side of the pool.

"Mind the tiles!" Jack called out, "We don't want you to trip!"

Laughter rang out.

Feeling the flush run up her face, realising she had been made to look the fool, Sheila thrust her way into the group of dancers and grasped Pat Greenwood's arm, jerking him to a sudden halt."

"All I can say, if you own this place then standards have definitely declined. Our villa will be on the market tomorrow."

Grasping the wide skirt of her gown, she lifted it slightly and flounced away, every inch of her portraying Queen Elizabeth in one of her bad tempers, unaware that her wig was askew.

Watching his wife disappear down the path, Jack could not believe his luck. He turned back to Antonio and grinned. "Champagne I think. Make that two."

"Well that was a stroke of luck for you, Jack old man," Pat Greenwood said, appearing at his side, Doreen on his arm. "Antonio, make that champagne all round, I reckon."

Jack laughed out loud. "I'll drink to that!"

"What's so funny?" Doreen asked, perching herself on a bar stool. "Have I missed the joke or something?"

"Jack saw me yesterday," Pat explained, "while I was at a meeting in the Old Square. He told me he was transferring ownership of that nice little single apartment overlooking the

Square to himself and the Villa to his mistress and the child to be."

"I do not intend," Jack added, "to ever bring my wife to this place again. My problem was how to tell *her* that fact. Ever obliging with her insistence on organising everything, though, she has just solved the problem for me."

"And here," Pat said jovially, "is just the person you might need if you want any legal advice. Simon, Chicky! Come and join us!"

The two men, smiles on their faces, hand in hand, came to the bar, accepted glasses of champagne.

"Meet my new employee," Pat said. "Simon has agreed to take over from Miles Griffin as my legal representative. I don't just own holiday camps you know, Doll, I do a lot for the United Nations, Amnesty International, Human Rights and that sort of thing. There is always some deserving court case I'm helping out with. Miles is moving on so I needed someone good in Court to take his place. Simon here came well recommended. Yesterday he accepted the job."

They all chinked glasses, cheered.

"There is one thing Pat," Simon asked, hesitantly, "you said I would be based here, in town. I was wondering, on the salary you are offering, perhaps I might buy one of these Villas?"

Pat nodded, "No reason why not."

"And," Simon added, a little more confident, "you said I could choose my own partner to work with?"

Pat laughed and good natured slapped Simon's shoulder. "Don't tell me. You have decided that you want to ask Chicky here? Why do you think I particularly wanted you? I knew you would ask your partner to be your partner!"

Chicky blushed. "I was thinking all sorts of silly things until Simon told me what had been going on. I can't believe that we are going to be staying here, in between flying off all over the world as your representatives."

Joining the laughter, Antonio refilled their glasses and they all toasted Bob as he elegantly waltzed Frau Hecks round the dance area.

“It’s been a great party,” Doreen said, “and I’m glad I’m not going to lose touch with none of you because you’re all lovely people.”

She looked around at the coloured party lanterns, the glistening water in the pool shimmering from the underwater lighting, heard the laughter and saw the smiles on people’s faces. She giggled loudly then looked up at the twinkling stars.

“You know something Pat?” she said.

“No, but I assume Doll, you’re about to tell me.”

“Sometimes,” she giggled, “it happens, the strangest, but nicest things happen don’t they?”

Pat laughed and kissed her forehead.

The End

To learn more about the Pauline, please visit www.paulinebarclay.co.uk

More Books by Pauline Barclay

Magnolia House

When Jane Leonard gave half of her house to her only son, little did she realise that within twelve months, she would be forced to sell the home she had lived in for nearly five decades.

The choice for this action was not hers, but the events that led up to her handing over fifty percent of Magnolia House paled by comparison to what happened after the ink had dried on the documents that named the new owners.

As Magnolia House is put on the market for sale, love and betrayal, hopes and dreams and ultimately family loyalty will affect the lives of all of those who become involved.

Satchfield Hall

When the news reached Henry Bryant-Smythe about his daughter's indiscretion, he not only dealt with it, but stamped on it with such a resounding thud, that the consequences ricocheted through the years and well into the future. Henry Bryant-Smythe cared nothing for the consequences of his actions and even less for the feelings of those involved, with the exception of his own, and these he cosseted.

Celia's Bryant-Smythe's disgrace set in motion events that would affect the lives of many people, taking decades to unravel. Lives would be lost and destroyed and it would take until the death of the one man who had callously started it all, Henry Bryant-Smythe, until it was finally over.

Satchfield Hall is not about gentleness, tranquillity and privilege; it is about, power, love, lives and in the end revenge

Lightning Source UK Ltd.
Milton Keynes UK
UKOW042124050613

211835UK00001B/4/P

9 781781 765487